THE POTATO EATERS

by

Richard Newman

Published by Lulu.com

Copyright © Richard Newman 2007

Richard Newman has asserted his rights under the Copyright, Design and Patents Act 1988 to be identified as the author of this work

This novel is a work of fiction. Names and characters are the product of the author's imagination and any resemblance to actual persons, living or dead is entirely coincidental

This book is sold subject to the condition that it shall not, by way of trade or otherwise, be lent, resold, hired out, or otherwise circulated without the publishers prior consent in any form of binding of cover other than that in which it is published and without a similar condition including this condition being imposed on the subsequent purchaser

First published in the United Kingdom by lulu.com

ISBN: 978-1-84753-323-4

Printed and bound in the United States by Lulu.com

Other books by Richard Newman

* *The Crown of Martyrdom*
* *The Horse that Screamed*

To the Dutch Resistance

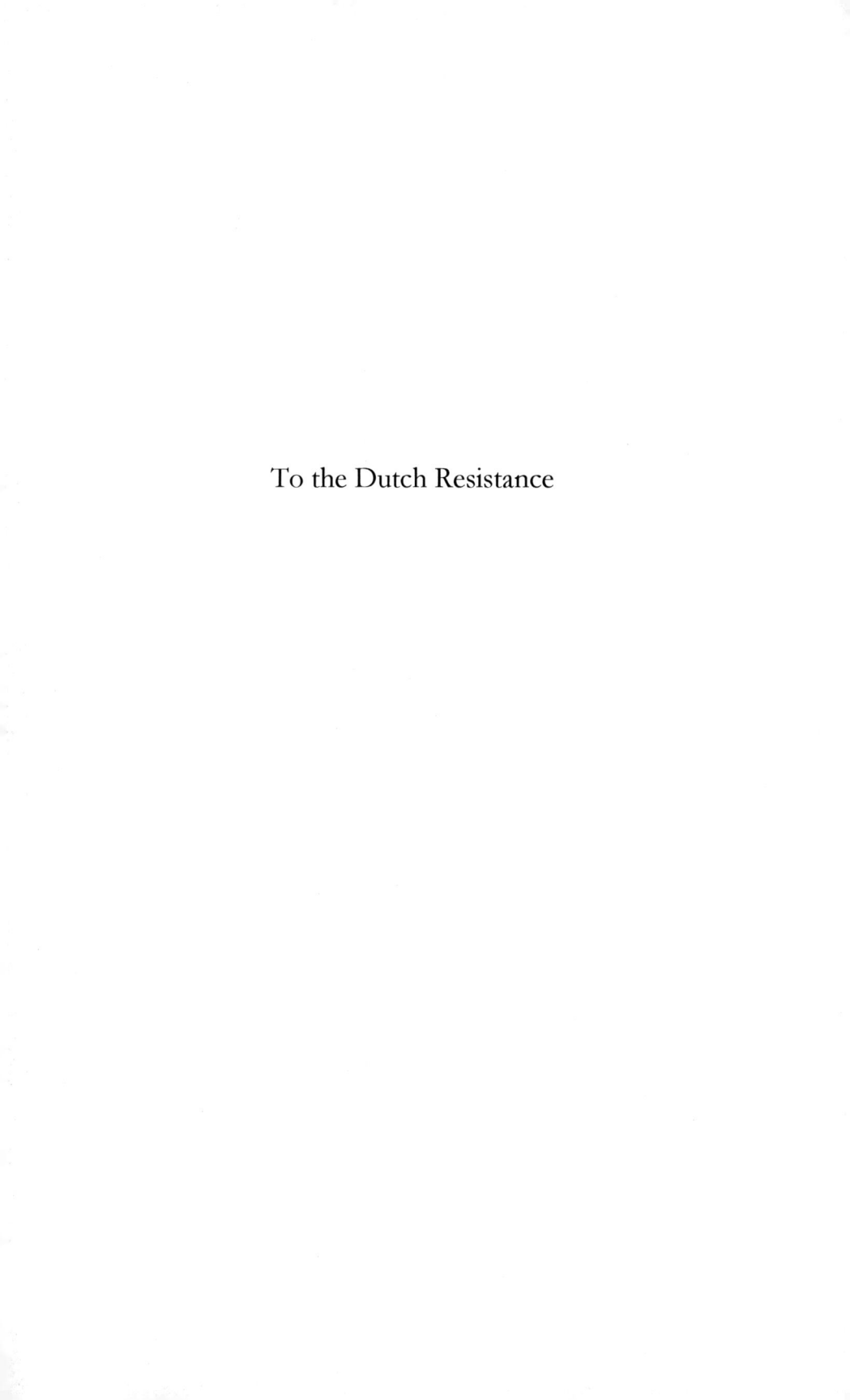

My thanks also to Michael and Pru Luke who inspired me to write this book while on holiday with them; and my family, as ever, for just putting up with me

A Safe Place

The air is as cold as the floor and the walls. It crackles and shimmers with frost, white crystals covering every surface. It mingles, briefly with the raw smell of sisal and hemp before being carried downwind. Old drums of oil, long discarded, with rust flaking in thin, jagged peelings from the rims, lie forlorn, forgotten. The mood grows like a cancer, unstoppable rot now that it has established itself.

Degrees of the dark, from North Sea grey to lampblack, smudge into each other, as if an artist with a charcoal stick is setting up to draft the outlines on a canvas, ready for work.

Oddly, however, it is a safe place, totally familiar. Each object has its own name and its own place, each with its station in life, with its own reason to be where it is. There is a gleam of light on the case clocks face. The light makes an absurd grimace, being bent, so to speak, around the glass dome, as if leering at its own gawping. But, it knows things are going to change. In a few minutes time, the moon is rising and the glass will sparkle and glow with pure silver. The insolent smirk will soften and melt and turn into the soft kiss of a child. After this promising start, there is a sudden reversal as the cold comes back again, and begins to intensify.

All at once the thermometer drops off a cliff. It is so cold that the man's breath condenses on the bedclothes. There are small ice droplets spreading away from his nose. In sleep, he hears, or imagines he hears, the scream of a particularly aggressive gull, followed by another, and another. The cry is wrung out, a tortured sound, wrought out of pain and terrible fear. The room begins to waver, before snapping back into line, like a column of soldiers being brought to attention, as the scream reaches his brain.

'Grand-maa! Grandmaa!' he calls out and she tells him what to do and he feels the stronger because of it. It stays, this strength, so it presses the corners away into the night and the day following. The rush of blood, released,

into the tiny corpuscles of the brain, is taking in oxygen. It clears arteries, blocked and crowded with the debris of the night, widens eyes and demands more of this life-giving breath.

It's the corners, you see; the corners of the harbour in which the boat is moored: the corners of the cabin, even the edges of the table. When the night comes, the corners curl and coil, and bend into fantastical shapes so there is a loss of all perspective and balance. There is no focus of the mind, because the daily elements, which make up the world, no longer relate to anything that can be recognised. This is why the fear is there.

Chapter One

One moment earlier, he had been alone on the street, the cool evening mist reminding him of happier, sunnier days. One split second in time, his thoughts had occupied a gentle space within his brain, allowing the soft night's dew to lie on his face to help relieve, if not remove entirely, the ice of the evenings horror. To be home safe was all he wanted.

He tried again to shift gear in his mind. He knew with awful certainty he had to get away from what ever it was that created his fear, a fear which he could almost sense pressing upon the fine hairs on the nape of his neck. So real was it he made to flick it away with his fingers, before realising it was his own hand that rested there. In making the action, the gear stick of his mind ground the cogs from fourth to first in one jolting pig-squeal, which frightened him further. The terror accelerated, dashing sensible and rational thought to pieces. As he fought against falling through a series of darkening black holes, unable even to see the bottom of the pit, he felt increasingly alone.

There was no one there to help him through the night. Just one person could make the difference between permanent madness and temporary sanity by supporting him until dawn. His greatest fear was to lose the final contact with the solid firmness of the real world he had been brought up in. He knew if he reached out his hands, it was there to grasp and pull him back into ordinariness, regularity and routine. His terror was the knowledge the walls were beginning to crumble under his grip.

His jaw worked in agitated motion. He found he was shouting out a babble of words: so much so, the street echo finally brought him comprehension. With understanding came remembrance and thus terror. And down he went again.

And so he ran.

This wasn't the horror we give birth to in our dreams, when words are choked off in a soundless scream, to disappear, almost always forgotten, on waking. Nor was it the fear of imminent death. Happily now, he would beg for death, so long as it blanked out all thought, an accepted wisdom creeping like dry-rot tendrils through wet wood into the curve of his neck.

So he called upon every God and Saint he had ever learned of at school to help him. He threw out his hands into the near darkness, his fingers spread wide as if to span a full octave.

'No! Not again,' he begged.

His voice bounced off the iron-hard cobbled street to skitter and collapse into the harbour. Faintly, across the water, there came an answering cry.

'No!'

He began to run again. A couple emerging from one of the port's many bars, who knew him slightly as someone who lived alone on one of the boats, shook their heads as he pushed past without acknowledgement. He was to all intents and purposes, blind, a blind man unseeing, a dumb man, gullet glued to the roof of his mouth. He had become a deaf mute, unhearing, and an idiot unable to think or even to answer to his proper name.

A girl in ragged clothes with her coat collar pulled up tight to her eyes, paused in the shadows, unwilling to go further, wondering if he was about to set about her, but he hadn't noticed the insubstantial, waif-like creature shading the doorway.

He ran to the dockside, familiar at least with each boat's registration number, an unthinking task like cycling, which required him only to glance at each stern plate in turn.

'Ah! Thank God,' he repeated, though this time it was with relief, as he leapt from the quayside into the blackness of the harbour with an air of finality. His feet struck metal plates causing his ankle to come into contact with the steel side of the capstan. The pain it caused inspired him. He allowed himself to slide down to the deck, to force his back against the side of the craft. The cold metal burned through his jacket as if it were heated by a summer's day. His blond hair blew in the bitter gusts from winds just beginning to shiver across the basin from the open channel beyond.

When he spoke, it was aloud to himself. 'I'm as real as anyone else. I'm sane! I'm sane!' He laughed aloud. 'I cannot be mad. People who are mad cannot say that, can they?'

He repeated the phrase rapidly several times, urgently demanding of the rigging and the mast answer him. The wheelhouse glass caught the faint gleam from a lamp out on the water. It winked back at him as it reflected a boat's wash from a late night fisherman returning to his mooring. Salt from the far off sea, mixed with tar, wafted across his nose to remind him he was home, home on the deck of his boat.

Gradually, fearful that any slight movement might change the improving situation, he tucked his feet beneath him so he could pull himself erect. His ankle throbbed from a sprained muscle and a bruised calf. He breathed in the smells, the sounds of the city and the sights across the water, thumping the gunwale with his hand as he did so. He knew every glitch, every indentation of its scored surface by memory, and he could recall how many of them had been created by his own activities. If he extended his arm sideways it would make contact with the short, sturdy forepost. By spreading out the other hand, he could reach out and touch the sea bunker, once used to store rope. Today, it was filled with wood shavings, timber flotsam pulled from the basin and logs bought from the local supplier, which heated the iron range. He could make the wheelhouse in four and a half strides. By twisting his body as he did so, he could enter and close the door in a single action, useful when it was blowing hard out to sea, not that this was an asset he needed just now. It also made him feel safe, protected from the world.

He hobbled to the doorway and glanced across to the boat moored alongside his own on the starboard side. This craft was about six metres longer. It was broader in the beam, 'fatter' as he saw it, the two craft rather like the Port Harbour Master with one of his junior apprentices, following a few paces behind. Even in the daylight, it would not seem as tired as the rest of the boats, perhaps because it did have a bit of style about its lines. The stern swept up out of the oily water at a sharply acute angle before returning back on itself, as it aimed for a point somewhere halfway up its black and white ringed funnel. The gunwales, though, of the two boats, were almost the same height off the water, allowing anyone who might wish, to cross from one to the other without having to use the two respective gangplanks.

He looked back at his own tug. Its funnel was taller than all of its neighbours. It could be clearly seen across the water, standing above the moored craft. It was like a factory chimney in many respects, though resemblances ended at this point, for it was painted near the top with a white band, edged either side with a smart blue ring. It was the most dominant feature of any of the boats in the basin, and brought inevitably, many crude comments from the Dockers. The hull was black, like all of its neighbours, the standard tint since the war had begun, with its name chipped and flaking in white: *Kuijpers-Amsterdam* on its stern-plate.

Alongside its nearby residents, it looked cocky, defiant almost, despite its battered appearance. The hull had survived two World Wars as it chafed at its hawsers, gazing out on the invading German armies marching close by along the cobbles. With hostilities ending, if not the shortages, his tug had begun to belch smoke of such a disgusting nature, oily and choking that it blanked out all vision in the street, so lorries found it difficult to see where they were going. In the past, neighbours had complained about the smell saying their children were coughing as a result. Diesel, they suggested, to match a city moving out of war, into a bright, clean future.

But, there was no incentive to change and no money anyway, so the *Kuijpers* remained at her lines, silent in her engine room.

Salt and rust crumbled together on the surface of her boilers. Two gauges, once polished brass with sparkling white faces and gleaming cover plates, were now dusty and dulled. The two indicator needles lay in parallel at their respective *STOP ENGINES* marks, two marionettes at rest, waiting for a performance that would never come again.

It was true he had, on a number of occasions in the past, lit the boilers with wood, not daring to use the cheap sea coal. Blue oak smoke had drifted across the harbour and brought an unusual glow to the boiler casings. The unaccustomed heat caused a series of creaks from the damp timber panelling covering the walls of the saloon as they began to dry and shrink. Engaging a gear, the boat had chuckled to itself, the water at the stern had foamed white, but there had been precious little wood so the smoke had died away, and the pistons brought once more to rest. The tremble in the hull, like an upset child, calmed. The onlookers had moved on as they fast lost their interest.

He pulled back from where he had wedged himself, pressed against the glass, and climbed down the almost vertical wooden staircase to the large cabin spanning the full width of the boat. There was a tin of corned beef on a shelf, which he took down. He stabbed at the lid with an opener before jerking the blade up and down to expose the meat with its white flakes of fat.

While he ate, he tried to analyse the reason why his mind had destabilised itself again despite his deliberate attempts to prevent himself being channelled down into the darkness. The reason why? He grimaced at the phrase. Had he any reason left inside of him? The early alarm signals he knew exactly. The creeping terror, so slow to start that he was sometimes mistaken, were he to be reminded, a few minutes later. The feeling the world was closing in, where the walls which pressed upon him were without windows or doors and the ceiling was lost in the gloom far above. Whether he was outside on the jetty or within his cabin, the fear arrived, just as he blinked an eye to remove a coil of smoke drifting from his cigarette. He might be drinking in one of the local bars or taking a snack. It came once as he had been gazing calmly at a wind-blown sky filled with crows, which had appeared like flak bursts above his head. It was always a different situation so he could never plan ahead and brace himself for the event. Analysis of the situations he had been in, the locations, even what he had been saying at the time, were of no use. It was always different.

The fear was two-edged, for when he came out of his mood, his brain was often hyper-active and alert, and he could recognise only too clearly that these occasions were increasing in their frequency. What if, he said to himself, what if they joined together so there would be no gaps between the good days and the bad? And, what if he found it impossible to climb back across the bridge, as if he were walking down his gangplank making for his home…and his safety harness? He might be forced to live with the terror forever, with no road to escape down. Each street in his mind would be a cul-de-sac as soon as he turned the next corner.

He pushed the awful thought from his mind. He had felt hungry that morning, realising he had eaten very little the day before. He had risen early, needing wood for fuel and food for the following week. His first call had been to the bank. The teller had been scrupulously polite, for he was a regular customer, but his untidy appearance at the counter made the staff look down on him as a rather strange and quirky man, maybe an eccentric was the kindest description, while those in the same queue often kept their distance, as though he were unclean. They would find themselves readjusting their hat brims, or would begin to pull at a buttonhole or appear to be engaging in some activity, which would require them to study their purse in detail. For, what if he tried to engage them in conversation?

He clutched the small stipend in his right hand, transferring it to a trouser pocket as he almost collided with a small boy standing outside a butcher's shop, as his mother argued the price of scrag end of lamb. His overlarge blue cap was pulled down, so he had to lift his head high to see under the peak. He did so as Theo, for that was the man's name wished him a good morning, subconsciously stroking the boy's soft cheek with the back of his hand. The woman smiled from the doorway, content. She knew Theo. The two of them had queued together throughout the long months and years of the war. He had entertained her to a steady prattle of his thoughts, mostly anti-German, pointing out the fat ones and the short ones, who seemed very little different to the Dutchmen who walked by on the same street. She, in turn, had described how best he could squeeze some flavour out of the stringy meat, by adding herbs which the butcher sold for a few cents; a twist of paper containing delicate scents and tastes.

'Good morning, Matt. You look cold.'

The boy, only three years old, responded by breathing hard from his mouth, the breath condensing in the early morning cold air. He repeated the action several times.

'You are a train, a train.' Theo whistled mournfully, and added the sound of wheels crossing the rail points.

'You should eat more,' said a voice in his ear. 'Your face is too bony.'

It was Matt's mother. She did not want to appear unkind, but she had seen the marked deterioration in his weight. 'You will be ill and then who will look after you?'

'The Family, of course. Pieter and Elizabeta and their children. That makes six people in all to help me.'

'My, you are a lucky man then. Come on Matt. Let's see if there are any flowers in from the fields yet.'

'Two more weeks, the Family says. The cold this winter has slowed up the growth. The buds are hardly formed yet, they say.'

'Perhaps some early daffodils. Goodbye Theo.'

He lifted his hat politely. She was a kind woman, always ready with a word or two for him. Matt waved back with his free hand, as he was hustled across the road away from a speeding tram. Theo shrugged his shoulders thinking of what she had said. If he was thin now, what about the terrible winter of nineteen forty-four? The Hunger Winter, the Amsterdamers had called it, when two thousand of them had died from starvation. Then he, like everyone that awful year, had cooked daffodil bulbs to make soup and bread.

In two weeks there would be daffodils in the shops. He watched the two of them turn back towards the Plantage Middlelaan. He felt better: a woman who never complained; a woman and a small boy, two out of one hundred and forty thousand saved by several acts of fate. Someone had smiled on her that day, allowing her to escape from the deportations through poor bookkeeping and lost records. The end of the war had brought her a husband, and, a little while later, a son.

He agreed for two sacks of coal to be sent to the quay-side, and bought a dozen tins of stewed meat and a jar of sauerkraut.

'I've got some potatoes left,' offered the shopkeeper.

'That's the one thing I don't have to buy,' Theo replied. 'The Family gives me all the potatoes I want...and they cook them for me as well.' The memory of the last potatoes made him pause in thought. It had been a long time ago, but he turned back as he was about to leave the shop. 'Have you some soft cheese? Cheese on the potatoes, nice eh?'

The shopkeeper nodded his head in approval and smiled. 'Watch the rats though. I hear the rats are back in force on the boats.'

'They are my friends. I may even give them a bit of my cheese, from time to time,' he said as he shouldered his purchases in an old army pack.

Relaxed and happy, mindful of the Jewish woman's comments on flowers, he turned towards the City rather than the Port. He skirted the marketplace to bring him into Dam Square.

Unlike Rotterdam, Amsterdam had been spared the bombing though the Germans had carried out a final massacre within the Square even as the Canadian liberators were at the suburbs.

There were hardly any flowers. Some hyacinths, brought forward by leaving the bulbs in heated cupboards in private houses. 'Soon, soon,' the stall holders all replied in unison, anxious to make money again, as they had done before the war. 'Maybe next week. The week after, surely.'

He didn't mind. He was suddenly glad he had made the decision to come into town. It made a change from the deadly repetition of his life. The streets were changing almost daily and his greatest problem was to avoid the hundreds of cyclists who filled every available space on the roads and pavements. It was their nonchalance, he protested. He could ride a bike himself, though not with the confidence, seemingly the rest of the world displayed, as they sped and wove their way through the other traffic. He hadn't practised since he was a child. After all, there was no place to go to on a boat, especially a small one. These shoppers sat well back on their saddles, arms extended to give themselves ramrod stiff backs, like women in stays in the old days. Bells rang, often in the imperative, so much so the sounds merged together, making him swing his head from side to side and fore and aft to prevent being run down.

After the hard, cruel years of the war, the City, he could see, was moving out of its forced captivity. Within the street scene directly in front of him, Theo could see two shop fronts being modernised, with two more being painted. There was a fanaticism for cleaning, as if the people needed to wash away the years of German occupation. The smells had gone; the painted slogans were being gradually scoured away and the posters long torn down. But, something more was needed before the townspeople could feel the invader had finally departed for good. The fear of seeing a German soldier approaching, perhaps only to ask for a light, or more frighteningly, the knock in the middle of the night at the front door would take longer to lose. But the deportations had ended and there was now a strong possibility of reaching home each day, bicycles not withstanding.

He had delayed his return to the jetty, allowing himself to be drawn as far as the *Rijks* Museum, before realising he had a way to walk. Quickening his pace brought him, eventually to the gaunt, bleak area where Matt's mother had directed her steps earlier in the day. Most of the streets were silent, the houses empty, front doors, where they existed at all, swung in the chill wind. Broken glass littered the streets adding to the general litter and weeds blocking the gutters.

As he shifted his feet faster in response to the encroaching evening, he knew, without being able to control it, his sickness was returning. Though he was surrounded by a series of grim streets, a ghost town where once, thousands of Jews had lived, he saw only an expanding black void, which sought to stifle and engulf him. The slight stress he had felt on seeing the darkening corners and alleys, had been a trigger for something far worse. It began in his imagination, where he began to see the shadows of unimaginable beings, formless, amorphous or dreadfully distorted, as they hid in the broken ruins, waiting. Even as he exhaled breathlessly, the horizon, whichever way he turned, began to roll towards him.

So he ran, allowing his happy thoughts to slip away from his mind as if it were mercury in his hands.

And he knew he was going mad. Not today perhaps. Not even this week, but there was a finality about it all which made him howl at the idea of being trapped forever within a world frightening beyond measure.

* * * * *

I never did like looking in a mirror at myself. The rain puddle acted as a reflector as if it were a theatre mirror in an actor's dressing room. It showed off the whole of my body, from the bare ankles, to my moth-eaten hat. My hair hung down in a straight fringe, cutting across my forehead in strict contrast to the whiteness of my face. There was absolutely no possibility of describing myself as slim. I was painfully thin, with any exposed bits of skin being blotchy red, more purple in fact, when it was very cold. My eyes, black and intensely nervous, seemed to consume my face with dark hollows as they sought to focus on the puddle.

None of this mattered, however, for it was so cold it caused the hunger in my stomach to rekindle itself. It felt sharp as a bite from a rat. It was the hunger I would always remember. The cold you could banish from your mind if you really tried, by thinking of a summer's day in Rotterdam when the sun would break up into patches as it shone warmly through the trees on the sides of the street. But, the hunger never went away, and brought memories to me of the terrible things from the past.

The *Middlelaan*, as the evening came on, was a dead place to be, so unlike the time before the war, before the Germans came and removed everyone like cattle, into trucks. Even the ghosts, had abandoned this awful place, left now to the yarl of stray cats and the swish of rubber tyres speeding fearful riders home across the short cut, some scared in case of being confronted with the actions of their recent past, some because of their guilt of doing nothing, some because it was just a frightful place to be.

There could be no future for this part of the City. The shame of the city folk for what had happened to my people was too much to bear. The only way they could remove the stain would be to raze the area to the ground and start again.

It all seemed so trivial. My mother had once agreed to drink a tin mug of her own urine to please a group of laughing soldiers, in return for a hard knuckle of bread. I remember the smell of her breath as she handed it to me, hands shaking but triumphant. Now, in Amsterdam, I saw what must have been a hundred loaves of white bread for sale all on one long shelf.

I shuddered to myself, knowing for the thousandth time that I had to stop myself from wandering into this time trap, where the past recycled itself every few minutes, repeating some event or other in an endless loop, until another took over. It was hard though, to put out of my mind, the shops I had seen today, filled as they were with food. The quality was better than Rotterdam, where the effects of bombing were even now, five years later, everywhere to be seen, and the people more numbed than the Amsterdamers.

I headed in the vague direction of the harbour, where I had landed three days earlier. I knew there was always some good neighbour in a boat, or a ship, willing to slip a piece of bread, or even a slice of sausage. Most of the men on the boats had seen hard times once or twice in their lives and understood the need when an empty hand was thrust into their face.

On the opposite side of the road, a man shuffled his way home in the evening gloom. He wore faded blue dungarees and a donkey jacket, which hung open despite the chill air. His head was thrust well down onto his chest as he carried an old army pack. His feet were jerking mechanically as they were placed deliberately, too deliberately, it seemed, one in front of the other; it appeared at first glance he had been drinking too much. He was like a marionette, but in other ways he acted as though he were sick rather than beered up. Surprising me, he accelerated his pace without warning, and shook his head several times as if he were a horse throwing off flies.

'No! No! No!' He kept on mumbling to himself. This was not in itself a particularly violent or peculiar message. It was a voice, tremulous and shaky, inwardly spoken and terribly frightened. He was quite clearly, addressing himself, with a tone which seemed to say he had reached the end of his tether. I had seen it all before, many times, and I was about to dismiss him from my mind, when, without warning, he began to cross the road towards me. It was fast enough to scare me, until he came nearer, when I could see his eyes were not focused on me, or on anything in particular. They were quite dead, though he wasn't blind. As he passed me by, he broke into a run while spreading his arms and fingers wide, as far as he could reach. A couple passing by had to step back quickly to avoid the flailing arms.

'Its poor Theo,' said the man.

'He's worse again,' his companion replied, though neither made any move towards him. Besides, the man called Theo was already vanishing into the dusk of the neighbourhood, a horrid noise curling from his mouth. I had heard the sound before in the camp, and I confess I never needed to hear another noise like it again. The combination of the sounds emitted and the reputation of the area, with its forlorn shadows, echoes of the past, its eighty thousand Jewish ghosts, dead and gone forever, made the two watchers hesitate before turning back in the opposite direction. The last time I had listened to a demented person was when they had made a woman kneel on the ground, while a group played Russian roulette with a pistol pressing into her forehead, firing the pin three times in a row. They had taken the bullets out of the chamber without the poor wretch being aware. At the third time, her mind simply refused to accept the situation anymore. A growl at first, rising up the scale beyond contralto and soprano it passed higher and higher until it burst with a scream as one used to hear screech owls when they flew off at night. It was a weird sound, nothing human about it at all. Because it wasn't human, it frightened even the soldiers who abandoned their awful game and walked back sheepishly and embarrassed to their quarters. The next day, unable to work, unable to give a rational thought to anything at all, the woman had snatched an officer's pistol from its holster while his hands had been holding a box, and placed it to her head. Her terror, at least, was over.

The couple who had known the man slightly, hurried on up the road as the noises floated above them. They seemed to emanate from the dark buildings themselves, through which led the only road. Theo they had called him. I wondered what sort of man he had been before the war. It must have been the strain of the war, for he appeared quite young: perhaps one of the camps I had known, a survivor like me, and one in ten thousand to come back. It was a ratio I knew by heart and each time it came to mind I wondered why it had been me rather than so many others.

The dead ghetto around me brought back the dreams again. Promises, promises I must keep. I must always remember, never forget, but the hunger and the tiredness were stronger now, so I staggered along the dirty cobbles where the rubbish of five years had compacted into a congealed mess.

The rubbish of *Auschwitz* had been formed out of human flesh, as often as not. There was never a chance of anything even remotely edible or having some sort of use, to lie on the ground long enough for the wind to blow it away. I grew used to death, though not of dying. When I saw an old man or woman in the street these days, I was reminded of the skulls, which had grinned at me with their bared teeth, making up part of the litter as they lay, half buried in the mud. Those people, at least, had cheated life. Death itself was blessed. It was eternal sleep where one was never frightened. It left only the manner in which this estate was to be achieved; that was infinitely more difficult. So, instead, we all continued to cling to life, however minute the straws were which floated by always out of reach.

My thoughts returned to the street, its dull yellow lights illuminated small circles of the pavement, absorbed quickly in the blackness. As I rounded an empty block of apartments in the act of being demolished by a local contractor, I could smell salt and stale beer on the night air. The rattle and squeal of trains moving out of Central Station above me, added to the lonely mood. Images of cattle trucks crammed with people, so full those who fainted remained standing up, trickled back into my mind. Each time I forcibly removed these images from my head, another pressed in to replace it, insistent, never caring if I wanted to recollect the shocks or not. It was only my curiosity to find out what had happened to the young man, which enabled me to continue to walk the greasy cobbles.

I shook myself shakily and eventually found myself walking alongside a quay. Rope hawsers bisected the granite coping stones every few metres. Small lights loomed out of the intense blackness of the water, tiny worlds of warmth and food. I heard someone laugh loudly, almost shocking in its contrast to my breathless silence, a sound followed by the clatter of plates and food being scrapped into a bin.

All at once I felt dizzy, so much so that the cobbles began to move and merge, one on top of the other. A lamppost, its gas mantle flaring and hissing, beckoned scarecrow arms at me like a policeman on point duty.

'Hey! *Mejouffrouw*! I've got you. Don't struggle; I'm not going to hurt you. Here, sit down for a minute.'

I did struggle, though the man behind me was immensely strong. His voice, however, was soft and I felt I could talk myself out of trouble if he began to get stupid. I tried to stand and found my legs buckling under me. It was ridiculous. 'This is silly. Let me up, please,' I demanded, but a mist had swum into my eyes. I took a deep breath.

'Who are you?' I asked when the land became marginally steadier than water.

'My name is Maas. Pieter Maas. I live on that boat…there.' He pointed in a vague direction to the east. 'Out there.'

In the mist I could see a larger boat with a light riding at its funnel, showing up as a white ring. 'You fell…in the road.'

'I tripped,' I answered feebly not sure why I had to make such a ridiculous excuse.

'I don't think so lass. I was watching you. You just fell down. Your legs gave way, just as if a cauliflower stalk had broken.'

It was a strange way of describing my descent to the road. I could smell raw earth on his clothes, yet he was a sailor to all intents and purposes, for he said he had lived on a boat.

Intuitively, he guessed what I was thinking. 'I pick vegetables. I work the fields by day with my family, and by night we return to the boat.'

'At this time of the year?' This was even more ridiculous. We were getting nowhere and, meanwhile I was lying in this man's arms feeling more and more awkward.

'There's always veg in the fields. We pull it up as it is wanted in the markets. Flowers also, in the summer, of course. After that, it is the big season.'

I was now curious. 'What is the big season?'

'Well, yes,' he appeared mystified for a moment, as if not understanding how I could not know what he was talking about. 'Potatoes, potatoes of course. Potatoes are my trade, really. And we get half a tonne for ourselves.'

The man, Pieter, smacked his lips as if with some distant memory. I couldn't see if it was connected with potatoes or not. It did not seem likely, for a potato was a potato, after all. 'Now, how are you feeling?'

I pulled myself up on his arm, which felt surprisingly strong for such a small man. He held me tight as the warehouses began to revolve. 'When did you last eat, lass?'

I could not remember. 'About four days ago…I think. Just before I landed. I got a lift on a boat from Rotterdam when someone gave me a bread roll.' The recollection of that precious gift made me smile. 'I've not been able to find work. Everyone seems so busy…cleaning up after the war, going about their work…no time to stop and talk. Perhaps it is because I am a Jew. My large nose and all that sort of thing. Its-'

'Now, that is silly talk. We've done with that. Hitler's dead, thank God. Eichmann's disappeared and won't be showing his head above the wall in this part of the world again. Besides, I stopped and talked to you, didn't I?

I laughed weakly, seeing the humour in his words. 'Rather forced upon you though, wasn't it? If I hadn't fallen over, you would have passed me by, neither of us seeing each other.'

'I'm not sure of that.' His response was quick. He was a man used to thinking rapidly on his feet, a man who had to struggle in life. 'I always look at a pretty lady. You looked rather ill though, with your head down, swaying as you watched the hawsers. You are not a boat girl, are you lass? I could see you were just about to fall into the water, and it's a cold night for a swim and for me to pull you out.'

The idea of anyone saving me from drowning was absurd. Only a few years separated me from a time when men might have fought to hold my head down in a barrel of water. 'You could drown too, trying to save me, in this cold.'

'That's not the point, is it? I would have to try; otherwise I could not look myself in the mirror in the morning. Would have spoilt my waistcoat of course,' he added mischievously. He slapped his stomach to show off a really magnificent embroidered vest. It had mother-of-pearl buttons and pockets edged with gold wire. As he did so, he let go of me and I began to sink to the ground once again.

'Hey now. You are coming home with me. Get some food inside of you.'

Home. Such a warm, comforting word. It painted so many pictures of the distant past. 'Do you live alone?' I said nervously. 'I can't go back with you if you are on your own.'

He laughed. 'Mama would certainly have something to say to us both if that were to be the case, and Hans and Jos, not to mention Anna and Suzannah. That's my family,' he underlined proudly. As he spoke, his eyes lit up. It made them gleam with pleasure. 'The thought of going back to an empty boat would be too hard to bear. Without them...without them...there's nothing, nothing at all.' At these words the yellow points in his eyes flared and spluttered.

I had seen such an expression before. Life guttering to a halt, the end of a candle, when the grease congeals on the side of the holder. You can see the heat bleed out into the air, hardening the drips into white, fatty shapes, smooth as if worn by the sea.

Pieter took hold of my arm on which I leaned heavily. We stumbled across towards his boat, both out of step with the other, made more difficult by having to steer our way round the ropes, rather than step over them. The ground continued to heave and the night air, now raw and choking with dirty fog, tasting of sulphur, clogged my lungs.

'Mama! Anna! Please come and help,' he shouted out as we stood on the quay-side, overlooking quite a large boat. It was just as well we went no further, for I could not have crossed the pitching gangplank on my own, and it was too narrow for two abreast. Three, not two women appeared out of the wheelhouse, one quite enormous in height, and bony. They took in the scene quickly, faces softening as they saw me holding onto Pieter's arm as if for dear life.

The larger, much older woman took immediate control. 'Anna! Suzannah! Stay this side. You take one arm each, understand?' They nodded, easily riding the slight swell with their legs braced apart.

'I found her down the street. She's starving,' Pieter whispered, though none too quietly, to his wife. The bony woman had crossed over the gangplank with practised ease. She took hold of me and held me firmly, quite strong enough to be able to suspend me over the water for a moment in time, while she regained her balance, before swinging me over to her two daughters. My arms were seized and, all at once I was aboard, though all this time, consciousness was slipping from me in waves of faintness, vision coming and going almost with each breath I took.

The younger, prettier girl's hands went up to her face. 'She looks so ill. There's nothing left of her.' I felt myself being lifted up with an effortless ease and transported to the wheel-house. Somehow, the four of them bundled me down a steep stair and onto a bed.

'Dinner soon?' Pieter enquired after he was satisfied there was nothing else he could do.

'Almost ready. The boys will be back at any minute. But, this one needs feeding straight away. I've some soup. Here,' she thrust a clay mug into my face. 'Sip this, its very hot, so be careful.' After a moment in which I found myself unable to hold the heavy vessel, she took the mug herself. 'Here, I'll help you.'

I shall never, ever forget the hot delicious taste of that vegetable soup. I could separate each flavour, one by one. There were leeks and carrots and cabbage, onions and chives all mixed in a thick flurry of potatoes. A bay leaf curled up from the bottom and floated on the surface.

'Steady girl, not all at once.' Mama's giant arms gripped my body keeping it in place as I tried to force the life giving liquid down my throat. For an instant I despaired as she moved away from my vision, though it was only to reappear within my focus almost immediately with another full mug.

I could feel the energy running back into my veins, down through my legs and ankles and circulating through my ear lobes and fingertips. My toes came back to life, but my hunger made me ignore the pain and then the maddening itch. They were no longer numb, so although I was very weak, like a new-born kitten I suppose, to my new-found friends, it was only a short matter of time before I was able to sit up and take stock of my surroundings. Before then I really had had no idea of where I was.

'Can you make it to the table?' Said the man called Pieter.

'Yes,' I replied. It seemed like such a silly question when the table edge was almost within reach. As I was pulling at the wooden arm of the side of the bunk, two young men entered the cabin. The place was rapidly filling up. They looked as if they were in their mid to late twenties, with roughened hands and reddened faces, characteristics of the Family it seemed.

Mama had left the room for a moment allowing Pieter to explain to the boys the reason why there was another woman on the boat. There was more concern from two further pairs of eyes, with much shuffling of their feet as they hung back with slightly embarrassed airs, as they made a route through for me to the enormous table which dominated and filled the cabin. Food and eating were obviously taken seriously here as I was about to learn.

'Anna. Set the table. Boys. Your hands if you please. Father, an extra chair.' Swiftly the commands were issued and as promptly answered, as if we were sitting down to a military dinner. Not a voice was raised in dissent as forks and spoons, bowls and clay mugs were thumped down on the scrubbed wooden surface.

I counted seven places. I was safe: for the time being.

A tureen, old-fashioned and blackened, which held the soup, was delivered by Mama, who hoisted the heavy receptacle to the centre with no apparent effort at all. I could hardly have lifted the blessed thing at all with two hands, and with all of my strength back. The youngest girl placed a tin plate with an entire loaf sliced up on a pile of crackling crust pieces, another with a lump of cheese which had been previously attacked by a madman with an axe or chopper. Pieces of cheese stood out in all directions with holes carved into its middle. I remember my mother placing a Gouda wedge on the table one day, where she cut an immaculate, creamy strip for those who asked, leaving an irreproachable cliff of cheese for the next meal. Here, probably everyone on board had carved a lump for themselves, the idea of any attempt at neatness abandoned to the winds.

'Father it is your turn to say grace,' Mama said firmly, brooking no argument. Her four children studied her face in disbelief, even as one of the boy's mouths froze in mid-bite, teeth still locked impolitely around a slice of bread.

Pieter took it in his stride. 'Of course, dear.' He cleared his throat rather dramatically. 'This simple meal, dear God, is all we have, but let us not forget those who have no meal at all tonight. Amen,' he ended.

'Amen,' we all murmured into our chins. Mama smiled like a woman coming out of church and seeing her neighbours walking by as she greeted the Priest.

'And…before we stuff our gullets like fledgling sparrows, I want to introduce ourselves to our guest.' Pieter spoke firmly, matching Mama's in strength. He looked slightly incongruous, standing up and facing me. He still had his peaked cap sat squarely on his head and his jacket was buttoned up as though to meet the Harbour Master.

'My name is Pieter Maas.' He rolled the 'r'. Some call me Papa. The magnificent lady on my right here is my darling wife, Elizabeta, though she is Mama to many, a wonderful cook and mother to our four children.' Again, he puffed himself up with pride. He swirled a hand across the table as if greeting a princess. 'And…my children, Hans and Jos, my two sons. My daughters here are Anna and Suzannah.' On completing this introduction he blew a kiss at the last named girl, as if favouring her above the others. No one, however, seemed to take notice or offence, far less care, nor was anyone upset for not also being singled out. Suzannah was certainly the prettiest by far. The hard work they were all engaged upon had coarsened the rest of the Family's features. Her face though, glowed life in the dim recesses of the cabin and brought light through her eyes, to smile shyly as she was introduced. She was the only one in the room, me including, with fair hair, the others being black, though Pieter's was now showing iron-grey on the sides.

There came a snort from the opposite side of the table. 'Papa, do sit down, there's a dear. Supper is ready to eat and will get cold…and…well have your cap off, I think.' Mama indicated for him to take his seat. Pieter snatched his cap off as though taken by surprise that it was still in place.

'Tell me dear, what is your name?'

'Ruth,' I answered, 'but my father always called me Mae, as my grandmother was called Miriam. Mae actually comes from Miriam and Papa was always very fond of her. It made Mother angry but he always continued to call me by that name, so in the end it stuck. I prefer Mae myself and my school friends called me by that name.'

Elizabeta leaned forward with her soup ladle, which caused her hip bones to move inside her dress. I was reminded strongly of a cow eating in Vondel Park in the early part of the war. Up and down, its hips moved. I looked up guiltily worried they may have read my mind. Up and down the waiting diners went the soup ladle as the steaming brew was farmed out equally to each waiting bowl. Carrots and parsnip rings swirled around the surface, inviting me to spoon them out but, I did not want to start before the elders had taken a first sip. Mother would not have liked me to break my manners just because I was starving.

'Where are you from, Ruth, er Mae?'

This was going to be difficult. Er…just south of the *Middlelaan*. Only a little of it left now of course, I added, finding it impossible to keep the bitterness from my voice. All the empty houses once occupied by the Jews have been raided for their timber and furniture to keep the fires burning in the awful winter of forty-four I suppose. I wasn't there but I heard about it.

The hunger winter, they called it, said Mama, her eyes reflecting that time and the experience. She shook her head recalling the time when so many Dutch people had begun to starve. Many houses fell down when the wood was taken away and burnt, but it kept many children alive, asked Pieter, what were you doing then lass…if you weren't here? What happened to your house?

This required another pause while I thought out a way to tell them without upsetting them. I had to tell these nice, generous people in the nicest way possible. I raised my head up. I wasn't there because I was in Germany.

Ah. Germany. You were a prisoner then…ah, I mean-

Yes. Sort of I suppose. I was in *Auschwitz...Birkenau*. The silence was oppressive and impressively long as I felt each pair of eyes on my face. I was a deportee, you see. I was taken from my house with my mother and father by the Dutch police and, eventually shipped to Germany, courtesy of the Dutch railway system. The carriages were not too posh though, in fact they were cattle trucks.

This time the silence was even longer. Jos attempted to continue to sip his soup but the rest of them had stopped eating. Embarrassment perhaps, or just unsure on how to answer. Pieter dealt with it by putting his head down close to the table as if to put my image away from him. But, it was Suzannah who broke the silence.

It was a shocking time which we seem to be forgetting. Its so easy to forget, I suppose, but we have a lot to answer for...but most of the collaborators have been caught and tried, haven't they?

Not at all,' said Hans, there are still many of them in hiding. I could not stop myself from biting my tongue in frustration. The collaborators lived. The Jews, the gypsies, the disabled, the weak and the children had all died. Like so many Germans who had escaped the Allies, there seemed no way to bring the guilty to justice: and, no-one had listened even after they had been told. Once someone was on the list, the quota had to be fulfilled. Everyone had wanted just to survive in those days. How could I blame an engine driver for shunting a line of cattle trucks across a border to Germany? There would always be someone else to take his place, besides, he could well have ended up inside his own train if he had refused.

Elizabeta was clucking like a mother hen scratching for corn. So Ruth, you have no family?

Pieter intervened before I could answer. Perhaps we should not-

No, it's alright, really, I answered as quickly as I could. No, no family left at all I know about. Mother and Father died after being sent to the camp. Mother and I were separated from Father as we got out of the train and we never saw him again. I learned that he was sent to the gas chamber the same day as he had arthritis and could not move quickly. She was never able to come to terms with the terrible changes in her life. Ive since learned that my two uncles, aunts and all my cousins are dead too. I had no brothers or sisters, thank God, I added.

So, you are all alone in the world, Anna spoke the words for the Family. She crossed herself in a curious semi-secretive way. Her lips were thick and her face lumpen, echoing her mother's characteristics. She was so different from her sister, not only in looks but the manner in which she conducted herself.

Gradually, everyone returned to eating me included, despite the earlier bowls. The bread began to pad out my stomach painfully.

Steady on, lass. Eat more slowly or you will bring it all up again. I've seen it happen all too often. Pieter's hand came out kindly and patted me on the shoulder. We wouldn't want that, would we?

His wife swung her body out of the chair and opened the oven door of the range. A delicious smell of baking potatoes filled the cabin.

Ah! Said the men in unison.

Ooh! Suzannah murmured more delicately while Anna smiled to herself, edging a small piece of carrot onto her spoon with the tip of one fore finger. One by one, the potatoes were delivered to the same bowls in front of us. Elizabeta led the way by carving a cross on each one in turn before depressing her two thumbs upon the hot brown skins. Like an earthquake in miniature, the scalding white flesh of the interior heaved itself into the lamplight. Steam poured out of the wounds causing an immediate withdrawal of fingers.

Tonight is special, said Pieter, grinning from ear to ear as he rose from his seat.

Elizabeta frowned. Sit down Papa. We are still eating.

One moment please, Mama. He went to a shelf where he had earlier placed a small newspaper parcel. He had been carrying it when he had found me in the puddle and had set it aside with some care. Proudly now, he unwrapped it to be greeted by a further chorus of exclamations.

Its butter, said Hans. Its real. I remember butter.

Where did you get it from? Elizabeta demanded, her voice decidedly hostile. It is far too expensive to buy.

I could not remember when I had last eaten it. Before the war, that was certain but never since.

It is a present from Mevrouw Linker. She wanted us to have it. She said the farm is settling down and producing well.

Somewhat mollified, Elizabeta's face relaxed. Carefully, as if unwrapping a nappy from a baby, she exposed the slab and divided it into seven pieces.

I should not be eating your butter, I said with some feeling. This was their prize, no doubt hard earned and to which I had not contributed at all.

Nonsense, said the Family as with one voice.

Seven pairs of eyes studied the bright yellow, slippery knobs of butter as they began the journey down to the bottom of each bowl, where it was retrieved and relocated on the top of the potato. It was difficult to remove ones gaze from the pile; like a pythons eyes it was simply impossible to look at anything else.

The soup had been wonderful but this was quite simply, delicious. Its taste, its saltiness, and the way it melded into the potatoes' flesh. The yellow showed off the white flesh like cream on ice cream. I leaned back for a moment, allowing the Family to cluster tightly over their bowls. Outside, the night was total, obliterating the world from sight until the dawn. Inside, the single oil lamp hung low from the overhead deck beam, highlighting a cheekbone here and an eye socket there. There were deep shadows under their chins and brows merging with the hard browns of their clothes. It formed a greyer swirl on the wall behind Hans and Jos where a vestige of steam still hung just below the cabin roof. The dish below them caused an immense amount of concentration of effort as, one by one the Family allowed the buttery mush to slip down their waiting throats. It was so good it drew saliva into their mouths and caused the sweat to start from their foreheads in a damp glistening sheen. There was a smell of body odour in the room.

Ahh! They all said at the end. It was fast becoming a stock phrase in this family. Mama began to poor the tea.

What else in life does one want? Pieter enquired of no-one in particular and no-one deemed there to be energy enough to respond. He began to fill his pipe and soon the room was responding to a new aroma as the tobacco took fire.

So, little Mae, tell us your story. He seemed to have forgotten his earlier comment, asking the Family to be sensitive in their questions. Why were you out on the dockside in the dark? There are a lot of strange things out there. People and the like, he ended rather lamely and without further explanation. Anna and Suzannah have to be in by nightfall any night of the week.

Oh, Papa, said Suzannah crossly. We can take care of ourselves. Besides, everyone knows everyone here. It is not like the town. What is there to be afeared of?

There's things, said Pieter knowingly without explaining himself. He shifted his cap which had reappeared on his head after the meal, to ease the sweat on his forehead, and winked at Elizabeta as if to say she well knew what he was talking about.

Things? What things? She demanded, spoiling the whole effect he had been trying to build. The girls need to know, Papa. You haven't explained yourself and I don't know what you are talking about either.

Come, come Mama. We know what we mean, eh? He turned back to me determined to end the conversation which was getting dangerously out of hand.

He meant rape, of course. But, no one used the word these days. The Germans had gone from Holland and there was nothing to fear from them now, better not to mention such awful things if one did not have to, for it only tended to remind one of the dark days and the trudge of marching feet on the cobbled streets.

So you lost your home, Mae and your parents. Was it as awful as everyone says? We've not talked to a… he stumbled over the word as so many did.

Jew? I replied, helping him out. Such a short, insignificant word of three letters, yet half the world, it seemed found it difficult even to speak it aloud without mumbling.

Er, yes.

No, it was far worse. How can someone who has never been to the Camps experience them? I replied with some misgivings. I dont want to appear rude, Pieter, but it is difficult to describe the indescribable. You would not want to believe most of the things I told to you and you would think I was exaggerating to make the Jews case stronger, even if you wanted to believe. Besides, most cannot be told in front of the girls-

Quite so, said Mama hurriedly. Suzannah pouted.

You must understand that for two and a half years it was the same as being sentenced to death for each of those thousand days. Every morning I awoke not knowing if I was to die that day. Here you might die by falling under a tram but you would not be expecting it. There you expected it and, if it did not happen, then there was the next day and the next...for ever. Seeing good people die in front of you, who we had endured the whole hell of it together, seeing the light fade for the last time from their eyes. Death was quite arbitrary despite the German thoroughness in their planning to exterminate us. A whim, a bad night, an indifferent breakfast was all it took for an officer to pull out his pistol and shoot someone and turn away as if they had been knocking tobacco out of their pipe. I turned to Suzannah, she being the most sensitive one in the cabin. Imagine, Suzannah, getting out of bed...here in this room in the morning, any morning for that matter, I spread my hands about me, unable to tell if you were to be on the receiving end of a bullet later in the day, unable to know if you would be here for supper tonight. For one day, you can get over the terror...eventually, but for a thousand days...you never get over it. It was not only death from a bullet which at least was quick, but many were injected with gangrene and other diseases to speed up the process of research. These people died in awful agony over a long period while the Germans watched with clip boards and recorded the process. And, I sighed, remembering, and even if you made it through the camp and were to be liberated did not always make it better. I came home to find my family's house gone and my relations all killed, nothing and no-one left. One day you can endure. Two years? I let my words drift for I had never spoken of this before to anyone. There was nothing to say after that. Besides, I had no right to spoil these good peoples dinner and impose my nightmares upon them.

Excuse me, I did not mean for this subject to be given new light. It's been over five years and I have tried to push it down into my mind where it will not see the light of day again.

The lantern jiggled as a boat passed close by, its large bulk catching the stern with its wake. Pieter rose again and came to sit beside me. He kissed my forehead. You need never talk about it again, Mae, at least not to us. Now, I suggest you go back to that bed. We all get up early here, even on a Sunday.

Suzannah's face was flushed and a single tear was drying on her cheek. Anna's bottom lip trembled and Hans's mouth gaped like a fish stranded on the quayside.

That's that, said Elizabeta. Sleep tight.

* * * * *

Before I eventually drifted off to sleep, my stomach full to bursting for the first time since I could remember, the image of the young man came back to me. Perhaps he also was home in bed, consoled by his wife, or a mother. Or was he alone somewhere, without any warmth to make him sleep? I would never know. There were so many pieces of human misery drifting around the cities of Europe these days, with no homes let alone a country or a nationality to bring that feeling of security and hope for the future.

During the night, a cat as black as the night itself arrived on my bed where it curled up in the angle formed by my body and my knees. It began to purr almost as soon as it arrived. It acted better than any sleeping draught. In the night, across the basin, the boats hawsers slackened and tightened in a rhythm as the wind died.

* * * * *

He pushed aside the empty tin and rose to glance out of the porthole. Alongside him, the Family were unduly talkative, he thought, though he could not distinguish individual words from the constant murmur floating up from the open door on the wheel house.

During the week, the sheer hard work kept them all quiet, or quieter. The weekend brought football and relaxation, while the ladies hung their washing out to gleam and dry in that order, for it was a matter of pride as to whose washing was the whitest. Caustic comments would be thrown across the water from boat to boat as they manoeuvred into the channel.

The sounds always made him feel lonely. He began to talk softly to himself, rambling, woolly words where he addressed the table and the clock alternately, contradicting each in turn. As he did so, he peered across occasionally at his good neighbours, hoping to see if they had noticed he was entertaining guests again.

If only- he mumbled to himself. If only he lived on a boat with a family such as was moored alongside the *Kuijpers*. They would hold his hand and cover his head when the world pressed in on him too imperatively, or, when he agonised over the meaningless of his life. At other times, he would find the love for his dead parents distorted by his own mindless anger.

And…the Family would say it was all a silly dream.

He went out on deck. The chill evening air had cooled almost to freezing point. He could smell snow on the wind coming down from the North-East where it had passed over the flat polders without any geographical constraint. It would mean he would have to find, or buy more wood for the locker: the cold, when it came, could last for four weeks at this time of the year.

Out on the water, the low, flat barges, rather like the polder itself, nestled bow to stern as far as he could see. Some had been wedged into narrow gaps so that their forepeaks touched the beam ends of others either side. Further out, a small tug went by, similar rings to its funnel and with the same stocky, almost cheeky look as its bow wave overtook the *Kuijpers*. Theo turned his head so he could see it better, silhouetted against the lights of the city. It made directly for the narrow gap between stone piers, its speed causing smoke to fan out over the moored boats. He made a fist as it reached the opening banging it down on the hardwood rail. The hard slap of flesh on wood coincided with the tugs stern neatly filling the space formed by the tunnel through which it had to pass; only at the last moment did the skipper lower the smoke stack to obtain sufficient clearance. It was a neat piece of navigation as, with a soft expression on its steam siren it vanished into the inky black of the tunnel mouth. Theo pondered upon the boats view on the other side: the Ij canal and the route to the massive North Sea canal.

His palm had split with the force of the blow, not badly and a plaster would suffice. It reminded him, however, that a normal man would not have carried out such a stupid and senseless action for an event as trivial as a boat going to sea. To any onlooker it would not have made sense, but then, it did not make sense to Theo either. Sense was reason, and Theo found little point in applying any sort of reason to what he did. By cutting off the view of the other tug as it disappeared into the tunnel allowed his mind to remain cut off also from the wide open space beyond the basin… his home.

WHITE WHITE WHITE

White, like sheets strung out on a washing line, wrapping everything up in sight. White sheets wrapping bodies in a morgue. Morgues, cold as snow. Snow is white, whiter than white...

The cold and snow wrap the boiler in an iron grip. So tight is its hold it freezes the tug in the sea to prevent it ever leaving port again. In fact, it is fundamental that it never separates itself from its warp attached to the stone pier.

The cold will last forever, so the boat remains trapped in eternity, as if a blacksmith has forged a weld between the decks' steel plates and the cast iron bollard on the shore.

There's a strange light across the water, not far away. It's not a light in fact...but a face perhaps, a white face. It wants to be friendly. It is trying to smile but the grin fades and becomes more of a grimace between two black holes staring and staring. It's rude, of course to stare, but the face takes no notice...bad manners mother had said, to stare. There's a grumbling sound as a corner buckles and twists in fantastic distortions. It collapses into the earth with a great shower of dust shooting skyward. The ice-falls in the Arctic do much the same thing though those are white ones.

Time to get out of the cold!

The face is there again, this time the black holes flash and blink white, black, and white again and again as if they are one of the occulting buoys in the outer harbour signalling the route for the tugs to the *Ij. There's no need for colour when there are such intense shades of black and white. They seem as red as blood from a fresh killed calf and as hard as a blue summer's sky in August.*

Someone calls Yoo-hoo: it brings sudden warmth and confidence into the small circle of ice walls. It has the power to banish the cold if only for a short while.

'Ahh! Potatoes!' comes a surprising statement. But it makes a lot of sense. Got to have more before the lights go out on the city walls, before the images return; images of blackened, broken houses with skulls teeth windows and agonised mouths for doorways. There's one, a thousand kilometres away…and another…and another, much closer. Now they are all moving forwards. So many they are beginning to crowd the boat.

The voices behind the warm steam echo like children in the tunnel across the water as they shout up to the barrel-vaulted ceiling of damp, mossy brick. The echoes are not clear though, damnit! Just when the voices begin, three or four at a time, they begin to merge, each time slightly more out of focus than the last.

'M-mea—tt…ttoo-dai?' Says Mama.

'Itt'-ss Ssun-dai,' all the voices say together in chorus.

The echoes are getting louder and longer now. Steam whistles like the Orient Express on the fast stretch through the Simplon. The sand, too, blows up against a hut. It will be strange, because the Marram grass planted to keep it all in place, will make no difference at all, however much they all work to hold it down. The fine round particles of quartz squeak as they blow away. They stream through your fingers like water and strip the paint from the grey hut door and walls until it is burnished into dulled brass.

I've seen it all before, a long time ago.

Cold again. The white is here. White, white, more white. Ice rears up to split and divide. It shears open to allow the savage sea to darken the cracks in between the blue ice. It's coming closer.

Below, the cold returns, surprising really because it prevents most of the light to shine where it is most needed. Shine the light; there's a sport… shine the light godamnit! Shine the light on the big black eyes…please.

There's a sound as when trains are derailed or trams collide so their sides run past each other. It starts as a groan, then, tails off into a high-pitched screech: a puppy dog being run over? At the end, what paint is left is whirled into the air. Bright red paint. It pretends it is all over now, yet it is ready to cut the air with another demented cry at any time. The sound is in the Kuijpers itself. It scours the worn steel plates and vibrates the deck heads transferring to the mast rising out of the wheel house like a submarines conning tower. There's a small, scratchy whine springing from the big, brass binnacle itself. It is all around, everywhere, but that is only to be expected for the room is on the move again. I mean…really on the move…coming at the speed of a galloping horse…the tide across the sands of Mont St. Michel, splashing through the mud flats. The cabin roof roars its approval for it is *guided by rollers so it can move downwards if it wants, when it wants. It is doing that now for it wishes to join the deck below.*

But…it is the corners to be really afraid of…

Chapter Two

He woke to find himself sprawled across the single arm chair, which had belonged to his grandfather. His ankle felt sore and weak after having collapsed untidily into his boat last night but, after a couple of tenuous try-out steps, he felt reasonably assured it would take his body weight.: the plaster on the palm of his hand he shrugged off as another one of his stupidities.

While he raked the fire and threw a few pieces of wood in through the open door of the stove, he banged down the kettle onto its top, allowing him time to study the weather. Like all the family before him, it had been a regular and necessary morning habit to see how the day was proceeding before making ready for sea. Old habits die hard, despite the fact that *Kuijpers* had not left the basin for years and Theo was not about to change now.

There was something different about the light in the cabin; something else had joined the dockside. He realised he had been woken by the brighter than usual light entering the porthole.

It was snow.

There was snow everywhere, covering the piles of sugar beet, filling the moored barges and clinging to the mudguards of the waiting lorries queuing to offload their goods. Porters stood in groups, waiting in abject misery as they tried to prevent the stuff settling down their necks. There is never a more unhappy picture than the one of men attempting to ignore the weather, having not expected snow, by hunching up their shoulders as if they were a series of herons on a river bank. The men pulled at their jackets and thin coats as the wind cut across the dead flat polder direct from Russia. All sound too, was muted, calming the traffic noises until a car went close by to crunch the flakes into rhythmic, zigzag tyre marks.

It was a strange sensation almost as if it were theatre, or like a circus act. As he peered towards the sky and the channel in the east, he saw a face appear at the port-hole of the moored boat facing him. It was a girl, perhaps a woman, though it was hard to tell from this distance through smeared glass and she had the sort of face that belied an accurate ageing, but it was certainly not one of the girls from the Family. This face was white, almost deathly so, contrasting starkly with her hair, as black as coal or a crow's feather. Her nose was quite large which would otherwise have marred her real beauty if it had not been for the pair of huge eyes. These same eyes now became aware of the watcher for the first time. He couldn't see much more, just a misty view, framed in the brass port, but she was new to the Family next door. He turned away, then, compelled to learn more, and leant his head back to catch another view. She was still there, uninterested in the snow, her eyes still in focus on the boat and, particularly on his porthole. Timidly, she gave him a half-smile, the kind of one that always is ready to die immediately if it senses no response and, also allowing him the means to reject it if he so wished. Anticipating his mood, she cut it off as if she had been caught spying upon some illicit deal or affair. It was almost painful to attempt to hold her eye and stare, but, somehow it seemed important and necessary. His smile stretched the thin skin over his cheek bones for an instant, before he reverted to his usual manner in which he nodded his head at her, once, twice before diving for safety to the floor below the port hole where he sat cross-legged on the blanket chest.

Who was she, for Gods sake? No one new ever came to the *Anna Rosner*. It was so unlike the Family to have visitors, in fact he could not think of another time they had had a guest to stay. She must have stayed for it was far too early on a Sunday morning for a caller. She was looking out of the portside forward bunk, hardly the place to entertain some do-gooder looking for a church offering. It meant the girl must have stayed the night before, when he had been ill. Perhaps she had heard him cry out in his sleep?

All at once the desire to see her again was upon him. It was urgent, a pressure on him as he had not felt in ages. He found he had to joggle his head above the brass rim, but she was gone. Instead, Mama, the tough old woman who ran the Family, could be seen stumbling slowly to the boat's edge, caution in every step she took, as the snow compacted into layers of ice beneath her worn slippers.

'Theo!' she called out loudly. 'Theo, I have *something* to say to you.'

It was quite a strange phrase to say; the word 'something' being stressed quite strongly, but a common characteristic to her, for Mama had always accentuated particular words to make a point of seeming importance.

Theo climbed up to the wheelhouse and slid back the door with difficulty for the slide had become frozen during the night as water had remained in the guide. 'Good morning Elizabeta. Not a good one for you, I think.'

'Winter's not yet gone and, yes, a bad one for us for no-one will want us to pick in such hard ground. The land will be like iron.'

'It's Sunday anyway.'

'Sunday, Monday, what difference does it make? Those men over there are working today,' she answered, shrugging against the chill wind and the driving snow as they pressed against her thin, worn-out dress with its large patterned hydrangeas. It caused her hip-bones to stand out. Her jaw was almost blue, as if she usually shaved, but not today.

'What is it Elizabeta. You will catch a cold standing there, not properly dressed for this weather.'

The old woman saw the sense of his words. 'Come to lunch today. Twelve o'clock. We have a guest for you to meet.'

'A guest?'

'Yes. A young girl. Came to us last night…all of a sudden. She's had a bad time of it, what with the war and all that.' Theo knew exactly what she meant. Everyone did. It was all that needed to be said to explain the entire history of the occupation.

So, this was the mystery face he had seen at the port-hole. He remembered her half-smile, entreating a similar response and some form of reassurance.

'Well? Will you come then?'

'Of course, I mean thank you very much for the invitation. I will be there at twelve.'

'Remember your manners when you arrive.'

Elizabeta grunted, though not unkindly. She turned and made back for the warmth of her own boat. Just as she reached the wheelhouse door, she threw him a friendly wave. He could see that the snow on her hair had prematurely aged her so he could picture what she would look like in later life.

Theo smiled. At that moment, two horses came towards him. The harness holding them together was covered in half melted ice from the heat of their bodies. They were hitched to a van, more of a square box sat on two axles, at the front of which sat two men in identical dark blue coats and hats.

'Bread? Today?' Theo shouted across the narrow gap of water at them while searching for a few cents in his trouser pockets. One of the Van Gerd brothers, the elder by five minutes, or so he was fond of telling everyone who cared to listen in the boat village, pulled at the reins.

'Tomorrow the channel might well be frozen over. No-one in mid-channel will be able to get bread and we won't be able to sell any. So today, Sunday I know, everyone gets bread who wants it.'

Theo jumped ashore and patted the two grey noses in turn. Pink lips puckered like rose petals as each sought a morsel from his hand. 'I have none for you today my beauties.'

One of the pair, thus offended, obligingly dropped an enormous pile of manure, which steamed in the snow. The brothers looked on unconcerned. Theo took two loaves feeling their heat through his jersey as worn as Mama's dress.

'You look hungry, Theo. Eat those quickly.'

'Ah! I'm going out to lunch today,' he answered with considerable pleasure, 'to the Family', he nodded back to the *Anna Rosner* half lost in the snow where only her rigging remained marked against the sky. He could see one of the daughters coming out to buy bread as well.

'Good appetite,' the brothers responded in unison waving back the impatient horses as they pulled against the brakes. He jumped back, acknowledging a cheery wave also from Suzannah and could see that the sea was beginning to freeze out in the harbour. The water was now moving as though in a slow-motion film: a tug making for a space between the boats to find the channel, turned in a swirl of ice, some pieces retaining fresh white snow on its crust. The boat caused the jet-black water to shiver and shake: not a day to fall in.

Theo passed the time of day until lunch by drinking tea, firing up the range to make it cherry red on the top. The heat rapidly reached the beams overhead which reacted by creaking and groaning in comfortable reply. Unusually, he began to tidy the main cabin, something he had not done in a long while. Even so, he could see the cabin needed, desperately, to be cleaned properly and not just the perfunctory dab and stab actions he was taking to justify the eternal wait until lunchtime.

Consciously, he turned and walked to the engine room. Behind the steel door it smelt of oil and raw metal. A bilge pump, set loose, clanked occasionally as the two boilers stared back at him, just as the girl had done earlier that morning. The two gauges were her eyes, disturbing him, and for a silly moment he thought of cancelling his visit.

'I must be stupid,' he said aloud, as he saw the engines staring rudely directly at him. 'Alright! Alright! I'll come and fire you up, soon.' He slammed the engine room door clips tight into place and walked back to the centre of the main cabin. It reminded him only too well of the main reason why he never left his mooring.

Theo found he often talked to his boat, or to part of it anyway. When, with the long days ahead of him, having nothing planned, and no one to speak to, he would attach himself to a particular section of the tug, a part needing his closest attention. He feared for the engines and knew they needed to be maintained yet, at the same time he was afraid of doing so. If they were never to be lit, the metal parts would inevitably fuse together irretrievably with salt and rust in a malicious combination. He was fearful of lighting the boilers for it could only mean he was preparing for sea. His sickness, for that is what it was, had sprung from a slow-growing, but an ever grittier urge never to leave the land again. Each time he had made fire in one of the boilers, the terrors hovering at the back of his mind, overtook the dam of his mind. At first, it would bring only breathlessness, as one is frightened by a barking dog or a gun going off close by; later, it expanded to a shaking hand and recently he had begun to hallucinate. It was totally irrational, he knew, for such a man to live on a sea-going tug, but the mere idea of passing through the tunnel on the opposite side of the basin, out into the *Ij* canal made him tremble. There was a sharp sour taste of bile as it slid quickly up his throat to cause his entire body to shake as if he had the ague. So, he was able to use the excuse, lightly given by the Harbour Master that he really should do something about the black smoke emitting from his stack, as the real reason for not being prepared for sea. He sometimes wished he had been served some sort of notice, a warrant with an official seal perhaps, declaring that the *Kuijpers* was not to fire up her boilers until they had been converted to diesel. And where would he get that sort of money from anyway? He was not able to translate his fears into psychological terms though the hawser linking *Kuijpers* to the quayside had become, to all intents and purposes, his umbilical cord. To cast off would be to make a leap into the unknown of such uncertainty that his mind refused to countenance the idea in any shape or form. It served only to reinforce his wish to stay anchored to the granite dock. He remained thus, trapped on his boat, destined never to leave the harbour, allowing the green blanket weed to cluster and grow thickly on its bottom, while the boiler room, wrapped itself in cold, stale air, as the once greased parts began to show the inevitable signs of rust and decay. Ice lumps clinked against the hull, breaking his reverie.

'I'm off to have lunch with friends,' he repeated to himself. 'Who wants to go to sea on a day like this…anyway?'

He sat down again and leant against the masthead which passed between the twin beams curving from one side to the other holding the deck with its towing winches in place. The brass-ringed port holes were long since oxidised and their glass scratched on the outside from a hundred mishaps from its past. Among all of these marks was a game of noughts and crosses, abandoned half-way through as if naughty children had been caught before they had time to finish.

He could see his mind was beginning to wander again, the fearful tendrils pushing at the back of his eyelids. He concentrated instead on the Family to occupy himself, to disconnect himself from the rising nausea when opening the door to his mind. First, he focussed on Anna who always seemed to be so straight-laced, peering down at her cheap novels with every opportunity she had. She was polite enough but…no fun and absolutely no humour. Was that the expression he was looking for, he wondered? And then, there was Suzannah. Dear

Suzannah. What a wife she would make someone. Although only two years younger than her sister, they could have had different fathers, mothers even. She talked so much she quite made up for Anna's silences, and made him want to be with her all day. She managed to make him forget his own dark broodings as he listened to her chatter. She would always make a point of enquiring what he had been up to since they last met, and would prise out of him any news he might have gleaned from the dockside. Being on the tug most of each day, he knew of every incident on the water and who was doing what with whom. From babies being born to barge collisions, fights on the quayside and the Harbour Master's newest uniform, he could report back to her with hardly a stumble in his words.

The boys? Well, they did not really understand him at all, and he only saw two young farmers with little to say unless it was to do with the size of a particular sugar beet or the latest football score. Hans was an extrovert nonetheless, fond of the ladies who liked to dance and a drink in his hand; Jos was moodier, much like his sister Anna, but he retained a reputation as a fine seaman and navigator, one of the best in the basin as his father was fond of declaring too often, much to his embarrassment. His skill in sorting out other peoples barges when they had got into trouble in the inner basin having caused a seemingly intractable problem, made the older men in the harbour shake their heads in admiration.

Gradually, frustratingly, the hands of the clock swung round to twelve where Theo's complex nature and taciturnity made him wait another five minutes. Finally, about to leave, he caught his face in the mirror. Humming to himself he slicked water on his hair, making it cling to his forehead in roman style, small curls in a row which set off his rather flat crown: he recalled his grandmother saying once, that his head had a double crown, whatever that meant. His cheeks were quite gaunt, framing the pensive and serious look, a characteristic not unattractive in his teenage years to young girls at the Saturday dance. He blew a clumsily formed kiss to the mirror.

Outside, the ice spicules clasped tight in the bitterly cold wind stung his eyes. He closed the wheelhouse door, sensing the snow on his still wet hair, but failed to lock it, a habit which had developed over the past two years as if to say he didn't mind if anyone broke in to the tug. Theo climbed over to his neighbour and wiped the wet slush from his crutch where he had sat astride the gunwale for a moment. He had seen the same strange face at the porthole as he approached and, this time there was recognition, causing her eyes to widen slightly, though this time there was no smile. The face disappeared from view after examining his own quite closely, her eyes unwavering. Theo called down the companionway, to be answered by a repeat cry.

'Yoo-hoo, yourself, Theo. Come on down.'

'Permission to come aboard,' he requested, snapping a lazy salute at Pieter who was holding a bottle of Geneva gin in his hands. The girls giggled. Hans and Jos shook hands, all correct and quite formal as music from some form of instrument wafted through the main cabin.

Theo was immediately full of admiration. 'Found it, 'said Pieter proudly, 'in one of those warehouses: just left there.'

'Course, you've got electricity these days, haven't you?' Theo replied with some envy.

'But, we don't use it, not until now. Never had the need 'cept for the lights.'

'And it's expensive,' said Mama, coming from the steam of her cooking and pecking him on the cheeks three times. 'Mind you, I don't say I don't mind the music. It's coming from *Hilversum,* and we can get England, the BBC Home Service quite easily. Can't understand it too well as they seem to speak so fast, but Jos translates for us.'

Theo was even more impressed. About to speak again, he was interrupted by Pieter. 'Our new guest, Theo. Her name is Ruth, or Mae, which ever you like.'

'Two different names,' he said confused and intimidated together. 'I-I like the sound of May, very English.'

Mae came closer, into the circle of eyes watching her. 'It is not May,' she explained in a kindly voice, holding out her hand, her face becoming more animated. 'It is spelt M-A-E as in Mae West the American actress.'

'Ahh!' he responded, 'I see,' not seeing at all. He knew nothing of films and had never been to a cinema, much less kept up with the names of the movie stars. 'That's a strange name, isn't it? Like the life vests I mean,' he went on hurriedly, feeling he was being rude. 'It is nice, it certainly sounds the same as May, but Ruth is your proper name I suppose?'

'You suppose right. Mae is what everyone calls me for Ruth doesn't do anything for me at all…does it?' She threw out a small challenge which Theo had no intention of trying to answer directly. He had never been asked such a straight forward question and her directness matched her penetrating stare. He looked round for support to find the Family watching them both closely.

'The first Ruth married Boaz almost three thousand years ago.' The offering from Jos relieved Theo of a reply at all. 'She was related to David, *the* David,' he stressed, completing the impromptu history lesson.

Ruth never was sure when someone was making fun of the Jews behind her back, but the boy seemed genuine enough and her bright smile, following his, which formed at the corners of her mouth and spread up into her eyes, transformed the whole of her face. 'You seem to know a great deal about the Jews, Jos.'

'Not really, only what every Christian is taught at school. I did not know the original Ruth was a Jew, only her relationship with David. I remember it from school, a long time ago-'

'So, you retain something in that turnip head of yours.' Pieter patted his son's head which jerked out of the way at the comment. Jos did not like to be patronised by anyone, least of all his father even though it was not intended as a snub.

Theo liked the Jewish people. There was the lady at the butcher's shop who was always kind to him, and the two bakers' brothers of this morning. Everyone, all Amsterdam knew of the Jews and understood what the City had done to them in the war by sending them away. He recalled now, her face staring, white and strained through the porthole at him… and somewhere else as well. His mind sighed within him: it was hard to remember anything these days.

Suddenly, she was talking to him again. 'You! You are the man who ran past me last night. You-, er, I'm sorry, you were in a hurry to get home, or so it seemed at the time. You were shouting out across the road to someone,' she quickly compromised on her words to try and soften the impact of the dreadful *faux pas* she had committed.

'What do you mean, dear?' Mama was not helping at all.

'Oh, nothing really. For a moment, I thought Theo was someone else-'

It was Theos turn to surprise her. 'But, you were right, perfectly right. I lost my head last night...as I do from time to time. It was me you saw, I am sure now. Sometimes it happens to people like me. I'm sorry if I frightened you.'

'Please, I meant only I was concerned for you, but you ran so fast you were like that black Olympic runner, and you just disappeared into the night, swallowed up into the dark.'

'I always run when 'they' are coming. I run to try and lose them but they always catch me up somewhere along the road.'

The Family listened with mouths agape until Mama rose and began to bang the blackened doors of the oven together. They tried not to stare at Theo standing with listless arms by his sides as Mae fiddled with the lapel of her blouse attempting to smooth it down, an effort which was proving rather pointless as it already lay completely flat on the fabric.

'I remember you now. You were tucked away in that shop front. You looked so ill but, you seem better today. Perhaps it was the street lights,' Theo added kindly.

He felt he had made a giant step by admitting his illness to a stranger but it was as though something inside of Ruth was willing him to speak to her in an entirely normal way. It made him want to try and explain everything to her. He hadn't been taught to speak to young ladies, especially ones with a well educated accent, and she certainly wasn't from the dockside. He wondered who she really was and this began to unnerve him. Luckily, Pieter felt they had monopolised the conversation too long and came to the rescue.

'Mama's soup, more likely. Young lass was half starving last night. Fainted right into my arms.'

Elizabeta snorted loudly through the steam, and turned to face her husband. 'Meal's ready,' she managed to say with some effort at grace.

The boys were on their stools in a trice before each of them suffered a none too light clip over an ear.

'Ere...what's that for Mama?'

'Think it over very carefully and it might dawn on you there are not three but four ladies present and, see, Theo here is still standing, the only gentleman among you with any manners.'

Theo found himself staring at the bulkhead. He never liked it when he was singled out for praise. He was directed to a proper chair at the huge table directly across from Ruth. Her deadpan face under the gas lamp showed up as a series of purple hollows and there were a number of thin, white scars on her face below one ear. She was wearing a black blouse with a warmer wool skirt. They were the sort of clothes which lay in huge piles on the street sellers' barrows alongside most canals in the City where much of the shopping had decamped during the war. They were all sold for a few cents each. No one asked any questions as to who had worn them last or what sort of person had worn a pair of trousers which now snuggled against one's crotch. It was enough to be warm and a good wash was all that was needed if one searched carefully through the mounds ready to argue a good price when the warmest piece had been found. As the city shops began the battle to win back the shoppers, displaying quality goods again in their new, large windows, the street vendors' days were numbered, but for Mae, she could still dress herself for less than a guilder.

Mama dished out more soup. There was a ham bone lying like a log on the surface of a river in flood. Bay leaves and rosemary added to the illusion as they crowded around the surface. Bread crusts cracked in the party's fingers showering the table with crumbs. The bread was still warm from the early delivery of the *Van Gerd* brothers. Silently, the bone sounded to the bottom of the pan.

'So,' said Mama cautiously, 'what is this, Theo that Ruth is telling us? Running down a stre-'

'I don't think so, really,' Mae felt obliged to interrupt; mortified the other guest on the boat was being subjected to an inquisition caused by her own foolish words. Theo, however, had little to lose for the Family were well aware of his illness and had experienced the effects of his attacks on several occasions. Besides, the Jewish girl would be gone in a few hours and would have forgotten him by nightfall.

'I felt one of my old attacks coming on. I was alone, in the dark, in the old Jewish quarter where there are all those old buildings being pulled down; spooky place, even in the day. I should have been home by then but it comes on so quickly sometimes,' Theo responded apologetically and turned to face

Mae away from Mama's curious stare, 'almost as fast as I can think about it. I have to run…to get home, before…' he ended by way of explanation. It sounded pathetic to his ears, but he did not believe anyone could have any idea of the crucifying terror it brought, as the horizons closed down and the buildings twisted and bent themselves as if they were trees in a storm.

'It's alright Theo,' Mama sounded strong by his side, realising she had asked the wrong thing. 'We understand. You had a bad attack last November, didn't you? You were in hospital for quite a long time.' By so saying, she communicated to Ruth that Theo was a sick man who lived on the edge of reason for most of his life.

'Yes, I missed Christmas. Five weeks in all. Then they let me out again but by then I didn't get any presents.'

Suzannah looked across at the two guests. They were so similar she guessed, in so many ways: both orphans, both half-starved and lonely. Both had had terrible experiences, the only difference between them seemed to be that hers had been brought on by physically administered mental torture which had probably affected her mind, though to be fair to her, it had not shown itself at the table, while Theo's was an internal illness of the brain, one he could not control. 'Are you able, I mean, can you…do you talk about it?' She asked of Theo.

'When it has gone from me, I do not mind. I can recall the pictures very clearly.'

'Where do these things go to?'

'Away beyond the horizon, behind the blackness of the sky, somewhere up there,' he gestured vaguely.

'How often do these attacks come on?' Mae was interested now, and her inquisitive nature did not want to leave it alone.

Theo paused unsure of how much he wanted to tell her though he felt a great need to tell someone, something so he could share the awfulness of it all. 'They come more often now. When they are with me, I see things as though at a great distance or at other times it is as if I am in some form of giant arena. It makes peoples voices sound as if they are under water, you know, when you tried to speak in the swimming pool when you were young.'

Mae wondered who 'they' were. It was clear Theo was as familiar with them as his own family had been. 'What happens if you get an attack when you are at sea…at work?'

'Oh, that can never happen.'

'Why not? Does the sea air stop it?'

If only, he wished and had to laugh. 'No, no. It is because I never go to sea. I cannot go. The Harbour Master won't let me fire up my boilers as they are very old-fashioned and produce too much smoke and bad smells from the coal. Besides, where would I go? I've lost my Master's ticket. It is out of date.'

Mae studied the young face in front of her. He had a seaman's face, the crows feet were already formed around his eyes, moulded from squinting into the sun when he had gone to sea. He had a sort of leathery look to his skin but she decided it was a kind face, free from any sort of malice. He was certainly thin and he walked, she noticed when he had come into the cabin, with a shambling gait, something she had seen the night before. That could have been due to the slippery conditions on the cobbles, she mused, but to her it was the walk of someone turned in on himself, a man who did not really care how he looked to the public. His pride had gone. Realising she had been studying him for some time, far too long in fact; she hurriedly turned to look out of a porthole.

'It's really snowing,' she said to break a short silence in the room.

'You don't have to worry about going out in this,' Mama responded, misinterpreting Mae's thoughts. 'You can stay here until you have your strength back and can find some work.'

Mae's face showed her thanks.

'Does this mean you will be a neighbour for a while?'

'Perhaps Theo, but I do not want to be a burden here. Food is scarce enough and–'

'Nonsense,' said Pieter interrupting forcefully while stabbing tobacco into his pipe. 'You can help us. There's a job going in the bread shop just past Central Station. We get our bread from the delivery van when it comes on Saturday; otherwise we get it at this shop on the way back from work. I saw a sign in the window. I'll enquire for you tomorrow.'

Mae was embarrassed at the help and kindness of these people. Her profuse thanks made Pieter self-conscious who winked to cover his discomfort and hunched his shoulders over the shower of sparks from his pipe which lit up the room with bright orange points of light.

'Leave your bowl in front of you Ruth,' said Mama. 'Meat today, and Papa, will you kindly put your pipe away. You can have that later.'

'It's Sunday,' chorused the boys in well-trained unison. It was obviously a ritual.

Theo didn't hear them. All at once he felt hot, hotter than was comfortable. There was the drone of far-off voices, muffled like summer flies on a window pane. The snow was dampening down all sound from outside. Mama went to open her mouth and began to speak to him, but she wasn't making any sense, for her words were developing into a strong echo which bounced off the walls of the room. He felt he was in a canyon, alone and no-one there to help and all at once he couldn't stand it anymore.

'No!' He shouted out aloud, making the whole family jump in alarm. 'It's coming. They're coming again.' As he spoke, their responding words of comfort clarified, the muzzled sounds sharpening. He felt foolish. What right had he to impose himself on these kind people? He looked across the table to see Mae's face full of concern.

'I'm sorry,' he said. 'I've had sufficient, thank you. I must get back to *Kuijpers*. I must do it now.' So saying, he rose from the table and began to climb back on deck.

'I'm coming with you.' Mae pulled back her chair. 'I think another attack is coming on.'

'Come back for meat.' Mama knew Theo too well to try and stop him, for it would only exacerbate the urgent desire to get home as fast as he could.

Outside, the snow was blowing almost to storm force, making the rigging scream and whipping the masthead. Theo was climbing back across the gunwale to the *Kuijpers* but a sixth sense made him turn back to see Mae emerge from the wheelhouse of the *Anna Rosner*.

'Go back,' he yelled and struggled across the icy deck almost slipping as he did. 'It's too dangerous.'

Mae made to cross where Theo had just gone but the two boats' sides were heaving and falling in an uncoordinated fashion. The rubber fenders squealed alarmingly making her change direction to the gangplank. Concerned to see he was safe in his own home she ran onto the narrow wood crossing and nimbly made it to the quayside but she hadn't realised that it was sheet ice. All at once, she was falling helplessly backwards towards the water, clogged as it was with lumps of mushy ice.

Theo was already running back to the quay. Without thinking, he jumped over the side, calling out loudly for Pieter and the boys to come as he did so.

'Oh God, save us,' Mama wailed, being the first to pop her head up over the coaming on hearing the cry. There was no sight of either of them. 'Papa, come quickly, they are both in the water.

* * * * *

I could not believe how cold the water was. I was paralysed, as it drove all rational thought from my mind, numbing me in the instant I went under the surface. Stupidly, my mouth was open to cry out perhaps, though what good it would do me heaven only knew. The diesel scum was the first thing I tasted as I hit the water awkwardly, one of my legs striking the side of the tug. I remember, vividly, the ice spouting up in all directions as it tried to get out of the way of my falling body.

The black water closed over my head, pushing me down, past the level of the ice where the weed hung on the hull of the boats. It was peaceful here; sound cut off as if cotton wool had been stuffed into my ears removing the need to struggle for although I knew I was drowning it did not seem to matter anymore. My breasts rubbed painfully against the keel of the *Kuijpers* before this pain was replaced by another. My hair was being pulled out; at least, it felt as if it was. The force jerked me backwards and up, away from the underside of the hull. A light burst into my eyes and I was on the surface gasping like a stranded cod.

'I've got her,' someone roared.

'Get a rope round her,' screamed another before I sensed a noose tightening around my waist.

Rather than a cod I felt now as if I was a rather large sea turtle being landed by a highly skilled fisherman…or was it a turtle man? My skirt had come off along the way so I tried to wrap my coat around me as I shook uncontrollably. My teeth threatened to come out of my jaw and lights started to go out again for the second time in two days.

More lights burst around me like fireworks and I sensed someone rubbing my thighs with a warm towel. More and more, the rubbing continued, expert hands causing the blood to flow faster and faster. My skin began to tingle. Once or twice, I opened my eyes for a moment or two which made them sting with the oil and petrol on the lids. Carefully then, I was able to see Elizabeta dabbing at my face and I was able to focus, take in the bony cheeks with their ridges of gristle over her brow and around her eye sockets. This close, I could see deep furrows across her forehead as if a farmer had ploughed up her face on command. God only knew how many years of hard labour had fashioned the creases in her body, making her the stronger mentally for it, if less and less attractive. But, still there, I could see the softness and care in her eyes, captured through the love she held for her family.

'There, there, little one. You are safe,' she repeated as if to a new born baby. 'Suzannah, another towel please.'

I felt again the warmth steal through me, invading the icy recesses, thawing out spaces which had stayed cold for years. As I tried to sit up Anna and Suzannah pushed cushions into my back to give me support.

'We almost lost you out there to the fish. You became caught up in the weed under the boats. Theo jumped in and pulled you out by your hair.'

'I know,' I said ruefully. My head felt tender but I was alive. 'He saved my life, didn't he?'

Suzannah gave me a hug, the first time anyone had done that to me since Mother had died. 'He is such a brave man. He jumped in without thinking, never pausing to consider how dangerous it was.'

Mae felt humbled. 'Where is he? Theo I mean.'

'He is on his own boat, the *Kuijpers*. Papa and the boys are building a big fire in his stove for him. He will be fine but we will have to wash all of your clothes, both of you as there is so much oil and tar on them. The water hereabouts is thick with it.'

I could see a big, steel bucket on the range, its galvanising shining dully in the light. Steam curled up from the top, my clothes replacing the cooking for the time being. This kind family's Sunday treat, the one time when they had some time to themselves had been ruined because I had disobeyed instructions and as a result, fallen into the sea. I could be so stupid.

'I'm so sorry I have caused all this distress to you all,' I wanted to burst into tears as much because of that first hug from Suzannah as from the aftermath of my swim.

Elizabeta studied my face for a moment. She smiled. 'Silly one, it's no trouble at all, and you might have died…easily,' she added, knowing the sea's temperature at this time of the year. 'Then there would have been real trouble, the police and all that.'

There came a knock from outside in the companionway. 'May I come down?'

I pulled a rug over me. I was completely naked. 'Come on down, Papa. Are the boys with you?'

'They are staying with Theo for the time being, at least until he has warmed up and has put on some dry clothes. We found his grandfather's long johns in a dresser. We put them on the stove for a minute or so before he pulled them on. That brought him round quickly.' He chuckled at his little joke.

'Don't be coarse, Papa.'

'Sorry dear. And how are you, little one? That was a close call, too close for comfort in fact. And you had to go and do it on the coldest day of the year. An hour later and you would have been trapped under the ice.'

'Is it that cold, Papa?' Asked Anna.

'They'll be skating on the canals in the morning I think, if this continues. They might even start the race again.' He was talking about the famous annual skating race across Holland.

I shuddered, seeing myself staring up at the iced surface, pressing it with frozen fingers as my air gave out and the water flooded into my lungs. I remembered the time at the camp when I had found a woman I knew, frozen in the latrine pit where she had fallen. She had been too weak to pull herself out and must either have frozen to death or suffocated in the stinking filth. The ice, mercifully, had removed all signs of her original personality and had allowed a light dusting of powdered snow to purify the shock of an arm stretching out above the frozen slime. I had always hated snow and ice ever since. Instead, I longed for Spring with its bright yellow-green leaves and the early promise of warmth in the air when the trees began to overhang the canals again, bursting into bloom with the reassurance of Summer to come.

'I hate the ice,' I said with considerable force, as my thoughts surfaced in the room, 'and snow...and the cold most of all.'

'And we all hate the winters,' Pieter answered. 'We cannot dig up the land. The carrots and leeks stay frozen in the ground so it becomes impossible to get them out without damage. The longer the snow and ice stay, the more the potatoes will rot. They go black you know, when they are rotten.'

'I know,' I said.

Pieter watched my face, realising he had nothing to teach me about blackened and rotten potatoes. I saw again, all the black potatoes my mother and I had eaten. After a year, it became a bonus if we found one with a part of white flesh. 'I'm sorry,' he said, and meant it.

Elizabeta shushed him out of the cabin while I pulled on a warmed vest and a long black wool skirt. I had never worn a brassiere for my breasts, small anyway through lack of food, had remained small. As I grew up, they had stayed firm, more attached to my body than flopping about like most of my school friends. Once, when I complained to my mother that my breasts were far too tiny, and anyway, much smaller than anyone else in the class, she told me not to worry. When I was middle-aged, she explained, I would still have my figure, while my friends would all have misshapen bosoms, sagging about their waists. I remember it made me smile at the time, a secret shared with her, which Father could not enjoy.

She, of course, could never have known or dreamt, that none of my Jewish school friends would ever gain the age of thirty, let alone enjoy middle-age. All of them in my school had been taken away at the same time. That awful day, when we had heard the squealing of metal wheels on the seldom used sidings, where the tracks had long rusted. There must have been sixty wagons, each with its wooden sides and white numbers stencilled on the planks. Inside, some of them had the smell of cows and the harsher ones of sheep. There was nowhere to sit but that did not matter for there were so many people packed into one wagon that everyone propped up their neighbour. If you fainted, or died, you remained upright until the doors were opened.

To think of something sensible I had counted the number of people jammed in to the truck: it was seventy-four.

'Are you warm enough?' Elizabeta's kindly voice broke through the camp's realities. Somehow, in the last day, I had been reminded more often of the war and the 'resettlement' plans we had had to endure, than in the past five years, since I had come back to Rotterdam.

I nodded. She went on: 'we want you to stay for a while. All of us do. You need to get your strength back, get a job, earn some money…find your feet again.' She gave my shoulder a friendly squeeze.

This time I did manage to burst into tears. I had not been treated so kindly for so many years. I had no energy to refuse and nodded my assent, unable to speak or see. My vision blurred as if it was raining onto my eyelids and the salt ran across my lips.

'Good, that's settled then. Tomorrow, we will find out if that job at the bakery is still open. Pieter is going up first thing when it opens.'

I lay back, letting the tears dry on my face as my mind began to relax again. The taste of oil was now the only reminder of the accident. Theo? What a strange man he was, yet, he had come to my rescue without thinking of the consequences, an automatic reaction to a situation as it arose, the kind of event which could have occurred when he was at sea. It was as if this was the real character of the man, not the mild, docile, creature on the deck. He had leaped into the filthy, stinking morass of ice with no consideration for his own safety. This Theo was a giving person, brooding perhaps as he had sat by my side as he watched the doling out of the food with fascination on his face, who, only the night before, had howled like a wolf at the moon. He had fought away imaginary demons threatening…what? What had Theo been so frightened of? And, if these things were as real as they appeared to be, was there something I could do to give him support as some small favour for saving my life?

Unlike Theo, my own secret demons had been born the day the Nazis had marched into the Netherlands. The mental fears had built up like a brick wall as the terror of being killed or mutilated remained an hourly guess. I had foolishly believed that with the demise of Germany, ending as the gates of the camp had been pushed open to reveal a stunned group of soldiers, I would forget, and eventually to come to some kind of forgiveness. The worst fears one could ever imagine would be freed from my mind to disappear like bad dreams always did in the freshness of the morning. I was strong, I knew: some from the past might have said, too strong, but it was now, five years later as I tried to find a new life I needed every gram of strength I could find. As I slept, the camp reappeared, in every detail, down to the way the nails had been hammered into the wall linings: it was real, tangible almost and an inescapable part of my life. It was not going to go away so all I could do was to keep it at bay to an extent where, at least I could get on with my life in the daytime.

This strange jumble of thoughts vanished as it had arisen with the advent of the cabin door swinging back sharply as Pieter re-entered, this time without knocking.

He was agitated, the grin gone to be replaced with wet lips on an open mouth. 'It's Theo, Mama. He's very ill again. Can you come?'

Elizabeta patted my arm reassuringly. 'I'll be back soon. There is nothing to worry about,' and, so saying, she heaved her bulk off the bed and moved off towards the steep stair leading to the deck. It was a hard climb for a fit person but she managed it without an effort, disappearing with the others off the boat.

I waited for a moment trying to make out the noises across the water but quickly became frustrated. I threw off the cover and pulled on my clothes. My shoes had been turned upside down on the range and stuffed like a turkey with paper. They were stiff but warm and I pulled them on as I hopped around making my way to the companionway. Having emerged onto the deck where the ice was still thick and slippery, I took extra care as I made my way to the edge of the gangplank. The water still heaved, grinding lumps of ice together in a spiteful, slushy sound so I bypassed the idea of going through the whole thing again by sliding my bottom over the gunwale of the two boats, surprising myself on how easy it was. This boat was much smaller, but had a jaunty look with its enormous funnel encrusted in seagull droppings around its rim. Suzannah emerged from the small wheelhouse of the *'Kuijpers'* as she saw me approach. She was quite breathless as if she had been running but I could see it was nervousness.

'Mae, it's you. As you are here can you come and help get a doctor with me? We need to get the man who knows Theo well. I know he will come.'

'Whatever is the matter?' I asked.

'It's Theo's illness. I think the dive into that water and the shock which came from it has brought it on again. It has happened several times before.'

'But, what is… it? What is his illness?' As I spoke we helped each other to the quay carefully and began to walk quickly in the direction of the city.

'Oh, he's-' she stopped, looking at me sideways. 'He has shut himself into a corner of the cabin and pulled the furniture around him. Theo is very frightened of something and he is always talking about corners coming in on him. When he did this the last time he was put into one of those hospitals for ten weeks. When he came back the doctor said he should not have any stress in his life any more. The trouble is, every day is a hard day here, even worse than it is for the normal Amsterdammers, as you well know. It is as well he does not have to work to live as his grandfather left him just enough money to live on, together with the boat, so he is lucky compared with the rest of us.'

She took my arm and guided me through the snow, navigating around the piles of rusting metal and drums as we cut diagonally across the yards towards the grand houses in the distance. The warehouses nearby contrasted with these fine buildings, their own blackened, gaunt shapes assembled like rows of giant skulls with their mouths closed. Blotches of dirty snow settled quickly onto our shoulders and clung in sticky smudges to our chests as we headed southwards into the wind.

'If Theo's grandfather gave him the boat, what happened to his mother and father?'

'His father died from the effects of gassing in the trenches, I think. He had fought with the British in the First World War and wanted to help them in return for what he said were the many things they had done for the Netherlands. His mother died in childbirth. Her one and only child, so, Theo came to live on the *Kuijpers* and became a tuggie, a tugboat man. Theo's grandfather was a much respected man hereabouts and he only died seven years before the war. He was a great character and very proud of Theo. He tried very hard to hide his grandson's growing sickness by keeping him more and more on the boat.

'What exactly is wrong with Theo, Suzannah? Is there something I could do to help?' I was still confused on the nature of his illness. It sounded like he was…mad.

'It is a sad little story, Mae, particularly for a seaman. Theo is sick, but only in his mind, not in his body. The doctor we are going to see is a specialist, of course. He only deals with what goes on in the head when you are sick. He says that Theo sees his boat and the harbour he is moored in, as his entire world.'

'But, isn't that natural? It has been his whole life from what you have told me.'

'Yes, he has, but you see, he feels that if he were ever to take the boat from the basin, cast off the ropes and go into the main canal he would fall into one of his attacks and never recover. So long as he has the boat tied firmly to the quayside he can always get a doctor quickly – and thus he is safe. The main canal here, on the other side of the basin, the *Ij*, is where he goes to in his mind when he is sick. It is a place outside his world of understanding, like, perhaps the camp for you? Anyway, it is a place so terrible he is unable to talk about it and becomes petrified, almost so he cannot walk or talk.'

'When he is mad, that is' I added.

'Hmm, yes but we don't use the word. It is too…hard a word. People think mad people are somehow…different, foreign, not worthy and Theo has so many good points,' Suzannah was quickly defensive. 'The doctor has said on a number of occasions he is curable but he needs a great deal of confidence building and the hospital is not able to provide the time or the money to make him really whole again.'

'I'm sorry,' I said, meaning every word. 'Where I lived, madness was a way to freedom. If one became mad, off your head as it were, as like as not you could be unaware of the real, awful world around you. You were no longer afraid of the Germans as you no longer recognised them as a threat.'

Suzannah nodded as if she had understood. 'Here we are.' She pointed to a brightly polished brass plate containing a single legend. *Doktor Hertz.*

'This is Doctor Hertz's home and is also his consulting room. Ludwig Hertz is a very kind man and has known Theo since his illness first started. He still believes there is hope for him, if only he can be separated from all his fears.'

We both stamped our feet as we mounted the five steps to the front door then shook ourselves as a dog would do. There was snow piled up on the door knocker which Suzannah blew upon before flicking the rest away with a finger.

I was curious. 'Why do you do all of this? For a man who is no relation to any of you. This seems well above and beyond the call of neighbourliness.'

Suzannah sighed. 'What is the alternative Mae? Leave him in hospital to be forgotten while his boat rots alongside ours. And, he is so appreciative of all we have done, not perhaps with bunches of flowers but, you just know he is very thankful.

The door opened just as a barge loaded with beer barrels sounded a lonely toot rounding the bridge support in front of us. 'Aah,' a woman said. 'It's Suzannah isn't it? It must be Theo again.' The woman smiled at me and held an arm out to usher us both inside to a large hall. She quickly shut the door to keep the warmth around us and turned. She was dressed in the sort of clothes of the greatest simplicity yet managed to convey an air of elegance in the most casual manner.

'Yes, do you think Doctor Hertz could come to *Kuijpers* straight away? We cannot get him out of a corner.'

'Come into the morning room. And, who are you?' She looked at me, studying my face and went on. 'My, you are thin, you need feeding up.'

'This is Mae, though her real name is Ruth.'

The Doctor's wife shook her head. 'Ludwig! Ludwig! It is the Theo boy again.' She had raised her voice but the doctor was already behind her pulling on a long, thick coat. He jammed on his hat until his ears began to splay out. Quickly introductions were made. He was about to say something to me when the Doctors wife interrupted. 'Yes, I have said how thin she is. Better get along.'

As we left I had another brief view of the inside of the beautiful house. Tall ceilings with green plants in Chinese vases, gleaming furniture and bronze statues filled my view. The hall had been filled with electric light and there was the steady heat from a central heating system hidden from view. It was so familiar to me though lost and forgotten for the past eight years.

Suzannah explained what had happened leading up to Theo's sudden deterioration. 'You should see a real Doctor,' he said with a half smile, turning to me, 'after we have dealt with a very brave Theo from what I gather. Heaven only knows what you swallowed along with the oil. Most of the boats discharge their waste straight into the basin.'

'I'm sorry, Doctor,' I had to explain quickly. There was no way I was in a position to pay anyone. 'I have no money at all. I have just arrived back into Amsterdam... from one of the camps in Germany'. I added this last comment to explain the reason for being penniless.

Apparently it did. Never mind the money. I know plenty of doctors who will examine you free of charge. Besides, it is I who should be paying you to compensate in some small manner for what happened to your people in the war.'

There seemed little point in replying to his kind remark. We both knew what he meant, so instead we trudged through the bitter cold and thickening snow wiping the flakes from our eyes as we went. All the water traffic had canvas covers over their deck cargoes, giving the barges the impression of enormous floating icebergs drifting down the canals sprouting dirty smoke from black holes. The snow muted the throb of the engines to a softer clunking sound.

'Mind how you go, Doctor. This is where Mae fell into the water.' All three of us gazed down into the slush on the surface, seeing the oil spew from a dozen cracks. He grimaced.

'That *is* dirty Mae. You will need to see a doctor as soon as possible.' So saying, he balanced his hands out wide as if he were negotiating the high wire in a circus tent. 'I am being careful, young lady.' He kept his chin up high, believing this would help retain his balance. I followed Suzannah down onto the deck of the tug and through to the wheelhouse. It was much smaller than the other alongside, but snugger, with its wooden grab rails polished smooth from years of rough seas and general use by Theo's grandfather.

'Ah! Doctor! What are we to do with him?' It was Elizabeta, her features hardened by the ice and snow and the events she had witnessed inside, who emerged from the stairway.

'This time he must come with me, certainly for some time. I must see if we cannot put this to bed once and for all and get rid of his paranoia.' This had been offered for Anna's benefit. She had come up behind her mother and her thick, almost Negroid lips were pulled back in protest. 'To help him Anna, we must give him a longer period of rest and treatment. We let him go too early last time.'

'I know that Doctor, but the longer he stays the more likely he is never to return to the *Kuijpers*..'

'Oh no! Surely not,' I let slip the words without thinking. Hertz, significantly, did not reply.

We all turned to the far corner of the main cabin where a door led to what appeared to be an engine room. Pieter had managed to push aside furniture heaped up on top of itself, leaving a small space to get through. Theo was at the far end of the cabin, studying us closely as we all advanced in two columns. At the last moment he jumped to his feet and leapt through to the engine room. The smell of oil and grease wafted back through the opening.

'Let me,' I said quite forcibly, hardly realising what I was intending to do, only knowing I had to protect Theo from all those eyes studying him.

Theo was totally naked but it did not upset me. I had seen so many sights that this was not one to make me embarrassed now. I did notice that he had been circumcised and wondered if he was a Jew. Many boys were circumcised even though they were not of the faith, but no-one had mentioned his religion to me. At this point Mama realised she had two young girls with her and ordered them back. Men with no clothes on, ill or not were not a place for well brought up ladies and there were going to be no exceptions at this time. The two boys, men I should say, looked on sheepishly unable to offer any sensible counsel.

'I'll get him.' I repeated my offer as I pushed through the steel door opening.

'Let her try, said Hertz nodding his approval. 'Theo feels trapped, surrounded. Give him space. Move back please:' and to me, 'slowly does it Ruth.'

I went ahead of the men. Inside the engine room, the dirt and grease lay on every pipe and dial. It was a gloomy place, unloved for many years with only the reflection of daylight bouncing in from the snow to outline the rooms several large unyielding pieces of machinery. Twice, on advancing, I banged painfully into unseen metal at low level. I made a mental note not to become a tug man's wife.

'Theo, it's me, Mae. I came to thank you for rescuing me today. It was a very brave thing for you to have done. You saved my life, Pieter says.'

There was the sound of hoarse breathing now close to me and I could see the vague outline of condensed air, short puffs clouding a large pressure gauge. 'Theo, please come and talk to me. I was frightened when I was in the water and you pulled me by my hair. I thought-'

'I didn't mean to hurt you,' Theo said unexpectedly. I was unprepared for any reply quite so soon, 'pulling your hair...and all.'

'Oh, you didn't hurt me. It was probably the only way to have got me out, wasn't it?'

I could hear the hash rasp in his throat. He could not have been more than two metres from me, close enough for him to spring upon me if he so wished. I had no idea if he had any form of weapon in his hand or how strong he was. All at once, the noise quietened, the white breath disappearing back into the darkness. I waited, squeezing my eyes together in anticipation, wondering what would be his next move.

It took almost a full minute before he spoke again. Somehow, I realised I had to let him speak at his own speed and not be accelerated by my own impatience to achieve a result.' There are so many voices here. They are all trying to whisper to me at the same time...it is so confusing.'

Now I saw him, vaguely caught in the half-light, his hands pressed tight one to each ear. His naked torso gleamed with sweat despite the ice-cold air in the room, his flesh a sickly yellow-grey like the corpses of Auschwitz in the early mornings.

'Listen to my voice Theo, just my voice. The others will go away if you concentrate on me speaking to you. Listen to me only and walk towards me as you do. You will find that you won't be frightened any more.' I began to repeat my words rather as if I were calling up a friend on a ham radio. I asked him again and again not to be scared and to listen only to me. He began to move. He turned, moving like a crab, sidling sideways, suspicious and expectant but left hand held out seeking to grasp mine.

'Theo, hear my voice. The other voices are growing fainter now, aren't they? Can you notice it? Fainter and fainter.'

Theo staggered as the Doctor's hypodermic needle entered his arm. He shouted out once before becoming still and docile. I hadn't seen Hertz come up behind me.

'I could have got him out, Doctor, really I could.'

'I believe you could have, my dear, but Theo is freezing to death and we must get him to hospital as soon as possible before hypothermia sets in. To get him out without sedation would have taken too long.'

I could understand his reasoning. Elizabeta passed over a rug which I wrapped around Theos body. His skin was clammy like a frog's belly. I shuddered. Mother's body had felt the same.

'Boys!' Pieter was back in command. 'You will need to help and get Theo onto the quayside. Anna run on ahead and telephone from the paper shop for an ambulance. Mama, get Mae back on to the *Anna Rosner*. She may well be suffering from shock for all we know, and she has had quite enough for one day.'

'A year, more likely,' Mama countered, managing to retain a wry smile on her face. The problem was over. Again, I felt arms enfold my shoulders. I could not have spoken, for tears were only an eye blink away. 'Come on my darling. Let's go and clean up next door.'

* * * * *

I hated hospitals. Even though this one did not have that lasting odour of disinfectant hanging in the air; nor was there the mandatory green paint on the walls painted up to an arbitrary line about waist height. Nor was there a clack and bustle of people going somewhere as if it were important. Here, the few people, all men, I could see were drifting aimlessly, hands hanging loosely by their sides and always, the vacant expression in the way they held their heads. The Receptionist, if that was what she was, seemed nice enough, smiling in an indulgent sort of way as if to acknowledge that this awful place was for people not quite of this earth, thus it was alright not to have a purpose in life and to dribble from the mouth and onto your shirt. I had asked her if I could see Theo, then realised I did not know the family name.

'He came in the day bef-'

'Yes, we know Theo. He has been here a few times. What a nice young man and so polite. He has been brought up very nicely by someone with such good manners. Are you a friend of his?'

I wasn't sure how to answer. Surely I must be a friend but, perhaps Theo might think me presumptuous in matters which really did not concern me. Or, he may have thought I had soft-talked him just so Hertz could stab a needle in his arm. Or, he simply might wish to be alone with his illness not wanting strangers staring down with pitying eyes, or fearful of making eye contact knowing the embarrassment it might cause. He might have forgotten who Ruth was, or Mae, or, or…there were a dozen other reasons not to go on.

'Say it is Mae. Spell it to him, M-A-E. He will understand,' I hope, I added to myself still unsure whether I should ever have come in the first place.

I waited in the Hall which smelt of cheap pine polish and old newspapers. There was not a single speck of dust to be seen anywhere and I wondered at the army of cleaners working their way down this enormous, cavernous almost, corridor. Was it really necessary to have such cleanliness in a hospital which did not have operations? I sighed. This was Amsterdam not London.

I could see several inmates watching me furtively, keeping their distance and always ensuring there was some form of protection like a piece of furniture to hold onto or to disappear behind, when they became too bold. One very old man, wizened face and thin lank hair hanging over his eyes was partly hidden behind an armchair. From time to time he raised his chin above the top as in a cartoon character before snapping it down and out of sight, giggling to himself. I found it funny myself, so I lifted my eyebrows three or four times directed at him which caused his head to vanish in a flurry of activity. My heart sank immediately after wondering if Theo had fallen to the level of the old boy. I could not imagine any way in which I could help, or for that matter, anyone, least of all the doctors. Elizabeta was strongly convinced I would be welcome and I wanted to tell him I had got the job at Bessels Bakery in the *Damstraat* right behind the flea market. I had been so happy to accept the small wage, and had been told to report the next day that I had willingly agreed to Mama's and Papa's suggestion that I visit Theo.

When I left the bakery after the interview, the queue waiting for the doors to open was four people wide. With such a business there would be plenty to keep me occupied. I needed, above all, somewhere to live. I could not stay much longer with the Family, kind as they were and warm and comfortable as it was, but the bakery might be able to help.

My train of thought was interrupted suddenly. '*Mejuffrouw Epstein*, please follow me. Please do not raise your voice when you go into his room and do not make any sudden movements. Theo needs words of comfort, no stress at all. Try to concentrate on good, simple things in life. Spring is coming, for instance…I hope,' she added glancing out of the corridor window where the City was frozen into an ice cube. Our feet rang in unison as we walked and I had to stretch my legs wider to keep up with the nurse's longer stride. She was a busy lady and clearly wanted to get back to her station as soon as possible. I felt as if I was a nuisance here, someone who was slowing up the ordered pace of the Institution.

He was standing by a window, with a view out to the cold, drab day, a wintry scene wherein a small army of workmen were engaged with their wide snow shovels. With each sweep of an arm, they jettisoned the contents in the direction of the canal where the brown slush was lost in the equally muddy colour of the water. Steel bars, rising the full height of the tall room emphasized the reality of the state of affairs and did little if nothing to the atmosphere of the hospital. It was, no more or less than a prison and the small vase of flowers on a side table was unable to mitigate the drear mood which clung to the walls and the floor as powerfully as any antiseptic. I was surprised he was on his own.

His short, brown hair gave him the look of a Roman consul, like the statues in the *Rijks* Museum though it was lank and greasy and I wondered if it had been washed since he had dived in to rescue me. His dungarees hung on his hips and down on the back of his shoes. For the first time I noticed that, despite his thinness, his body was still powerful; no doubt a carry over from the days when he was working with his grandfather. I guessed he was in his early thirties.

Theo turned to study a lazy trail of smoke which curled out of a factory chimney. The flue was black which made me wonder if he was daydreaming of the *Kuijpers* and the good days when he had sailed into the *Ij* every morning. Suzannah's words came to me at that moment: 'He cannot leave harbour. He could have one of his attacks.'

But, he *had* had one of his attacks without ever leaving shore, in fact a long way from the entrance to the *Ij*, and moored up close and tight to the quay. She wasn't right, at least not on this basis. For that matter, had the doctors been right? It seemed arrogant even to think of challenging their diagnoses. If they were right, Theo's future was bleak indeed. But, behind the emptiness of his eyes, I had seen the spark of intelligence when I had talked to him. If it was there, perhaps it was just hidden, sheltering a while, waiting for an opportune moment to push itself back into reality. I wanted to believe this was the real situation so much I burst out quickly. 'Hullo, Theo.'

It had not mattered. He stayed remote, continuing to stare out of the window as if I was not there.

'That chimney,' I went on, 'it looks just like the *Kuijpers* funnel, except yours doesn't have any smoke coming out of it, and it doesn't have a blue ring around it.'

At that he turned with a half-smile. 'Why should I need smoke? My boat's going nowhere. It is my home, not my place of work.'

The nurse had disappeared as soon as she had opened the door, so I sat down uninvited. 'I came because I wanted to thank you for saving my life.'

'You are welcome,' he said listlessly. He might have been talking about buying groceries. 'Anyone would have done the same.'

'That is the whole point, Theo. I very much doubt if anyone would have thrown themselves into that icy, stinking water without first thinking of their own safety. And...if they knew they were risking their life to save that of a Jew-'. I did not finish my sentence. It all sounded rather self-pitying. Again, that hint of intelligence crossed Theo's face, an instant in time, but, nonetheless it was there.

'What has being a Jew to do with this? The war is over.'

'Perhaps,' I replied, 'but, I don't think our problem is over. Some people do not think it will ever be finished where Jews are concerned. They wanted Hitler to finish the business before they stepped in.'

Theo changed tack. 'Why are you here?'

'I told you, to thank you.'

'So you said. Now you can leave if you wish. You have done your duty.'

'It is not a duty. Do you not want me to stop and have a chat?'

'Why?'

Theo was becoming exasperating. 'To pass the day quicker, the quicker the days, the sooner you will be home on your boat with all your things about you.'

He started to shake his head and open his mouth, both in an unenthusiastic fashion, so I hurried on. 'Mama and Papa have found me a job.'

He was curious, despite himself. 'Where?'

'Bessels, the big bakers... on *Damstraat*.'

Theo's muscles in his cheeks twitched as he fought back some hidden fear which had surfaced as if he were trying to keep a lid on a boiling pan. As quickly, the ripples quietened as the drugs took over. 'That's the big bakery not far from here...uh from the boat. It's a good job, I expect?'

'I hope so. I shall be serving in the main shop. I get training in all of the departments in due course so I can talk to the customers better: like boxing up the cakes, and how apple strudel is made.'

His eyes gleamed for the first time. Intelligence flooded in, bringing character instantly to his whole expression. 'Cakes? With icing?'

'Yes, lots of icing on all of them. Some with red cherries on top as well. The lady in the shop told me they were called glacé cherries. French word, makes it rather posh don't you think? Of course, I haven't started yet so I don't know any of the special words, but I will learn quickly, I think, so I can do the job better. If I come and see you again I can tell you about it. We could save and buy one, a cake I mean.'

'Why are you telling me all this?'

'Because Theo, in so many ways we are the same. Both of us are alone in the world with no-one to care for us. Both of us are ill-'

'You are not ill like me-'

'I have a sickness in my mind as well, a sickness of what I have seen. You Theo have a sickness in your mind of what you cannot see. There is very little difference as I see it. But you are luckier, that's for sure. You have your own home, a lovely home, warm and friendly with all your possessions around you. You have a little money coming in each week. How precious is this? Me? I have no home, no belongings and no security.'

'You have a job.' He smiled, properly smiled for the first time.

'Yes,' I realised he was right. I was so used to saying otherwise.

'I have a job,' I repeated the phrase more firmly. The feeling was so good, I wanted to be alone. I turned to go.

'Goodbye, Theo.' He did not answer.

As I reached the door, he suddenly ran forward, frightening me. 'Why don't you stay on the *Kuijpers* until I get back…if I get back? You could keep the place clean and-' He was breathless and finding it hard to speak. His control was beginning to weaken. 'Just do it…eh?'

He shuffled to the window and took up his, by now familiar stance again, of staring out at the workmen and the snow. I was not sure whether he could even recollect what he had said. An idea, however, had already formed in my head but it would mean I would have to take up his proposal.

For the first time in my life, I had a purpose. I almost skipped to the Receptionist to say goodbye and reconfirm I would be back, and then walked hurriedly through the wet slush where even the air seemed warmer.

* * * *

The boys arrived back first, chattering noisily as they ran across the gangplank. I had made a big pot of tea in Mama's brown teapot, at which Hans and Jos thanked me profusely before diving aft into their bedroom shouting out as they did about getting changed for a dance in town. Five minutes later, Mama and Papa appeared on the steps. How easy it was now for me to add the nicknames rather than the formal Pieter and Elizabeta.

'My, oh my, no-one has ever made a cup of tea for me in my life before today,' Mama said, giving me a big hug which threatened to swamp me in her generous bosom. 'Do you hear that Papa, and you boys? Why can't you do this for me sometimes?'

'Because you wouldn't let us,' chorused the three men together, singing, seemingly, a well worn song. She shook her head in mock dismay though knowing it was the truth. 'Theo? How is he?'

'He is calmer, better maybe, but very withdrawn from life. But,' I paused, 'he wants me to live on his boat, the *Kuijpers*, look after it, and keep it clean, only until he is better, of course. By then I will have a room of my own.'

Pieter, who had entered, and was listening to me gabble on, looked at Mama to gauge her reaction before responding. 'It sounds an excellent idea Mae. Did he really think of it himself? He must be better.'

'It was all his own idea. It quite took me by surprise in fact. I would not have wanted to suggest such a thing, not when he is ill but it does seem to make a lot of sense. Someone needs to look after his boat especially in this sort of weather. But, I have time to give it a clean, polish the brass; the lace in the portholes is almost black and the deck needs a hard scrub.'

Pieter laughed. 'Scratch a Dutch girl and you will find a scrubbing brush.'

Mama was about to open her mouth when the two boys clambered back into the main cabin. Their hair was slicked down with some sort of scented grease. Each had a cravat tucked into their shirts and their trousers appeared to be much wider at their bottoms than the tops. It was obviously the fashion, though it made them look like English sailors. They grinned rather owlishly at me as Jos brushed his jacket self-consciously. Hans passed over the two tea mugs.

'Here,' he said, we've brought these for washing.' They made for the companionway.

'Hey!' said Mama, remonstrating at both her sons with a raised finger. 'You haven't eaten.'

'Well find something there, and heat up supper when we get back, Mama.' He paused before returning to the room and kissed both her bony cheeks.

'Don't be late,' said Papa beginning to unwind from the day. He had pulled out his pipe and the room began to fill with the warm, sweet aroma of tobacco.

'There's a funfair on the *Amstelveld* tonight,' Anna threw at their departing backs. I felt an unfamiliar surge of jealousy. All to live for and young enough to enjoy it. They hadn't a care in the world, while I sat and thumbed through old magazines passed on third or fourth hand from other boat owners in the harbour. But, I had a home to go to and a job, food in my stomach and friends by my side.

Papa handed me a key and I climbed aboard the smaller tug feeling my way carefully across the icy surface. It was nice that he did not try to come with me, for I wanted to be alone this first time. I wanted to make my own mistakes in private and learn the ways of a boat for myself. I knew almost nothing about tugs except what I had learnt from Pieter and the boys.

The snow had not melted on the deck, reminding me that there was no heat in the cabin below. The wheelhouse door too, had frozen in its slide-gate. I had to kick the end with my foot before, grudgingly it gave way. Protesting it slid back and I hoped the wooden frame had not been damaged.

I stood in the tiny space, seeing my breath condense in the damp air and spread across the glass panels. It had been three days since we had had to take Theo out of the cabin and up the steep stair in a semi-conscious state, his arms catching on every protrusion and corner possible. Everyone had crossed to the quayside just in time, for Theo had slumped to the ground his weight pulling Hans and Jos down with him. Now I was alone, looking down into the darkness of the cabin and wondering if I was doing the right thing, a trespasser into his private world. I could not even be sure if Theo had understood the implications of what he had proposed to me in the hospital, albeit at the time he had made it very clear what he had wanted from me. The blackness too, was eerie and uninviting: with Theo in the asylum, *Kuijpers* lacked a spirit and the boat was a witness by telling me that as I did not understand boats, I wasn't welcome.

'Tish! Tish! My mother had always said when I had been frightened of something when I was very young. 'Just concentrate on whatever you are doing and you wont be frightened any more.' It had always worked in the past: I saw no reason why it would not work here.

I took a match and lit the lamp hanging on a nail by the stair bringing me much needed light as I climbed down the steep steps with its tarnished polished brass rail. I had had my eye on this particular piece of metal when I was first aboard three days ago. It needed a lot of loving care and attention, nothing else. I reached the main lamp switch in safety seeing the shadows skitter away ahead of me, creating an instant bright glow as I turned the little brass wheel controlling the wick. My breath steamed so it bleached the colour from the furniture and the covers. White frost lay on the sills and the blankets to the bed. As I stood, taking in Theo's grandparent's knick-knacks, photos, pipes held in racks, mugs, more brass lamps and horse brasses, the square table with its rounded edges and turned legs, all at once I felt secure. This cold, bleak room could yet be home.

I found paper and wood shavings, but the stove had died, half full. I spread out an old newspaper on the floor and pulled out the half-burnt logs, cinders, pieces of wire and metal, stones and other hard rubbish, all tinted with the same reddish dust. It was clear it had been kept going week after week without a proper rake out.

The fire sprang into life returning life to the cabin, the early flames licking the polished timber panelling so that the heat was reflected back onto my face. I found some fine steel wool and an old tin of metal polish by the sink in the galley and began to rub the metal face of the stove. It had a laurel wreath with the number 109 impressed into the surface. Rather smart, I thought as it glowed like the fire from the steel polishing. I cleaned a little shovel with its wooden handle and then a poker with a brass knob.

I leant back on my heels to ease the pressure on my thighs, seeing around me the frozen dew begin to retreat from the bed covers. The crystals on the port holes showed their fatigue as they slid towards the small curved sills under the effects of gravity. My breath no longer condensed each time I breathed in and out. *Kuijpers* was coming alive again and as if to confirm the statement her panelling creaked and groaned as it began to tighten to the frames. I still had my coat on, one that had been lent to me by Suzannah, and I now hung it up carefully as I looked round for the next job.

'Mae! Mae!' I heard Mama call. 'Come and eat.' An hour had passed in a trice and it was almost with a snort of annoyance that I acknowledged her summons.

'This is stupid, Ruth,' I said aloud to myself. 'I have to leave here anyway when Theo returns.' It was stupid as well, I told myself, that I wanted to stay…badly.

Despite my wish to continue to clean and complete the burnishing of the fire surround, the *Anna Rosner* was snug and warmly lit with its lanterns. Anna and Suzannah were already sitting down, still wearing their head scarves around their heads. The boys, long gone, were probably carousing around the city which made the boat considerably quieter and more peaceful. When they were on board there was always a tense air and argument just round the corner. They were like all the young, knowing better than their elders, wanting to fly the nest, impatient to see life.

'Mama's decided Spring is coming early this year and, as she did not have to make the tea, out came the cleaning cloths.'

Pieter nodded his head lugubriously, letting the air in his cheeks exhale with an exaggerated sigh. 'This is planned to be done in March some time. Heaven help us now it has begun so soon.' As he spoke, Mama was pulling out a pile of potatoes coated in cheese and sprinkled with chopped onions. At the same time, her other hand slipped a cloth along the back of his chair.

'If we get up half an hour earlier tomorrow, we can wash the rugs and leave them to dry over the range while we are at work. Mae, you start work tomorrow as well. It is going to be so nice for you with money in your pocket. Can you tell us more about the job?'

It was easy to sit in the happy room, chatting over ideas for the future. The Germans had gone for good, peace was overtaking the city again, more jobs, more money more everything. Pieter traced a route for me around Central Station and the girls asked me if I needed an apron for my work. I was able to tell them I was provided with an apron and head dress.

It was getting late. Mama glanced once or twice at the clock on the cabin wall. 'I'm going,' I said. 'I must keep the stove alight tonight to let the boat thaw out properly. As I rose to go there came a commotion on deck coupled with the sound of running feet. The wheelhouse door slammed back on its guide. 'Papa! Papa!'

It was Jos sliding down the stair rail in one leap. 'Papa! Mama! Hans has been arrested!'

'Oh my god!' said Mama, quickly crossing herself.

'Whatever for?' Pieter demanded thrusting himself to his feet. 'Has the stupid boy gone and got himself drunk again?' His eyes flickered across the table at the two girls, to see they were not frightened, as Jos, now in the cabin stood with hair wild and eyes staring out of their sockets. His shirt hung half out of his trousers making him look like a tramp. He was strangely frightened as though the event was much more serious than it might have been otherwise.

'Calm down, Jos. Let's have the story from the beginning.'

'It's Hans. We went down to the dance. Lots of people there. One or two old school friends. Do you remember Gretel? The very rich girl. Blonde haired girl, tall, one of Hans's old girl friends, well, sort of girlfriend. She saw us but instead of coming over to say hello she ran out of the room crying. I forgot about it all and went off to dance. We had hardly had a single drink at this time. Almost half an hour later Gretel returned, this time with not one, but four policemen. 'There he is,' she screamed out, so loud it stopped the music. She pointed a finger at Hans. Everyone had to stop dancing and they kind of made a circle around him.'

By now Jos was firmer, making his speech more convincing. 'The police arrested Hans right on the spot and are charging him with being a collaborator, you know, one of the war time collaborators.'

'Ah, God help us all.' Elizabeta collapsed in a pile of untidy clothes like washing ready to be hung up to dry.

'This is ridiculous,' Pieter replied, for once ignoring his wife's efforts at drama. 'Hans never collaborated with anyone in his whole life. Besides, that is all over and done with five years ago.'

'No it isn't,' Jos was much quieter now. 'The police said they think Hans is responsible for the death of the four men who were arrested and later shot in forty-five; the ones on the bank of the Amstel. It was right at the end of the war. They need never have died.'

I knew about the collaborators, of course. Like France, there had been some Dutch people who had believed they would be better off if they worked with the Germans, making money on the way, and to achieve this, all they had to do was to let the Gestapo know when they saw something suspicious or even, not quite as it should be. Something a little out of the ordinary was all it took. The story of Anne Frank was beginning to come to the light of day not only of Amsterdamers but further away in Europe.

'This is crazy.' Pieter jammed his hat on his head as if he were squashing a wasp and began to pull on his long coat. 'Hans worked with us every day in the war. He never left us. What possible reason could he have had?' Nonetheless, Pieter looked pinched in the jaw as his own nervousness began to take hold.

The pile of clothes stirred. 'What are you going to do, Papa?' Elizabeta's bony face was more gaunt than ever, if this were possible. The life had drained out of her face. Her bottom lip trembled.

'Go and see the Police, get it sorted out, that's what. Jos, you come along with me and show me where they are holding him.'

The cabin mood had changed abruptly. The air felt cold as the girls and I washed the plates, leaving Elizabeta to sit for once in a chair, shaking her head from side to side. She muttered under her breath like a dog seeking attention. Eventually, I said goodnight wishing the whole family success and luck with the Police. Suzannah gave me a hug promising to keep me up to date with the news.

Back in Theo's boat, the stove had gone out. Around it were discarded cleaning cloths and steel wool, lying where I had dropped them so much earlier in happier circumstances. So much had happened and in such a short time. I relit the fire with far less enthusiasm than the first attempt but was cheered with the returning warmth and glow.

While I waited to ensure the fire had taken I expected someone from the *Anna Rosner* to call but no-one came and I drifted off to sleep on Theo's pillow wondering where Hans was and if he had managed to get home after some sort of silly muddle.

I woke the next morning to the tinny rattle of the two alarm bells on the clock by my head. Snow gleamed blue- white outside the port hole in the pre-dawn moon and I could hear the first traffic of the Monday morning already making its way carefully along the glassy-looking quayside road. Mist condensing from the radiators caused the warehouses to fade into the distance, hunching shoulders on those that walked and chilling the general mood. There were the regular dray horses hauling full loads, having to work that much harder when a drayman pulled on a brake: they too puffed the air as if they were engine shunters, which, I suppose they were. The grey sky showed no signs of changing during the day so it was a case of wrapping up with what ever I could find in Theo's boat.

No-one had come to me in the night, though I had woken twice, each time with the cold, to stoke the fire. There had to be a way of keeping it in all night. I never had had a problem with Mother's, or at least, the maid had never complained and we had always been warm in the morning. I pumped urine into the harbour and glanced across to the *Anna Rosner*, but it was all quiet, silent even and rested in darkness. I dressed carefully, taking my time with my hair. Mama had pressed my skirt, bless her and my blouse was as white as the pile of snow on the overhanging eave of the bargees' hut. I had left plenty of time so as I waited for the kettle to boil, I climbed over to the other boat and was about to call out when I noticed the wheelhouse door was locked and the deck frozen with a deadness in the air that I knew there was no-one inside. Pieter would always have been astir by now. The absence of the entire family disturbed me the most. Although they were away in the day for long periods at a time, there was always the certain knowledge they would be back in the evening spreading their cheerful banter ahead of them as soon as they could see their home in the distance. It would come alive within minutes as they called out to each other and their neighbours, in exasperation or merely pleading. It was usually the boys who were on the end of the commands which they followed up with a, 'Oh Mama'... or 'in a minute Papa...' The smell of hot bread and baking potatoes was as normal in this area as tar and diesel. It was the trademark of the Family, as usual as the morning coming up itself and as essential to the well-being of the boat as life.

Today, however, the tug was silent, rocking gently on the swell from the workmen going to sea, the air unscented and still as the grave. I didn't like my description and told myself not to be silly. I could not stop and find out what had happened. I had above all to survive, and today was probably the most important in my life so far. If I messed up today and lost this job I could not begin to think how long it would take to find another, and I had no money to buy food. I could only pray the Family would return home that evening after work.

My route took me past the entrance to Central Station then back across the bridge to the *Damstraat*. Twice a week, I had worked out, by going another route to work, my steps would take me past the market. I would be able to find something to eat for lunch close by and cook myself a meal on the boat in the evening. Two meals a day was something entirely new to me, well... since before the war.

At the bakery there was already a small queue forming, blocking the entrance and pavement, but I had to go round to the back anyway, now I was an employee. The lady in charge of the shop smiled at me glancing as she did up at the clock. I was early. She nodded approvingly at my clothes. She handed over a white overall which I had to button up to my neck and a stiff lace band for my head. It made me look a bit like a nurse. I undid the sleeves of my blouse so I could adjust the arrangement.

'Er, Ruth. I am sorry but we do not allow tattoos to be displayed.' The Manageress was rather shocked by the idea of a young lady with such a brand on her forearm even though it was to be covered up.

'I'm sorry Madam. It is the mark, put there by the Germans...at the camp...when I arrived. It will be hidden by my sleeves, honestly.'

The Manageress looked back at me, mortified. 'I am so sorry Ruth. I had no idea.

'I suppose in a way I was lucky. Those with a tattoo lived, at least for a while. Many who arrived with me that July did not receive a mark at all, for they were destined for the gas chambers the same day.

The silence which followed was comforting, but time was pressing and I had a new job to hold down. I knew she would not ask me again but she had seen in some tiny way just what the Jews had had to endure in those dark days. The woman shook herself mentally and I smiled to show her I was ready for the work.

'Just listen to me during the day. Watch exactly what I do. Learn the prices by heart. Smile always at the customers no matter how rude they may be and, most important of all, try to remember their names and who the regulars are. The big spenders will soon show themselves and will need special watching. They are usually the most difficult as well.'

This appeared to be the end of my training, so I followed her into the shop front. The ceiling was quite low but the room was large and everywhere painted a fresh white. Eight shelves behind the counter held rows of different breads. Below the glass top to the counter were steel trays: these contained buns. There was icing sugar on them all. White, some pink and some mauve. They looked nice to eat but I thought they could have been presented better. I noticed one of the girls having to step up on a block of wood to reach the bread on the top shelf. It made her seams shows off to the waiting customers and reminded me to keep them straight if ever I could afford to buy a pair in the future.

'You'll get used to seeing these. Those left over at the end of the day are divided between us. We cannot sell them the next day, you see.'

I didn't see. I thought of all the times I had fought for a crust of dried bread. Here was bread so soft you could press it until it was flat. 'You will get a share of the buns yourself.'

I could not believe my luck but reminded myself they might all be sold before the end of the day. That, after all was the end reason for the business here and anything left over represented a loss of further profit. My father would never have permitted his Manageress to make a statement like that.

All at once came the clunk of two bolts being pulled out of the floor, followed almost immediately by a gaggle of voices proceeded by a wave of overcoats, scarves and hats, into the shop. I could see expectant faces, faces which had filled out since the end of the war. Fat cheeks now and fleshy jowls to replace the common gaunt look when everyone had had to struggle to find enough to eat. A number of men in the queue had smart hats. Children hung on their mothers' arms each dressed in clean socks and polished shoes. There had been a time not long gone when some of them had had neither, or at best, crude home-made sandals even in the winter.

'Can I help you Madame?'
'Two brown malt loaves, wrapped please.'
'Of course, Mevrouw-?'
'Mevrouw Goldstein.'
'Anything else I can get you Mevrouw Goldstein?'

It was the beginning of my first day. The first day of my first job I had ever held. I was absolutely determined to hold on to it. All morning I served bread or fetched more supplies from the bakers' ovens across the yard. They were heavy, twenty-four loaves on each tray. After a time I was able to regulate my thoughts. The panic of doing something wrong had evaporated, replaced now with a growing confidence and conviction I could do the job and do it well. I felt I could learn quickly how to handle Bessels clientele. Some did not thank you or even give you a glance, but it didn't matter. Mothers had much on their minds balancing budgets while seeing their children did not put their fingers on the cakes. What, I wondered, had happened to the other family, my family, in a manner of speaking? Surely one of the six should have remained on board in case a message was delivered or, if only to watch for Hans arriving from another direction.

At lunch, I was given half an hour as a result of which I managed to slip across the road for twenty minutes. I chewed a piece of bread Mama had given me the night before. Outside, the icicles had gone from the gutters and it was now the turn of the piles of shovelled snow to begin to melt, each with its blackened, frosted crust from the diesel fumes of the lorries. It must also be inside our lungs I realised with a start.

In the afternoon the shop was quieter so I was sent behind into the bakery where I swept up spilt flour. There were dozens of small cuts of trimmed dough risen up with yeast so they looked like a whole brood of yellow slugs. There was an enormous slab of marble which I had to scour making the stone glow translucent white. I scrubbed, happy in my work and wondered again about Theo and what the Family was doing.

There was, you see, nothing else in my life to think about and it stopped me thinking of the approaching night when the past would come back and the souls of six million people return to haunt me.

You Don't Owe Me Anything

The corners are retreating. Although they make no effort at all to redistribute themselves into the positions which are recognised as normal, in a proper order as the world understands it, or as an Architect would draw it with set square and Tee-square, they are nonetheless, moving roughly to the approximate locations expected of them.

The place, you see, is made up of corners. Everything, in fact, is made up of corners in a building like this. Corners, long corridors with more around each end. Corners, where their ends are blurred by poor light, and, the sheer distance of these soulless connecting spaces, makes it impossible to judge them accurately. It is difficult to comprehend if they just end or break to the right and the left into…more spaces? There's no shadow to give the game away and there may be another way out, or another series of formless, identical rooms, where the inmates dress in identical clothes and identical haircuts. Their faces have no modelling…no shadows, you see.

The air is filled with curious squeaks and squeals as if a thousand mice have been released to occupy the, otherwise, empty atmosphere. The noise solidifies to become a furniture shape, or a picture perhaps, something else to consider as progress continues relentlessly towards the blank ends. There are other noises too: short, rapid clicks; rough breathing, buzzing and occasional baying, the human variety.

Rising like the dawn sun above it all, is the even drone of authority. It covers everything in its sight, in a typical aerial disinfectant. It brings instant obedience and silences the babble and stammer of the inmates.

Down in the foyer, too large for such an institution, for it is easy to be lost here and who wants to be misplaced when you have only just arrived? Few people stop and wait for very long. The space resembles a liner, the sailing variety, with white painted rails running in parallel threes. The waters break about it but softly now, after the storm of the past week. The waves almost chuckle with the undemanding current of the ebb and flow of the tides: thus, they cancel themselves out with their opposing energies leaving this little world becalmed in its centre. If a yacht was to arrive it would be marooned, 'in irons' as they call it down on the quay leaving the mainsail to catch an occasional shiver in the clew, just as a man urinates when he is cold.

There comes a morning when he is awake…sensing life. He watches his hair tumble to the ground in small spirals. They fall quickly like rain though the fine spray of tiny hairs, each a few millimetres long, float in the beam of light radiating from the sun, gold light as it too, falls to form a pattern on the floor.

'I-I… s-ssmell…the…Sprr-ing.'

It is easy to understand for this person speaks slowly, with a black hole for a mouth and two more, coal black again, this time for eye spaces.

'Ly-kk-e a co-al min…e'

There's the tug, steaming by very close. It is in the hall, the vestibule. It has just appeared for it is painted white, like the walls and ceilings. It can only be seen now because it moves. Chameleons give themselves away like that, stupid insects, and then they are eaten. They go to such lengths to camouflage themselves…then pouf! They blink their enormous eyes and you see them and wonder why you did not see them before.

But…she is nice, very nice, no doubt about it. Kind, gentle even, makes him think of grandpapa and grandmamma and home made biscuits as warm as the glass of milk at night.

As quick as the flash of an eye, the corners become sheer, vertical all the way to the ceilings where they collide with each other in perfectly formed right-angles. Look left and right: the corridors are beginning to rationalise themselves into door patterns, door numbers, name plates and handles; directional signs and arrows, all about fire. Each door breaks the run of the black skirting board which runs for kilometres, so they too become part of the patterns making up order and sense. It is as if Picasso was here, explaining the rectangles and squares to make them understandable.

'You u-h…don'ttt…owe me anythinggg- you know-'

It is important that she grasps his point. It means freedom, not owing anything to anyone, so you hold your head up high… anywhere. But, she is complicated, not like the others. He cannot recall anyone like her before. She insists there are dues to be paid at least if not now, then in the future. And, there is no future; he knows that well, so what is the bloody point of saying it in the first place?

But, she makes him think that there could be a future: her force and energy radiating out of her words are all directed towards a long future, a *future which is bright and hopeful but, he cannot see it and it confuses him more.*

'I-oh-we…you my life,' she says.
It says it all, you see but he remains bemused and perplexed.

Chapter Three

The tug rolled lightly as the huge Rhine barge out in the main stream navigated its way towards the sea in the West. Its bow wave surged through the narrow opening into the inner basin, which lay below the railway lines, in a long, creaming bore. Oily water surged up the vertical sides of the granite walls before dropping again to expose the limpets and fronds of seaweed.

Ooster Dock held so many boats it was hard to see the water at all for a distance of three dozen metres or so out from the dockside. Instead of the grey canal with its random craft plying up and down the man-made waterway, here there were rows of bow-sprits and hawsers all tied regularly to the black-painted bollards which corralled off the stone quays from the water. Each boat was secured with the same figure of eight knot, tied without thought to how it was done, an action so often carried out that its owner might have been hard-pressed to explain how it was achieved. A thousand pieces of discarded, rusting steel plates, bolts, nuts, washers and cans lay half-exposed under the sloppy snow. It slid untidily off barrels and drums to splash eventually into the harbour, each time with a slushy sigh of accomplishment. Some, the coldest bits in the north-facing yards remained stubborn and unyielding, resting as they did indolently in the glare of the sun shining smugly upon the City.

A man and a woman, followed closely by two girls and a disconsolate younger man walked wearily along the granite cobbles, unheeding of the new sun or its effects upon the white mantle which, until the day before, had kept this quarter of the City wrapped in a cloak of respectability. The warmth of the day was beginning to expose the debris and unwanted bric-a-brac discarded and conveniently forgotten when the snow had begun to fall. The younger man kicked aside an empty can and shouted something unintelligible to the backs of his parents.

'Let's get home first, Jos. I'm worried about little Mae. What ever will she think of us, leaving her without letting her know where we were?'

'She's the one who will survive us all,' Elizabeta replied. 'After what she has been through in the war, our problem is but a gnat's bite on the back of a horse compared with hers.'

'She has been totally dependent upon us this last week, Mama. She almost starved to death you know, until I found her and brought her home. She's alone now on that dirty boat with his piles of unwashed clothes. The place smelt, didn't it?' Pieter managed a certain pride in his voice. He might be poor and without much education but his boat sparkled every day of the week. They ate well and wanted for nothing. Well, not a lot, he considered on reflection. More lights lit by electricity and one of those gas cookers perhaps but, each day he pulled on a clean shirt and his daughters' skirts were always stain free.

'I have a mind that that young lady intends to do something with her life. Why else should she leave the warmth and security of our home?' Mama ground her teeth to drive home her point. Men could never seem to see these things.

'Perhaps she felt she has used up our hospitality,' Suzannah said brightly, causing Anna to nod in agreement though she kept her head down while she said it, almost always in accord with her sister's sympathies.

'It's alright for one day, and then it gets awkward. Mae's not the type to use a friendship without wanting to give back something in return. Mark my words, she left the *Anna Rosner* for a reason and the reason is she wants to be independent. Remember, she has had nothing for eight years, nothing at all. Now-'

She stopped. The whole family came to a halt just as they turned through a pile of timber to reveal the *Anna Rosner*. They stood by their own gangplank just a few metres away, mouths open and eyes focussed.

'Good God,' said Pieter.

'Good heavens,' countered Anna.

'You were right, Mama.'

Suzannah just gawped in astonishment.

Suspended in the cooling night air, on temporary strings tied not only to each other but to the masthead, the shrouds, from the forestay and the funnel and from the wheelhouse roof grab rail to the stern post eye, Theo's entire wardrobe hung aloft. It was as if the *Kuijpers* was a yawl under full sail as it displayed itself to all and sundry passers-by and now, to the Family. Cream long-johns, underpants in a variety of old-fashioned designs, some with buttons, and some stretched with age, dark-blue oiled sweaters, an off-white jersey with a thick rib collar, socks perhaps two dozen in number but making four pairs with some hard work, swung together. The tiny porthole curtains were there and the nets, drying cloths and coloured handkerchiefs, two pairs of English striped pyjamas and all of his Sunday white shirts, buttoned close and standing stiffly as if in deep conversation with one another. Some of the arms overlapped by necessity as each fought to find enough room on the lines.

'Mae! Ruth! Are you there?'

As they all looked across to the *Kuijpers*, the wheelhouse door rolled back easily to reveal Mae with her hair tucked up inside a headscarf. 'Oh, thank God you are safe. I wondered if you had all been held by the police... or something,' she faltered, as she realised Hans was not with them.

'I'm so sorry Mae. We had to go out. Hans has been held and they are not going to let him come back to the boat, at least not until this whole mess has been cleared up. It is all some dreadful mistake but, until they have proof they won't let him back on the boat. It is something to do with the current kafuffle where collaborators are being smuggled out of the country. There's a real witch hunt going on right through the country. Last night late, we all went down to the police station so we could tell them about Hans and the fact he never could have done something like the awful things they are claiming he did. We all told that policeman in turn, but he wasn't very nice at all and just told us to get a lawyer for Hans. A lawyer, for goodness sake! Where would we get one of those?

The problem is the girl who denounced Hans at the dance says she knew him very well during the war and could not have been mistaken. There is a small bit of truth in this as Jos confirmed Hans had stood her up badly at a dance in front of all her friends. She is moneyed, very rich in fact and that counts for a lot with the police.' Pieter's mouth was hard and set as he relayed the story. That a woman could do this to one of his sons was beyond belief.

'I cannot believe anyone would do anything so wicked,' Mama protested as the words spouted out of her mouth, venom-tinged on every syllable.

Mae shook her head. 'A woman can do such a thing very easily in my experience. Her trouble will come, if she has made it up, or even some of it, when she is questioned further. She will get deeper and deeper into the lie. Probably by now she has seen how far her words have gone, how seriously the police are treating her accusation. Combine that with the hysteria going on at present and she has a major problem on her hands. I am sure she has no idea of how to get out of it without disgrace on herself and the likelihood of a charge of wasting police time. She can see that if the lie were to be out in the open she in turn will be the one in trouble, and serious trouble at that: which is probably right.'

'Oh dear! Hans looked so pale and young. He was shaking with fear all the time.'

Pieter tried to change the subject. 'Come on, Mama. We must cook some food. We are all hungry and life must go on, mustn't it?'

'I'll come and help,' Mae said generously. 'I've come to the end of the washing anyway. There's nothing left. I boiled it all up in buckets. It stank, some of it,' she ended lamely for the second time feeling she was being rather disloyal to Theo.

'So we often thought,' Mama looked up at the washing lines festooning the boat. 'looks a good deal cleaner hanging up there.' This was said approvingly as she eyed each piece in turn. 'It'll not dry tonight though.'

'That's alright. I am going to bring them in and hang them round the stove.' Remembering her important news she reached inside the wheelhouse door and pulled out a package which had been thrust into her hands after her first day at work. 'I have some cakes for all of you.'

'Ooh!' said the Family in unison able to forget their worry for a moment. The grim mood which had touched them all melted slightly with the revelation they were being offered iced buns. Iced buns were not a pleasure the Maas family could often afford.

While the women prepared food, Pieter and Jos sat either side of the glowing range, discussing the events of the night and the long periods of waiting in the day. The entire Family had lost a day's wages.

'There's nothing in this, is there Jos? Nothing I should know about?'

Jos hesitated before replying. 'I don't think so, Papa, but he was forever going out on his own in those days. I know I did as well' but Hans was almost never with me, but… no…he could not have done such a thing. I am sure he would have told me something, and, helping collaborators to escape, surely I would have had some idea. But,' he paused, deep in thought, 'but he did have some funny friends, didn't he, not least of which is that cow-'

'Watch your mouth, Jos.'

'Sorry, Papa, but that Gretel woman needs a good spanking in my opinion.'

Pieter inclined his head to acknowledge Joss's words as he felt the heat of the fire on his thighs. 'This is what I feel also. The problem is, though, he is my first born and is as secretive as Anna. I don't know where he gets it from, certainly not from me or Mama. She has the same charac- char- the same charac-,' he gave up eventually having quite forgotten the formation of the word he wanted, 'as Hans.'

'What will happen to him, Papa, if it is proved he did these things?'

'He could be tried as an accessory for murder.'

'What's that? What's that?' Mama had pricked up her ears from the food locker. 'Whose murder?'

'No-one Mama, you must have misheard.'

Mollified somewhat, she came into the kitchen laden with food. Mae realised she had set a place for Hans and hurriedly removed the knife and fork, but the empty space in front of the chair was more damning than if she had left his space set. To try and prevent them all being reminded of Hans's predicament, she placed a cork mat, half in and half out of the area which he would otherwise have occupied, to allow the vegetable dish to fill the gaps.

'How was your night, Mae? Did you sleep on that cold boat with the ice only a metre above your head?'

'On and off. It will be better tonight as I have managed to keep the fire going all day. The stove was full to the brim with clinker. Tomorrow, I'm going to scrub the floors and wash the woodwork.'

'I asked,' said Pieter, 'because when I came back to collect Mama and the girls I thought I heard you cry out again, as we left the boat.'

Mae shrugged her shoulders. It was nothing new. 'I suppose you must have heard me right across to the Anna Rosner. I still dream of the camp, you know, in fact it is not possible to get through a night without the whole nightmare coming back into my mind. It will be with me forever though it is worse at night because there is nothing else in my thoughts at that time of the day. I have nothing else for my brain to occupy it. Yesterday, the panelling was frozen. Just as I was falling asleep, the cold wood planks brought back to me vividly the walls of my hut: then there's the smell of boiling socks. I was back, six years ago, just before Mother died in Auschwitz, She paused. 'So many people cried out in their sleep: we slept three bunks high, many women desperately ill close beside you, coughing, vomiting and voiding themselves. Sorry, we are just about to eat,' but she went on, haunted, driven now, needing to let the memories out.

'It was the, not knowing what the new day would bring. Every single night, everyone was terrified. Not frightened you understand? Fear goes, after a while and you come to terms with what scared you. The terror of the camps was not in what you could see; death, after all was all around you every day, bodies rotting in the mud; corpses propped against the back of a wall like so many shop dummies waiting to be dressed or women sun-bathing. But, it was what you could not see, no picture at all, which made us cry in the darkness. As one inmate put it, the Sword of Damocles wasn't hanging over our heads; it was hitting us in the face, every day. Those memories cannot be erased so that is what it will be like for the rest of my life.'

Mae stopped, seeing everyone else had also stopped what they were doing and were listening intently. The laying up of the table had been temporarily abandoned so they could all hear what she had to say more clearly. Anna had put her fingers in her mouth as she lived out the dreadfulness.

'And we once thought we were scared,' Mama broke the silence in the end. 'Do you remember, Papa, when those German pigs came here one evening looking for that English pilot? They believed one of the tuggies was hiding him.'

She hoisted the tureen of vegetable stew onto the table with a single heft of her arms. A huge shinbone wallowed on the surface trying to turn on its back, much like a sea otter in a kelp field when it is preening itself.

Despite their worries, the Family turned to the serious part of the day to eat. As Jos picked up his spoon, Pieter held out his as a barrier, preventing them from starting.

'God bless our son, Hans, and keep him safe until he comes home to us.'

Anna was already turning tearful, causing Suzannah to give her a quick squeeze on her shoulder to prevent her from further sob. 'Do you want to tell us more about your family, Mae, rather than that awful camp? Perhaps it might help and we won't have to dwell on our own misfortunes, seeing as how, at least, yours are over.'

Mae smiled. 'There is so little to tell, really. My mother died when I was sixteen. My father, I am told, died in the same year, but he was transferred to another camp because he had expertise in industrial diamonds. He would have had plenty of work as the Nazis had stolen so much from us. I still have no confirmation he is dead but he has to be so, or he would have come home by now. I must assume he is with my Mother up there somewhere in a far, far happier place. He always said it would be like going home when we died and I always thought of his words when the days were particularly bad.'

'But, before the war, I mean. Where did you live?' Pieter managed to ask even while sucking noisily on his spoon at the same time.

Mae began to feel uncomfortable. 'We had a nice house in the *Jordaan*, all gone now. Father was a very successful jeweller with a number of shops. His father started the business from nothing. Father always worked so hard. Mother lived at home in comfort with a number of servants…helps I mean. It was so hard for her…when Eichmann began his resettlement programmes for she simply could not come to terms with her change in station.'

'Were you rich? Your family I mean.' Jos asked.

'Tsk! Tsk!' Mama hit out at him none too lightly with the palm of her hand. 'You don't ask such things in nice society.'

'But, we are not nice soc-'

'Shut it, Jos,' warned Pieter. Jos immediately lowered his head, furious at having been put down in such a manner.

'I really do not know. We had servants and things, two cars. Mother's jewellery was nice, that sort of thing.

Her words began to stir the interest of the group huddled around the stew-pot. The shadows had lengthened to draw the dark-browns on the walls almost to touch the chairs. The electric light flickered like candlepower as the overloaded harbour wiring reacted to the jury-rigged installations on the boats. Elizabeta was absorbed in Mae's story. Cars, jewellery, servants, a big house with a nice address in Amsterdam, albeit Jewish, such things were as if they were on another planet; certainly not on a tug-boat in Amsterdam in 1950. And where had it all gone? Where was their house, their furnishings, the two cars? Had the Dutch people really allowed this to happen and, even so, at the end of the war, why had they not been given back to the rightful owners?

Did you go to a Jewish school?'

'No, not that is just for Jewish families. It was a private school. Then, I had to leave as the other Dutch families, not Jews of course, got together and said there was too much pressure from the Germans. We were influencing other children, how, I do not know. At first, we began to be teased, some of my friends joined in, then more.' Mae almost snorted with the memory, 'After that, came the dirty Jew comments being thrown at us, followed by the yellow stars, that sort of thing.'

Mama's big, bony frame stirred uncomfortably. She shook her head in disbelief, hiding her shame as her own memories flooded back, recalling how she also had scorned the local Jews even if she had said nothing. She kept her head down as she spooned out more stew into the bowls, still half full, without asking if the recipients needed more. 'What a terrible thing, what a loss of honour for this country to bear. It is one thing for an invading army to do the things they did to us. They were, after all, only animals from the north, no different from the times of the

Romans, without minds as it were, rutting pigs driven by nature. It is another thing entirely for our own people to disgrace the name of the Netherlands-'

'But what could we have done, Mama?' said Jos earnestly.

'We could have resisted, refused to go along with them, or at least hidden them.'

'We would have been shot for refusing, then what?'

'Then we would have died with honour,' ended Pieter.

'And the Germans would have done the job themselves. We would all be dead and the Jews would still have been sent away.'

'Perhaps,' said Mama annoyed with the turn in the conversation. 'I'm so sorry, Ruth.'

'It is quite alright. You have done more for me than anyone else has ever done since I was taken away. Too many awful things have happened, none of which can be altered how ever I deal with the future. We cannot bring back a single life, not one relation. Nothing probably will ever happen like this again, so we must try to forgive, mustn't we?'

That statement caused the longest silence. 'When were you taken away by the police?'

'Nineteen forty-three. We were brought together and isolated in the *Joedenhoek* ', Mae pointed over her head towards the quay and beyond, 'to contain us like rounding up cattle in a Wild West film, to be branded later on, on the arm. Then we were sent to the theatre there. A little bit later, we went by cattle truck to *Westerbork*. We lost track of Daddy there.' Her lip trembled for the first time, as her firm control held in over months and years began to slip. 'Mother and I were sent to *Auschwitz-Birkenau*.'

'Is it still very fresh in your mind?' Pieter wondered. 'Is it fading at all?'

Mae paused. She had explained this before. How on God's earth could she make these nice, homely people understand the horror. Seeing the clean lace in the windows, the bright, polished hearth and the well-fed, if not fat, faces around her, it simply was not possible. 'Most people had been Lithuanians. Mother and I were kept to wait on officers' tables as we both spoke good German, Hoch-Deutsch, which, they said, sounded good at the dinner table, for Mother spoke with an upper-class accent.' And, recalling Suzannah's similar question of the day before she went on: 'I remember the end, though, when the Americans came. I walked down the street into town. So neat and clean, spotless in fact, like the houses here and all so near to the camp. Trim hedges to the gardens, yet a kilometre away or so...' she paused, as so often in her reflection as another image rose up to meet her images that rose like waves in the sea, they never ended, 'they must have smelt us, the smoke from the crematorium... in the wind. They must have known we were there, hearing the trains squeal into the sidings at night and the stench of the trucks.'

Pieter played with his meal. It had been a stupid idea to raise it just as food was being served. He remembered also, the shouts and the taunts in the streets across from the canals. Dirty Jew had been his favourite.

* * * *

It was the same stench. The socks boiling away like cabbage on the stove, but at least the filth would drain out into the basin and eventually find its way to the cleansing North Sea, replaced with clear, clean water to fluff up the wool and bring brilliance to the colours again.

I had walked home from my first day at work, pleased with life for the first time I could remember, almost chirpy and content as I clutched my bag of buns. The fact I had been on my feet all day had not worried me in the slightest for it had become a way of life and my legs were the stronger to carry me through the days. I was happiest because I knew I could, not only handle the work, but could improve upon it. Fathers training in business had given me a basic understanding in how it was all put together. Life in the camp at least allowed me to add to that knowledge so now I could see glaring holes in the way the bakery was organised. The problem lay in the fact it was run by a family, who had had no chance in the last ten years to examine modern business practices, so it had remained frozen in the nineteenth century. Profits would never increase until major changes were made, of that I was certain, but how could I hope to make the owners alter their way of thinking?

So immersed in my thoughts was I that I almost ran into Theo's boat, noticing straight away that the Family had not returned. It was all to do with Hans's arrest, I was sure, but there was little I could do here except check their boat for security and sweep the slush from the gangplank and deck.

I wanted to light a fire for them but I did not have a key. Instead, I crossed back over to *Kuijpers* and began my own small battle. I badly wanted to help someone, anyone, for the kindnesses, and Theo especially, but I wasn't sure if he would approve, pulling apart all his most intimate clothes as I shoved my fingers into all the corners of the drawers which had clearly not seen the light of a Dutch woman for many years.

I had decided his clothes came first, for I could take some of them up to the hospital on my next visit and bring back his dirty linen. I wanted to continue through the boat as I had started, and to make it gleam and glow with polish and metal cleaner, something to match the home next door so to speak, and for the one I had lost eight years before. To start with I had pulled out items, too dirty to be anything but in urgent need of a wash. It began to dawn on me, however, that they were all in the same condition so everything came out in piles on the floor. I had committed myself.

While I waited for the last two buckets to boil, I opened the steel door which had remained closed since Theo's sudden departure to hospital. The engine room retained the chill of winter within its steel walls; there was a tangible air of abandonment, nothing was as sad as the sight of powerful engines standing forlorn and silent. A piston, I assumed from its shape, had come to final rest in the up position resembling the leg of a giant grasshopper, with its steam gauge forming the eye of the insect. My feet stuck to the film of thick grease and oil on the floor and, annoyingly I knew that the cabin's newly cleaned floor would be covered in black grease once again, repeating the episode when the whole quayside population, it seemed, had tried to enter this small room. The only feet which had not touched the floor were those of Theo for he had been carried by Doctor Hertz to the gangway.

I could imagine this space as Theo's grandfather had looked upon it and worked in the heat. Almost certainly with pride, his possession and his home, working for him in the day and giving his family a place to eat and sleep at night in the safety of the harbour. I could see the dials sparkling in the flame of the boilers' mouths, running cotton waste over the brass work, a piece of which would have lived in his hand all day, almost as if it had grown there, and all orchestrated to the music of the hissing steam and the clank of the propeller shafts. I wanted so much to start work that I was momentarily upset when I heard a shout from above. Someone was using my name, and my nickname. The voice was heavy in accent, broad, and deep but not coarse.

It was Pieter. By the time I reached the wheelhouse I wondered what had made me think it was anyone else in my small world. I could see the Family staring up at the *Kuijpers* masthead. They were all there except Hans. He was still missing. Pieter began to tell me of the arrest which was obviously important to them so I kept quiet about my first day in my first job and the cakes I had brought back with me.

At last I managed to find time to pull the bag of iced buns from the wheelhouse and hand them over. It was though I had given them frankincense or myrrh. The joy lit up their pinched, unhappy faces and I knew it was the best thing I could have done. It brought instant cheer and made me pleased I had not downed them all myself despite the Manageress saying I should eat as many as I could for six months to put back the weight I had lost.

I crossed over the gunwale, lifting my legs gingerly above the sloppy wet cap. Most of the slush had slid into the water, though with evening the frost had begun to crackle again on the surface. Across the harbour, I could smell Dutch soup and bread being prepared in fifty boats. It mingled with the cheap tobacco from a number of nearby tugs, where their owners were making fast for the night, smoking the last fill of the day. The night air was so still it carried their voices to me, allowing me to eavesdrop on what each of them was saying in turn. If asked, I could have restated their conversations verbatim so clear were their words. Other sounds too, the chink of china being washed, a toilet being pumped out, and the harsh scrape of a besom on a deck, all the sounds of a harbour packing up for the night. It was all so peaceful, the war such a long while ago, almost as if it had never happened yet behind me a Family was in shock with the events of that war catching up with them. What ever the truth and I desperately wanted to believe in Hans's side of the story, there was a great deal of anger out in the city led by the avenging Nazi hunters. Mistakes could be made in the heat of the moment, reason blinded by memories of the families lost in the camps, not a time, I realised, to rush into making any decisions without clear proof one way or the other.

'Come on Mae, you are making the boat cold.'

I climbed down the stair, breaking the magic spell of the peace hanging over the water, where it lingered as if God had drawn his eye to this particular part of the world for a brief moment in time.

While we ate, the conversation moved from the worry of Hans back to me, in the hope, I suppose, of trying to forget the dilemma he was in. Mama's face said it all but she bravely attempted to change the subject. The Family wanted to know more about me, about the early, happier days at home. Elizabeta moved like a bony cow, not meant rudely, but, as she turned her face towards me each time I opened my mouth to speak, I could see her own jaws chomping from side to side, over and over.

Jos was more open in his interest, pointing his spoon at me from time to time. His questions were meticulous, too detailed really, and I began to feel I was not one of his favourite people.

My problem was to tell them gently, and it was here that I think Jos resented my previous wealth, my background. It had been a time when servants made life for me, my Mother and my Father, very comfortable. I was young enough not to know anything else and to take for granted the fact that my bed was made in the morning and meals were cooked and brought to the table by a girl in a white apron. Until the war, I hadn't realised how a fire hearth came to be cleaned and relit each morning in the winter. For me it just happened, miraculous perhaps, before I was dressed and downstairs. Food, warmth and nice clothes, I took them all for granted. When the fall came, I had so much further to slip than many others. Eventually hitting the floor, I came to appreciate how hard the surface was and how much more difficult it would be to climb back up. By the time the Germans had quit the country there was no-one to steer me in the right direction.

'After the war,' I told my listeners, I found my way to Rotterdam as the Allies were repatriating us to one point. The City was in a terrible state having been badly bombed. Here in Amsterdam it is so different. I knocked on the door of a gentile woman, a help from my mother's past, the only name I could remember. She, God bless her, took me in because she was alone as well. Her husband died the year before and her only son killed on a Royal Naval frigate on D-Day.'

I recalled, vividly, the day when Mary, that was her name, had said simply, you had better come in. I was told you had all perished. She hadn't been shocked, hardly surprised to see me. I think her mind was so dulled with the losses in her own life, she was incapable of reacting in either direction: despair or happiness. She just...existed, but that was better company than on my own in the streets. We lived together, Mary and I, in a house on the edge of the slums. We ate herrings and cooked them in fifty ways and talked of the times when she had scrubbed the kitchen pans in our house and emptied chamber pots from under our beds, one at a time. You couldn't carry two at a time, they were too heavy. Mary never complained of the way life had dealt her a rotten hand and told me that Daddy had been a kind, gentle man and Mother had been a good person to work for.

'Why did you leave her?' asked Jos, curiously.

'I didn't leave her, Jos. She left me.'

Suzannah wrinkled her nose in an endearing movement of her face and one which future Dutch boys would fall in love with, given half a chance by Mama. 'Where did she go?'

'To heaven,' I replied. 'One day Mary decided she had had enough of her life. She had been quite happy that day, I remember clearly. The street musicians had stood outside her apartment seeking a few cents. She loved accordions you see. And a trumpeter, a good-looking boy with his hair slicked down with hair cream. It must have aroused memories, happy ones of her son, and her husband when he was younger. She felt it was time to join them, I'm sure.'

'What did she do?' enquired Suzannah rather breathlessly, living the whole event in her mind.

'She went to bed as usual and cut her wrists. For good measure, she also slashed her throat.'

'Oh good God above! How dreadful,' Mama choked on her own words. 'Who found her?'

'I did, of course. There was no-one else in the house. She did not come down for breakfast so I went up to find her, thinking she might have been ill.'

'You found her? Like that? All covered in... blood...?'

This was not a conversation for the meal table, another taking the course of all the others. 'So, I was alone again, rather suddenly. I couldn't stay in the apartment as an Aunt arrived on the doorstep and told me to get out. She didn't even give me twenty-four hours.'

I often thought of that day. Mother's death was beginning to fade, at least it was now tucked into a corner of my mind and Mary said I had not been crying out so much at night as I had done when I first arrived at her door. Finding the Aunt on the doorstep, hands clasped tightly in front of her with her hat jammed down over her ears, had made a forbidding picture heightened by the lack of neck, so that her head had seemed as if it was growing out of the collar of her coat.

'There's work in Amsterdam young lady,' she had said without a hint of an introduction as to who she was, 'but you'll not be blood-sucking this house any more after today. I never did hold with Mary's ideas.'

After that, there was not much point to ask for more time to look for some other place, let alone argue my rights if ever I had any. I walked away with a paper carrier which the woman searched before she would allow me to go. There had been a frost in the air, and in my mind, and I really did not mind in which direction I went.

It was Suzannah who always listened so carefully to me. Sometimes, when her back was turned, or perhaps when bending over to clean the stove or brush the floor, she would cock an ear, or incline her head, the better to hear the story being related. She absorbed them like a sponge, whereas with Anna they would flow more easily over her like water making a path to the harbour.

Elizabeta was deeply troubled with what I had had to say. I could see the way she turned her head to stare at a chair, the one which Hans usually occupied every evening. All at once, as I was describing the countryside around Auschwitz, her shoulders dropped and began to heave. Two huge tears, one to each eye, began a long run down her cheeks. Pieter was immediately at her side. He held her head and crooned. 'There, there,' over and over.

Outside, the frost crackled fiercely again and the little tug close by began to cool down. It was time for me to go and stand on my own feet again.

The Potato Eaters

* * * *

Theo stood at his window, unaware the soft light silhouetting his body, blocked the view for any others who might want to watch and stare. He had thrust his hands deep into his pockets so they pulled at his shoulders in a big shrug, causing the linings to stretch to their limits. There was no collar to his shirt, nor a stud visible at his neck, allowing two or three blond hairs, the same colour as the back of his hands to curl out from the Vee of his chest.

He knew he was better. The hospital had told him so, but, better than this was the fact he no longer saw the images as harshly; pictures which had pushed insistently into his life since he had become ill. Now they broke upon his shore, still intrusive, still cold and wet, yet without the frightening noises. The sounds of the sea roaring at him as in a storm had lessened and he knew he was distancing himself from them almost by the hour. The waves broke, at times peacefully in his ears, reminding him of his boat and the harbour: his home. Most of all, he knew he could control his rambling tongue when Mae came to see him. In the bad days he had gone off into long discussions on theology. Mae, however, had not been prepared to listen politely to the painful words. She had not shown any embarrassment as she challenged each utterance, each phrase with: 'Why?' or 'How?' demanding almost, needing to know why he had raised the subject in the first place. He believed she was stretching his mind, freeing it up from the years of solitude when he had had no-one to talk to for hours, days even: it had activated his mind, thrusting his brooding ideas up to confront his existence. So he strove to reply sensibly. It made him think, a process he had not had much experience of aboard his boat.

One day, a steam pile driver had been driven directly below his window at the hospital where it had started to pummel long, shaven tree trunks down into the mud alongside the canal. He had let his voice rise above the steady whump...whump frustrating himself in his attempts to oblige her to listen. She, however, waited for the inevitable pauses, these being introduced every ten minutes or so. As the vibrations on the windowpanes had quietened down, she would replace them with her counsel. As she did, he noticed how she would unconsciously almost, brush hairs from his jacket or pick specks off the collar, or run her hands up the back of his jersey to pull out pieces of fluff. And his clothes were clean and smelt of soap and fresh air, air from the harbour, so he longed to be on the deck of *Kuijpers*.

The next time she had called, she had arrived with a pair of scissors borrowed from Mama. Theo had had to sit quietly, and without complaint on a high stool in the middle of the polished floor. Because cut hair had always made him itch for the rest of the day, he had taken the option of sitting stripped to the waist, examining each fine blond shower of clippings as they were generated, falling past his face to the floor. Individual hairs caught the light as if there were gold motes in the room, bringing a shimmer to the atmosphere. The room was always warm though the heat of her body in close contact brought him immense pleasure. He had been minded to lean back on her chest so he could drown in her body smell, but almost as though she knew he was about to do it, she moved away tantalisingly, to start on a new section. She passed on, to trim around an ear, or crop his front when he closed his eyes tight and recalled when his grandmother had done the same thing to him. He felt Mae's gentle breath blowing the hair from his eyes, telling him he could open them again, but it was nicer to stay with his eyes screwed shut, dreaming of the past and better days. It also sanctioned another issue. While in hospital he had found few people to talk to, other than when Mae came to visit. At such times, he found the need to speak of burning issues in life, not to gossip or to chatter, determined to be heard with his own simply formed questions. His deliberate, halting voice became firmer, the structure and syntax more defined and daily, he became stronger in accent. Mae sensed the haunting quality of his expression, a reminder of the past, hidden behind his illness until now. It was almost…beautiful, she realised, although she was not at all sure if one could apply such an adjective to his prose. Living with his grandparents, isolated to a degree and repeating their words and their mannerisms from the turn of the century, he had had few other role models to copy from since schooldays. During the last visit, he had become almost poetic as he described the life of the workmen below his window. He always asked of news of Hans. The report though, had always been negative. Today, however, as Mae stood behind a nurse finishing off the cleaning, not wanting to disturb Theo's reverie, she had more detail to the news, if more alarming.

He turned his head with a smile as he heard the squeak of leather on the waxed floor, appearing genuinely pleased at her coming.

'Mae, come in, come in.'

The nurse left, patting down her apron and adjusting her headgear, content in the knowledge her visitor was able to provide better therapy than any doctor.

'Hullo.' She always gave him the same, quiet greeting, as if not knowing how she would be received. Up until recently that would have been the case, now, things were changing. 'Are you well?'

'Much better... thank you,' he added, turning to face her. 'It is warmer out, is it not? I can see the workmen: they have taken off their jackets.'

'I smell Spring.' The phrase excited her as she spoke it as if it heralded a brand new change in herself, let alone the weather outside. It was warmer, she knew, such that the hard pinch in the air that made the hairs in her nose itch at times had vanished to be replaced with a softer feel as if her mother had given her a fine cotton handkerchief to blow.

She held out a small bag of buns. 'I was told yesterday that the bakery is very pleased with my progress.'

'I'm glad for you. Much better to work, than be shut up like here, performing for the doctors like a chicken having to lay an egg every day for the hungry farmer.'

She ignored the comment. 'Soon you will be out of here, cured, back on *Kuijpers*. You will be coming home just as the weather becomes nice to sit out on deck.'

He liked the notion. 'How is *Kuijpers*?'

She wasn't sure what she should say or what he really wanted to know, or even how much to tell him. Some times, over the past weeks she felt she had gone too far in the treatment of his boat, his home after all, melding it as she had done to her personality, rather than that of his own. She had learned that he had never really cared in looking after his belongings, how he looked or what he wore; he did not care how his furniture was set to the room or whether the curtains were hung or were clean, but, it *was* his. He might well think it was a personal invasion of his privacy. 'Hans? Is there any news?' He had interrupted himself as usual.

'Yes,' she replied gravely. 'There is more news, confirmation, I am afraid of what we all knew but did not want to believe in. Hans is being held, without bail, on suspicion of collaborating with the enemy and indirectly causing the deaths of three Resistance fighters in nineteen forty-four. The reason he is not being allowed bail is because one of the Resistance fighters was a national hero and the government are determined to be seen to be co-operating with the international witch hunts from so many countries.'

'What are they hunting?'

'People, collaborators, who allowed so many Dutch Jews to be sent to Germany without a fight and those that exposed Dutch Jews who had been in hiding, to the Gestapo. The police think Hans would try and leave the country the moment he was released despite the bail, if it could be raised from Mama and Papa. But, on the good side, it is becoming more difficult for the prosecutors to hold him without a trial, and they may have to release him soon if they do not find enough evidence to bring a trial.'

'Well, that's good, isn't it?'

'Maybe, possibly, but that will not solve the problem.'

'But, it is a start. It means there really isn't enough evid-' He gave up trying to pronounce the word. Theo turned to the window again. It had become his counsellor at times of decision. He had formed a link to the outside world via the window which framed his entire waking day. By gazing through the glass he was able to steer himself into making the right choices for himself without the feeling of making himself silly in front of others.

'This is always going to be with us, isn't it? The winners want vengeance, however long it takes to find them all. In a few years time the old people will be dead, but their children are being taught to remember it all so…the hate and violence will start up all over again.' He paused: 'It is so much easier to hate than it is to love, I think.'

Mae was silent, hearing his words, understanding them, seeing only the long lines of Jews queuing up to climb into the cattle trucks. Those few left would never forget so long as they lived and their children would be taught to perpetuate the knowledge of the horror. In another fifty years the whole cycle would be set in motion again, subtly at first, then more directly as the mobs became more confident and more numerous. It would not take too much longer for a leader to rise above a disillusioned populace, to make a policy statement concerning the need for re-housing their Jews to a particular quarter of their city, the better for them to live together…for their own benefit.

'No! She replied very firmly. 'You are wrong, Theo. To love does not require any effort at all. One only has to listen. Listen to the sounds of the grass in the dunes on a windy day. See the first daffodils poking through the tram tracks in *Leidesplein*. Watch the lips of someone who loves you.

'But, to hate, hate needs effort, great effort. You need effort to stamp on someone, to brutalise their mind when you know there really is no need to do so. Hate shrivels your heart like a dried prune, leaving the centre rotten and crumbly, quick to turn to dust: it turns you in on yourself until, finally, it destroys you.'

As she spoke, Theo continued to watch a barge negotiating along the canal with its cargo high enough to brush the tips of the branches hanging down from the trees which lined its route. She knew him well enough by now to know he was digesting her words carefully. Afterwards, he would rehearse them when he was on his own, to see what he could make of her ideas: later still he would bring his own halting words to challenge hers. This was the paradox. To the world he presented himself almost as an idiot, certainly one whose mind had long been lost. But, below the blank stare, intelligence hovered, waiting to break out into the world. He would never be as fast as her he knew, but with time he found he could come up with strategies which made simple, commonsense.

While she waited patiently, not having been asked to sit down, Mae wanted only to take him from this unfeeling room whose history had absorbed the madness of its inmates almost into the plaster itself. She could feel the fear and the emptiness, without a gram of warmth or personality. Why, she asked herself, were all hospitals universally bland, universal colours and identical layouts? The walls here departed from the main corridor, being shiny gloss paint, dark green below the dado line set at an arbitrary height above which it took upon itself to change to the palest hint of green. The paint reflected the white glass coolie shade hanging from its cloth-covered flex. The ceiling was so high that the cable appeared to rise up forever, where, out of reach of interfering feather dusters she could see a fine layer of dust on the shade. A series of finer, lighter lines caused by fingers, showed where a hospital porter had left his mark when he had replaced a blown lamp. There was a single picture in the room, a standard image repeated throughout most hospitals in the country, one of Christ in Agony. How unthinking of the Nuns to add such a depressing scene in a mad man's den.

She checked herself sharply. He wasn't mad, of that she was certain. Not Theo. His condition, the doctor had taken the time to describe to her, was schizophrenia, a new word to her, but the official title of his illness. Schizophrenia, she had learned was a state of being when a patient had a split mind, when his thoughts were not focussed but divided into real and non-real worlds so that Theo jumped like a hurdler from one to the other. Each world, in turn was the real world confusing him more.

'Will he be like this forever?' she had asked Doctor Hertz on one of his visits when she had been there.

'Not necessarily,' he had answered as carefully as he could, seeing the desire for honesty in her pinched face with its dark hollows enquiring anxiously. 'As you know, he skips in and out of this state. It only takes a small event, a tiny pressure point to set him off in the opposite direction. He could, one day, come permanently out of this half world he occupies so reluctantly. He must want to do so, however, and for that he needs considerable care and personal attention on a daily basis; someone to share his concerns and remove them as they arise by taking on his responsibilities.' If only someone could do that for me, she thought. 'If not...?' he let the words dry on his lips, unwilling to continue.

'If not...he could remain in the other world, for ever?' she completed the words for him.

'Quite so,' he replied quietly. He patted his lips delicately with a spotless handkerchief, unused to the girl's directness. This was not what women were good at doing, nor, usually would they even attempt to reply to such a query. This remained men's talk, and for this slip of a girl to stare him in the eye with such steadiness was unnerving as he was never sure what would be her next subject.

Mae repeated the words she had been told by Suzannah to the doctor, of Theo's link with the shore, his absolute terror of leaving the land. 'That is very interesting. I can actually see the nucleus of an idea there, but,' he added with a pout, shrugging his shoulders, 'there is so little money for research, and no time at all. If you think Theo is a bad case, come to the rear wing of the hospital one of these days. I'll show you what man has done to man. So many are shocked by what they have seen, and did—'

But, she knew all about kicks in the teeth…and sights for that matter sights to amaze even the good doctor. He suddenly realised his error. 'I'm so sorry, my dear. You must have seen some terrible things yourself. It was so stupid of me.'

Mae found herself laughing. 'It is a wonder you are not treating me as well, Doctor Hertz.'

'In fact, I think you are a very well-balanced lady, with a fine brain. You could be a doctor too, you know. You will get through this in the end and the nightmares will start fading after a while. It is time you need, time and calm.'

Mae recalled that conversation now. It brought fierce motivation. She wanted to apply her own ideas, not as a doctor but in business. All at once it came together, as if she had been working on a thesis for weeks and the answer had come to the front page. Words came tumbling out.

'Theo. Why don't you come back to the boat? I'll take care of you, cook for you in the evenings, and wash your clothes…and things.' Again, she had ended rather lamely unsure if she had said too much, unsure even if he was listening properly. He had a habit of looking just over her right shoulder, eyes just averted and slightly glazed.

But, he *was* listening. 'Why should you do all of this for me? You don't owe me anything, you know.'

'I owe you my life, among other things, or have you forgotten what you did for me. But, that is not the point I am making—'

'I would have jumped in the water for anyone, Mae. You have no idea what it would be like, living on *Kuijpers*, the two of us, that is. I know you have been looking after her for me while I have been here, and I am grateful for this…but, I shout out at…at night s-sometimes. I am awake quite often and walk about the…the c-cabin.' His earlier, stronger voice was becoming more strained and hoarse; he was tiring, and so the phrases were more confused, running into a stutter. Objects change their s-shape in front of me, move even,' he added looking at her for a reaction as though his words would surely put her off. Seeing her tranquil and waiting for him to finish, he went on: 'You would not believe how, how they do it…this would not be the place for you when it happened.'

Mae was laughing again, much to Theos concern for he was unable to fathom just why she should be taking his words so lightly or was it simply the way in which he had thrown out his hands to ward off unseen demons as he explained it to her?

'I'm sorry, Theo. I'm really sorry. I only laughed because I can see how little you know of me, far less than I know of you. Do you know, for example, I sleep for only three hours a night or so each and every night? I wake with sweat pouring down my body so my eyes ache. I scream aloud as Pieter will avow, as he says he can hear it from the *Anna Rosner*. He says I cried out at night, even when I was living on board with the safety of the Family all around me, When I am alone-'

'Well, you wouldn't be alone, would you, if you were on *Kuijpers*.' He smiled, almost cheekily, a complete turn around.

This was the first positive step he had made. Mae would remember this point in his healing process for a long time, a moment when his mind had made its own decision. He had reversed his original thoughts by one hundred and eighty degrees just because he wanted to. It was positive because he had been pro-active…and curiously, protective.

'I suppose not,' she said, smiling broadly. 'We appear to be a couple of misfits in life, don't we?'

'One day, Mae, the war will go away from your mind. You will not see the things I will continue to see-'

No!' her voice almost whip lashed him in its passion. 'You are going to get better, completely better. I am not going to let you believe you will always be…ill. I am told you can get better, so you will, I will see to it.'

Despite himself, Theo loved the strength in her voice. He smiled again transforming his face into an intelligent being. The very idea made him feel better and brought a desire in him to see his boat again.

'I would need to get permission from Doctor Hertz, and the hospital. They would have to sign some form of, er, release I think it is called, like they did last time.' He smiled for the third time. 'When they think I am not dangerous, I presume. And, I would have to continue taking the medicine.'

'Of course, naturally.' Her heart began to beat quite painfully. 'You must complete the course of treatment whatever you do, otherwise it will all have been wasted. I could collect the medicine on my way back from work in the evening.'

'Ah, yes. You have your job.' He was silent for a long time. His eyes flickered across the few objects not considered hazardous, in the room, then out again to the city at work. A flat barge, its deck loaded with wooden crates and showing off a rust-coloured, rectangular sail standing up like a funnel, moved past his line of sight, almost as if it were in slow motion. 'I would like to have a job, very much, just like you. It would stop the boredom and keep my mind from straying to… to… you know where. At least, I think I would like to work.'

'You could Theo. There are so many jobs going in Amsterdam at present. The city is finding its feet again and companies are expanding.'

'But, what could I do?'

'Sail your boat. Use it for–'

'No! Never! It cannot leave shore you see. I cannot use the boiler.'

'If you found a partner, you provide the boat, for example. He provides a new diesel engine.'

'You do not understand Mae. I…cannot leave the harbour. It's not possible. God…its God,' he was grasping at straws, 'He will not permit me to leave.'

'Well,' she replied, keeping her voice light yet controlled, pausing to sum up his statement. 'Your God is different to mine. My God wishes me to be successful in life so I can help other people in turn, and in what ever I wanted to do. You know, your God's son spent most of his time with fishermen, so I am surprised your God does not allow this.'

'Ah, but you are a Jew, you see. He has different principles to work to. Mine, well, it is not possible, he says.'

Mae was enjoying the sort of fencing between them, unsure whether Theo was fully in belief of what he said. There was sweat, she could see on his top lip. 'That cannot possibly be the case, Theo.'

'Why?'

'Because you are a Christian, are you not?'

'Yes, I am.'

'Well, Jesus was a Jew, have you forgotten? He came from a family just like my own.'

It was time for Theo to have a shuffle about with his feet. He did not speak as he tried to come to terms with what she had said. His shoulders felt uncomfortable as though someone had placed a sack upon them. 'You make so many things so much more clear,' he said eventually. 'When you talk, the walls move back, the corners become right-angles and the horizon doesn't dip and dive all the while.' His voice was stronger again, likening it to having had a half hour cat nap. He looked backwards to where she was standing. Finding it hard to smile so often, he twitched his nose in an effort to communicate he was not at all upset by the drift of the conversation.

It was strangely quiet in the room as if all the patients and staff had gone shopping without telling them. The only noise was a coin rattling in a beggar's rusty cup out in the street where he jiggled his coins with the toe of his boot each time someone passed him by.

The germ of the early idea had taken root climbing like a creeper towards a blue sky. 'Wait, Theo, wait here, I am going to find a nurse.' Mae was already half out of the door as she spoke. She found the duty nurse sitting stiffly erect in her starched blouse, laboriously entering a row of figures from a hand written sheet into a ledger.

'Excuse me, could you tell me if Doctor Hertz has to be informed if Theo wants to leave the hospital? I am now able to cook his meals, see he gets clean clothes and I can check he takes his medicine each day…that sort of thing.' She almost garbled her words, so anxious was she to tell the woman what she wanted. Two grey, serious eyes studied her for a moment. They were not unkind but they wanted to know more, seeking a reason behind the request. Eventually, the cheeks cracked open in a half-smile. 'Theo is much better. I know he needs to get back to his boat, but Doctor Hertz has been attempting to affect a more lasting cure than those he has tried in the past. It could set him back a-'

'Oh, I really don't think so. Perhaps,' she paused, 'should I call at the Doctor's? Do you think that would be a good idea?'

'Bring me an authorisation note from Doctor Hertz and we will get him home for you.'

Saying goodbye rather breathlessly, as if she were a child again, thanking an Aunt for a present, Mae ran down the street until, suddenly feeling quite foolish and annoyed with herself for showing such emotion in front of someone she hardly knew, she slowed her pace. Why was she doing this anyway? Theo meant nothing to her and after all, he was mad, well, distinctly strange, with a prevalence for tearing his clothes off in the middle of winter. But, that sounded harsh, too truthful. Theo was a good man, attractive in a physical sort of way, only needing direction and care to allow his true nature to return. Mae liked the sound of the last one. She found she could come to terms with her plan to bring him back home with all the encumbrances that would arise as a result. And, she had dismissed, until now, the thought of living on board the tiny tug with a man, healthy in all other ways and armed, possibly with an appetite for…sex. The word even, quite shocked her. She knew absolutely nothing about it other than what she had gleaned in the camps and most of that was wrapped up in coarseness and an assumption she knew all about it.

'He's a sick boy, that's all… man I mean,' she said aloud. She could find a room on her own, let the Family keep an eye on him and get on with the rest of her youth. Calming herself she managed to maintain a steady pace towards the *Prinzengracht*.

The two dray-men she often waved to, each responded to her signal as they continued down the road. They were dressed in their Sunday clothes having been to church, so they looked very different to their normal weekly boiler suits. The scene reminded her that the Doctor might not be in but she was absorbed in apple strudel and cakes and cabbage soup and welcome home signs.

'Is Doctor Hertz in?'

'I'm sorry, the doctor is resting. He has had a tiring night with a patient, and has been up all night.'

Mae's face fell down the steps hitting the pavement. 'When will he be awake, please? It is important.'

'Who is there, my dear? I'm not asleep,' came a disembodied voice from the drawing room nearby.

'Tsk, tsk, his wife mouthed, her face in open dismay. 'You must rest.'

'It is perfectly alright. Ah, it is you, Ruth. Have you been to see Theo?'

'Yes, Doctor Hertz. He is so much better. I want to take him back to his boat where he belongs.' She rushed on, not waiting for him to raise a single objection.

'I have cleaned his boat, scrubbed the deck and all his clothes are washed and ironed and put back in clean drawers. The Family…next door… want him back as well. They will help to look after him. Between all of us, we can do everything he receives in hospital except what you do for him, of course,' she added noting the need for considerable tact at that moment. 'And make sure he takes his pills.'

'Of course, young lady,' he replied evenly and gravely at the same time. Hertz held up a restraining hand to prevent Mae from continuing, or at least, from running out of breath. 'I was going to call on you at the quayside later today as I knew you would be there. I came to the same conclusion as you. I can do no more for him, at least, not without time, time which is not available to me. I thought I could cure him in the hospital. What he really needs is a Family around him and to be well looked after. There are so many others needing to come into a bed I could do with the room urgently.

'I know you will look after him and I will call once a week to bring his pills. It is very important you see he takes them daily. It might be dangerous if he misses out, so you need to continue the routine of the hospital. Can I depend on that?'

Mae wanted to kiss the tired, old man, whose eyes were shadowed in purple. 'Thank you, thank you, Doctor.'

'One more thing though. Theo must stay in tonight. You can collect him tomorrow, after work perhaps?' He examined the pinched face in front of him seeing the first signs of a slight fleshiness beginning to round her cheekbones and under her chin, weight he had not seen there when he had first met her. A pink tint, as light as the reflection of an apple on a tablecloth, suffused her skin and he marvelled how nature was bringing its own healing process to a body, which, to all intents and purposes should have died a few weeks ago. He had mentally confirmed Theo should be let go the day before. Now, seeing the strength of Mae's will to help him, he knew it would be the best treatment Theo could receive.

Mae arrived back at last on the dockside eyeing the *Kuijpers* critically. There was still a pile of old snow lying here and there where shovels had heaped the snow up away from the quaysides to keep the moorings clear. 'He's coming back tomorrow,' she shouted, climbing down the companionway to the Family. They replied by asking her in for Sunday lunch, but she declined the offer.

'Too much to do, but thank you all the same.'

Suzannah laughed delightedly. 'What! But everything's spotless.'

'Ah, you are wrong. There is one more place I haven't been to yet. It is the worst, greasiest place I have ever seen but it has to be done so I can say the whole boat is clean. 'She held out a grease-proof bag. 'A spiced cake? I don't want it.'

Mama, who had lumbered in from the galley, took it with a smack of her lips and pulled out the offering. The sweet aroma filled the wheelhouse. Her jaw chomped up and down on the morsel she had prised from the edge. 'Hmm. That is a good bakery you work for, Mae. Almost as good as mine.'

'Never,' echoed a chorus or voices from behind. Mae chuckled, pleased to see their spirits lifted. But Hans was still not with them.

'No news?' she enquired. Pieter shook his head.

'They won't release him. At least not with this girl's testimony holding up and as the case revolves around her word they have to make further enquiries. Her father is very rich, one of the biggest shippers here in the harbour and the police tend to believe her rather than Hans. Also, there is a crusade going on right through the country with the newspapers taking the high moral tone. I am just pleased there is no picture of Hans in the paper.'

Mae nodded her head in reply. 'It will come right in the end, just you wait and see.'

'Thanks for the cake,' said Pieter no longer believing in such platitudes but recognising Mae's loyalty.

Mae closed the wheelhouse door and climbed back aboard *Kuijpers*. She raked out the stove and relit the wood. She had a box of wood chippings collected daily from the yards around her and they caught quickly, sending a flicker of light through the red glass of the stove's vermiculite window. She frowned. The whole affair over Hans and the police was not making sense at all. Normally, someone would be released on bail within a few days if no evidence of any substance had been offered. Hans had been held for four weeks on the word of one girl with only further confinement to be expected. She wondered what sort of girl, if girl was the right description, to have laid such a charge against an ex-boyfriend. She must have hated him very much and, again it made her pause to think of what Hans had said or done to her, for her to maintain her accusation. Although she had known Hans for very little time before he had been arrested, he did not display the habits of a traitor. The tug-men were a loyal band, held together by the sea and their trade, steadfast in their devotion to the Royal House and their country. The whole affair did not make sense.

She turned purposefully and walked to the end door and swung it open.

A draught of oily, cold air met her. She wrinkled her nose in distaste to be replaced an instant later with a grimace as she pulled on a head scarf and abandoned all thoughts of a meal.

The grasshopper sat exactly as she had seen it that last time. She switched on the fluorescent light only to snap off the metal control as soon as she found her bearings in the room. Standing on a stool, she managed to release the two tubes from the light fitting and take them down. They were covered in a film of grease, to which clung balls of dust. These she washed almost lovingly, running her encircling fingers down the full length of each tube, then back up as soap creamed between palm and thumb. She felt hot, softer and more aware of her body than she could remember.

She dried the tubes, twisting the linen cloth to polish each one before fixing it back in its box. This time, when she depressed the knob, the machinery jumped out at her, the pieces stark, grimy, highlighting each grease mark and thumbprint.

She forgot about making a snack for herself, or to go to bed at a reasonable hour. Mindful of her work the next day, she covered her clothes as much as possible before tackling the steel plates on the ceiling. Underneath the filth, the paint was surprisingly white and in good condition. It was as if the deck overhead had been removed to let the sun pour down into every crevice of the engine room. While she washed, nagging ideas jumped into and out of her mind. They nagged her because she knew she was thinking of interfering, this time, in the Family's affairs. She tried to free her mind by concentrating on the brass rims encircling the dials which she burnished with fine steel wool she had found in a box, once used to hold all the cleaning cloths of the boat. The floor had once been a mixture of red and green paint coming to life as she scoured the oil and black tar. At half past two in the morning she stopped to survey her work, feeling dizzy from lack of food. She shook her head for the fiftieth time at the ridiculous situation she had fashioned for herself. What possible point was there in cleaning this area, manned by a madman who would never go to sea again in his lifetime? The engines would never be fired up, those sparkling pistons would remain at rest as if the insects they resembled had grown old and tired of jumping, frozen for ever in that position. She relented on the word madman and substituted the word schizophrenic. It was easier to accept.

When she switched off the electric light, the room vanished back into the night. The grasshopper glowed with energy as it picked up reflected light from the main cabin, contradicting the view they would never move again. She shut the door and leant against a wooden panel in the cabin allowing her eyes to travel round the spotless compartment.

'Tomorrow, Theo will be here again. Theo will be sitting in his chair, *his chair*...and we will talk of the future.'

* * * * *

As much as worrying about Theo's homecoming was the matter of how I could become involved in helping the Family with Hans. Alone in the boat after saying goodnight to Pieter and Elizabeta, I had asked myself what I could do to help. When I had been cleaning the engine room, ideas had sprung to mind that I might get involved in some way. Privately, I realised that this new pre-war world continued to be biased against the poor: this Family was relatively poor and with little if no influence at all with Authority. Money, influence and a good lawyer might have allowed Hans to be released on bail by now, whereas he languished in prison accused of the terrible crime of treason. The Family had given me warmth, comfort, food, security and found me a job when I had needed them all and had none of these. It was now a time of reckoning. It was my turn to do something for them.

When I woke, slightly stiff from my exertions in the engine room, I smelled of oil so I stood in the tin tub with a copper of hot water which I had left on all night and soaped myself over. I wondered what it would be like for a man, my husband, to wash me while I sat, or better still, lay in the bath doing not a lot, to enjoy every sensation he created with his hands. Marriage was like this, or so I imagined. Not Mother though, she would not have permitted such things I fear.

It was so early even Pieter was not about, one reason for my early rise as I did not want him to see me going. Oil-free and smelling of soap I climbed ashore in the dark, the air, ice on my nose, and the cold clamped around my clothes. Frost muffled the sounds of the quay as the City hesitated slowly into life once again, disturbing the pigeons and causing the, usually, self-confident cyclists to slow down on the cobbles. The burble of exhausts under water orchestrated themselves alongside the clank of the heavier engines and the shouts of *'Goeden morgen'* from a number of boisterous men being taken out to the outer harbour in the small ferries. It looked a day where the sun would shine and that was important for me.

The Police Station where Hans was being held was on my way to work, behind the Royal Palace on Dam Square. The outer office was lit by a single lamp in a cracked shade casting deep shadows behind two settees, the only seating in the room. There was the sour smell of vomit and stale beer coming from a corridor running off at the rear of the room.

'Yes?' said a disembodied voice from behind a hatch which had opened in the wall. And then, more considerately, seeing me: 'Can I do something for you?' The tone was applied as if it were quite natural for a girl of my age to be entering a Police Station at this ridiculous time of the morning.

'My name is Maas, Anna Maas,' I said as quickly as I could. I had learnt to be proficient in lying at the camp but I still hated doing it. 'You are holding my brother, Hans Maas here. I would like to see him for a moment please.'

The policeman's eyes narrowed. 'You have been here before, with the rest of the family?'

I was in with a chance. 'Yes, that's right, officer, but I felt it was better without the rest of the Family together. They are, well, a bit noisy and disruptive, aren't they when they all get together. Last time was, well…a bit embarrassing, wasn't it?'

The officer nodded grimly, recalling the difficult night. He relaxed, slightly. 'All that argument. I said to them it was not up to me, it was up to my Superior, but your parents would not listen, would they? Your brother is being held now under the Special Powers Act Nineteen forty-six, for those accused of treason. There is no bail for those charges. They are very serious and the whole thing is becoming political. The young lady who made the accusation might not have realised just what she was getting into when she made the allegation. So, I have no right to let you see him without higher authority permission.'

'But officer,' I wheedled. 'Just for a minute. I have to go to work very soon anyway. Just five minutes, no-one would know except us. Please…'

The man began to hesitate, scratching at his night's stubble. He glanced at his watch and pursed his lips. 'I go off duty in exactly seven minutes. I want you out of here before my colleague arrives. Understood?'

'I promise,' I urged giving him what I thought was a winning smile ensuring that I would rather die than let him down. We started forward.

Behind was a wide corridor, each side holding a number of steel doors which stood in pairs opposite each other. Hans's name was scribbled on one of the panels by the side of a door in purple chalk. The door opened easily on its oiled hinges. He was sitting on a small bunk bed, feet splayed apart a newspaper in front of him.

'Mae! What in Gods name are you doing here? Is it Mama or Papa?'

'I thought you said your name was Anna,' the officer was now suspicious.

'It is my nickname,' I said truthfully.

'Yes, it's true officer,' Hans reacted quickly to the situation.

Mollified, the man walked off shutting me in the cell. 'Neither,' I said smiling at Hans's immediate concern. Would a traitor have first thought of others if he were really guilty? These were not the words of a collaborator. 'I'm on my way to work and wanted to find out if there is anything I can do to help. I only have five minutes at most.'

'I'm innocent Mae, totally innocent. It is all to do with an old girl friend of mine. She always said she would get her own back on me one day. I stood her up at a dance once. The problem is, she is very rich, or rather her father is very rich and she has never had a man do that to her before. In all fairness it was wrong of me, but it is easy in hindsight to see these things differently, but we were so far apart in our lifestyles anyway it could only be just a fling, a bit of fun which was going to go nowhere. She wanted to control when it would finish and I anticipated the ending so I left her. She was extremely angry with me.'

'But, she has to have some form of proof, doesn't she? For you to be held this long, I mean.'

'This is the whole problem, Mae. She says she saw me several times coming out of a meeting room of a man who lived close to the University building. This was in the war of course. This man was involved in the shooting of three men on the banks of the *Amstel*. What she says was quite true but it was just coincidence that I was there with the man. I think I asked him for a light once. That's all I know. The problem is made worse because she is very plausible and uses her father's name to get what she wants. Her father is big in shipping, and in Amsterdam that counts for something. Money talks, doesn't it?'

'Did you go to this house, the one you were talking about?'

'Yes, several times, I have never denied it. It used to be a meeting place for young people such as myself. Hundreds must have gone there in the past, but it is all nonsense for they could all be accused along with me on exactly the same charge.'

Hans studied the concrete floor which smelt strongly of disinfectant, like Theo's hospital. He looked despondent as he listened to his own words. He could see how weak it all was and, as a result he was still locked up. Why indeed, had no-one else been charged? It all hung on this girl's testimony.

'What was this meeting room all about?'

Hans hesitated for a moment. 'Well, the Germans tried to make the young Dutch men have a different attitude towards ...Jews. They brought girls in to dance with and supplied us with beer. It was all a bit of fun as we knew that we would not change our ideas... except a few stupid ones.'

I had heard of these meeting places where the Gestapo had attempted to make informers of the locals so that more of the hidden Jews would be brought to light.

'How is all the Family?' He threw at me, changing course into easier waters.

'They are all well, worried about you naturally enough, especially Mama.'

'And your job?'

'Good thank you. Theo comes home tonight. With a bit of luck, that is. I'm going to pick him up-'"No more Miss. I'm going off duty in a minute or so.' The officer placed a light hand on my shoulder though firm enough to know that I had run out of time.

'I'll come and see you again, Hans. I know this matter can be cleared up soon, it has to. It just doesn't make sense.' 'Give my love to Mama and Papa, and Suzannah,' Hans ensured my relationship with the officer was re-secured. As I was escorted back to the outer office, the policeman said in a conversational tone: 'He's guilty, Miss, guilty as hell. I'm sorry. There's more to this than just one informant you know.' I just could not believe him, and the strange mood of conviction stayed with me all day as I swung loaves around in their paper bags to twist the ends tight.

I saw Hans, his eyes almost closed against his eyelashes, and the wispy moustache pushing against his top lip. His healthy face was permanently freckled, so dewy young in his way...and so totally innocent to my way of thought. I remembered about three years ago when groups of the Home Defence Force, rifles at the port, had marched along the streets of Rotterdam, encircling small groups of civilians who held their hands up tiredly from their elbows. Some of these men had looked flashy, black-marketers, others just rough. Others again though, were as if they had walked out of University doors a little earlier in the day. And young! The same age as Hans. There had been reports of these collaborators in column widths, stretched shoulder to shoulder as they held out wooden poles in front of them, nervously prodding the grass in front of them as they sought out land mines and old booby-traps which had been laid in the outlying fields during the end of the occupation. And sad days followed, when a huge mass of people had come to a halt in *Haarlem* as *Hannie Shaft* the Resistance fighter was laid to proper rest. We had been a vengeful nation then, understandably perhaps. Today, five years later, it seemed as if the war had come to revisit me and to cloud and complicate the otherwise bright future held out in front of me.

A train, pulling into Central Station whistled particularly loudly as I was leaving work. It reminded me there were other things to do. Theo was coming out in a very short time and I worried if I was able to cope with him…or him, me?

Whatever the truth of Hans's past, it was certain in my mind that Theo was not involved in any way. He, as opposed to the Family brothers, although openly unrefined, had a gentle manner which communicated to the world through his eyes. This character of his surfaced quietly and at times quite unexpectedly, the intelligence, masked for most of the day until a trigger allowed it to show itself. Theo's nature could not have involved itself in betraying his country for an ideal. His was that of a compatriot, without the flag waving and chest beating. Hans, rightly or wrongly would be standing in court on his own,

At the hospital I had to wait in the bare hall while the nurse clacked away in her utility shoes, leaving a door to bang testily behind her. The double-clunk, magnified by the hard surfaces, left me all at once suspended in silence, broken only by the drip of a tap nearby. Even the inmates seemed to have gone, back to their rooms perhaps and I realised now, that for all the times I had been coming here, I had never seen another visitor. It was a place where the insensible desperately needed the sensible to maintain the thread of normality but had been abandoned by the very people who could best achieve this: who understood that anyone, I perhaps, might end up here in the future when their own particular brand of luck ran out?

'Hullo Mae.' I was startled out of reverie. My short suspension of time had temporarily closed off my senses, a trick I had learned in Germany. He stood beside me, a quizzical smile on his face, his head cocked to one side, as if listening for something.

'So, you came.'

'Of course,' I replied. Now I was here I had no idea what to say to him, though I had rehearsed it for most of the day. He wasn't my brother, or my father, neither my lover nor my husband, he wasn't even, if I thought about it, a close friend, more of an acquaintance only. We had spoken words together on my visits to the hospital, mainly trite comment about the weather, what food there was in the shops, jobs about, that sort of thing. But, this man had also saved my life. He took my hand as he shouldered a small bag of clothes.

The Receptionist hurried after him. 'Theo, Theo, you must sign this form please. Here, and here… and here also, next to Doctor Hertz's.'

Theo ambled back to the desk with her to lean on a flat surface. Surprisingly, his signature was quite a flourish, his mind automatically over-riding his slowness as it remembered the curls and loops before he had become ill. The nurse smiled up at him. 'We are going to miss you, Theo.' And to me, 'Take good care of him please, Miss.'

That was strange as well. Since when had I been called Miss, a mark of some respect in life, certainly well off the bottom rung? It gave me a tremendous feeling of confidence and all at once I felt I could handle any situation that might arise between us.'

'Goodbye and thank you for looking after him.'

The nurse gave a half wave, her hand jerked down again as soon as she had raised it as if it were not quite proper to show such emotion.

He held my arm again in a show of determination that he had at last found a friend. I had never had a man hold my arm before except only to force me to go in a particular direction, or, as the policeman had done, to ensure I would comply with an instruction. Here it seemed the most natural thing to do.

As we walked down the steps and out into the cold air, I covered my lack of responses by reciting my experience of the morning. 'Could he be guilty, do you suppose?'

'It's very hard…to say, isn't it? He was always out in the evenings and, he is Pieter's favourite, so we only hear the good things in his life. Perhaps,' he was getting slower, 'perhaps there are only good things to hear, anyway. I would have thought, if he had given these people away that he would have said things about…the Government perhaps, or the Jews which might have given me a clue as to what he really thought, but he only ever discussed football and music.'

These were the words of an intelligent man, not those of an imbecile. As I recall them now, I have removed the long periods of time between the words as he struggled to form them: they were jerky and out of rhythm, but the logic was sharp and to the point.

We walked back over the bridge. The massive bulk of the railway station reared up in front of us, familiar now as it deflected us to the right, towards the harbour and home. Theo began to quicken his pace as we rounded the last pile of lumber and took in the full length of the moored tugs and smaller craft. We both smelt the water, the oil, the dirty smoke at the same time. The air was warm, almost as if it were welcoming us back. One or two caps were raised as we passed a row of men sitting on the steel gunwale of a canal freighter. Though they all wore jackets, none had a coat. Spring was in the City.

Before us lay *Knijpers,* riding at her moorings, her tall funnel with its distinctive blue band pushing cheekily above many of the other, larger craft. The glass in her wheelhouse sparkled in the sun and the brass gleamed with the care I had lavished upon it. She passed muster with any of the other owners. Theo slowed his walk until he was picking his way across the hawsers, almost like a cat will do in advancing towards a bird, his feet placed carefully between the rope hazards. He let his eyes travel upward to the funnel, then fore and aft the full length of the tug. He must have noticed where I had managed to tie a brush to a pole and clean the blue and white bands on the smokestack, though he made no acknowledgement of the fact to me.

The Family must still have been in the fields taking advantage of the softer ground, or on their way home on the lorry, for they were not at home. As we climbed aboard I suddenly felt terribly scared as when you wake from a nightmare, wondering if the shadows really contained something not very nice. All Theo's clothes had, after all, been taken out of his drawers, washed, replaced, and clean I know, but without his permission. I had pried into places perhaps he may have wished I should not have gone. I had agonised over the decision as to whether I should have started in the first place. Would he, for example, have done the same for me? As we climbed down the companionway, his hand lightly brushed the brass handrail which gleamed and sparkled in the light of the wheelhouse lamp.

I decided to remain in the well at the bottom of the stair while Theo continued of his refamiliarisation tour. 'It's so good to be back,' he exclaimed after a hollow silence. While I stood there, his eyes I could see from the turn of his neck missed nothing as he took in the full extent of my meddling.

'Where have you been sleeping?'

'Oh here,' I said, pointing to his bed with some shame, 'but I have washed the sheets and I have moved to the front-'

'The forepeak.' It was a statement.

'Yes, the forepeak, if that is satisfactory?' It sounded pathetic to my ears. God! I was quite unable to handle this situation; one I acknowledge freely was solely of my own making. Again, there followed one of Theo's long silences, an idleness of talk that made one have to offer something to fill in the deafening gap. I heard the clock chime on St. Nicholas's Tower; the Family would be home soon. Theo moved back to the range and opened the door.

'I'll get some coal,' I said, anxious to do something, anything. I moved to the engine room door.

'No. Let me. Where have you been keeping it?'

'In there,' I pointed, hardly daring to breathe. This inner sanctum was without doubt a male place, one where men worked and women had no leave at all.

'That's where Grandpa always kept his bucket of coal. It always kept dry there and it was no distance to carry it. That's good.' He smiled back at me. I couldn't even manage a grimace.

Theo opened the steel door, so I sat down and riddled the fire into life.

* * * * *

The room was strange, for it shone white. Light bounced off a hundred angled surfaces and slithered across the floor as it reflected off the walls and ceiling. There was a star-burst of multi-coloured fire where the communication pipe curved up to the wheelhouse being painted red and green for some reason. Dial faces gleamed as if they had once been choirboys performing for their parents. The room was strange to him because for a moment he could not recognise it as belonging to the tug. It was as though he had walked on board another boat by accident and found himself in with the boilers. Theo walked towards the giant pistons dragging a splayed set of fingers behind him, caressing as he did, the steel walls. As they encountered a line of rivets he allowed his thumb to pass over them as if they were spring-loaded levers.

Mae, in the main cabin, listened to his footfalls. They were deliberate as always, often stopping, pausing from time to time, the better to catch his reflection in a dial face. She realised he was making an examination of each part of her work, chewing it over, inspecting, assessing and perhaps, she wondered, marking it out of ten. Perhaps, again, it was just too much for him, too many intrusions into his life, this hermit-like existence he led.

It proved too much. She just had to know what he thought, whether she had done the right thing or not. Any reaction was now preferable to waiting longer, looking foolishly into the fire as if there was something wrong with the flames or engaged in a very busy task.

'Theo,' she called out. There was no reply. 'Theo!' Again she spoke his name, rising from the hearth as she did to walk over to the engine-room. Her feet stepped forward cautiously unwilling to beak the silence first. It was his turn to respond.

'Hullo Mae,' he answered. He was sitting on the painted steel floor. His knees were hunched up with his arms spread wide, palms turned towards the deck. 'It almost makes me want to go to sea again. This is just how Grandpa kept the place when he was alive. Its like…stepping back… ten years He liked to paint the floor every year about this time, one year red, the next year…green.'

'So that is why I noticed two colours everywhere,' Mae still could not bring herself to ask him what he thought though his reactions had become very positive. 'Bits of red and green.'

'I can see the floor is green again…thank you… ever so much,' he emphasized the last few words, testing them in his mouth, unused as he was to exercising them in conversation.'

A warm glow, a rush of blood spread through her thin face. The dark sockets of her eyes lightened and paled to a softer brown away from the pallid whiteness. She brushed her skirt with both hands, unsure if she should reply. The moment was snatched from her, a decision made from above.

'Ruth! Ruth! Are you there?' It was Elizabeta, home from work, banging on the wheelhouse door.

'We are here, Mama.'

The bony frame, moving down the steps like a series of pistons in slow motion, dropped into view, her potato picking boots still laced tightly. 'Theo, my dear boy. You are home at last, God preserve us all.' She gave him a hug which necessitated a deep breath before he engaged with her.

'It's nice to be back in my nice clean home.'

Mama gave Mae a conspiratorial wink. 'Did you have a good day, dear?'

'Yes, I did Mama, thank you. And I have special news for you this evening.'

'Very special,' added Theo caught up in the mood.

Mama wrinkled her brow. 'What is it?'

'It's about Hans…I've been to see him.'

There was a total lack of comprehension. No one in the Family had been able to see him except once on a planned visit permitted by the police under strictly monitored conditions. Elizabeta assumed it was under these circumstances now. 'But, it is not the end of the month. Besides, you are not Family and thus not perm-'

'I've been to see him, Mama and on my own, and alone with Hans.'

'God in heaven, child, how on earth did you do it?'

'I asked the duty policeman if I could see him and, well, I said I was Anna. In I went, although only for five minutes.'

'How is he? Is he well, poor boy? He must be half starved by now, shut up in that awful place and what is he doing all day?'

Mae laughed as the barrage of questions rained about them. Theo looked on, bemused. 'He is well Mama, surprisingly well, I would say. They bring him things to read and he has three meals a day. He says he is innocent of the charges and wants to talk to a lawyer. He says it is all a terrible mistake.'

'I know that,' Elizabeta brushed aside the comments. Oh, my poor boy, sitting in that fierce prison, and unable to work.' Mae hadn't realised the reduction in income the Family had had to endure. It had seemed irrelevant before.

'One of the policemen here is kind. We shook hands,' she slipped in the last comment as if it were important to show she had established some sort of relationship.

'My Hans, my Hans. Where do we find the money for a good lawyer?' She repeated her son's name several times over, her bottom lip trembling. 'And tonight, he will miss another of his mother's meals.' She paused, taking in two faces in front of her. 'Tonight you must both come to supper to welcome Theo home. No buts,' she ended, having taken firm control of herself again. What ever she held in her head, it was now locked away as the evening chores pressed upon her. 'The thaw has enabled us to earn more money again. Vegetable prices are staying high though.' Despite herself, she gave them a grim smile. 'Tonight, we eat potatoes.'

'And, tonight we will go to the *Zuider Zee* afterwards for a drink or two.' Pieter had arrived down the stairs behind her unannounced as he took Theo's hand. Theo chuckled. He was almost human again, Mae realised, happy for him and for herself in a silly, school-girlish way.

'A drink? Alcohol you mean?'

'Well…yes. Drinks often contain alcohol. Beer is good. Geneva is better,' he responded cheerfully. 'We might have two.' This second proposal was followed up by a quick glance in the direction of his wife to ensure he had her approval.

'One is quite enough,' she countered.

'But-'

'We'll see.' That managed to stop the conversation fairly rapidly.

'What time is supper,' Mae wanted to know. 'Do you need some help?'

'It looks as if you have given all the help possible here, and to us by seeing dear Hans.' Mama's eyes roved admiringly around the cabin, taking in the spotless surfaces. 'Almost ready for sea.'

'Aye, aye, Captain. Slip the springs.' Theo sprang to the voice pipe. After all, it was only a joke. He wasn't going anywhere. They all laughed but Pieter looked more than thoughtful as he climbed the companionway steps with the rest of the Family. 'See you in one hour.'

Theo returned to the cabin with a bucket of coal and began to drop it on the opened fire, lump following lump, using his thumb and forefinger rather than the gleaming brass tongs. Finished, he was about to complete the operation by wiping them on the back of his trousers.

'I can see what you are doing. Stop playing with your fingers in your pocket.' Hearing her own words she was embarrassed. 'I mean, stop poking your-'

Theo laughed aloud, not attempting to help her out of her predicament at all. 'I often play with my pockets. You should see the inside of them.'

'I've seen them all,' she blurted out.

'How do you mean?'

When she didn't reply, he went to the chest fixed to the end wall and pulled open three drawers in turn, from the bottom up. As each was pulled clear, the contents exposed, the wool jerseys rose like warm dough, out of the drawers.

'You've washed them all...you've done everything.'

'Yes, and all your shirts as well, and your sockets and long johns. Seems you wipe everything on your bottom.'

He pushed the drawers back carefully so the clothes did not catch on the cross rails. He was kneeling, his hair curled onto his forehead, almost like one of those ancient saints in history books from school, where the picture was painted in red and blue, always with a gold halo.

He paused a long time in reflection. Then: 'It *will* come back,' he said shortly, returning to the old theme. It was as if the happiness of the past half hour had never been. 'It can be very bad-'

'But I can help you,' she answered, refusing to accept his objections.

'Why should you?'

'It is because I have nothing to lose and everything to gain. I had no home; I was starving, no family or friends to help me, no job to bring in money to eat. When you were away in hospital it made me want more. You are ill in the head, but...so am I. Sometimes I want to kill myself. You remember the day I fell in the water and you came and rescued me. That day I didn't care if I drowned. It was almost peaceful you see. The cold water numbed me, my mind, everything. I could see Mother and Father calling out to me and I wanted to join them.' She paused for breath. 'Then, you pulled me out and I wanted to live, and I am pleased you did.'

'But, you are young, with…. everything, so many things to do in the future. You are clever…I think you will make a success of whatever you decide to do.'

'I grew up in a camp, Theo, and aged a hundred years in my mind if not in my body, but I'm still…a virgin.' Why she said that she had no idea. She felt stupid again as her will took over from senses. Her words had issued unchecked, like a train ticket out of a machine, after the button has been pressed.

Theo looked her full in the face, something he rarely did. He was surprised and embarrassed at the revelation. Such things were never discussed, not even in the bar. Somehow, he had felt the Germans would have taken care of her virginity. 'I would have thought…you know…in the camp and…all that-'

'The Germans were not permitted to touch us Jews except to push us out of the way. We were unclean you see, like pork to a Jew or a Muslim. We were dirty as pigs. Silly isn't it when you realise that Germans are one of the biggest pork eaters in Europe if not the world and Jews are not allowed to eat it at all.'

'That is crazy. They are terrible people…why do so many people hate the Jews do you think?'

'There were once many reasons. We are often successful in business. We lend money. We get on in life. These days we are hated simply because we carry the label Jew, once having to carry it around our necks and display a yellow star: now the label has gone but the tag stays.'

Mae crossed to the stove where the handles of the doors gleamed with blued metal. The heat poured out and into her blood warming her legs which straddled the fire. 'I want you to know Theo, that when you are sick, I will nurse you back to health. When I scream out in the night, you can tell me not to be a silly billy, and it is all a dream.'

'Living here on the boat, what will people say?'

'What people?'

'Everyone. This is a small com…community,' he struggled with the word pleased with the end result. 'Many of them are religious, very churchy, and very…proper.'

'Tell them the truth. That I will be living in the forepeak with the ropes for company, just like a rented room in an apartment block. You will be in the next cabin, the next apartment, like most other people in Amsterdam. What's the difference?'

'But…they will not believe us.'

'It is the truth, isn't it? What else can we say? If people choose not to accept the truth, then they are cheating on themselves. The real truth is they do not want to accept the truthful version as it makes a better story the other way round. Does this not tell you something about such people, Theo?'

His reply showed his acceptance of her words. 'The forepeak is very cold. Hard. It smells of tarred rope. The harbour slaps against the sides much more loudly there.'

'You seem to know a lot about it?'

'I slept there myself every night until Grandpa died. There are rats there sometimes,' he added as an afterthought, glancing at her sideways and wondering if he had said too much.

Mae ignored the comment. If they had been there before she had started on her clean-up, they had certainly made the decision that another boat might be more preferable to the constant heaving around of boxes and ropes to disturb their nests. 'It seems you are making excuses, Theo.' She levelled her eyes at him until they focussed in on his own. 'I should leave right now, I think.'

'No! No! I mean I did not want you to sleep, live in this tiny space. I will sleep there.'

'Now you are being silly. This is your home. I've made up my mind anyway. If I am to stay, then I stay in the forepeak. Besides, it will be home from home. My bunk in the camp was very similar, if not as large as yours.' She smiled at her own joke quite lost on Theo for the moment until he caught her face. The ensuing peace was broken by a snort followed by a chuckle. They both began to laugh.

'They'll never believe us though.'

Mae felt she was on a roller coaster like ones she had seen in her early youth, her heart and mind both wanted to leap and fizz at the same time. Everything was good, everything possible now, and everything in the world. Her wits rushed down an accelerating track, then up towards a clear blue sky where the sun exploded in a yellow flash of colour.

'Oh! I'm so pleased.

To prevent any awkwardness arising out of her words, for he still found it easier said than done to control such difficulties and respond to such happy lines without stammering or blushing, he turned his back to close the door on the engine room.

'Its time we went to lunch at the *Anna Rosner*,' he said over his shoulder.

As they climbed up on deck they found the Family waiting for them. Pieter was pointing out something on one of the giant cranes in the distance which stood like fishing herons behind the row of moored boats. Elizabeta was stroking Suzannah's hair just for the sake of stroking it. As he heard the voices, Pieter turned. 'We need a drink now, not later, what with the trouble with poor old Hans and Theo fresh out of hospital.'

'I have some money, for Mae and me.'

'No need, but it is very kind of you to offer, Theo. We have had a good week despite Hans not being with us. Besides we have saved quite a bit. Papa says we are probably the richest boat in the basin. We shall be able to retire one day.'

Pieter fairly strutted across his deck aware of the admiring glances from his Family. He felt tall, important, as if he were the Mayor receiving the plaudits of his respectful citizens. He fervently wished that a couple walking close by on the quayside had heard the announcement. As he reached the end of the gangplank he saw indeed, that the woman had glanced back for a moment. Good, she must have heard something.

'Come on then, *ZuiderZee*?'

'No, no, no!' Said Mama quickly. That's a dirty place, just for men. There are ladies present don't forget. We'll go to the Three Windmills.

'They are next door to each other,' Jos said, smiling. He didn't mind where they all went; it was enough to get out of the stuffiness of the boat with its deadly routine. But...it would have been nice if Hans had been there as well. At least Mama had folded her mind inwards to close out the worry, if only for an hour. The trouble was, she had also locked out any undertones which might, otherwise, give her some pleasure at the end of the working week. It left a tighter than usual jaw line leaving no-one in any doubt she was not to be argued with today.

Under the railway lines, a row of buildings lifted themselves to a height where their owners had felt they had achieved something in life. The enormous warehouse stacked everything from hardwood from Africa to sacks of rice from the Far East, surviving two World Wars. Now, one or two spaces had succumbed to other pressures, the need for a drink after a long day being paramount. The *Zuider Zee* and the Three Windmills were only two of the waterfront bars, all catering to the same trade, mostly identical in looks; brown stained wood walls, stone floors and a blue or green tiled boiler in a corner. The smell of beer permeated the street, even overcoming the odour of diesel.

The party of seven trooped inside, considerably brightening the atmosphere where a knobbly, heavily veined man leant across the counter in deep conversation with two seamen. All three were smoking strong tobacco, the combined effect causing it to hang about their heads like cobwebs. The seamen turned away from the noisy group closing them out from the quiet conversation that had been taking place. Their smoke by now, had haloed along the ceiling the full length of the bar, wavering in its attempt to stay together as the door opened. On the opposite wall was a fire, recently lit, casting shadows on their faces.

'Good day to you,' said Pieter importantly. He faced his troop's expectant faces.

'Geneva,' said Mama.

'And me,' replied Anna and Suzannah in unison.

'One Geneva and two small beers, small ones,' Pieter countered causing a grimace from Anna but both accepted the proposal on the basis it was the best they were going to get.

'Large beer,' said Jos.

'And…me please,' Theo matched the mood. 'I mean, first I must ask Mae what she would like.'

'I really don't know. I've never had alcohol before.' The barman smiled indulgently. 'Why not try a sherry? It's from Spain. It's sweet. I have a bottle somewhere.'

'Yes please, I'll try some of that.' Theo looked pleased.

'And a large Geneva for me.' It was Pieter's turn.

'Papa,' this is not going to end up with you being too drunk to have your dinner, is it?'

'Mama! What a thing to say. Don't you worry now.'

'That's what I am worrying about.'

Mae watched, fascinated as the barman pulled the brass handle, the liquid frothing in its release from the wooden barrel.

As the foam rose above the glass edge he expertly sliced it away with a wooden spatula. He took down a slim stone bottle and poured out a clear liquid into two glasses one twice as large as the other. Pulling yet another bottle, this time from a cupboard, he poured fluid amber which sparkled in the glass.

'Your sherry, Missy.' Mae noticed the bar man had polished only her glass before he filled it. She smiled at him. The others were more interested in taking hold of theirs as soon as they could.

On the far wall, opposite the lit fire, was a huge stove, clad in green glazed tiles. It sat on the paved stone floor like an enormous toad and rose up towards the ceiling where swastikas and German script covered the plaster infill between the beams. 'The German sailors used to come here a lot in the war,' explained Jos.

'And you Jos,' reminded Pieter.

Mae remembered the swastikas, especially in her previous life. The red, black and white emblems on long banners had hung in festoons everywhere, even flying on tiny flagpoles on the front wings of the staff cars. They had been pasted to cattle trucks and the steam engines which pulled them. She shivered involuntarily as if someone had opened a cold doorway behind her.

The bitter thought vanished as they all sat in a ring of stools around the open fire, the heat of the flames beginning to redden their faces. It made silhouettes of their heads causing the Landlord to surrender any idea of enjoying the heat himself, for his new customers effectively blocked any heat at all from reaching the bar. He sighed, grunted and lit another cigarette. On the opposite side of the bar, one of the men was staring at Jos or Pieter, Mae could not tell which, as though he recognised one of them.

'So, try your sherry,' Pieter's insistence broke through after a long, relaxed silence each within their own thoughts while the two men quaffed long and hard on their beers. The girls were almost as thirsty, but Mama, surprising them all after her original comment on control, drained her glass at one swallow.

'This is how you drink Geneva,' she said demurely, batting the side of her hair into place. Jos laughed into his beer while eyeing his father who had decided to sip his gin. It was infinitely too precious to drink all at one go. Mae lifted her glass to her nose and breathed in the heady scents of grape and clay soils, curling the aroma around the fine hairs of her nose. 'I remember,' she smiled, 'Father had a bottle of this in the dining room. He kept it in a glass decanter on a sideboard. We didn't drink but the level went down one day. Father suspected a maid so he stuck a piece of paper on the back and marked the level with a faint pencil line. The level stayed the same ever since which was surprising as we did offer drinks occasionally. In the end, of course, one of father's friends told him his sherry was so watered down it was quite tasteless.'

Pieter roared with laughter, joined in by the rest of the firewatchers. The sound filled the quiet bar and made the flames flicker as if in appreciation of the joke. Surprising them all for the second time, Elizabeta made an offer. 'Here, I have some money. Let's have another.'

Jos was at the bar almost before she could thrust a bundle of soiled notes into his fist. 'Change please,' she demanded. Surprising them all, Jos began to talk to the two men and fell into deep conversation forgetting the drinks.

'Come on Jos, we are waiting,' said Pieter.

Theo waited for his beer patiently, seeing the dark corners of the bar without fear. The walls remained firmly in place, holding back whatever had been out there. He turned to look at Mae, who was close by his side. He leaned out from his stool and caught sight of her flushed face. She smiled back happily at him her eyes reflected in his own. Her legs, like the other women were apart to let the heat soak into cold bones. Hers had felt the chill of a whole decade of winters without real warmth; with almost no flesh on her thighs the frost had been able to pinch her to shades of purple and blue as soon as the first snap of winter had declared itself.

She felt a pressure on her shoulder for a moment. Theo had risen to help Jos carry the drinks back to the table. He used her for support though he was perfectly able to manage without touching her. For a second, she imagined his fingertips had caressed one of her ears, but then again, perhaps not, and he had returned to the counter. Had she invented the touch in her mind to suit her mood? Perhaps he *had* touched her but only by miscalculation rather than it being a deliberate act? She decided she could afford to settle for the first option after all, and allow her to make up her mind as she so wished.

'Who was that then?' Pieter asked. 'I've not seen them before.'

'They are from the upper basin, I believe. They had heard about Hans and were asking me how he was. I told them little as I don't know them.'

'Seems you were telling them a great deal,' snorted Mama taking her drink. 'Rough couple.'

'Do you like it then?' A voice penetrated Mae's bliss.

'What? I mean, what do I like?'

'The drink, the sherry.' said Pieter.

'It is very nice, quite a strong taste, earthy, smells of the autumn leaves, but nice.' She nodded her head affirmatively.

'The leaves are used to sieve the sherry to make it clear. And you, Mama. Are you happy?'

'Yes, my love.' The bony jaw opened to reveal a row of strong, white teeth. She smiled warmly at her husband, anxious to make him feel it had been worthwhile spending the money.

Pieter expand almost visibly. His shoulders rose, rising up, brightening, as he took hold of one worn hand with his own cracked and split fingers. His eyes, Mama could see, were moist as they gazed upon his wife.

Mae had grown up with love stories in her nursery, with tales of Princes and Princesses, or at least, rich, good-looking heroes and heroines. The reality was almost always very different. The couple in front of her were gnarled like thorn trees on the edge of the dunes. Bent twisted, ugly, they resembled more the troll under the bridge than the sleeping princess, but they clung, like the bent tree, tenaciously to life, and to each other. She tried to imagine what they had looked like at the start of their lives together. She would have already been big-boned but tall, good-looking probably in a handsome way. She would have outgrown her only pair of shoes quickly to the despair of her parents. He, diminutive in stature would spend the rest of his life looking up at her, with the same bright gleam in his eyes, already built stocky and firm, ready for the hard life ahead. Both had taken that decision to spend the rest of their lives in the job, seldom wondering what might have been. Pieter could not have been much of a catch, despite owning his own boat, so he must have had something else to offer. Mae knew instinctively what it was. It was love, or rather loving, that had maintained the bonds through the freezing winters when fingernails split into bloodied sores and backs had crooked like an exhaust pipe in the engine room until, one day, they would refuse to straighten in the next Spring.

'You seem quiet, Mae. Do you not like it here?' Theo was sitting down, wiping beer from his hands onto his trousers.

'I love it here, Theo, but I don't like to see you making your clothes dirty. Remember what I told you.' As soon as she had spoken she kicked herself mentally. What did it matter what he did with his clothes or what he looked like as a result? She did not own him, nor was she married to him…and in front of his friends! The truth was she wanted him to be seen in a new light: refreshed, clean clothes, looking sharp and tidy, an employable person in fact.

'Yes, but, they were dirty before I came home,' he added after a pause. 'I won't wipe my hands on your clean clothes, see if I don't.' He sounded sincere though there might have been a trace of a smile playing around his lips.

'I'm sorry; I should not have said th-.'

Mae did not trust herself to say anymore on the subject for she enjoyed watching him, she realised. Any excuse to study his eyes, to see the gold flecks change to brown as intelligence flowed back again into his face, was gratification enough. He would have been in the hospital still if she had not got him out; of that fact she was sure, the first positive result of doing something herself since leaving home.

'If only,' said Elizabeta, 'if only Hans were here to share this with us. He loves to have a drink,' this she said, turning to Mae.

'Now then, Mama, we said we would have a good drink before we eat. And Theo is home and our guest for today.'

'I know, I know.' She held up her arms helplessly in frustration, as much with herself as to anyone else. She rose quickly, squeezing Pieter's hands together.

'I'm going home to finish the meal off. You can have quarter of an hour, and then you must come back and wash your hands if you want to eat today. There's work tomorrow as well, don't forget.'

As she wended her way through the tables followed by the two girls the two men glanced casually across. One of them then caught Jos's eyes causing him to turn away quickly. They looked rough and drunk.

* * * * *

As Elizabeta walked out of the door, I realised I was witness to an enduring love story, one showing absolutely no signs of diminishing. There was a subtle relationship between the two of them, far ahead of the normal everyday dependence of one to another. It radiated out to enfold the children and, in so doing, touched Theo and myself. Mother and Father had loved each other, of this I am sure, but they rarely showed their affections in front of me, and certainly never in front of the staff. Sometimes, Mother would give me a clue as to how she handled her marriage. I would catch her, standing in front of her bedroom mirror, staring at a photograph of Father mounted in a silver, oval frame. She kissed one of her forefingers and placed it on his lips in the picture. Another time, I had been watching the ice-skating race on the canals, one cold winter. We had been huddled up in clothes when the wind had caught mother's wool scarf and had blown it away from her cheek. Almost as if he were waiting for it to happen, Father moved forward and tucked the scarf back into place allowing his fingers to stroke her neck for an instant. Only I had noticed the small gesture, but it made me wonderfully happy at the time. Five years later, they were both dead, perhaps happy again somewhere far away from the gas chambers.

Suzannah and Anna had run off behind Elizabeta, leaving me the only woman in the group, and in the bar. I wondered if I should leave too, but I did not know the correct protocol at the time so instead, I just put off making any decision. The men did not seem to worry.

'You stay,' said Jos generously, reading my mind. 'There are enough women to cook the meal. You seem to fit into this bar quite well, I mean-'

'You mean, I look like an alcoholic?'

'No! Of course not! I mean…well'

We all laughed but, as we did, I noticed Jos take another glance at the bar. He definitely seemed to know one or both of the men, though at the time he had been asked, he had been dismissive as if he had not known them at all.

'I like what you say, Jos, 'I kissed him on the cheek, just a peck, of course, but he pulled back from this display of affection, embarrassed. He glanced around the room wondering who had seen him. The two men smirked.

'Don't I get one?' Pieter pleaded, and received a similar peck. Theo fell silent.

'To be fair, and, so you men don't get any ideas of favouritism, you too Theo.'

His cheek smelt good and I found it somewhat hard to withdraw. My lips too, had pressed against his flesh, rather than bouncing off quickly as I had with the other two. Theo did not pull back like Jos.

'The sherry is working, or so it would appear,' he said, managing to smile, but, he looked uncertain of his next stance and looked around for support.

'Tell us about your job, Mae,' said Pieter. The other two waited impatiently for me to begin. Such news cut across their dull lives. They did not read a newspaper unless they found one discarded and I filled a void on what was up-to-date in the city, what was being worn by the young and which shops were redecorating.

'I meet all sorts of people, rich and poor, though the rich often send a maid to collect the bread for them. A bread shop is a great leveller for they are all buying the same, cheap goods at the same price. It is only the cakes they pick up themselves. I suppose they do not trust their staff. Think they will lick off some of the icing.' I remembered Mother instructing Emilie, our front of house maid, in exactly this manner every day.

'They all wait so patiently. Their faces stare forward so they won't miss their place in the queue. They study the trays of cakes going down like water in a glass, or sherry,' I added. 'That is the only time one or two of them become anxious. When they want to buy something, something they have fixed their minds upon, like an almond cake, for example. There's two left on the shelf, say. You can see their thoughts almost written on their foreheads. Their eyes never leave the cakes for a moment, as if, otherwise, they might disappear into thin air. If the cakes go before they get to the front of the queue, a small light snuffs out in their eyes:

wind on a candle. It leaves just a stony glare as they reform their ideas, beginning to concentrate on something else, an orange bun, perhaps, and the whole process starts over again. I've been watching in the shop and I can see where improvements could be made. Profitable changes, that is. Those ladies with the cakes: why could they not order the day before? The cake is waiting for them all fresh and the shop has a sale, perhaps an impulse buy, as well, and the company has nothing to throw away.'

The men studied her warily. This was talk they really did not understand. Pieter and Jos were fascinated with what normally might be an ordinary day of shopping, not seeing the cut and thrust of the housewife out to get the best she could for her family. It was Theo who broke in first.

'What if everything goes off the shelves?'

'It happens, sometimes. Fridays usually. Then, those that are left clench their lips together and buy flour and rice paper. It is one of the things in the bakery I do understand. For some reason, the bakery makes the same amounts of each item for sale, every day, irrespective of the history of the sales. So, why don't they make more on a Friday? I always go back to the bakery at the back to see what is left and sell it for a few cents. The customers are always pleased as it is personal attention to them and to them alone.'

'To have nothing is awful,' countered Theo, drinking down the last of his beer and causing the glass to hang inverted from his mouth, clenched in his teeth. It guaranteed he would glean the final drop from the bottom.

I had had nothing for seven or eight years. Now, I had a bed and food, friends and a job. Before, there had been hope of something better as the war began to draw to a close, that is until Mother had been killed. Afterwards, I had not even hope. I lived from day to day, hour to hour, not daring to consider I might have one or two days of life left. Just to get to nightfall and the doubtful security of the hut was the only goal to plan for.

Pieter refused to enter into my morbid world of thoughts. 'Come my children, Mama awaits us. There's hot potatoes and soup.'

THE LIGHT, THE GLORIOUS LIGHT

The wall stretches as wide as an aerodrome. There's a hole in the exact middle, through which echoes the laugh of a madman. These laughs are not the funny kind, these are frightening ones as one cannot imagine unless you are here to witness them.

Beyond the wall, are fields and fields of bright flowers. There are blue hyacinths, yellow daffodils and tulips of every hue and shade. The flowers are in rigid lines as if an engineer had staked out the seeds, one after the other along a theodolite. The harsh laughing is high-pitched and eccentrically in contrast to the flowers wilting where they are exposed to these discordant sounds falling on the petals like rain. This causes them to vibrate spilling their perfume into the air as if they were women walking down a catwalk. There are other smells too: spices, apples and fresh bread, good smells, every one of them so it takes a long time to separate one odour from the next, eliminating the dreadful, to leave the good, to bring the calm, quiet light.

The flowers spread over the water, colouring the swell so they reflect upon the hulls of the moored boats. Each is coupled to its neighbour and to the quay as well, so none of them can go to sea unless they receive orders to do so. They seem to smile, like Cheshire cats for their hawsers curve like lips up the sides of their bows.

There is pressure to bear, for no reason in particular, but it comes, nonetheless. It comes, because there is an insistence from just behind the watcher. Left or right, which ever way the mind turns there is cause to wander, wavering under the wish, the desire almost, to leave, and a craving to pass on. There is a reward, you see, a kiss even, perhaps a hug or a caress, worth all of the stress and strain of the long, desert years when the voices whispered and the walls creaked.

A storm threatens every time a boat ventures near the tunnel. Sou'westers, thigh boots and yellow oilskins are in demand and are donned in frantic haste as the adrenalin spurts in a fine, microscopic spray into the bloodstream.

Beyond this storm, away on the horizon, as if it were the very first minute of the very first dawn, you can see the light, pure, glorious radiance formed out of its own urgent desire.

It can be connected to, of course. You can almost touch it if you want, but it takes enormous effort, enormous nerve...but it is there to try if you want.

Such is this wish to stretch out and touch the light; it brings physical orgasm and the cry of soft release.

Look up, astonished and surprised, for the room has stayed in place, the walls positioned where they should be and the lofty ceilings no longer threaten to roll down until they reach the floorboards. The terror of the night has passed by.

Beyond the furthest point of imagination, beyond interstellar space and time itself, the yellow light extends itself to strike the soaking granite cobbles. The light touches everything, warming each surface in turn. There's work to be done before the day is risen, much work, he knows, but, for once there seems a way through the briars...and there is no longer the need to be frightened.

Chapter Four

'I have a great idea. No, I have a stupendous plan,' said Pieter, correcting himself, sitting back, replete after his evening meal. Stupendous wasn't a word he used very much, if at all, and he could not think of the last time he had uttered it. Even here he had used it only to underline the importance of what he had just said. He must have borrowed it from someone in the street; it was like so many words he had picked up as strays going to or from work. Liking the sound of it, he had stored it away for future use. They were often too...grand...too exalted for the humble family, so they became pushed to the back of his memory, forgotten until a need of some importance needed to be aired.

Smoke curled from his pipe and his lips in a lazy coil. Reaching the low beams it spread out where it lodged in the frills of the curtain tops. The central lamp bored shafts of light through this smoke to make it a miniature setting sun on a Spring evening.

Anna had propped her chin up with her two hands as she pored over a cheap paperback, occasionally licking her top lip with her tongue as she sought out the remaining morsels of food from the supper. Pieter, however, had engaged his mind into gear before the meal was finished as he had put the finishing touches to his plan. It had made him uncustomarily quiet, causing Elizabeta to think he might be coming down with a cold.

Now, he opened his mouth with the proclamation. 'I think I can help Theo with his problem. Well, better perhaps, by removing it forever. We all know Theo has this problem of not wanting to leave shore ever again. His mind, the doctors say, is tied to the quay as surely as if it were moored with a sisal hawser. Hertz has confirmed it now, hasn't he? The excuse Theo gives of his engines making black smoke in the harbour is only a defence.' He was going to say smoke screen and would have enjoyed the pun but doubted any of the Family would have seen through it. The subject was, also far too serious for him to let it occupy his brain for more than a few seconds.

'You don't take the *Anna Rosner* to sea, do you Papa?'

'Don't be difficult, Suzannah. You know perfectly well we have no need to go to sea, or even into the *Ij*.'

Suzannah sniggered, triumphant, but her father remained serene, determined to conclude his speech before the washing up dispersed the group. 'Theo needs to go out into mid-channel at least: better to go further to make absolutely certain. It does not have to be his boat either, does it? Any boat will do. The *Anna Rosner* for example.'

Slowly, his proposal began to sink into his family. 'You mean, take Theo out one day when he comes aboard?' Mama pouted suspiciously. 'Like a pleasure trip?'

'Exactly,' Pieter liked the phrase, patting the tight cloth of the waistcoat encircling his waist, rather pleased they had picked up the idea so quickly without having to mention the actual deed himself.

'How would you do that, Papa? You haven't fired up the boilers for ages, last year in fact.' It was Jos's turn to question the scheme.

'The engines are due for a de-coke and clean anyway. We usually do it in late Spring, don't we? I'll just bring it forward a few weeks. You can help, like always-'

'Hans was the best at-'

'Hans is not here,' snapped Pieter quickly as Elizabeta began to raise her head in interest at the turn of the conversation. 'We can manage by ourselves. It will just take a little longer.'

'And then?'

'And then, we invite Theo on board. Get him down here. While he is eating, or talking, we reverse out into the basin. A small trip, maybe on the *Ij*, half a kilometre perhaps. It'll do him the world of good and, afterwards he should be cured. He will be able to-'

'You mean,' said Suzannah with incredulity, 'take him out to sea without telling him?'

'Don't interrupt. As I was saying, he will be able to see for himself it was all in his mind and he has nothing to be afraid of ever again. He can take the *Kuijpers* out by himself of an evening, some fishing, call on a few friends or he could take Mae out for a cruise in the summer. Just think of that. There's plenty of cheap coal and wood about. He probably will never have to go back to that horrid hospital.'

It was breath-taking in its simplicity. 'Oh, do you really think so, Papa?' Suzannah wanted so much to believe in it, changing her mind several times while he had been speaking. Mama smiled in anticipation of the help they were going to bring.

'Is it possible? Is it truly possible?' Suzannah stretched herself to stand behind him, both arms locked around his neck.

Pieter asserted himself again. It was his idea, a pretty good one too, one the doctors' had not thought of either. He could show the hospital in days to come they were pretty much a waste of money and time. This would cost nothing, well, only a little coal.

'But, what if he doesn't like it, and what about Mae? Are we going to tell her?'

'No!' On this, Pieter was adamant. 'We will keep this a secret between ourselves. She can come and have lunch with Theo. That way, he will be more relaxed.'

Anna was still not sure. 'This could go wrong, seriously wrong.' There had been one or two disasters in the past, well covered up and forgotten with the passing of time. She looked up, marking her place in her book with a finger as her father continued.

'He may not be absolutely happy, not to start with, that is. But, as soon as he is under way, away from the quayside, he will be able to see how safe it all is. He will understand it is just like the old days when his grandpapa took him to sea every day. I'm surprised Doctor Hertz has not suggested this himself. We won't tell either of them when they come on board, just pretend we are de-coking the engines as we do every year. We are not telling stories as we shall, in fact, be doing just that. This will be quite natural to him.'

This settled the matter. 'When?' asked Mama.

'Next Sunday morning, if the weather holds fair, and we have been able to clean out the boilers by then.'

'It means plenty of hot water. Baths all round. Such a dirty job, isn't it?'

'Remember, not a word to anyone outside the boat. We don't want to upset either of them next door.'

* * * *

It was late. It was Theo's habit, I had been told, to stay up till the small hours, advancing his day so he lost the early mornings. I, on the other hand was the other way around, a habit I was obliged to learn from *Appel* in the camp when we had to stand on the iron-hard ground before the dawn, as men with piggy eyes and fleshy lips detailed us for the day's duties. Tonight though, Theo was home. He had spent a couple of hours roaming his boat, noting everything I had done. He would walk across the cabin seeing a chest or a drawer, delighting in the surprise each time he opened one. The brass catches still gleamed in the lantern light despite the damp weather. The smell of clean clothes and the heat of the iron on the linen were caught in the drawers. Theo would breathe in, recalling the days when his grandmother had done the same.

'Good, good,' he muttered to himself, ceaselessly.

Finally, at one o'clock I was too tired to go on. 'I'm going to bed. I have work to do in the morning.'

'I'm sorry, I forgot. You start early.' It was a statement not a question.

'Yes. Goodnight then.' I got up from the blanket-covered chair and walked self-consciously across the cabin floor towards the forepeak lockers. I felt his eyes on my backside and wanted to turn sideways.

'You don't have to-'

'Yes, I must, I'm fine, really, your reputation as well, Theo.'

'And yours,' he said a trifle too quickly. Now I had made up my mind to go it was becoming more difficult. I did not think Theo would have raised any comment at all.

'I'm nothing; I'm a Jew, after all. I don't exist for most people.'

'Don't ever say that! Ever! Please, I'll make a reputation for you, wait and see. I'll work on it,' he added as if it were a bit of hardwood off-cut to be carved over the next few days to polished completion. But his defence of me had been considerate. I reached the door. 'Good night, Theo.'

'Goodnight, Mae.'

The cabin was bitterly cold, for the heat had remained in the main cabin together with the smell of tar and rope tainting the condensed air around me. At least it was clean and I had made the bunk up so there was little to do. The walls were planked horizontally, to which was attached a cot bed. I lit a candle and, as I did, the shadows flickered into life around me, almost alive and threatening. The less the movement I made, the less urgent were the mirrored movements above my head and behind my back. I undressed, having checked the door and climbed in pulling a warm rug tightly over my shoulders. A feeble light filtered in through the scuttle so as I blew out the candle the outline of the cabin jumped into clear focus. Instantly, I was transported back in time. I lay, as I had always lain, hoping the night would never go, wondering if I was to be turned far left or just left as we paraded on the ramp for the officer after we had arrived off the train. Far left meant I was not recognised as a child with a mother and stood alone, then to be deployed into work. Just left meant Hut 25, the holding base before the furnaces and the gas chambers; children and mothers a speciality. Right was for the men. Sick, old or infirm meant they were destined for Zyklon-B treatment immediately, no wasting time, not even to say goodbye to a wife and a child.

Tonight though, there was a difference. Now I had a reason to live. Before, left or far left had been almost immaterial, for death was much easier than survival. Both merged, inevitably, it was just a matter of time. Having something to lose made it worse, far worse and I just wanted to cry.

'Mother! Mother!' I sobbed.

The door crashed back against the cot. Theo stood, holding a candle. 'God! It's cold in here. What ever is the matter?' And, receiving no reply, he came over to the bunk.

I gazed up at him, my eyes clearing. 'I'm sorry, Theo. I have woken you and on your first night.'

But he refused to accept this. 'I wasn't even in bed, and I'm going nowhere tomorrow.' He reached into the bed and took hold of my hands. For a panicky moment, I thought he was going to place them between my legs but it was only to pull me from the rug and lead me to the main cabin which still retained its warmth.

'You are going to sleep here. You had a blood- a bad nightmare.'

'I was dreaming of the camp.'

'But, such a terrible camp, Mae. You were screaming your head off.'

'I'm sorry to have scared you.'

'Not as scared as you were. I…I felt somehow… you had never left the place.'

'I'm free of the physical restraints, but my mind is still tied to the hut where I spent so much time. It will never go. I hope that in time it will, at least soften, and I need to have my strength so I can help you get better.'

'We are a couple of crocks,' he mumbled gently. 'I wonder who has the most frightening experience. We should try and find out one day.'

His comment made me smile and I felt better.

He pulled the two big armchairs together so they faced each other. Numbly I climbed in and felt the soft cushions take up my bodyweight. The arms, butting close together, formed a protective barrier to the whole world.

'Thank you,' was all I could manage.

Theo climbed into his own bed, only the length of his body between us, but it didn't matter any more. I felt safe and secure; this time the boat was my fortress. As I drifted off, I watched the candle flicker yellow and steady, until it fused and dimmed as I closed my eyes.

* * * * *

Theo smoothed the front of his shirt, tucking in the long tails into the back of his trousers. He pulled on a sweater which, he could see, showed as red and blue in the early Spring light. He had forgotten its colours, imagining it to be navy blue for years.

I hadn't any other clothes, but I washed my hair, adding vinegar to make it shine. I wished I could colour my cheeks as Mother had done every morning, but I didn't know where to buy the stuff even if I had the money in my purse.

'Here,' he said, pulling back the dividing curtain and holding out a red patterned handkerchief to all intents and purposes like a husband in a bedroom, dressing before dinner, to his wife. We had abandoned all idea of using the forepeak as a second bedroom so Theo had rigged up a curtain on a rope which divided the room almost into two equal halves. In the day we took it down to leave only a couple of brass hooks in the bulkhead.

I took it from him. 'Round your neck...knot it,' he suggested. It must have belonged to his grandfather, for it was huge and old-fashioned, the type of material he might have knotted at each corner and dropped onto his head to keep the strong sun off in the summer. But, it was colourful so I tied it round my neck and let the two tails hang down my chest. It brought a touch of blush to my clothes.

'Good, good,' he said, quietly approving as if working from some master plan I had not been made party to, the first item perhaps, in a design to redress me completely. 'Shall we go?'

Outside on deck, the palest sun removed the chill from the steel deck-plates. Next door, a steady thumping from below made me start. 'Time of year,' said Theo as he swung a leg over the gunwale to the *Anna Rosner*. 'Pieter always warms his engines up about now. Turns the pistons over, and things, to stop them seizing up. He's early this year as he usually does it next month.'

'Why,' I asked. 'He never takes his boat either, to sea, does he?'

'You have to keep the moving parts in good condition in case you want to sell one day. I do the same to *Kuijpers* even though my boiler is so old I cannot go to sea.' I took no notice of that one.

'When do you do yours?'

He hesitated. 'From time to time. I used to, up until last year, until I was ill, that is. I haven't done it for almost a year...or so. I suppose it needs doing badly.'

'Perhaps I could help you, one of these days.'

'Yes…one day perhaps. Here's Jos. Hullo, are we early?' They shook hands. It was a Sunday after all. 'No news of Hans?'

He looked down at his feet and shuffled them clumsily. 'No. No news. It is getting a bit precarious now. We do not believe the police can hold him much longer. It is against the law. We have been told that there is no legis…leg… no law to hold him for so long. The Government wanted to bring it out but has failed to do so, meanwhile the Police are using the possibility as the means to hold on to him while they seek more evidence.'

We climbed down the steep companionway which I was now able to do quite expertly, throwing out one hand to the bulkhead to shield my head and the other on the rail to prevent myself from falling to the bottom. I often wondered just how Elizabeta was able to pull herself up so easily. If she were to slip, there would be an awful accident below.

We were greeted by the girls and Mama, all busy at the table which had been set up specially, tidier somehow with a first daffodil in a jam jar. It was such a pretty splash of colour. I could not help noticing that Hans's place had disappeared in the re-arrangement. Mama gave me a hug.

'That scarf looks lovely on you, much better than on Theo.' It made me feel so good. Anna asked me about my job while stirring a vast pot. Pieter arrived, wiping his hands on a large piece of cotton waste.

'Theo and Mae are guests of honour today, so they are to sit at the top of the table, here and here,' he indicated with a flourish, chuckling to himself as if he had a secret joke. He led me to the chair with its back to the portholes instead of the usual stool. For some reason, they had pulled the curtains across on the opposite side making it darker, but someone had lit a candle on a shelf. The girls were nudging each others arms and Anna was looking nervous or more nervous than usual. There was an air of forced gaiety, the chatter louder, rising to merge with the sounds emanating from the engine room. I had never heard an engine turn over on either of the boats for it vibrated the steel walls, bringing the sense of a real ship to me rather than just a home. It was almost by accident that the home happened to be on the water. It was quite exciting, but I felt concerned we had prevented them from finishing their work on the servicing.

'Aren't you going to close down the engines?' Theo wrinkled his brow.

'All in good time. I want to check one or two things after lunch. You need to be thinking about the same thing on *Kuijpers* soon, Theo.' Pieter smiled again still retaining the mystery to himself.

'Let's all sit down.' Mama pushed sundry children into their newly allotted places. I could see we now all faced different individuals. Hans's chair sat forlornly alone in the corner, an old magazine lying on the seat as if it had always been a reading table. I wondered if this was why everyone was so jumpy. Pieter looked as if he were working himself up for one of his rather important speeches.

The huge bowl of potatoes arrived. A draught caught the steam instantly frosting Anna's round lenses on her glasses. Impatiently, she wiped them clear with a drying cloth as she placed the second heavy tureen, this one with a knucklebone floating in the broth. It was so hot it was like having a miniature stove on the table.

It was towards the end of a rather stilted meal, with no speeches from Pieter that I saw him rise. He had raced through his meal, hardly stopping for conversation, intent only on stuffing his stomach as fast as he could. This engine work had obviously worked up a big hunger. Jos, also, failed to live up to his reputation of talking nonsense even as he filled his gut to bursting. He got up from the table as soon as he saw his father wipe his mouth with his cuff, and, together they left the room with an apology about completing the job in ten minutes.

'I'll be back to talk then, lass.'

Mama continued to eat and smiled at me, and then Theo, as a broody hen will do checking her offspring. We were part of her family these days. She glanced at us again as her hands moved to the tureen. 'I expect they need to see if the engines are overheating. We are earlier this year as we want to get the work out of the way before the season starts properly: the demand for vegetables is growing and the export trade is developing nicely.'

'Perhaps,' I said, 'they are going to close down the engines. If they don't do something soon, it will be a waste of good coal.' It did go against everything I knew of the Family's character.

All at once, the flicker of worry which had been gnawing away at my consciousness since I had sat down burst into full understanding. The key notion was the 'family character'. It was, *totally* against the nature of the *Maas* family.

The swell against the boat had increased though, unlike a passing craft which normally caused a double roll, one to port and one to starboard, this time it had continued, gentle as the motion was.

'No!' I shouted out, getting up too quickly and spilling my mug. I knocked over the chair to make more space. 'No, you mustn't, you simply mustn't.'

Theo looked up in alarm but saw no answering fear in the girls' faces. Mama had clenched her jaw tight but was saying nothing, nothing at all which was strange, almost as if there was a tacit understanding with what was going on.

I ran to the companionway, shouting for Theo to stay put. In the wheelhouse, Pieter puffed at his pipe while taking hold of the wheel in both hands. Out on deck, in brilliant sunshine for the first time in ages, I could see Jos pulling in on the warp, gauging the widening gap of black water between the tug and the quayside with a practised eye. He rode the swell as a horseman rides at a canter, flexing his knees as the swells hit the boat. The reverse swirl was pulling masses of flotsam, timber, tins, bottles, all covered in oil, back out of the winter trap which had ensnared them all. Below and behind me, I heard a howl of anguish to realise my worst fears.

'You mustn't,' I screamed at Pieter this time, surprised at the strength of my own words. His pipe dropped out of his mouth.

'It's perfectly all right, lass. We know what we are doing. We want to make Theo better.'

'You don't understand. You will drive him under, forever. He will never get better.' And when he didn't stop his steering I added: 'Stop the fucking boat, damn you!'

Pieter was shocked but remained in control. 'Now look here Ruth, you-'

All at once, a vile taste entered my mouth and something stirred in my bile. Like a toad or a rat, it wanted to get out. The past was rising to the surface, unstoppable, relentless and with it, absolute evil.

'No, *you* look here. If you want to be responsible for his permanent madness then you are going the right way about it. Take your bloody, fucking boat out to sea. You think you will cure him by forcing his mind to accept the inevitable. If you try and go any further, I will rip your bloody balls off and then I'll turn on that bastard son of yours and he will never sire any children.'

'Get me back, get me back,' came a groan from behind me. It was Theo having arrived in the wheelhouse, staring aghast at the quay, now one hundred metres away. Below, Mama could be heard crying out alone. Around me was total pandemonium as the girls started screaming.

I pushed back the door to the wheelhouse. On deck, Jos stood gazing at us, unsure what to do. 'Turn the bloody boat back, Jos you bastard, or I will fucking kill you.'

The long suppressed agony, five years old, began to move. A black slime crawled into my mind and began to settle across my eyes. Jos's face began to pucker as he saw mine literally change shape and took in the words he had never heard from a woman. This was 1950, in a country which still put adulterous women in dung carts in some parts of the country, but I no longer cared. I could feel my face distend in horrendous rage to push me totally out of control. Reaching him, I began to kick him in the groin hoping I was connecting with anything soft.

'Alright! Alright, let me be,' he groaned. 'Papa, put the boat about, for God's sake. The Jew girl's gone mad. It isn't going to work.' As he spoke, I saw the tug moving now in forward power towards its berth again, a dozen boat owners looking on in amazement. This was not the usual Sunday afternoon antics of the *Anna Rosner*. Mama and Suzannah where restraining Theo as best they could, for he was struggling like a madman and I wondered if my words were to be prophetic. Pieter did not look at me for he was concentrating on negotiating his re-entry to the narrow berth so he kept his eyes focussed on the gap created by the *Kuijpers* and an old wooden barge on the other, ignoring the surrounding chaos. As soon as I felt the jar of the boat coming into contact with the oak post providing the mooring, I leapt ashore towing the heavy rope warp. I found the strength to slip it over the bollard and tied a figure of eight to prevent it from slipping. The tug held firm as I braced myself for the impact.

Mama and Theo had both fallen onto the deck with the jolting. It had not been Pieter's best berthing, I would imagine, but he now had to contend with Anna's hysterical sobbing as she threw herself into his arms. Jos began to climb up from the engine room where he had gone to close down the engines: the clanking had ceased, leaving only a faint whisper of steam to curl out of the funnel.

I took hold of Theo's arm and pulled him to his feet. I knew I had to get him off the Anna Rosner as soon as I could and home safely. He clung to me his eyes glazed, the glints dulled. 'I don't want to go to sea, Mae.'

'You don't have to, ever. You'll never have to go to sea if you don't want to.'

Slowly, we walked back across the gangplank, my arm round Theo's shoulder while a mass of people watched sympathetically; beginning to gain some idea of what had happened. I did not look round until I had Theo in the main cabin, where I sat in shock myself, aware, yet not aware of the events of the past fifteen minutes which had overwhelmed us all like a tidal wave.

What possessed Pieter to dream up such a stupid plan I could not begin to think of an answer which would make sense. He knew, just as we all did, how sensitive Theo was to the water especially the open sea.

What was as disastrous was the probable loss of the Family, possibly for good. Dear kind Pieter, so proud, so in love with his wife, his jaunty walk proclaiming his self-assurance to the world. Mama, dear Elizabeta, who had clucked her tongue such a short while before, as if I were one of her clutch, who had taken me in when I was starving. And what of Hans? After the fuss of today had died down, would he still want to see me while he was in prison and waiting trial?

Theo shook his head up and down, rather as a horse will do when his nose is inside its nosebag. His eyes were narrowed as he examined the corners of the cabin one after the other. It frightened me, as I could not gauge how far he had gone. There was one thing for shock I could administer.

'Tea, tea with lots of sugar. Have you any sugar, Theo?' He nodded, thank God, understanding me. 'Good for a shock, I am told.' I began to rake the coals of the stove, blowing on the embers in an urgent effort to heat the water quickly. The stove began to glow comfortingly in a matter of moments. I had mastered the range, if nothing else.

Theo sat, his hands around the mug, shoulders sagging, to all intents and purposes like a sailor just rescued from the sea. He allowed the brew to spread through his mind. His entire body shook in spasms so he had to hold the mug close to his mouth to prevent it from spilling down his front. Once or twice, a single tear ran down his cheek to hang onto his chin, expanding until it eventually dropped to the floor.

It was a time for decisions. I put my empty mug down and set Theo's on the sideboard. I took him in my arms and, together, we fell onto his bed. I held him as tight as I could, so his body, tense though warm, clung to mine. His head rested on the pillow with his grandmother's red and white check cover, his nose pointed towards the bulkhead. His cheek was against mine preventing tears from falling further so a pool collected and cooled, until the change in temperature became a caress, barely there, yet at the same time like an electric shock, a tingle to my skin. I relived the time when my mother's hands had brushed my face, or my father's cheek, roughened after a day's work had touched my own smooth down, making contact when I was sad or frightened.

This though was different. I was aware I was engineering the situation to suit myself, not one Theo had sought or asked for in any way. He had never stroked my cheek nor caressed my arm and had barely smiled, while a laugh was rare. It didn't matter to me because I knew he knew, and felt as I felt, the chemistry of two alien skins coming into contact for the first time.

Gradually, the tears eased, the trembling spasms ended in one long final sigh, air exhaled as if he would never stop and Theo slept. For a long while, I felt the regular movement of his body beside me, examining the planks in the ceiling as if I had never seen them before. I traced the knots in the wood with my fingers, twirling them in patterns to match the wood rings and tried to guess if one plank had come from the same tree as its neighbour. It seemed important, at the time to find out.

He stirred, turning until he faced me, his head very close, his thighs to mine, his iron-hard stomach pushing against me. I held him though my arm beneath his body was numb. And then, I too slept.

* * * * *

The smoke from a dozen stoves collapsed onto the surface of the water as soon as it cleared the funnels of the tugs. The sunlight, stronger than the day before, and the day before that, threw progressively slightly shorter angles of shadow as they glanced off the cobbles which felt less inflexible than they had been the day previously. There was a mood in the air to send a signal: winter is over – official.

The two tugs, one larger and longer than its neighbour, remained moored touching each other as usual. Despite the friendly intimacy of the scene, as the boats rubbed gunwales together, the mood was quickly dispelled if one was to examine the people who lived aboard. The wheelhouse door of the *Anna Rosner* slid back. Pieter Maas looked across to the *Kuijpers* almost furtively, not wishing to be seen, and then only for the briefest of moments. Seeing no-one there he rapidly crossed the gangplank without another glance in its direction. He was followed shortly by Jos.

'We'll be back at lunchtime, Mama. Jos and I are going to see if there is any work in *Noordwijk*. If we keep our noses clean, it could mean permanent work in the future. I have heard the growers are expanding, supplying to the British markets again,' Pieter had explained to Elizabeta before leaving home. 'We'll take the train.'

Mama had, in fact, discussed the ideas the night before. This was a repeat performance to enable Pieter to try and come to terms with the idea of moving the berth. The Family had chewed over the need to move the boat closer to where their work was; to move away from the basin and all the life around them, life they had known since Pieter had first arrived in the mid-war years and settled down. 'The boat's been here for ever,' said Anna, taking an interest in the proceedings for once. But Mama was thinking only of Hans. Moving away from Amsterdam meant leaving him on his own, with fewer visits.

'It cannot be much longer,' Pieter had confided, artificially bright. 'They have to put him on trial by the end of the month or his lawyer can claim unlawful arrest, despite the emergency rule.' Mama's heart had banged quite painfully at the last part and she had wept more tears to fall in a stream down her leathery cheeks.

'It's only the girl, Gretel's say so. If she hadn't opened her mouth that night, none of this would have come to light. It would not have been picked up by the police at all. As it is, this delay should mean compensation for us for what we have had to go through.'

'If he is innocent Mama, then he will be set free. And, yes, he should get something for being held illegally.'

'It is so unfair. My poor boy, shut away in the darkness, And then, there's poor Theo-'

'Mama!' Pieter raised his voice in a rare display of annoyance towards her. The unaccustomed pitch and volume brooked no argument whatsoever and all of the members of the Family sitting around the table knew he meant what he said. 'Those two are not up for discussion,' he snapped.

'We should never-'

'Suzannah! I repeat, for your benefit only, we do not discuss the er...incident. Such language, and after what we did for them both.'

'Scratch a Jew and you will always find trouble,' said Jos to Pieter's gratification. 'Somehow, the Jews always find themselves where there is a situation and try to win an advantage.'

It was Suzannah's turn to cry. She was silent in her tears, turning away to one side to hide her feelings from her father. What an awful day that had been, when Mae had screamed out like some banshee, a maddened witch whose every word had been a foul accusation against her father and brother. Her fists had beaten at Jos's chest as if to claw her way through his body, if necessary, to reach the engine room. The thought of what would have happened if her father had disregarded her pleas and continued out into the channel was too awful to contemplate? But the tears were not for her father. Her frustration was because she knew Mae had been right and the Family wrong, quite wrong in their behaviour. If Theo had been taken out to the *Ij*, Theo might now be locked up in a padded cell.

And the stillness following, with the engine engaged in a final burble before shutting down. Mama and daughters had clutched each other as Jos bled from the mouth in a small trickle. It had left Pieter with his head hanging down in shame and embarrassment, unwilling and unable to look up at Theo and Mae as they had left, holding hand to shaking hand. Men on other boats nearby, some moving out into the channel and passers-by had turned to stare at the scene, some almost rudely. Cries of shame had floated out across the waterfront, for Theo was a member of a well-respected family and it had not reflected well on the Maas family to be seen to be bullying him. Mae had pushed her way through the knot of people looking neither to one side or the other, ignoring comments from Jos who was regaining his composure. She simply had no more breath in her body, no wise counsel to dispel. So, instead, she clutched hold of Theo in a tight embrace, terrified less he might howl again. He had shown her the long corridors and she had seen the green painted walls and smelt the disinfectant and the spilt urine. He had witnessed the same walls moving in like a giant vice, and experienced the ceilings buckling and heaving like sheets on a laundry line in a high wind.

'It's alright, Theo, really. You are safe, you are safe.' She repeated the phrases, over and over as if a gramophone needle had become stuck in its groove. He had never had such attention, never heard the care in a person's voice since he had lost his grandfather, causing the glare in his eyes to soften and managing to relax his stomach muscles. So he had slept and stayed sane.

Now Mae smelt the smoke as it lay drifting just above the water a few centimetres of clear air between the two layers. It reminded her of long ago, before the war when the gardener had burnt the autumn leaves at the bottom of the garden. The smoke had always lain on the air in a paper-thin band, rolling drunkenly with the exploits of the wind.

She hurried on to work, keeping a measured distance from all other early walkers, with her mind set on other matters. At lunch, she managed to slip out as quickly as she could and walked over to the Police Station. It was the same officer in charge as before. He must have changed his shift to the day-time.

'He's been moved, Miss. We couldn't keep him here any more.'

'Oh, I quite understand officer. This time though, I only need information. I could do with the name of the girl, woman, Gretel, who laid the charges against Hans.'

'And why should you want that?' Again he was not unpleasant but there was firmness in his voice.

Mae looked innocently at him and caught his eye. 'I need to build up a file for Hans. We have no money so we will have to defend him ourselves. We need to have a file on all of the witnesses.'

'Very well, it is Gretel Neumann. She lives up in the *Vondel Park* area.'

'That's a nice address to have.'

'She comes from a very good family. She speaks as you do, if you don't mind me saying, quite different from the rest of your family.'

Mae smiled sweetly. 'I had a different schooling from the others. I was lucky, I suppose. Perhaps, we have one thing in common.'

'Perhaps,' the policeman replied. 'She is your age as well.'

'Mm, thank you. I don't suppose you have her address as well?'

'You know very well I do but you will have to go through the courts for that. She is a material witness, the most important one, in fact. You might try and interfere with her statement and everything hangs on ensuring she is not intimidated before the trial. None of the other witnesses want to move until she does.'

'But, we shall need to send her our documents.'

'You will be able to send them through the Courts. No!'

'No?'

'No.'

As Mae turned to go, he called to her at the door. 'Nothing to stop you calling in at City Hall. Every inhabitant is registered there. Cost you half a guilder, though.'

'Of course,' she beamed at him, an act to banish the hollows under her eyes. 'Thank you very much.'

The City Hall lay on her route back, and her lunch money for two days would now have to be spent instead, on buying information. Eating did not feature in her mind at all, as she asked, breathlessly, for the address. She found she had to wait for the information as she had to fill in a form which required her own permanent address. Here again, she never hesitated in her determination, writing down the number of the berth and the quayside name.

The plain, bespectacled attendant handed over a piece of paper upon which was written, in neat script, a name and address, and even a telephone number. Mae took it from her as if it were smuggled goods, feeling like a fence with stolen merchandise. She suppressed the desire to cast her eyes around as if to see if she was being watched by anyone. As it was, she *was* being spied upon, although it was only a city drunk, in from the cold as he clung to the meagre warmth being given off by a single radiator, waiting for the inevitable order to get his backside out of the building. He smelt of drain water and cheap beer and Mae felt sorry for the clerk who probably had to put up with the man every day.

Outside, she held the address up, hand trembling. She now knew where Gretel Neumann lived.

The afternoon was the first time since she had started at the bakery when Mae found it difficult not to be impatient with the customers who seemed to dawdle with their purchase decisions and fumble with their change. At last, it was five o'clock and she was able to hang up her apron.

'Goodnight,' she called to everyone in the shop, leaving before anyone else had had time to pull on their coats. Instead of turning left immediately outside the shop to take her back to Central Station and the harbour, she stepped onto a tram taking her south until it stopped by the Singel Canal and close to the Rijks Museum. The twin towers blocked out the sky with their bulk as she passed one of Amsterdam's most prestigious diamond shops before crossing the road keeping the Park Hotel in her sights. It had been a long time since she had been away from the boats, the port and even her old home. Here, the houses were five stories in height, each with a different gable frontage. From the street, laid down with bricks, big steps led up to massive doors with black lions' heads as knockers and windows twice or three times her own height. She wondered who did the cleaning these days of all that glass, but presumed there were plenty of people still about to provide in-house services as it had been before the war. The street was lined with tall, well-established trees reminding her of the days when there would have been daffodils below them in the Spring. The lower windows were barred in decorative wrought iron in a manner suggesting there was plenty to hide, and wealth to tempt the most affluent of burglars.

She came upon the house suddenly, the adrenalin shocking her sufficiently to make her mentally unprepared. Walking on quickly, she turned her head away in case she had been seen from one of the giant windows.

'Silly,' she said to herself, but, nonetheless, allowed her feet to take her to the next junction where she turned and stopped. A cyclist rang his bell to remind her she was still in the middle of his road. She had no idea if the woman was in the house and, if so, what would she say. As she retraced her footsteps, a plan began to evolve in her mind.

'Yes?' said a pretty, young woman, her hair immaculately coiffed up onto her head. Her clothes were expensive and modern, bringing a rush of perfume with the opening of the door. 'We don't buy at the door you know.'

'Are you Gretel Neumann?'

'Yes. Who are you?' This was said impertinently as if the speaker assumed everyone would know of her.

Mae's heart was hammering so hard it felt as if it were blocking her tongue. 'I'm a friend of Hans. I know your secret and your problem and have come to help.'

The woman's eyes narrowed sharply and she paled visibly. 'I don't know what on earth you are talking about. Who is Hans?'

'You know him well though these days better through your lawyers I understand. You reported him to the police a few weeks ago and he has been in prison ever since. Look, can I come in. I know Hans is innocent and-'

'No! I do not want to discuss it. I suppose you are from his family looking for money. Well, if you think you can blackmail me let me tell you who my father is.'

'Hans is innocent.'

'Innocent! Hah! He is just a dirty little collaborator.'

'But, I know he isn't. I have proof. If you will not talk to me, I must take this evidence to the police. The judge is not going to be too happy that you perjured yourself, and it will set Hans free, after which he will sue you for wrongful arrest. It will be in all the newspapers.'

For the first time in her life Mae had lied deliberately and consciously for gain. She had crossed her fingers behind her as her grandmother had taught her, and swore on her mother's grave, trusting and hoping it would provide sufficient protection and that it was for a good reason. After what seemed like an eternity, standing on the top step, an interval when she did not breathe, the other woman broke the silence.

'You had better come in then. Follow me.'

Mae entered the house, as nice, if not nicer than the one she had glimpsed down the corridor of the one belonging to Doctor Hertz. Only her parent's house had been as grand. She should have realised what it would be like by the fact there were six steps up to the front door. Houses in Amsterdam were rated in the past by the height of the main entrance doors above the canal level.

The walls were a soft cream in colour and to touch almost as if the wallpaper was covered in silk. Her feet sank into wool carpets and warmth enveloped her. She slipped back easily in time, home to her father's house, every object familiar to her. The walls *were* silk, to balance the Dresden china in the glass-fronted cabinets.

'You have a lovely house,' she said not being able to stop herself as the other woman indicated for her to sit, on the basis if you must sit down you had better sit there.

'Thank you. Now, what is all this about?'

'I want to help Hans's family as they once did for me. They need to know what he has done and...more important to them, why he did it?'

The others immaculate make-up twitched. She appeared totally bewildered, exactly as Mae had wished it. 'But, you just said he was innocent and you had proof.'

'I said those things to get you to listen to me. I don't know if he is innocent or guilty as I met him on only one or two occasions. I know his lovely family, though.'

'They are just common potato pickers.'

'Yet, you went out with one of them all the same, didn't you? Why, when you have all this money and...your station in life?'

Gretel was becoming curious, despite herself and realised she had been boxed in by a girl far more intelligent than her clothes supposed. She knew she had been duped into letting this hollow-eyed, badly-dressed girl into her house and she was already losing control of the conversation.

'I...I found him attractive. Don't you? He is different and very good looking, in a brutish sort of way,' she added. 'Most of all, he is a very good dancer, very light on his feet. It was fun, just dancing, nothing else. There was no way I would allow him to come home or meet my friends.'

'Yes, very light,' said Mae putting on a dreamy look.

'Have you danced with him then?' Her curiosity had become intense and Mae imagined the woman was showing the first stages of jealousy. She feinted with another question. One lie was enough at a time.

'I enjoy his dinner talk mostly. He has much to say on so many subjects.'

'You've had dinner with him?' Gretel found it hard to keep the incredulity from her voice. How could such a slip of a girl have attracted Hans?

'Oh yes, on six occasions in fact. Right up to the time you called in the police.'

'So, the little pig. He was dating you, while taking me out dancing: serves him right, if he is now in trouble.'

'You don't understand Gretel. May I call you Gretel? I was just one of a bigger party. But, I sat next to him each time so I was able to talk. And, all he could do was to chat about this other woman, a young woman he called Gretel. It was very rude of him as he claimed he had lost his heart to her and asked me how he should deal with the problem. I became very bored with the whole thing in the end because he only wanted to talk about her.'

Gretel blushed and became flustered, realising she should have let Mae finish what she was saying. Eventually, she got up. 'I have some proper tea. Orange Pekoe. Do you like it?'

Mae nodded. It was a name from the far past and threw a smile at Gretel. 'But no milk thank you.'

'You are a strange girl. You have been brought up well, speak well yet dressed…if you don't mind me saying…poorly.'

Mae waited in the comfort of the drawing room allowing herself to revel in the sheer luxury of the cushions, softness in her back she had forgotten.

'I have no maid today, you understand,' Gretel was explaining the need to do the chore herself. She placed a silver tray on a table between them. 'As I was saying er… what is your name?'

'Mae. My name is Mae.'

'Mae? You do not look as if you have any money, no makeup, yet you speak as if you have attended the most expensive school in the Netherlands.'

'You are perfectly right on all three counts.' It pleased Mae she could now speak the truth, though she refused to enlarge upon her story. Her hands were still shaking slightly, making her worried she might spill her tea on the rug.

'So, why are you really here? Not really to help Hans.'

'Yes it is. I told you when I came in. I don't know what the truth is in all of this. I believe you do. The police say you are a material witness, the most important witness, in fact. Goodness, just think of that. You will have to go up on a stand and swear in front of a court full of people, a judge and those awful newspaper men with their cameras. I could never have the nerve to do such a thing. You are very brave…and it is soon, I believe?'

Gretel had lost her blush and her lips took on a pallid blueness burning through the glossy red seal. While she drank from her cup, she caressed the gold rim with delicate movements of her little finger. Mae could see she was trying to gain time. 'I only want to be able to tell his family the truth, such lovely people Gretel, poor but honest, salt of the earth types. Good citizens in fact. If Hans is a collaborator, they will need to know. They are very proud and this is hurting them dreadfully. The mother has been in tears for most of the time.'

'I saw the father once. Hans pointed him out to me though he wouldn't introduce me. Said his father's hands were too rough and cracked, they would spoil my own.' She turned her beautifully manicured nails on display, then back again as if to reassure herself it had not been a delusion. 'Look,' she went on earnestly. 'There is nothing I can do. He is guilty and the evidence is all stacked up, so he doesn't have a chance.'

'Thank you. Then I will tell Hans's family later tonight. I expect you will see him and the family in court. They will all be there, of course, to give him support.'

'Even if you tell them I said he is guilty and saw him coming out of this Nazi building on several occasions during the war?'

'Of course, he is their flesh and blood after all, particularly if he goes to prison for the rest of his life. The family will come to some sort of justification for it all in their minds. They will have to, wont they?' Mae took a cup of tea, sipping it as she studied Gretel over the rim of the cup. She held it automatically, just as Gretel did now, a habit not lost from the years of having it drilled into her at home and at school. Gretel shook the hair out of her face, now ashen in its hue. 'Yes.' She could hardly utter.

'Of course,' Mae went on relentlessly, 'the nice police sergeant at the Police Headquarters said in all truth he will be shot as it has become political and gone up very high in Government. They want to send a message to all collaborators left in the country that they will be found and dealt with harshly. It will be a war trial; after all it is a war crime isn't it? Apparently, he caused the death of three Dutch heroes-'

'Stop!' Gretel collapsed on the settee, bent over sideways. 'Please stop,' she added, her head coming to rest on a silk cushion. 'I was going to tell them, you know. The police, I mean, but it all got out of hand and, as you say, it has gone up the Government and Daddy has become involved. I wanted to s-.' Tears coursed down her lovely face, carrying a good deal of mascara with it to the curve of her jaw. The blue eyes, lifted up for help, were tinged with pink. 'You must understand, if I tell Daddy the truth, he will kill me.'

'Your father lives here?'

'No, no. Mother died some years ago, in forty-four in fact, and Daddy lives in *Baarn* close to the people who matter in this country. He is in shipping.'

Mae felt an enormous surge of relief. Hans was innocent but, she had yet to convince Gretel to report the facts to the police. She now recognised the name. 'Everyone knows the Neumann shipping line. Surely your father would always understand if you told the truth. Angry for a while perhaps, but…think of the alternative.' She turned the screw tighter. 'Hans shot for a murder he didn't do, disgraced, and you having to live with that truth for…ever.'

There were more tears. Gretel's slim frame shook, as her mind attempted to come to terms with a dreadful truth she had tried to bury. To Mae, she was clear glass to look through, the room, with its collection of idle purchases, so soon after the war, given no doubt, by an adoring father who had no wife left to lavish presents upon. The woman, probably for the first time in her life found she could not purchase one man's life, or to control it, nor, how to buy herself out of a dilemma. They had all come together. How pathetic and how trivial her empty world was. The old, complicated ways were already beginning to replace the simplicities of living that war had brought. It was not to say that war was good, but somehow many of the everyday problems were removed, as necessity brought the real issues to the front and removed triviality from one's livelihood.

'You have to tell the police, Gretel. I cannot do it.'

'I cant! I cant! My father, you understand.'

Mae rose to go. 'Only you can do this, Gretel. Thank you for the nice tea.'

'What can I-'

'Goodbye.' Mae cut her off firmly and walked down the brightly lit hall where the lights continued to burn unchecked in a far room while they had been talking in the drawing room. She eyed the brass trays from China, the camel stool from Arabia where a pair of leather gloves and a pill-box hat rested. She thought of the *Kuijpers* with its cold stove and the floorboards, ice-cold to her feet in the mornings…and knew which she wanted more.

* * * *

I knew I could not attempt to force the rich young girl into confessing her sin to anyone but myself. It would take enormous strength of will after her first mistake in accusing Hans in a silly show of pique. For a moment, I believed Gretel might have asked me to go with her to the police station. In the end, her body had shaken so much that her teeth rattled in her jaw. It had turned her lips blue making me think she might suffer from a heart attack. It frightened me to think I might be responsible for her premature death and I could not press her further, but my only consolation, as I walked away was that in a court of law, a good defence lawyer would break down her story very quickly.

So I walked back to the boat. Theo was on the gangplank, repairing a broken forestay. His skill with the soft wire was obvious in the way he laid each turn against the previous bend, tight as the splice beneath it.

'Hullo.' His face lifted as he saw me approaching the quayside. 'Good day?'

'Good to start, shitty towards the end,' I replied, tired and irritable. It was a throwaway remark.

'Mae! What a word to use. It's terrible, like in the army or something. I have never heard a woman use that word before…'

He was right, of course. He had put the whole thing in perspective in his own, simple way. 'I'm sorry.' I was genuinely remorseful. I went below, followed by Theo and rolled up my sleeves to wash. 'Did you know the Family are planning to leave the basin, even Amsterdam?'

It was the worst shock since I had left Rotterdam. 'No, I did not. Why, for goodness sake?'

'Pieter wants to be closer to the bulb fields…he says. But, Suzannah told me he cannot come to terms with himself over the awful incident after the fight. He blames himself but is unable to admit it to anyone, not even Mama. There's silences…and things.'

'This is dreadful Theo. I should never have-'

I stopped talking for he had placed his fingers in a simple, moving gesture, lightly over my mouth. He was lost for words, but this was a much more effective way of communicating. He wanted to help but did not know how, so he merely stopped the flow of words. 'You came to help me but you must see that Pieter and Jos were only trying to do what they saw was right. Suzannah told me they planned the whole thing. They thought if I was to go to sea, I would be cured…like taking the waters.' He laughed ruefully. 'After all, it is all in the mind.' He smiled thinly but sincerely and I felt better.

The amazing thing was that Theo did not seem to be affected by the trauma of the experiment, albeit cut short as it was. 'That was a plan? What an idiotic thing to have done.'

It was an ill-advised blunder though it had been typical of Pieter to see how he could help. He was, deep down, an extraordinarily kind man and I am sure he would have been quite reckless in drumming up support from his family, setting it all up even to the extent of bringing forward the date of his boiler service. I could see him with his finger stuck into his waistcoat, standing in front of the fire, legs spread apart, ready to put on a show, his grand plan to restore Theo to health once and for all. 'We'll cure him, Mama, just you wait and see,' he would have said, calming the doubters and the magnified pouts of the ladies. Jos would have done anything his father told him, anyway and Hans was still in prison.

'Perhaps I should go and see him.
Them? I can't let him leave here because of me, can I?'

'They won't see you Mae. They are too ashamed. Pieter has put it about the basin you are not welcome aboard the *Anna Rosner*.'

I felt sick in my stomach though I was certain I had done the right thing in preventing the boat from leaving port. God alone knew what could have happened to Theo. In an instant, I had lost the only people who had stepped into my life and really helped me out of sheer kindness. Our lives had crossed for such a short span of time. We had touched, briefly held hands and now they were waving farewell to their old home because they could not stand being around me.

I cooked Theo's meal of beans and sausages, made into a stew. I hardly touched my plate, seeing only the Family on the other side of the table. Instead, I pushed my food from side to side of my plate occasionally collecting a single bean on my fork. Eventually I gave up on the congealed mess.

'I have to see them, Theo. You wash these things up and get some more wood. It's cold this evening and the wind is coming up. I wouldn't be surprised if there was a storm coming in from the Atlantic.'

'He won't see you, Mae. None of them are allowed to talk to you.'

'I must try,' I said, meaning it.

It was dark outside the wheelhouse and the deck was beginning to heave from the low pressure storm coming in from the North Sea making its presence felt in the basin though it had begun thousands of kilometres away. The big tug alongside burnt with light at the waterline portholes though there was the absence of any laughter or even of conversation. Often, when I had come on deck for some air, one or more of the Family would be making themselves heard, until Pieter's voice would rise above the general level and peace would descend again like the dusk, for a short while. Tonight, only the wind was being heard as it moaned through the rigging covering up for the lack of any chatter.

'Hullo,' I said, committing myself.

'Who is there?' Pieter replied. I heard whisperings from below. 'It's Mae, I think,' said Suzannah. More whisperings ensued.

'If it is Mae, you are not welcome here. We have nothing to say to each other.'

I took no notice and continued to climb down the companionway steps and into the main cabin. The light was turned down, casting shadows across the room as if Pieter had given a command to his Family that if he was not enjoying himself, they, neither were to apply themselves to reading or sewing. Suzannah and Anna threw me uncertain smiles, half caught between their wish to make contact and the nearness of their father who had taken up his usual stance in front of the fire, his arms folded in front of him like a barrier. 'Very well, as you have pushed your way into our home, uninvited, have your say, then leave.'

Mama sat down. Her hip bones moved in a familiar fashion. It was as if I had never left. The pans remained bright. I noticed Hans's chair had been moved to a far corner of the cabin in recognition, I supposed, that he was gone and thus less of a reminder in their lives. Mama saw me glance in its direction.

'I heard you may be leaving. Leaving the harbour that is, Amsterdam also perhaps. Could you tell me why, please?'

'And why should you want to know?' Pieter replied haughtily still not making eye contact with me. He had found a fascinating mark on the ceiling to study. 'Who told you this?' Suzannah blanched and anxiously tried to catch my eye.

'I hear these things on the boats. You know how stories travel here.'

'It is nothing to you, whether we stay or go.'

'But it does, Pieter if you are leaving because of what I did. If this is the real reason and I don't expect you could bring yourself to confirm this, I shall be leaving here, tomorrow morning at first light, I promise you. You will never see me again…ever.'

Mama caught her breath in an inward choke and put a hand to her mouth. 'It wasn't really-'

'Enough, Mama,' Pieter cut her off as if with a whiplash. 'I can assure you, I would not be moving my family because of you. But, I agree,' his voice rose, warming marginally as he saw a way out of his dilemma. 'It would be better, much better for the whole harbour if you were to leave. You don't fit in, you are not a tug man, er tug woman.'

'What about Theo?' Suzannah was crying openly, defying her father's edict to keep quiet. She looked at me for guidance.

'It is his boat, his life. I came into it for such a short while that I am sure he will have forgotten my name in a week. It is not as if we were lovers…is it?' I ended by fixing Mama's eyes, holding them to my own, challenging her to repudiate my statement.

'If you say so.'

'Yes, I say so, Elizabeta. It happens to be the truth. And I have never lied to you before.'

'Alright, alright. Tomorrow you go.' All at once, Pieter held out his hand. He could afford to. 'I wish you a safe journey to where ever you go.'

'Thank you.' I took the toughened, rough hand in my own. 'I hope Hans is returned to you, safe and sound: and soon.' Again, I looked across to the forlorn chair, standing alone in the dark corner. It had a drying up cloth draped across its back, already finding a new use, any use in fact, but what it was bought for. I turned to go. There was no point at all in saying anything more. I had talked my way out of my little home, my friends and my new life. I would have to find somewhere new to live quickly. I turned my back on the Family.

'Hullo Mae.'

I stood rigidly to the spot on the polished floorboards at the bottom of the companionway, my passage skywards blocked by the stocky frame of a young man who looked so much like his mother. There were dark lines of strain under his eyes though otherwise he looked well enough. He was still wearing the blue canvas smock he always wore on board and a pair of dungarees.

'Hullo, Papa, Mama. Girls.'

There was an electric moment in time when everyone in the room came to an absolute stop. No movement at all.

It was Hans. He walked up to Jos, the nearest, and gave him an awkward hug with a curious mixture of fondness and embarrassment. Tug men did not normally show this sort of emotion.

Mama had been gazing out across the water unwilling to look at me as I left. She turned as Pieter almost shouted out Hans's name, almost in annoyance at her son's name being raised, particularly as I was still on board. Then, she caught sight of her son being kissed by Anna and Suzannah, seeing his broad back enfold them in his arms.

'Ah! My darling boy. They have let you out.' She heaved her enormous, angular frame towards him with surprising speed to clasp him to her. Pieter attempted to hug him also, realised what he was doing and instead, thrust out his hand. Hans's arms, however, were trapped by the bonds entwining him. Suzannah and Anna, released, clapped their hands in delight.

I was already in the doorway, finding myself forgotten, as the Family reunited in a joyous ring of hands and arms which reached out to touch him, to see if she was real and solid, some specimen in a zoo. I climbed back on deck and swung my legs quickly over the gunwale to Kuijpers. All at once, I felt something was wrong despite the happiness I had witnessed.

'Mae? How did it go?' It was Theo to meet me, anxious for news.

'Hans. Hans is back. The Family have agreed to stay I think-'

'That's two good pieces of news,' he said, smiling.

'One, Theo. I have had to agree to leave. The Family want this.'

I felt so tired I sat in Theo's chair, full of tears, yet unable to shed a single one. Theo came and sat down, puzzled shadows chasing his face. He touched my shoulder, once, lightly as if he were a dog after a smack from its master.

'I do not understand any of this. What is going on? Why do you have to l....you mustn't leave...you simply mustn't. It was Pieter's idea to try and get me out to sea... and Hans. What has he to do with all of this?'

'Nothing, nothing at all. It is just chance, an extraordinary chance maybe, but nothing more. He arrived as I was leaving for good. Pieter is terribly embarrassed by the whole thing, Theo. I think he finds it difficult to live with himself at the present time. My presence here reminds him every day of his stupidity. He helped me so much when I needed it that I have to do something in return for him. It is only right, because he is a proud man and he will not be able to bend towards me.' I picked up the kettle and filled it from the bucket. The fire caught and roared into life as soon as I riddled the grid. It was ironic: it had taken so long to learn how to do it, now being perfected I had to leave in the morning. I would probably never have to riddle a ship's stove again in my life.

We sat close together, allowing a single corner light to illuminate the room. There did not seem to be any need to turn on the main lamp, and it saved fuel.

Theo finished his tea and placed his mug quite deliberately on the table, searching for an exact position that he appeared to need as if he were a blind man, or a very drunk one. He studied the table top, seeing the wax shine dully, the spotless white crochet mat, once stained with tea rings.

'No!' He shouted out, making me jump in the gloom of the room. It had caught me unawares, for his voice was not only loud, but harsh, though quite controlled, unlike the ramblings of the past when I had first encountered him in the *Middlelaan*. 'No! No! No! You are not leaving Mae, not, at least, because of the Maas family. That would be completely wrong.'

'I have to go, Theo. Pieter...his mood...my promise.'

'Pieter!' he struggled with the word and then another caught in his tongue. 'Fuck Pieter!' The enormity of the word choked him to silence, and he collapsed in a fit of coughing. I had taught him the word I am sure, for his grandfather had not been the type of person ever to have sworn at all, not least in front of his grandson. Whatever, I had rekindled a flame inside of him.

'Hush,' I said, moving towards him. I put my arm around his shoulders but he turned further to face me directly.

'You must not go Mae. I don't think I could go back again to the old ways if you were to go. There is very little else in this world that I want to hold on to, if you leave Kuijpers.'

And there it was in a nutshell. If I did not leave, I would have broken my promise to Pieter, Pieter the man who brought me back into the real world. If I left, I might even have the death of a good friend on my conscience, certainly almost madness, and a permanent room in the madhouse. I hung my head, my mind cracking around me as I tried to think of a way out.

'Hey there, you aboard Kuijpers,' sounded a voice from the wheelhouse, 'Permission to come aboard.'

* * * *

'Come and sit down here, darling, as close to me as you can get. Why are you out? The police have let you out, yes?' Mama's querulous voice climbed above the general hubbub, 'and you look so thin.' She stroked his face.

'Of course, Mama. I haven't escaped from prison, if that is what you thought. The police withdrew all charges. Without the testimony from Gretel Neumann, the police said the other witnesses would not be strong enough to make a conviction. . They say the case would be dropped before it ever got to a trial. So…I'm free, I'm clear.'

Elizabeta stroked Hans's cheek again before clapping her hands in delight. Pieter frowned. 'I don't understand. You could never be held for so long on just the word of a woman. There must be more to it, a lot more.'

'Circumstantial?' asked Jos quickly.

'Yes, it was circumstantial, Papa. They built up a picture about this man taken from many sources, especially members of the Resistance. I happened to have been seen in the area of the City where they were particularly interested in and kept a close watch. I was there, at this house, several times, Jos as well, in fact. Jos and I were always down there, by the University in the old days. It was where all the pretty girls used to be. So, along with about a dozen others, we were all put on a list of suspects at the end of the war, apparently. Gretel did the rest, for when my name came up it tallied with that on the potential collaborators register. Gretel must have had access to this list.'

'But, why was Jos not put on the list, as you say, or pulled in at the same time?'

'I think the police only examined those over a certain age.'

While he talked, he was being stroked and patted continuously as if he were a lap dog or a cat. Small animal noises were emitting from Elizabeta's throat. 'What a wicked, wicked girl. She will burn in hell for this.'

'There, there, Mama. All's well that ends well. No harm done,' Papa patted her head condescendingly while sucking on his pipe hard. Her words were too…hard for his boat.

'Why?' asked Suzannah, 'did Gretel change her mind?'

'Well, you know, because of Mae. Where is she, by the way?'

'She's gone.' There was an uncomfortable silence. Hans looked around, a puzzled expression developing on his face as the tide exposes sand.' What's going on Mama? Papa?'

'She's leaving. Mae's leaving in the morning.' The silence increased.

'Going? Going where, Mama? She has nowhere to go.'

'There was a row, an argument, sort of. She's leaving tomorrow as a result. But…she suggested it. She'll be away from us all.'

'It was her or us,' said Pieter, trying to lend weight to the discussion but needing the subject to change for the better as soon as possible. 'That's what it came down to. So, here you are, you've lost some padding round your gut.'

Hans, however, was not to be deflected.

'You've turned her away' I cannot believe you have done such a stupid thing!'

'Now hold on, son.'

'She said some terrible things about us, darling. Just when we were trying to help Theo. Mae even hit Jos in the mouth and made it bleed.'

Hans held up his hands, mortified at the news. He held his hands up high above the group encircling him. 'You simply do not understand, do you? You have no idea what you have done. You cannot have heard the news. The reason I was released is because Mae went to see Gretel. Gretel must have been made to see how wicked her actions had been and she must then have gone to the police. I was released about half an hour later by a sheepish Police Inspector.'

The stillness following this statement could almost be touched and felt. The only movement was the orange light from the range where small flickers might otherwise have reminded them of the supper cooking away. Pieter's features had collapsed into a putty-grey knot of jowls and chin. His cockiness, normally keeping up the shape of his waistcoat buckled into a deflated beer belly. Hans smashed a fist into the doorframe, making the girls wail with fear. Jos shook his head in disbelief.

'Damn! Damn!'

Suzannah shook her head over and over again. 'I should have known nothing would have deflected Mae from helping us, even when we turned her away. We have made a dreadful mistake, Papa, dreadful.'

'Now then, sweetheart-'Papa began.

'No, Papa! You must accept we have all made this awful blunder in trying to take Theo to sea. Only Mae saw the danger. She was the only one who understood the problem. All she did was to try and protect Theo in the only way she knew and she answered us in the only way possible, the way she was taught in the camps. We were the ones who made the mistake. We *have* to go to say we are sorry and she must be allowed to stay in the harbour.'

'And thank her for bringing my boy back to me.' Mama reinforced her daughter's affirmation. Pieter was bewildered by the sudden and total about turn.

'She must not leave; Mae, I mean,' repeated Suzannah. 'It would be very wrong of us if she was to leave now, when all the time it was our fault.'

Pieter had managed to shrink further inside his clothes as he felt the measure of his inadequacy. They were nails of his crucifixion. Each clout shrivelled him further. He found it physically impossible to look any of his Family in the face. Instead, he gazed dejectedly with cloudy eyes at the floor, seeking a single kind word to provide a route back into the fold.

It came eventually from Hans. 'I don't know what has been going on Papa while I have been er…away, but I am sure that if you had planned it, it was because it seemed like the best thing at the time. Looking back, wishing you hadn't done something, well…, Gretel is in the same boat, isn't she?'

Pieter straightened his back, as renewed energy flooded his spine. 'I tried to take Theo to sea, to make him break his fear he has of leaving the harbour. You know how he is? As we were moving into the main stream, Mae literally went mad, like a dog with rabies. She attacked poor Jos and said dreadful words to us all.'

'She had a very good reason to do so, Papa. She saw that it would drive Theo into permanent madness, didn't she? Then his state of health would have been on all of our consciences. It was a risk strategy which, luckily Mae was able to see was absolutely wrong for Theo, and some bad language is a small price to pay, don't you think?'

'It was a mistake,' said Elizabeta, 'but it could have worked.'

'We will never know, Mama. We were taking the place of the doctors, without any training at all, even thinking we knew better than God.'

Suzannah held out her hand to her father. 'Papa, we must go and see her. She has no home to go to, and a new job to worry about. If we do not, we will put her back where you found her, in the gutter.'

A small relay tripped in Pieter's mind. A synapse closed creating a new channel of thought. Though the idea chastened him, a now determined Pieter whirled about to seek five faces. Then, changing his mind yet further he continued towards the companionway.

'No, it is for me and me alone,' he shouted over his shoulder.

'I'll go with you,' said Hans.

'No! No, I'll go alone if you don't mind. I began this, I must rectify this.'

Mama put her hand to her mouth again as if this was becoming a regular habit. She transferred her anguish from one member of her Family to the next. 'Oh dear, as soon as something good happens to us, there is always something else to push it aside again. It comes up behind us every time.'

'So, therefore by your reasoning, Mama, it will be another good day tomorrow for us,' said Hans with a smile. He had no idea what had gone on that Sunday lunch when Mae had lost her reason but knew there had been an over-reaction by the Family. What on earth could Mae have said to have shocked them so much? He watched his father pull on his Sunday jacket then mounted the steps without further comment.

Pieter climbed over the gunwale of *Kuijpers* brushing water from his trousers. His first knock on the wheelhouse door was so ineffectual that he slid it back and stood in front of the wheel summoning up the courage to call out.

'Hullo,' he shouted down the stairwell, a frog catching his throat so the end result was little more than a chick cheep so he turned to climb down backwards. This way he would not be the first to have eye contact and would give him time to recollect his thought. Theo and Mae were there, sitting in half dark, very close to each other as if they had just parted. He wondered, as Mama had intimated, if they had become lovers. Alone, here on the tug, with only one bed from what he could see, he could not imagine Mae's emaciated, naked body, cold white, in contact with Theo's own muscular frame. But, there was no accounting for taste and Mae was a very determined young woman with plenty of backbone in her. She had achieved what he had not done, to free his son and it gave him a bitter taste in his mouth. He remembered the first day he had met Elizabeta. It had been in the bulb fields, her broad shoulders bent to cut the heads of the tulips. She had been heavy-boned then, with a massive head and bulbous breasts already beginning to sag in her thin, cotton dress. His face betrayed the event fleetingly.

'I have come to apologise,' he waded in immediately, standing, both feet together, both hands clasping the buttons on his jacket. 'I've been told how you managed to get Hans out of prison, for which I shall be forever in your debt. It goes further though…' he paused to lay emphasis on his words, 'I realise I was very wrong, terribly wrong in what I tried to do for Theo.' He turned to face him. 'I thought only of trying to make you well again, to help you out of your illness. You must believe me when I say I did it only because I hope we are friends and neighbours. It is extremely important to me you understand what I am saying, Theo. I did it for you.' He repeated himself, so earnest were his words, almost making him lose his drift. There was no response from either. The three of them stood in the soft light of the cabin as the boat rocked to a new swell. Mae remained in thought.

So Gretel had gone to the police and Hans had been set free as a result. She felt a prickling at her eyelids.

At last, Mae spoke. 'There is no debt, Pieter. You did more for me than I could do for you if I live to be one hundred. As you helped me, you tried to help Theo. I just knew if you had gone to the main channel, Theo would have lost his head and might never have been the same man again. I felt I could go to Gretel as you could not, one woman to another, educated at similar schools and brought up in similar circumstances. I was sure she had lied, and in the end she admitted it to me. She is a brave girl for it must have been incredibly difficult having to tell her father and all of her friends she had put someone in prison just to spite a man.'

Theo broke in, his speech halting but determined. 'Does it matter, Pieter, whether…I stay on shore…or go to sea? It is much more important to me I keep my friends about me. I haven't anyone left of my family, just you. I'm not a fisherman…nor a tug man, I'm just…' he was at a loss for words. Mae longed to fill in the gaps but knew what he was trying to say was central to his reasoning. Pieter, whose face was red and pricking with tears, held up his hand in supplication.

'You are just our very dear friend. We are your friends, Theo. Never forget that.' He stared straight ahead of him, knowing what was happening but unable to control the single sparkling drop of crystal as it oozed out of his eye. It rolled down onto the floor unchecked to catch the light of the stove. Too late, he attempted to brush it away as if he had walked into a cobweb. 'I'm sorry to both of you,' and, directly to Mae: 'Please do not leave on our account. The whole Family wants you to stay.'

Mae smiled for the first time since he had come aboard. 'Only if you agree to one condition.'

Pieter eyed her warily. This girl always had a trick or two up her sleeve. 'What is it?'

'That you and your family stay here also. Keep the two boats side by side, like a pair of lovers.'

Pieter relaxed the tension in his face, allowing the stress in his body to soften. 'God bless,' he ended and, before they could say another word, he turned and climbed the steps. Theo went to see him out but Mae put a restraining hand on his arm.

'He's a proud man, Theo. It took a great deal to bring himself to admit he had made a mistake.'

'Just also remember, Mae… if you had not gone to the Family in the first place, we would all still have been out in the cold.'

'Let's make some tea,' she said, ending the matter.

* * * * *

She woke early as usual and pulled back the curtain dividing the room. Theo was still asleep, his face rested and at peace. One hand was flung out, grasping an old scarf which had belonged to his grandmother reminding her of the piece of lace of her mother's which had provided the substitute comfort when she had been in trouble. She smiled, recalling also the late evening when Theo had mulled over with her the fine detail of Pieter's visit. The earlier mood, when she had felt so close to him had disappeared following the removal of the threat of separation. Pieter's confession, if that is what it was, had taken the overriding worry of where to live, out of her immediate mind. She knew it would be all the more hard to leave in the future, as a result but, all of this was a temporary affair, just until Theo got on his feet. Meanwhile a new bond, a three-way bond between herself, Theo and the *Kuijpers* had replaced her mood of desperation.

It did not mean she had lost the deep relationship she had forged with Theo, merely, she had parked it like an Amsterdam bicycle, shackled to a lamp post, secure until she came back to unlock the clasp, and set herself free again to do as she wished with her emotions. Today was too soon to think about it.

As she walked back across the gangplank once again, she received a wave from Pieter climbing into his working boots covered in mud. The air smelt warmer, somehow closer. Spring? Spring, she repeated to herself. How she wanted the short nights and warm evenings when she could sit outside and darn socks on the deck. Down in the cabin she had had to live like a mole, seeing the boat in daylight only on Sundays.

Busy at the counter, she hardly recognised Gretel queuing for bread, waiting until Mae was free. She allowed another woman to go in front of her to another server.' I have to see you. Are you free for lunch?'

'Yes, I am, but only for half an hour. What can I do for you?'

'I'll tell you then. I can't speak at the moment. I'm so upset by the whole thing, and I do not want to get you into trouble here at the shop.'

Mae could see the woman was literally shaking with fear, or illness, though from which she could not tell. A bead of sweat on her top lip contrasted sharply with the smoothness of the makeup and the sophistication of her dress.' I *must* talk with you.'

'Very well, I will be outside at twelve. I will meet you on the opposite side of the road and we can go to the Square. There are seats there.'

For the next hour, while Mae dealt with a steady flow of customers, she pondered on why Gretel would want to see her now she had been to the police. How also had Gretel found out where she worked? They had absolutely nothing in common, save for the expensive schooling, and she could not see how she could help further, if it was to do with Hans's release.

Gretel was waiting for her, hands clenched to an expensive leather handbag, despite the shoulder strap.

'At last. Well go to this Square? It's safe there?' This, in itself was a strange comment to make, thought Mae, but, dutifully followed the other girl to Dam Square. Mae found she had to struggle to keep up with the other's long, graceful strides once the Square was in sight. She felt like a puppy attempting to catch up with its taller mother.

They found a bench and sat forming a reasonable space between themselves. It allowed the two to face each other rather than to talk to the *Krasnapolski* Hotel on the opposite side of the Square. Gretel continued to turn her head as if watching for another friend to arrive.

'Now, what can I do-'

'Oh Mae! What on earth have I done?' Gretel was instantly in tears. 'I had to let Hans go, especially after what you said at the house. They might have shot him, or put him in prison for the rest of his life. I went to the police as you advised me and I hear Hans has been released. It was done so quickly it was almost as if they were waiting for me to come.'

'So,' said Mae, feeling coolness in her chest.' You did the right thing. You know you did.'

'You don't understand. I *know* Hans was a collaborator. It wasn't just that I saw him mixing with those awful men they caught after the war. Quite by chance, I think I saw him slipping out of an office one evening before it got dark. The Gestapo occupied the building in those days, not far from my Daddy's City house. Hans was with someone else and they were acting in a relaxed manner, as if they hadn't a worry in the world, which, knowing the Gestapo as we all did, made me wonder why they were not more apprehensive. They were speaking German, not Dutch which was strange too. I didn't say anything at the time because I was far too frightened, besides it was a Gestapo house and you know what they were like. You never went anywhere near there unless you were taken. I was much younger, but he was always a good-looking man, so like his brother in many ways. I am sure it was him. After the war, the Germans were gone and I had forgotten about the whole incident, trivial as it was anyway, until I met him again at a dance and we began seeing each other for dances and have a few drinks together. I remembered him coming out of that house but did not say anything at the time. You know…'

'So,' Mae interrupted, 'you think Hans really was a collaborator after all?'

'I think so, Mae.' She stopped, as the need for a cigarette became too urgent to carry on. Her body continued to heave in spasms as she attempted to light up, but failed three times before Mae took hold of her gold lighter for her. In the midst of the confession, the people of Amsterdam swirled around the two of them, oblivious to the conversation, going to lunch, meeting friends, unaware of the drama unfolding in the Square.

'Are you absolutely sure of what you are saying? You don't give the impression this story can be substantiated, that is, strong enough you could swear on a bible for instance, as you would have to in Court. The police anyway, will find it very difficult to believe a second story, and, is it a story anyway? Might it have been Hans, but was he there on a genuine mission for some reason or other? Or Jos perhaps? You said they were similar looking then and they still are.'

'No, no,' Gretel was at the point of self-torture again, seeing the whole event entering a new cycle, like a nightmare returning just when one thought it had gone away. 'Hans will never come out of prison.'

The real reason for the woman's agony struck Mae as she spoke. 'You love him, don't you?' she said, taking hold of Gretel's hands to comfort her.

'To distraction…the bastard. He dumped me just when I fell for him.'

A thousand concerns swamped Mae's head. It was ironic, she reasoned, that a Jew, tortured by the Germans, was seeking ways, any way, to save a man who had sold Dutch Jews to the same master race.

'Look, Gretel, I have to get back to work. I cannot be late, but I'll think of an idea. I promise I'll meet you tomorrow, same time, and same place. Here.' She gripped Gretel's hands tightly, feeling the rings on her fingers, making sure the message had entered the distraught woman's head.

'Please don't be late. I will be waiting for you,' she implored.

'I've given you my promise. I will be here, right after twelve.'

That evening, after Theo had cleaned his plate of beans and sausage with the last pieces of bread and sat back with a contented sigh, she broached the subject carefully. She ate while she talked, as Theo had sped ahead without thinking of slowing his pace to match her mood.

'Tell me, Theo. Just supposing Hans had been a collaborator.'

'He would have got his…just…deserts, isn't that the word? He would have no friends in the Courtroom, least of all, me. You've lost all of your family, Mae, through such people as him. Things could have been, well, different, without these types of people spying for the Germans. I heard that twenty thousand Jews were hidden by our people, but eight thousand of these were denounced to the Germans by collaborators, or at least, people who thought they were doing the country a service. Anne Frank? You heard of Anne Frank? Maybe not, as you have been away but you would not forget her story.'

How could anyone forget her story, thought Mae? One day she would become a legend to Jew and non-Jew alike.

The tug creaked in sympathy as it settled down for the night. Its deck, heated by the blazing stove below, expanded the wooden beams tight against the sides of the tug. Theo patted the bulkhead. 'It stands to reason,' he went on, 'he would have been sent to prison for a very long time. Why are you asking, anyway? The girl, Gretel, went to the police and explained she had made up the whole thing just out of spite. A wronged lover,' he was sure he had seen the phrase in one of his grandmother's books. 'I hope I never get into a situation with a woman.' He ended this long speech gloomily.

'Yes, but what if she said it to get him freed, because she loved him?'

'You said she hated him because he stood her up at a dance…or something.' Theo had no idea where the conversation was leading, but he knew Mae well enough now to know she was not going to let the story go. He could see her eyes were full of frustration as she attempted to work out a problem while listening to him at the same time. He closed his eyes but found he could not match her in doing two things at the same time. It was hard enough to follow her at the speed of thought she travelled at as it was. He did, however, want to understand it all as he felt it would strengthen the growing bond of friendship between them if he tried to identify with her discontent, so he leaned forward, closer to her as if this alone would help.

'It doesn't mean she fell out of love. Love and hate are as close together sometimes as a sheet of paper between them. Gretel could hate Hans for rejecting her but, it doesn't follow she automatically fell out of love. It might make her desire stronger… not weaker.'

'Maybe, maybe…she didn't love him in the first place. Maybe…she made a genuine mistake; maybe…it is just one big mix-up.'

Perhaps Theo was right, wondered Mae. Maybe Gretel had been mistaken, seeing Hans come out of that house. And what house? In a German occupied city, one's mind could play tricks: the house might just have been, say, an office to administer fishermen, or tug men. Hans could have been registering the boat. But then, why was Pieter not there? Disturbed again she saw little point in continuing.

'Did you like your meal?'

He nodded and patted the arm of his chair. She sat on the edge, her large, dark eyes like big pebbles at the bottom of a river. 'You are not going to leave here, are you?' he asked querulously.

'Not for a while, if you can put up with me and my strange habits, and anyway, not until you are completely better.'

'You don't have to leave, ever.'

'I must, one day. One day you will want this place for yourself…and a wife. I will be in the way.'

He found the statement deeply upsetting, not just because her words always rang with the truth. His thoughts had failed to touch upon the subject before: there had been no need and no-one to exchange a few words to extend and fill the day for him. Now she was demanding he look into the future, and it frightened him.

'I will never marry. No-one would have me; besides, it should not make any difference between us.'

'I think your wife might have something to say about that.'

As she changed later that night behind the curtain, all at once she took off all her clothes together. Always the routine at night was to remove her top and slip on a cotton nightie followed by her skirt and pants, part of a pattern her short life had dictated to her. Tonight, she stood close to the temporary screen, breathing heavily, believing Theo must hear the sounds. Once, she brushed the curtain deliberately where they were joined together. For the time it took the cloth to drop back into position, she was exposed to view, naked from kneecap to neck. But his back was turned as he sought to fold the quilt back as he had been taught by Mae. Resolute to meet her smallest request for tidiness, he had begun to fold the cloth exactly as shown. By the time the ends were joined together, Mae's body had disappeared from view.

And why, in God's name did I do that? She wondered at her stupidity. 'Why on earth?'

As she heard him climb into bed, she tucked his grandmother's goose down quilt about her, fluffing it up in a mood of extreme comfort, thinking back to the last time she had felt as good with herself. Theo's bed creaked as it took his weight with a long suffering sigh.

'Goodnight, Theo,' she said aloud for the first time on the boat.

'Goodnight,' he answered immediately. 'Don't worry about Gretel. I'm sure there is an explanation for it all and she has a lot of money to get her out of any trouble.' Mae felt strangely comforted by his words.

'Please tell Pieter, tomorrow before he leaves for work that I am seeing Gretel again to get a full explanation. If I have any news, I will stop off at the *Anna Rosner* on my way home.'

Theo, sensing how close she was to him that night, felt warmed. The reasons for his illness began to seep as gently as whey through a muslin sieve, back into the past. Little by little, they both drifted into sleep, turning noisily once or twice to remind the other that, not only were they still awake, but aware and close, ready to part the curtain, if only the other were to call out.

THE SKY IS THE COLOUR OF SEPIA

The tug rides at her mooring, the morning swells tossing her short foremast in an erratic circle as her neighbours take to the main channel one by one. The sun is now at its strongest, it being July, the almost white light blinding the couple who stand in the wheelhouse. He is gnarled like a thorn tree on a sea cliff, bent away from the wind, but still iron hard and stubborn, taking whatever he can draw from life. His clothes show the wear and tear of hundreds of washings, making the colours fade to a universal blue green, like the water of a deep ocean he knows so well. The man places a pipe on his lip as he proceeds to light it, the first indication of a smile playing along his mouth as the tobacco rasps at his throat. The woman is bent also, but frailer than him, wispy grey hair falling out of a badly tied bun and her skin is wrinkled like a dried apricot. She is firm, even so, for she is at the side of her husband, who she has lived with for almost sixty years, but she knows her time is closing down soon when he will be on his own again.

The sky is the colour of sepia, as are the warehouses and the street, bleached colours as in a photograph album. There are no strong contrasts here, simply the levelling signs of toil and graft for small reward.

At the forepeak stands a young lad of perhaps sixteen years, his age difficult to pin down exactly, as he is strongly built and dark shaven already. He rides the undulations of movement with the easy balance of a man who has lived all of his life on a boat, his actions in getting ready for sea unthinking and instinctive though the old man keeps a discreet watch through the glass of the wheelhouse at his grandson's preparations.

The lad, for that is how we describe him, suddenly puts his hand up to his head, and blinks several times. His grandfather sees the act and grimaces at his wife. They both shake their heads, an automatic gesture brought out from a lack of understanding.

Around their grandson, the walls and cobbles, the colour of malted barley take on darker shaded colours, then, all at once change back to lighter tints as the summer sun chases the clouds. But, on summer days such as these, the oldsters don't see the cobbles heave and shout out, forcing the sand joints to open up and spit pebbles at the lad's flailing hands. He tries to protect himself as much as he can, until he feels his grandfather's steadying support and the gull-like screams die away in his head.

'Another turn?' The old man asks. He pulls at his pipe, nonetheless, to keep it alight as he does not understand the symptoms of the lad's illness. His wife clucks into the wrinkle of her chin, seeing far more than her husband, but afraid to say anything which would go against his authority.

'Slip the springs,' he says at last. 'We have to meet the Shell Conqueror in half an hour and she will be well up the Ij.'

The lad stumbles to his task, but as he does so, it makes the street become stable, and the tall buildings rise up, straight and square. As the tug heads for the open water, the episode occupying a few minutes of the day is forgotten in the need to watch for sea-going traffic. It's a passing phase, the oldsters believe, like glandular fever and puberty; as the boy becomes a man it will disappear leaving him strong and ready for the hard life ahead.

Chapter Five

When I woke, a phrase which had been running through a jumbled dream remained in my head. I had been trying to lift Elizabeta over an immensely high wall, a barrier seemingly placed as a deliberate obstacle by someone hidden from view. Better the Garden of Eden, she had said, pointing to a muddy potato field covered with ice, than the desert of Auschwitz. I was agreeing with her, as I tried to raise her enormous bottom, magnificent and magnified as it was in the dream, to where she was able to see the horizon. Upon successfully climbing over, I found Hans waiting, smiling up at me, though, on recollection it might have been a sneer. I woke up as the alarm sounded off.

I made Theo a cup of tea, having raked up the coals to a cherry red. 'Wood, Theo, and coal and cheese, please.' Suddenly, unable to control myself, I bent down and kissed him on his upturned cheek. He smelt of warm sheets. 'Goodbye.'

'Take care,' he shouted after me. It was a strange comment. Of course I would take care, though perhaps he was, after all, only thinking of me.

The air on the quayside was almost mild, that special gentleness of the early dawn; the pores of the City were creaking open again after the hard winter. Chattering teeth and blue lips would be forgotten for the next nine months as Amsterdamers threw off their heavy clothes and replace them with summer shirts and light skirts. The brown skins of the buds on the trees also seemed looser, as if they were testing the wrappings, ready to cast them off on a signal. I smelled sap and wet wood, fish and tar, brine and seaweed rising over the winter blanket of soot and smoke generated by the trains above my head.

I pulled off my beret and undid the top button of my coat. The air intruded on my chest, causing my body to shiver for a moment reminding me there was still a way to go before I could call this summer. Above, in the sky, there was a ragged tear of blue, which sat between the twin spires of the station, criss-crossed a thousand times by the bare branches. In a short while, this sky would fill with yellow and green leaves and the Spring flower aroma would blow in from *Noordwijk*.

At lunch I got ready quickly to go out again to meet Gretel. She had looked so wretched and forlorn. I did not want to be late, making her worry further.

'Don't be late, Ruth. We are Spring-cleaning this afternoon.'

The same bench was free, which allowed me to relax, head up in the sun, coat off and sleeves rolled up. I might have drifted off for a moment or two except my concern of getting back to the bakery in time for the afternoon shift. Besides, I had a plan to talk over with my superior, an idea arising out of listening to Theo in the evenings.

All at once I snapped open my eyes. There was still no sign of Gretel, and I had to get back. It was strange, for she had been so insistent on the meeting, and to continue the discussion. It would not, I am sure, be the first time she had stood someone up, as her mind wandered over a new shopping trifle or a drink with a new boyfriend.

I walked back quickly, shrugging off a nudging worry. I could not fight more than one thing at a time; first and foremost was how to find Theo a job he could hold down.

That afternoon I scrubbed floors and walls, cleaned out ledges and crevices of old flour, which had turned black and mouldy and removed dried pastry cut-offs. It was no different from the cleaning I had done on the boat, though this time I was being paid for it.

'You've done enough for today, Ruth. This is excellent work,' The Manageress appeared genuinely pleased, making me blush with pleasure. I did not get enough compliments in my life.

'Perhaps I could have five minutes of your time, Madame.'

'Come and sit down, Mae,' she used my nickname for the first time and pulled out two bentwood chairs from a table. She smelt of hot body odour for she had been just as active as me. I noticed the other girls had all gone home some time ago.

'I have an idea to help the shop and, at the same time help a friend, my friend Theo.'

'Er, yes. Tell me Mae, there are rumours you are living with this man on a boat. Is this true?'

The news that she knew I was on the *Kuijpers* was quite shocking. Someone must have made a point of telling her, almost as if it was a deliberate act to get me into trouble. I had to remain calm. 'Yes, if you mean do I live on the same boat with him. But, no, I do not live with him in the sense of man and wife. I do not sleep with him and I am still a virgin. I just needed somewhere to live after I came home.'

The Manageress seemed slightly shocked by the use of the word virgin, but I saw no need for her to pry further into my private affairs; besides, it was the truth. 'Theo is a very sick man, Madame. In the head, that is. I want to help him. He once saved my life and I want to see if I can help him in return. By doing so, the shop benefits as well. I owe him something, don't I?'

'Well, if you put it like that, yes.'

'I have an idea,' I repeated. 'I want to buy the bread which is left over at the end of the day. All the loaves you throw away, or give away. At present, you get nothing for it; do you, so it is a loss element on your balance sheet. This is right, is it not?'

The Manageress nodded in confirmation. 'You sound as though you have had training in accounts. Yes. It is wasted, most of it, that is. Not a lot, of course, because we control it well, but there can be six or seven loaves each day. The little cakes which do not last go to the staff.'

'I will pay you half the selling price on the bread. Cash. Each day when I leave work, when the shop is closed and you cannot get any further sales.'

'Oh really. Half price but-'

'Otherwise you get nothing, Madame. When you close the shop for the day that is when the business closes itself off for sales. Bread has a shelf life of just one day. No Amsterdamer will buy bread which is twenty four hours old, will they?' I tried to speak politely, so as to make sure she was always in control of the discussion. 'If I buy the bread, your sales will increase and there will be no wastage at all. Your production is guaranteed, each day, every day of the week and you can report to your boss you have no wastage. If you were selling volume bread to a client, he would probably ask for a discount anyway.'

There was a very long pause during which she scanned my face as if to see there was a flaw, some devious plan perhaps which a Jew was trying to hatch.' An idea came into her head. 'What about payment? We would need guarantee of payment.'

'It can be deducted from my wages, so it is also a guarantee in itself. If I don't work I wont be needing the bread, and vice versa. Also, if I do not pay you for the bread on any one day, you do not give me the bread: you are twice insured, that is a lot more than some of our account customers who seem to pay when it suits them.'

'And what are you going to do with all of this bread?'

I plunged on, like a swimmer going for a gold medal. 'I am going to make them into sandwiches, like the English soldiers were always doing. Two slices around a whole range of fillings.'

'And who is going to eat all of these? Your man?'

'No, no, Madame. His appetite is big enough as it is already. No, he is going to sell them to the boat villagers, the fishermen, the tug men, the pilots. Theo will go from boat to boat taking orders for the next day when he delivers the sandwiches. This cuts down from two to one visit each day. More efficient, you see. The next morning early, before the men go to sea, he will deliver them all ready for their lunch.'

This time the silence was even longer. The woman was astute, the reason why, no doubt, she was in charge of the shop. 'This is an awfully clever idea, Mae. It could actually work, you know. What does you friend, Theo think of all this?'

'Er, he doesn't know about it yet, Madame. You see it is no good getting him excited if you won't sell me the bread in the first place. I need to buy cheaper bread to start with, if I am to be competitive with my customers making sandwiches themselves.'

'I don't suppose they have much time to make anything in the morning.' The manageress shuffled uncomfortably in her chair, unused to making such a decision. Finally, she stood up. 'Very well. We have an agreement, but only if I deduct the cost each day from your wages. When do you want to start?'

'Tomorrow,' I answered, feeling a great pressure lift from my mind.

'Where did you get such an idea?'

'It is hard to believe, Madame, from the camp, in fact. Time was the one thing we had in abundance. Because I was a bit fitter than many others, especially towards the end, and a little bit fatter due to the fact I was a serving girl, it became my job to run errands for the sick and the dying, a cup of water, a crust of bread. Often, I had to choose whom I would go to help. Help someone, for example, who was too weak, who then died, meant I had nothing for another who might have made it through the night.'

'God preserve us. You had to make those sorts of decisions…and daily…and at your age?'

'You get used to anything in time, Madame. Anyway, it allowed me to think of how I could deliver food and drink to lots of people at the same time. It took my mind off the awful days, the reality of my life. It made me dream that one day I could run a business, doing just what I have described to you. Here I am, hoping to put it into practice.'

'Hmm,' said my immediate boss. 'I shall have to watch you. You could be managerial material one day. This bakery is going to have to expand soon, what with the peace and more money in people's pockets. There is a big market out there to tap.'

'Exactly, Madame. What ever else the Dutch people do, they will always have to eat and drink. It is the last thing you do before you die.'

'You have your bread. Don't let these activities get muddled with your proper work here, will you?'

'No Madame. The idea is to let Theo do the work. I will supply the bread.'

As I walked back to the quay, I channelled a dozen phrases through my mind, each one an alternative way of introducing Theo to my plan. Selecting the best one from the rest was essential if he really found it difficult to understand what my plan was all about.

I arrived back at the tug, to find a police car close to the *Kuijper's* hawser. Two men inside, were smoking, and had made the windows mist up, making it difficult to see out at all. The black car, black uniforms with their peaked caps made me shudder, Dutch insignia though they were.

'*Mejouffrow Epstein?*'

'Yes,' I answered, terrified and turned around to make eye contact. I heard a door open and waited for their rough hands on my shoulders. Often, it had been a rifle butt into the small of my back; instead, they merely paraded around me to check my face.

'Do you know a Gretel Neumann?'

'I have met her twice,' I could answer truthfully, so I took it into my mind to stare the first man out, challenging him to hit me. I remembered then…this was after the war, police did not go around hitting people, not unless they were hooligans in a strike. They were Dutch people, not German pigs. 'But she is not a friend.'

'An acquaintance then?'

'Hardly. I have talked to her, twice,' I persisted.

'You were to have met her here, today?'

'In town, not here.'

'I'm sorry. She left you a note.'

'I don't understand. Why give you a note instead of meeting me-' I stopped talking. I did understand. 'She's dead, isn't she?'

'Why do you say that?'

'Because there would be no reason for the City to tie up two policemen and a car just to hand me a note.'

'I'm sorry,' the first one repeated. 'Yes, she is dead.'

'How did she die?'

'She threw herself into a canal. Left her bag on a bench, inside which we found a note. Both were handed to us. It was difficult to know if she died first of drowning or exposure. We will find out later, after the autopsy. Could she swim?'

'I have no idea.' I knew so little about her I could not see how I could be of help. I thought of the lovely dress she had been in the last time I had seen her, only the day before. Now it could be muddied and soaked, covered in canal slime and filth. 'Oh God,' I wept silent tears. Two women I had known, both dead, both at their own hand. I took the note. 'Thank you for telling me.'

'We need to have the note back…for evidence…for the coroner, you see. But we thought you would want to read it first.'

'I see.' It was addressed to me correctly.

Mae Epstein   Quay 4. Berth 114
Sleep boot Kuijpers

I shall not be able to meet with you today. You are the first person I feel I could trust and I really wanted to talk more with you in the park. I am very frightened, as there is someone else involved in the problem we talked over, who I did not tell you about.

Having thought it over, I have changed my mind on everything I said and I do not want to discuss it any more. There's no point going on any further...

It was unsigned and I could not make out if there should have been further text as the paper was almost reduced to pulp before it had been dried. The policeman took the leaf of paper back from me as soon as he could see I had read it. He proceeded to reread it himself, several times. 'What does she mean by this, do you think?'

For some reason, based on several years of survival training, I suppose, I became cautious.

'I have no idea, officer. She was going to meet me today, at lunch, to ask me to try and help solve some problem or other, the subject of which I don't know.'

'It is curious, don't you think, Miss, when you hardly know her, your words I believe, for her to ask you to solve an important problem of hers?'

'I don't know, officer,' I was beginning to sound like a parrot. 'I didn't meet her, you see. Besides, she did not say it was important, your words, I believe.'

The officer looked sharply at me for a moment, but did not rise to my bait. 'Did you know she was the girlfriend, at one time, of Hans Maas...of this boat next door, er berth.' He jerked a thumb towards the *Anna Rosner*. 'It was she who put him in prison in the first place.'

'I know of the story, officer. But, as I say...'

'Alright, alright. I get your drift. But, we will need to keep this,' he held up the sad little scrap of paper. 'Do you live here?'

'Yes,' I replied, suddenly tired and weepy. It felt as if my period was coming on.

'Is there something the matter, Mae?' It was Theo, thank God, arriving from the wheelhouse.

'No, nothing, Theo. The girl, the one who knew Hans, she's killed herself.'

Theo gave me an incredulous stare. 'That is very sad, even though I never met her. But you were talking to her, only too recently.'

'So, you couldn't add anything to this matter, Sir?'

'I suppose…having to face up to an enquiry… with all those newspaper men in Court, charged, perhaps… with wasting police time, and worse, accused of lying…'

As usual, he had not finished his sentence, but, surprisingly, he had directed himself into the main thrust, which had passed also through my own mind. This could have been the main reason, after all. It certainly made the two police officers frown in unison. Perhaps they had recognised this could be the real motive, rather than the casual implications they appeared to have pulled down from the sky.

'You mean,' the senior man said, 'the embarrassment of having to own up to having made the whole story up?'

'I said just that.' Theo began to shamble about, his shoulders hunched in a familiar way, eyes out of focus.

'She had a powerful father, influential and very rich,' I added helpfully. 'Imagine what he would have said, or done when he found out. How awful for Gretel.'

I saw again her body, drifting in the black water, her hair like tangled seaweed, pulled from the canal with hooks and ropes. Laid out on the quayside, her beautiful face washed of makeup, the bitter cold of the water would have ironed out the soft features, into a rigid mask. None of this made any sense, despite what I had said previously.

Then I said something stupid. 'Are you absolutely sure she killed herself?'

The policeman was turning away, considering the interview was over. He stopped. Damnit! I could have bitten my tongue off.

'Why do you say this?'

I panicked. 'I have no idea, officer. It just came into my mind.'

'Look, officers,' said Theo. 'Can we go inside. It's getting cold and dark.'

'She wrote a note. If the handwriting is hers, this will close the case. You can go in, Sir.' The man sniffed as he shrugged himself deeper into his coat. 'We'll be in touch, but do not leave the area unless you first contact our office. We may need to talk this over with you again in the future.'

'We are going nowhere,' said Theo, unaware of the double meaning behind his words. He pointed towards the *Kuijpers*.

Once inside the cabin, with the stove doors wide open, Theo tackled me. 'What on earth was that all about?'

'I don't know, honestly I don't. I told the truth out there. Gretel never kept her rendezvous with me, because she was already dead. It must be suicide, mustn't it? Whether she couldn't face a Court, because she made up the entire story about the war or, if she didn't want Hans to go to prison, because she loved him, doesn't matter, does it? Either could have pushed her to the edge.'

Theo shivered involuntarily, and took several deep draught of air into his lungs. I hated the signs. 'I'm going to make you something special tonight. I bought some Indonesian spices. They are quite cheap.'

Theo's stomach and nose became simultaneously aroused, and his thoughts switched from the death of an unknown girl to more relevant matters. 'How long to wait?'

'Half an hour. And, I want to talk something over with you, something important for you. Can we go to the bar again…for a small drink?'

He was puzzled by my words. 'Of course,' he replied. 'The money goes further now, what with you buying food as well. We could have two drinks if you like.' He chuckled, his earlier fears banished to the forepeak where we both were minded to dump the problems we couldn't handle.

He was quiet while we ate, like a man preoccupied, enjoying his food more even than his large appetite normally permitted. He kept saying: 'Good, good,' privately to himself and, occasionally, letting out a thin, continuous noise, as if I were not in the room. His attention to his food let me ponder over the sadness of the news and my own, silly words, spoken, I suppose in reaction to the shock. I had no idea if the note was in her own hand writing, though I had to assume it was, otherwise it could only mean someone had forged the letter deliberately before killing her… and that was stupid. Of course, if this *had* been the case, he or she knew she had been coming to see me. Who had told this person, and how did they know about me? I was a nothing, not known here, a non-person. I gazed at Theo. He looked up suddenly, smiling, seeing my troubled face.

'It's good, its bl-, it's very good. Never have I had such a meal in my life. There is no need to worry. You are such a good cook.'

He had no idea of the reservations, rushing in, churning up my mind. What frightened me most was how my thoughts continued to return to the single aspect of Gretel's death. Other than Theo, and I could discount him couldn't I, Gretel's death would have benefited only one person that I knew? But, that was before she told the police she had made the story up, so he had no motif but, again, Greta had said he was guilty all along. Her double lie made everything totally muddled. Hans: it kept coming back to him, and he was alive, eating not five metres from me in the next boat.

'Stupid!' I said to myself. 'Come on Theo, we'll wash up later. I want to talk with you.'

As we walked along the quayside, side-stepping a new delivery of hardwood planks, he took my arm again naturally, as if he had done this all of his life. I pressed my arm to hold his tightly. I did not want it to slip away.

'What is all this mystery, Mae? What do you want to talk about? Is it about Gretel?'

I laughed shortly for it must have seemed to him it was the only subject on my mind. 'No! No! No! It is not about her at all, honestly. It is about you, and you will have to wait until I have my glass of sherry in front of me.'

The Three Windmills had a bunch of noisy sailors gathered around the bar with as much beer on the floor as inside their bellies. The fireside was clear, however, and I took a seat watched by the hungry men eyeing me up, sizing up Theo. Realising I was, at best, plain, with no breasts to speak of at all, they returned to a very rude joke about a Dutch boy, preventing a dam being breached. The Landlord acknowledged my stare with a slight nod of recognition to his head.

'So, what is this all about?' Theo couldn't wait any longer.

Instead of replying, I sipped the sweet liquid to collect my thoughts. 'Do you always want to do the same thing all your life?' I began by asking a question. 'I mean, wouldn't you like to have a small business for instance?'

'What! On my own? I don't think so. The responsibility, you see.'

'No, I don't see, Theo. What if I were to help you?'

I knew how to handle him despite his fear, and I proceeded as carefully on the matter as I would handle a piece of fine china.

He was curious. It was the very fact I was prepared to be beside him, which caused him to look up over his beer.

'What sort of business?'

I launched myself into the main theme. 'Every night, the bakery throws away the bread it has not sold during the day. It always makes extra in case of a sudden demand. I have arranged to buy these, each evening…at half price.'

Theo looked bemused. He let the bar clock chime, nine times, a clear, though tinny sound against the sailors' crude laughter. 'That is good for one loaf, Mae, but what do we do with all the others? We cannot eat more than one loaf a day, surely?'

'We are not going to eat any of them, Theo. We are going to turn them into sandwiches, like the English eat them, with two pieces of bread around a filling. We will pack ours with all sorts of different fillings and then we go and sell them to the tuggies and all the other owners of the boats out there. They cannot have much time in the morning, before they go to work, to make up a bite to eat and certainly not enough time to go into town and buy something. There are so many boatmen like us…you I mean, then there are visitors in the summer especially, and it is growing again each year now; even the Custom boats, and the pilots. Amongst all of these, there must be thirty or so sandwich orders we can get.'

'But, you are working. You have a good job. When would you sell them?'

'Not me, Theo. You. You will sell them. We will make the sandwiches together at night, after I come back from the bakery with the bread. Next morning, you will deliver them and take the next day's order at the same time, saving you a trip. You can have a list of fillings and prices with you, so they can choose themselves, and will only have to look at one column to select what they want. Your most important job will be to make sure the right sandwich gets to the right boat…and in time before they leave to go to work,' I added.

He sat, legs apart and swinging, his lanky body swaying slightly to the rhythm of the movement, arms hanging, as always between his thighs as he gazed at me trustingly. He was attempting to come to terms with my plans. I wanted so much, for him to agree to the idea I stopped breathing for a time.

'Well…' A long pause followed.

'See here; imagine you are a tug man, off up the *Ij* early each morning. You leave at quarter to seven, before the shops are open and you get back after they are closed. Besides, if you like to lie in bed until the last moment you have a real problem. No time to make your lunch, only time to get into your trousers and pull your braces up. This is how you sell the sandwiches to the men, Theo. Paint a picture to them of how easy it will be for them. Imagine, Theo, as you are pulling on your boots the shop comes to you, with fresh bread and your favourite filling already wrapped, just to your liking, like your own favourite cheese, or sausage.'

'Well-'

I pressed on before he could waver. 'Fresh onion, sauerkraut, mustard as an extra, smoked ham,' I battered at his will, knowing I was making his saliva start working afresh. He took a quick sip of his beer. 'Hang on, hang on, Mae. I was just going to say, if this is your idea, why don't you do it yourself. You are so efficient, so strong. You could argue with the tuggies.

'Because I want you to be that person. As you said, I have a job; now it is your turn. Something for you to look forward to each day. You know the people in the basin, from the Harbour Master down to the smallest tug. You will find new customers, expand the business, and watch it grow. Delivering the special requests, like birthdays and anniversaries. Tell you what, why don't I come with you on the first evening or so? No one has anything to lose. Cash on delivery for the customers. If they don't like them, well, we'll eat them ourselves, for supper.'

Despite his fears, Theo smiled at me. 'Later, we could sell hot potatoes with different fillings for these, in the evenings, when they come back from work.'

My heart ached painfully against my ribs. I smiled also, and kissed him on the cheek. 'We must think of the fillings, and how much to charge. I will work out what it will cost…and add in the profit, of course. We must keep records as well.'

It was my dear Father talking. I could hear him at that moment as if he were in the room. He would always write everything down and calculate expenditure and profit, no matter how small the transaction. That way he was able to work out if it was worth doing, before he lost any money.

It was only later, as I sat at the table under the single light, writing out menus on pieces of card I had found, I was reminded of the earlier events of the day. Poor Gretel, how easily she was being forgotten. I imagined the scene again: being hauled over the edge of the police boat, as water drained from her open, gasping mouth, and the grim policeman who asked strange questions, as though this was not an open and shut case for him. Perhaps he always treated cases like this? Would they have asked so many questions if it had been an ordinary suicide? Possibly, this was quite normal.

'...course, many of the boats are moored in the middle of the harbour.' Theo broke into my thoughts, echoing slightly as he raised his voice to make sure I had heard him.

'Yes.'

'Well, how do I reach them?'

'You, Theo, are a boatman. You will have to work out a plan, wont you? I'll help you,' I added, deciding this was too big a leap for him to take on his own. Doubts had begun to furrow his brow. 'All problems are there to be resolved.' It was my Father again. Strange, how he had begun to feature more strongly, now in death than he had before he was taken away. His quiet way of teaching was beginning to mean something to me, even above those of my Mother.

As night fell, my worst fears returned in a shocking nightmare. I was back in the camp. I could read each rough knothole in the planking of the wall next to my bunk. I could recall every texture of the wood. Suddenly, without warning, the hut door had crashed back against its hinges. My Father stood, framed in the doorway, dressed in the uniform of a Gestapo officer. His hands were on his hips and he kept repeating the phrase: 'Get up and work.' He pointed to someone on the bunk below me. When nothing happened and no one moved, he strode, with enormous goose steps to where I lay and reached down to pull out the miserable wretch below me. He was mouthing vengeance all the while.

It was Theo, with seaweed hair and blood gushing from his mouth who was being strangled by my Father. A light burst into my eyes, and I screamed out, 'Father!' realising as I did, my dream had already ended. I had shouted out, after the cabin lantern had been illuminated. I was awake and Theo was holding my shoulders, trying clumsily, but sincerely, to calm me.

'You've been dreaming, screaming as well,' he said by way of explanation. 'I thought that was *my* job,' he added, trying to bring a glimmer of humour to the scene.

I turned my head fearfully, searching for the German, but my Father had disappeared into the night and the back of my head. The forepeak door was closed, shutting off the place where Theo and I kept our secrets.

'I had a bad dream,' I ended stupidly, aware both of my breasts were half exposed to his eye, for I seemed to have torn my nightshirt buttons off the cloth. Theo though, pulled the cover over me with a curiously gentle action of a hand.

'You were twisting so much; the cloth got caught around your neck and was choking you.'

This time, I laughed aloud as I wiped the drying tears against his bare wrist. 'I am such a silly Billy at times.'

'No, you are not,' his response was immediate and very positive. 'I know you share the same place as me at night. We walk along the same paths at times. When you are afraid to look at the end of the bed, so am I. Often, when the walls creak and groan, I know they are the same demons leaning on the outside, waiting to …to,' he couldn't describe the experience, 'swallow me. That's silly too.'

'Maybe, the demons are not demons, but a friendly wind knocking on the hull, waiting to blow you across the sea to where ever you want to go?'

'Hmm,' he smiled,' that's a bit far-fetched,' he was pleased with the word. '

'But you see what I mean. These things you see at night may not be bad at all, just that you…and I for that matter think they are evil. Maybe we should challenge them sometimes, see if he react.'

He kissed me on the forehead, like a brother would, and tucked the blanket tight to my body. I felt safe, safer than when my Mother was with me. I could feel the heat of his legs through the cloth spreading to my whole body.

When I woke in the morning, I found myself in exactly the same position as when he had kissed me goodnight. I hadn't stirred, nor had I had a repetition of the awful nightmare. Theo pulled back the curtain screen shyly. It had always been me before.

'Tell me some fillings of sandwiches. I want to go out and try and sell some.'

'Hang on, Theo.' I tried to get out of bed, but my nightdress had ridden up to my stomach as it always did every night. 'We have to buy the fillings; you have to show them the menus I have written. What about the prices? I haven't decided on those yet. For the first few mornings, we will have to accept what we buy may not be wanted, or our customers may ask for something we cannot supply. We can't start a business saying no can we?'

Theo shook his head in amazement and concern at his own lack of understanding of modern commerce. 'I'm no good at business things, but you seem to know all about it.'

'Scratch a Jew, Theo. But, you are wrong. You are the person who knows the waterfront, the people who live on the boats, and the food they like to eat. You know their names and how to talk to them, understand their businesses. You know who leaves really early in the morning and those who come back first after work…that's important. You cannot say, hey, you. You must say, Meinheer or Mevrouw of course. Better to address them as Good morning Michiel- or, its a nice day, Mevrouw Anna'

'I thought I would offer them herring, pate, sausage, you know, the raw one, cheese, cheese and pickles, onion,' Theo might have gone on dreamily for some time.

'You've been thinking about this, haven't you?' I answered happily, catching his mood.

'Ever since I watched you go back to sleep…' He stopped, realising what he had said and was too embarrassed to continue for a moment. 'I was worried you might have another bad dream and strangle yourself like the first time. His behaviour would certainly have been frowned upon, by his grandmother I am sure, while his grandfather would have smiled behind a hand while trying to reinforce his wife's morals: I liked the idea… a lot.

'It was awful, the screaming, I mean. It frightened the hell out of me.'

'You are quite a dear man, Theo.' I meant it and the fact astonished me. I could not believe I was becoming fond of this demented soul, a spirit as uncontrolled as my own, but he was becoming a regular feature in my daily life, and it felt good. 'I think that range will do well, for a start. We can change the list as often as demand makes of us. Now, I must get up and go to work, while you have to go off to the boats with the menu. Later we can get the menu printed to look professional. We will price them all at twenty cents each. Once we find which are popular we can put the price up to twenty five cents…or so,' I added the rider, to cover myself, but spoiled it with a giggle.

Theo looked at me in a new way. 'What time do I deliver?'

'It's for you to decide, boss. If we make them tonight, wrap them well to keep them fresh through the night, then you must get them delivered before the first boat sets off for the day, and certainly before your clients leave.'

'Of course.' Theo was annoyed for not having seen the obvious. 'First boat out is usually half past six.'

'All you have to do is to write down the boats name, the sandwiches they want, and the time. And…you must never make a mistake. Repeat the order out loud to the customer to ensure you have not misheard him, or her. Mistakes mean less business.'

'There's a great deal of responsibility in all this,' he replied, biting his lips in stress. I noticed the chrome of his dungarees buckles were worn to rust and made a mental note to buy some new buttons. His blue eyes had trapped the light to such an intense degree, they seemed to shine out directly, almost as two beams, which held my face, just as a torch at night on the polders, will freeze a rabbit into submission.

'Good luck,' I said, pulling the blanket about me firmly. 'Off you go.'

* * * *

When Mae left the *Kuijpers* for work that morning, her heart was embroiled in a thousand differing thoughts. As ideas bubbled to the surface, she failed to notice the police car parked discreetly, though not deliberately, behind a row of steel oil drums. The two men inside were cold, though it did not prevent them from casting their eyes carefully over her, for the time it took to cross the gangway and turn her back on them, before returning to study the *Anna Rosner*. A crack of opened window allowed a continuous stream of grey-blue cheroot smoke to leak out in a tangled ribbon, into the early morning mist. One nudged the other.

'Here he comes.'

It was Hans, leading the Family out to work. One of the officers' made a note of the time and yawned. 'Off to work,' he exclaimed, making an obvious remark. He was not the most highly paid official, nor with the highest degree of intelligence. 'Do we know if he works all day with his parents?'

'Yes. He's been checked out. What ever he did in the past, ended on the same day the Germans left the Netherlands. This surveillance is just a waste of time.

'Little you know. What if, just what if he has pushed the pretty lady into the *Singel*? That's murder. Modern, up-to-date murder, not something which may have happened eight years in the past.'

'The girl from the other boat. She was smiling when she left. She didn't appear too upset about the death of her friend, did she?'

'I noticed that, as well. Perhaps she has something to do with it as well. They live very close by, don't they? If we get him, well get her as well. He will talk in the end, just to get a lighter sentence. She made up some story she was his sister when she came to the Station but, it became obvious, pretty quickly, she was not related.'

'Jew girl, isn't she?'

'Yeah. You never know what they are up to, always planning something and never happy just to let the world go by.'

Further down the road, unaware of the surveillance team, the Family had caught up with Mae. Hans took hold of her arm from behind, making her start out of her daydream.

'What's Theo up to, today? Out so early, he beat us all this morning. What are you doing to him, Mae?' Pieter asked, with the inquisitiveness of a badger on his evening round of the molehills.

'I'm not doing anything to him, or for him. He's doing it himself. Theo's starting his own business, selling sandwiches to the boatmen.'

'Hardly a business,' said Jos without thinking.

'Twenty cents a sandwich. I reckon thirty to thirty-five a day. Say three hundred and fifty days a year. That's three thousand guilders a year. And we are buying bread at a fifty percent discount to cut down overheads.'

Pieter whistled, arching his eyebrows in amazement. '*That's* a business. But it assumes you sell thirty every day of the year.'

'True, but it is an average. Theo aims to sell more, much more but there will be holidays and high days to deduct.' She hadn't told Theo about the holidays yet. 'We intend to expand later: of course, we are talking minimum numbers here.'

'Of course,' said Jos. 'Your father was a good business man, wasn't he? He seems to have passed it on to you. You are something else,' he went on. Mae didn't quite know what he meant by that. 'This is just what might work in the harbour. No one is doing anything for the boat owners, and that goes for the big boats up stream of Central Station as well.'

Mae turned to face them all so they had to stop in mid-step. 'Tonight, you must all come to dinner. You will have to bring your chairs…and plates.'

'Glasses too, forks and knives,' said Mama solemnly but pleased with the invitation.

'Yes, perhaps so. I am not sure what Theo may have stored in the trunks, the ones I haven't opened yet. When we are eating, we can tell you of Theo's plan. The idea is the more people in the basin who are in the know, the more who may want to buy. Selling forward, my father used to call it. Well…sort of.'

'We'll come around at seven. It will give you time to cook, if that is acceptable?'

'Baked apples for pudding,' Mae said, turning to cross the street, before a tram rumbled down the slight hill and cut them off from sight for a moment. The spur of the moment decision had cast her mind into turmoil. The tram passed close by, clanging its bell in alarm while it ground its steel track into a bright polish. The driver had seen the young woman standing on the pavement edge as if to step off at any time. You could never tell. It had happened so many times before.

Focussing on the opposite side of the road, Mae saw a news billboard. From this distance she could still read the headline:

MYSTERY OF RICH GIRL'S DEATH.

The Potato Eaters

It had to be the story of Gretel, she knew, but why was it all a mystery? She had killed herself, perhaps for all the wrong reasons, though in the end, she had decided to end her short life. No mystery in that. Maybe the mystery lay in the fact she had done it at all, when she had everything to live for. It made Mae frown as she threaded her way through the hundreds of travellers spilling up the steps from the station onto the Square. Preoccupied, she ploughed through the stream at right angles, ignoring near collisions and the glances of annoyance from those latest for work.

'I shall be out this morning, Mae,' said the Manageress, on her arrival. 'I want you to take charge of the other girls when they arrive.'

'Yes, of course Madam, but does this mean I am not to leave the shop at lunch? I need to buy some things for a supper party this evening.'

The older woman studied the anxious face across one of the marble pastry tabletops. 'I will be back by then. I thought you might like to try the responsibility.'

'I do, I do, Madam. Thank you very much and there is no need to worry while you are away.' Mae realised she had not responded as positively as she might have done.'

'Very well then, and no, I shall not worry. I have every confidence in you. And, don't forget, you will be buying our left-over bread this evening?'

'Yes.' She remembered her plan all too well and wondered how Theo was getting on. She hoped he was already busy walking round the boats, one by one, knocking on hatches and wheelhouse doors, being polite but selling hard.

She enjoyed the morning and found she was in her stride within half an hour. By now, she knew all of the regulars by name and made sure her girls looked after them first. Her eye missed nothing, and, having less need to look after the customers directly, made several small changes to the presentation of the goods, such as the location of the bread rolls and the jars of honey, which had begun to arrive from overseas. She re-sited the till so the girls would not keep bumping into each other. If only we had another till, she realised, selling could be speeded up. Mae could see the queue did not have so long to wait for service, which meant the operation could reduce the number of staff and work just as efficiently or…she stopped in mid-thought. Last in, first out, as the old maxim on employment went. If she went on like this she would, effectively, sack herself.

At lunch, relieved of responsibility, she went out to shop, taking her time in choosing the best ingredients, while balancing these against her meagre resources.

'There are five loaves over,' said the Manageress as she locked the door at the end of the day. 'Twelve slices per loaf, gives you thirty sandwiches. That is quite a lot to sell.'

'We'll have to see, Madam.' She paused. 'Have you thought of doing it here, Madam? In the shop, I mean. Think of all the businesses around here, practically within touching distance. Fresh bread rolls, one girl out the back preparing the orders and a pile of them ready made under the glass shelf here.'

'Oh, I don't think so. We keep the cup cakes there. They sell well.'

'Certainly, but the mark up is sixty percent, I would imagine. A sandwich is two hundred. We sell fifty cakes a day. I reckon we could sell over a hundred sandwiches each working day. Besides, we can relocate the cakes in that empty showcase I saw in the flour store. We could put it on the side of the queue so they can study them while they wait. They won't be able to resist them, will they? Buying on impulse, my father used to say. So we get additional income, an additional outlet for the bakery and improved sales for the cakes.'

'Where on earth do you get all of these ideas, Ruth?'

She shook her head. 'I don't know, well, Father, I am sure. He was a very good businessman, but certainly not from my Mother. By the way, did you see the move I made of the till?'

'Yes. Why did you do that?'

'I have speeded up service. The customers do not have to queue for so long. Means we can get rid of a member of staff in the future, or, better still, we can sell more and keep all the staff.'

This time it was for the Manageress to shake her head. 'I see.'

As Mae stepped from the bakery delivery door, she realised it was still daylight for the first time in the year. There was a scent in the air as a million blooms trapped the evening air and blew the tangy result in from the coast. Across the road, women were still sitting under hair dryers or were having their hair washed in the smart salon. She watched, wistfully, as a client, hair now shining, emerged, the door respectfully held back by a girl,

'One day,' she said to herself. 'One day.'

She shouldered her purchases and her large bag containing the bread. She prayed Theo had been successful. Apart from the waste, her plans to help him would collapse before they ever had a chance to succeed.

If she had turned her head, she might have noticed the two policemen who had questioned her, were back, sitting in their car, smoking in long, deep draughts as one does when there is a long wait ahead.

'Theo! Theo, I'm home,' she called before she reached the wheelhouse. The door was locked. Anxiously, she opened it with her own key. Immediately, she knew he wasn't there. The tug was dead. 'Oh, Theo.'

She was so disappointed and so much to do. The meal for the Family and the need to find out how many sandwiches had to be made…if any. And where on earth was he? On a whim, she went up on deck but there was no sign of him on the *Anna Rosner*. Nor were the Family back from work.

Bitterly upset but promising herself he would be back soon, she stoked the fire until the range glowed red. Into the oven she laid the big cooking apples soaked in treacle and stuffed with currants she had bought from the bakery. Her eyes roamed the table, estimating, with a squeeze, she could fit everyone around its edge…including Hans. Now he was back, he made eight.

All at once, she was happier. She dismissed the sad episode of Gretel's death and the strange questions from the Police. Here was home; here was a place of peace, a house sparkling and shining with beeswax. She turned to her stew, still wondering where Theo had gone, perhaps to a bar, where he could forget the fear of going out on the water. Overhead, she could hear the Family clattering tiredly across the gangplank already planning to take off their muddy boots and stretch their toes. A few minutes later, there was a knock on the door overhead. It was Mama.

'Chairs…and plates,' she said by way of greeting. She stood aside as the men folk carried in the stools. Mae received a kiss from each of them in turn, smelling the dank, raw smack of the earth, which blended moodily with their sweat.

'Anything we can do?' Despite her tiredness, Elizabeta found it difficult to restrain herself as her eyes darted across the pots. The smell of hot cinnamon and black treacle drifted in the cabin, making Pieter's mouth water in anticipation.

'No thanks. It is all under control.'

'Where's Theo?'

'I don't know Pieter. I was rather hoping you could tell me.'

Suzannah and Anna exchanged glances. 'I'm sure he is close by. He has got distracted for he is never away at this time of the day.' Mama answered for them all reassuringly.

'Maybe,' said Mae. 'See you in an hour.'

'Very well then.' Pieter ushered the Family out of the cabin allowing the room to expand to full size again.

It was twenty minutes later as she was pulling the apples from the oven, she felt a touch on her shoulder. Jerking up in surprise, she came face to face with Theo.

'So, where have you been? Apart from cooking for eight, I thought you might, at least have been here to tell me how you-'

'What do you mean eight for supper?'

He had, at least, a right to be told he was entertaining that evening, before the guests arrived. And in his own house. She burst into tears at her discourtesy.

She remembered, only in a dim and distant past, the sort of reassurance he now brought. Like her Father before him, when she had been upset, Theo's encircling arms, clumsy though they might be, held her in an embrace, where all she had to do was to let her head lie on his shoulder. It smelt of flowers, hyacinth perfume.

'You've been to the fields,' she said at last, not wanting him to move.

'I smelt them blowing in from the coast. I wanted to see the colours after the grey of winter. So, I thumbed a lift.'

'I should have asked you first. Pieter and the Family are coming to supper in about thirty minute's time.'

He wiped a half dried tear from her cheek. 'Excellent. We can repay them for all their hospitality. Your cooking and their company.' She raised her head for the first time. She could hear a new confidence in his voice. It was still hesitant, the stumbling sentences, the faint lisp were there, but it was stronger, not the whisper of yesterday when she had had to bend down at times to

The Potato Eaters

hear what he had to say. Like the coming of Spring, Theo was throwing out a new shoot.

'Hello. We can't wait. Can we come down?' It was Suzannah, closely followed by Hans and Jos. Anna held glasses. The others grasped knives and forks; Jos held aloft, a stone flagon of the fermented apple juice. Each one kissed Mae three times, for the second time of the evening and shook hands with Theo.

'So, you are back,' Mama directed her stern gaze, though it remained so for a fleeting second before opening into a smile. She was halfway down the steps, allowing the rail to take the weight of her broad shoulders. Theo's blown kiss reminded Mae of a child's action.

'You smell of hyacinths? You have been to *Noordwijk*, haven't you?' Suzannah was quick to notice the smell.

'How do you know I have been to *Noordwijk* rather than some other place?'

'Because the hyacinths are concentrated in the fields, east of the town this year.'

'You should be a detective.' Theo laughed out loud, a hoarse sound, one he still found difficult to control. 'Which reminds me, those police are back? Have they been speaking to you, Mae?'

'No. Please sit down where you want, only leave me a seat by the stove.'

The Family needed no bidding, breaking the bread into a spray of crumbs on the red and white checked cloth, whose ironed creases stood out in parallel ridges. Mama grunted approval to herself, and cast barely concealed covert glances in Mae's direction.

'Why,' asked Theo,' are the police here? I understood they had all the information they wanted.'

'It's in the paper. Headlines on the billboards all over the city.'

Jos looked up sharply. What? Gretel's suicide?'

'Well, her death, at least,' said Mae.

'But…why are they still here then? A suicide is a suicide, isn't it?'

'Except when it turns out to be murder.' Mae had a knack of throwing all conversation into disarray.

'That is silly,' said Jos, shrugging his shoulders at the proposal. 'She was found in a canal with a note on the quayside.

'Why else are the police here, still snooping around the harbour, unless they have made a mistake. How did you know about the note, Jos?'

'It is in the papers. There is a transcript. The note is addressed to you.'

'Really?' said Mae. 'A suicide note made out to someone she hardly knew. How sad she had no one better to write to, her father for instance. He should have been the person, shouldn't he?'

'Not necessarily,' said Hans. 'Suicides do strange things at times. After all, they are no longer rational at that stage are they? Imagine yourself, about to take your own life. All normal reasoning, surely, would have gone completely. All washed away–'

'Yet I hear suicides often take great care to ensure, not only are their deaths comfortable and pain-free but they make a full explanation to their loved ones of why they are doing it. Even in the camp, many people who killed themselves told us when and how. I accept it was a bit different in those days for it was only advancing death by just a few days or weeks.'

Anna sniffed. She hated this sort of talk. 'Nice soup. What is it made from?'

'Motza meal, cabbage and onions mainly. I got some ginger from the bakery.'

'Hi, yi,' Mama wailed. 'And I smell the honey and cinnamon. You are so lucky working at the bakery.'

'We all love your cooking, Mama,' Hans chirped in defensively.

'But it would be nice.' She studied every move Mae made as she cleared the soup bowls, replacing the spoons, hastily washed, by each place. 'This is good. Everyone together again. Theo, Hans, Mae, everyone.' Suzannah positively beamed, stroking the arm, first of Hans on her right, and then turned her attention to Jos. Mama smiled at her daughter, content all was in its ordered space on the shelf. 'And what have we now?'

'*Cholent*,' Mae replied. 'Jews serve this on the Sabbath, but I cook what ever, when ever. It is made from brisket and butter beans, dumplings. More butter beans than brisket, but it will fill you up.' The men raised their noses to the hot aromas, different from the ones they knew, strange, exciting and slightly…foreign? Pieter licked his lips comparing each ladle portion,

'Who taught you to cook?' Mama demanded this time.

'Cook?' Said Mae, delaying her answer, knowing full well what she had meant.

'Yes, who taught you?'

'Cook? Oh, I see. Well, our own cook, in fact.'

'You had a cook? Just for yourself?'

'Well, all the family actually.' Mae realised she had got herself into another problem.

'I hear you are cooking for the whole boat community,' Pieter added archly, swinging his eyes across the table as if not believing the gossip he had picked up on the way home.

Theo, who had been quiet, decided to enter the conversation. He had enjoyed the atmosphere of the boat, the warmth of the cabin, alive and full of good people.

'Not cooking, you must understand.' He adjusted the light over the table to bring the source closer to the tablecloth. 'Only sandwiches.'

'How many have you sold today?' Asked Pieter.

'None today.' It made Mae compress her lips together. 'You see,' he went on,' we take orders one day, ready for the next day. Today being the first day we cannot have sold any until tomorrow.'

'So, how many tomorrow?'

'Forty-two.'

'Forty-two!' Mae almost screamed it aloud. 'You never told me. You went to see the flowers, you told me.'

'Yes, I did. But, only after I went round the boats. That's what we agreed, wasn't it?' He ended with slight alarm on his face. 'Seems everyone in the harbour thinks it a very good idea.'

Mae was behind his chair, meal forgotten, hugging his neck as she ran her fingers through his hair in unashamed delight and joy. She wiped away a tear. 'Theo, Theo that's wonderful. I really believed you hadn't bothered. Besides, you said nothing when you came in tonight.'

'You didn't let me speak.' He nuzzled his head into her cheek. Anna turned away, slightly embarrassed, though Suzannah gazed on raptly. The men had turned back to the food. It was far more interesting than the rather soppy, and slightly discomforting sight of the couple openly embracing, the sort of thing the French were reported as doing in some newspapers.

While they sucked the bones with their fingers and sliced through the fragrant dumplings, Mae's head was again in a whirlpool of ideas. Placed on temporary hold when Theo had not turned up on time, she was now committed to forty-two sandwiches, eighty-four slices of bread. 'What fillings?' She asked, as her thoughts surfaced without warning in the middle of a conversation on post-war politics.

'Here's the list,' said Theo, pulling a hand-written list in spidery writing. It had been much folded and was well creased. 'It's mostly cheese.'

'I need more bread,' said Mae.

'I've got plenty,' said Mama, seeing Mae's face. 'You can replace it out of your enormous profits.'

'You are going to be rich.' Suzannah smiled at Theo. 'Soon you will have a fleet of vans delivering sandwiches across the city.'

'Could be,' he answered slowly, realising the enormity of the venture about to unfold, at least in his mind. He batted his eyelids several times. It was too big even to contemplate. Mae, meanwhile, kept quiet. This was Theo's day. She couldn't have been happier for him. 'You'll have to get up early and I'm going late to bed, cutting all this bread.'

'I have a stone,' Pieter offered, making actions in the air as if to explain his words the better.

'Pity it is not already cut. A machine could cut it very fine, couldn't it?'

'Silly lady. It would make the bread go dry very quickly.'

'No, hang on. You could have an airtight bag. Machine wrapped. Greaseproof, perhaps and then sealed.' It was Mae off again on her production ideas.

Pieter still did not think much of the suggestion. 'I don't think it would last long, would it? Dutch people like their fresh bread each day.'

Mae went silent. It could work, she told herself, only how could she convince anybody of any of her ideas. She was a woman after all, and not a very pretty one at that. Pieter continued to suck noisily on the apple skin, refusing to let any remain on his plate, studying his Family from the rim of his spoon. He had enough money to be happy.

While they were undressing for bed, the sandwiches in stacks of greased paper wound tightly around the bread and covered in damp cloths, Mae called out to Theo through the curtain wall. 'Have you thought anymore about how to reach the boats in the middle? There are so many moored out in the basin.'

A long silence ensued. As always, when a new barrier was being considered, sometimes over several days, Theo often retreated back inside himself, while he examined the fence from every aspect. It took so long for him to reply, he could have been asleep, but he appeared through the curtain joint without first making sure she was decent. She was, luckily. Her shift fell demurely to the floor, leaving only her ankles exposed to his view.

'We would have to go out in my boat, row around. But, I'm not ready for that, Ruth, I don't think.' He used her proper given name. It was essential that she was able to grasp his viewpoint. 'One day, maybe. I feel I could ...I want to at times, you know, but Pieter's silly mistake...it scared me. If I took a boat out, you would have to be there.'

She felt strong, her thin chest thrust out against the demons, not only in her life, but his own. She knew she wasn't cured, probably never would be, for they were based upon real events, real terrors. But, his were imagined and could one day melt like the harbour mist on the promise of a hot day.

All at once, her wild character took over again, unthinking, she said: 'Do you want to make love, Theo?' Shit, shit, and shit she screamed inside herself.

He was still standing half in and half out of the blanket screen, which divided the night for them. He went back to his bunk and sat down, looking up at her. His eyes squinted in purpose, his arms hanging loose. 'Yes, one day Mae, but not until I am cured. I want to believe I am not imagining the whole thing.'

She felt hard and soft at the same time. She was standing by her bed, the only light from a single candle, which she kept by her bed. The thin nightdress was all that separated her flesh from his hands. He went on: 'I've never been with a girl, like you say, before. They used to laugh at me at school because I hadn't been with the one or two girls who would let you touch them for a packet of cigarettes.' He got up and kissed her on the forehead very slowly, leaning forward so he was able to sense her body was only the thickness of a cotton thread away from him.

The moment went as quickly as it came. She still felt hot and slack around her thighs, with her need. It wasn't rejection, and the idea of putting the want on hold, made her more determined to succeed sometime in the future.

'Those police,' he said, as he turned to go, 'It's all very strange, isn't it?'

'I don' know what to think, Theo. It is probably what the police do for every suicide, to see if there are any unusual circumstances. They were all around the house in Rotterdam, asking me strange questions. They even suggested I had had an abnormal...relationship with my mother's friend. Like, homosexual.'

'I thought it was only men who-'

'Apparently not. I think it was the awful woman who made me leave so quickly, who put them up to it. They were quite embarrassed themselves and it upset me a lot at the time, but they went away quite quickly and I have never heard from them again.'

'That's horrid.' Theo found it quite impossible to imagine two women together. He had enough problems seeing how a woman and a man could do what they were meant to do. 'Tell you what. Why don't we take the curtain down? It makes the room larger, not so pressing in on me.'

'What about...changing...in the morning?'

'I am going to change in the boiler room. It is so clean I could eat in there if I wanted. Besides, I will be up well before you. Or, you can just turn over in bed.'

'Just for tonight then.'

It was an almost surreal conversation. They had removed the last physical barrier between themselves leaving a clear path to change their relationship with each other. But, neither seemed willing to be the first to break the bond of the loop.

So, she lay in her bed, the aroma of toasted cinnamon and the residue of baked apples still in the cabin. Just after midnight, the moon rose, its light bringing the room into clear relief. Across the bed he lay spread-eagled, with the down quilt, half off his body, his steady breathing almost metronomic. She remained on her side, absorbing the swell of a rising storm in the main canal, content to lie, safe and snug, as if her own father was there to keep her safe.

Above on the quayside, the police car had long since gone, leaving only a pile of cheroot ends scattered on the cobbles. It appeared to draw a line across the case.

* * * * *

'Theo! Theo! There you are.'

He was up, emerging from the boiler room, hair slicked down tight to his skull though the curls on his forehead would only stay down until they dried. By the time he was across the gangplank they would have risen like dough, to bounce across his forehead. 'I'm off,' he said. And then:' Did you sleep well?'

'Yes,' I lied. I didn't tell him of Gretel, haunting the cabin, nor the howl of the storm in the rigging. The rain had soon blotted out the moon, so the shadow of Theo was lost, washed away in the darkness of the wall. 'Have you got your waterproof?'

'Yes.' He shrugged it on. It smelt of tar and long dried salt.

'Don't forget tomorrow's orders. I'll buy a bit extra today. I'm going to take a chance.'

'I like bread pudding, anyway.' He had packed the sandwiches into an old canvas sail bag. 'Wish me luck, Mae.'

'I wish you luck, Theo.' And I wished it as I never wished for anything before.

I went and lay on his bed, still warm from his body. I put my face down on the pillow, and tried to draw up his sweet smell. I pressed my body into the mattress as hard as I could, until I imagined it was his leg and stomach muscles I sensed beneath me.

During the tea break, the Manageress came through to me. 'So? Did you sell any bread for sandwiches?'

'Yes, Madame… but we had a problem. Not enough fillings. I had to borrow.'

'Well, that is a good problem to have, Ruth. Did all of the bread go?'

'Yes. We had to slice the loaves thinner than normal to get the right number. Forty-two in all.' I felt quite proud in replying.

'My goodness. We are going to have to increase our bake production here.'

'But, that will mean I will have to pay full price.'

The Manageress laughed. 'Not necessarily. We already have a discount on the unsold bread. We might be able to arrange for you to have a discount on the volume sale. It means the more you buy, the more we are able to agree some sort of reduction in cost.'

I knew all about discounts. My father had always sought it while not wanting to give one himself. 'It is very kind of you, Madame.' I couldn't think why she was doing all of this. It didn't make good business sense to me. 'I know all about discounting,-'

'But you do not know why I am doing this. Well, how would you like to do the same thing in the shop, as you suggested? You would be in charge of the operation, production and selling, orders, all of it.'

I didn't know what to say for the second time, though I could see if anything were to go wrong, it would be me who would have to accept the responsibility. Theo's welfare was important, but I was being offered something so much larger, exciting and a bit scary.

'Mae, of course you must go on helping Theo, after work. Your skill will help him to develop confidence. But, the bakery needs new directions so it can keep ahead of the rest of the competition. If this woks here we can repeat the operation in all of the other outlets.'

'I was thinking of quiches as well, Madame. Sell them by the slice, or whole.'

'You had better write it all down for me. A clear plan is what we need, before we can present this to the Company's Directors. Take an hour off at lunch and see what you can do.'

The storm had lessened its force by noon and I walked to the same place I had met Gretel. I brushed off drops of water from the bench and sat, a pad of paper in my hand and a pencil, chewed at its end despite the indelible ink.

'Hullo. It's Miss Epstein, isn't it?'

I looked up to see one of the policemen standing in front of me. His rain- coat was belted tightly to his body showing the build up of fat on his waist. The scant years of the war were gone.

'Mind if I sit down?' He swept a place for himself, having made the assumption I would automatically agree to his suggestion.

'I'm working,' I said. 'I'm very busy and have a deadline for the bakery to write a report by one o'clock.'

'My, you have an important job. Reports, deadlines, I must assume you are in management. Reports are all what my own job is about, it seems these days. Do you know, for every hour we are out on the street, we have to spend two hours writing it all up.' I nodded my head, not wanting to be drawn into the conversation.

'I would like to discuss one or two points with you concerning your friend's death. Shall we say five this evening?'

He knew what time I finished work, and where I spent my lunch hours. I nodded again. 'By the way,' I added by way of dismissal,' she wasn't a friend. I have told you that before.' He inclined his head in my direction by way of acceptance.

'I will see you here. Good afternoon.' He touched his peaked cap and walked off quickly, tucking his hands into his raincoat. I turned to my task. Though the words were easy to put down on paper, the day had turned curiously dull, as if there was another storm in the air. More rain, perhaps, I decided. A tram barrelled past, making me think it was thunder. 'Damn!' I shouted out. An elderly couple gave me a pitying stare.

The shop was busy in the afternoon, which allowed me to take my mind off the man's intrusion into my life again. The Manageress had said she would discuss the idea of going into production of quiches, but wanted trials made, and research on old recipes. I suggested one or two names and she went away, apparently highly pleased. At the end of work, I bought eight loaves, which appeared excessive, and hefted them towards Dam Square. There had never been eight loaves left over and I wondered if Madame had had anything to do with this. I was taking quite a chance in buying the lot, for, if Theo had had no success today, all of our profit would be wiped out at one blow.

The policeman was waiting for me. He had changed, though I could tell he was in the force despite his city clothes. He was now wearing a black leather jacket with a scarf tucked inside his lapels. His shoes were well worn, particularly at the heels. He obviously walked a great deal, despite the car I had seen.

'Miss Epstein,' he said for the second time that day, touching the brim of his soft hat without lifting it. 'You are punctual.'

'This is on the way home. I leave at five. It is now five past.' I couldn't think of anything else to say, and I wanted to be as coolly precise as he was, to make him understand I objected strongly to the intrusion into my life. For the first time since Gretel's death, I pondered on what I was getting into. I wanted Theo at my side. It would have made me that much stronger.

We sat on the same bench, the one with the peeling green paint on the knotholes, facing the Palace where the Royal Family had stood on the balcony window to meet their people after the end of the war. So much had moved forward since that day. It was only me who was drifting backwards in time. Theo, I said to myself, help.

The policeman was holding out the note, the same note I had seen before. He went straight into his questions. 'Notice anything strange about this?'

There were several, but I was not going to be the one to raise them. Nothing annoys a policeman, in my opinion, more than the public playing amateur detective.

'No.'

'There are several, Miss. First, suicides almost always make it clear they are going to kill themselves. Yes, she does say she is very frightened, but that is not enough in itself. She is frightened of someone else, not of the act she might have been committing to herself. Second, what is she frightened of? Third, Who is this someone else'?

I had noticed all of this when he had first shown me the note. It did not add up, making the policeman quite correct in pursuing his enquiries further. I pulled my coat tighter as the evening began to darken Dam Square. A wind had got up again, blowing last years leaves into yet another corner. They rustled impatiently, out of place with the coming summer.

'There is something very strange though. She did not sign it.'

'Is this strange, officer? I mean, do we know if it is her writing in the first place?'

'Yes, we have had it checked out by her father. He says it is absolutely hers, by a characteristic curl to some of her letters and not others.

'Of course.' He would not have mentioned it otherwise. Rule One: always check the evidence first. He thrust the note closer to me, right under my nose, in fact so I could smell the paper and the slightest touch of diesel.

'Something very strange indeed, it's only half a note, isn't it?'

This time he stopped me in half-formed reply. The trite, polite response had been already planned, though I should have noticed it before. I reached out to hold it, only to examine it closer, but he snatched it away. I suppose it was prime evidence, the type that hangs you. 'What do you think was on the other piece of paper?'

'I have absolutely no idea, at all officer. How could I? Perhaps she went on to say goodbye to her father. It would only be natural, wouldn't it? An apology for what she had done in the past, asking forgiveness? I simply did not know her well enough to answer you. You keep forgetting, I only met her twice.'

He ignored my words as he had ignored them in the past. 'Or... it could be to describe the person she wrote about, and to name him...or her.' There was quite a stress on the last word. 'She could have been telling us who she was frightened of, and why. If she had written more about this person, he or she might well have wanted to kill her, or make sure she did not talk in some way-'

It also meant this person could wish to do the same thing to me, but I wasn't going to get involved in murder. 'But she was going to kill herself anyway. The note is there for anyone to read. All they would have to do is to steal and destroy the note.'

'As I said, suicides almost invariably leave a note of some description or other. Certainly, someone as educated as Gretel Neumann would have wanted to tell the wide world she was leaving it. No note could be construed as murder. By tearing the note in half and leaving the non-incriminating portion in her bag, we are led to believe she has taken her own life, thus, no more investigation. Clever, isn't it?'

'Have you thought, officer, how this murderer would know what she was going to write and... arrange for her to stop precisely at the right point on the sheet? And, she might not have had another piece of paper. The back of the note is covered in an advertisement, or something, so it would not have been clear, would it? It might have been a last minute thought, so she tore off a sheet of paper, say, from a shopping list.' I had done it again. I had reminded myself not to get involved and my comments annoyed him because they were frustrating him. I had done what I had arranged not to do – annoy a policeman in his duty. 'But the note is unsigned, that is very unusual if this is the entire note.'

I was as baffled as he was. I understood most of his reasoning, though this would mean Gretel clearly, was being followed before she killed herself. 'I don't know what to think, officer. Gretel's dead, leaving a note. End of story, I think.'

'And this connection, the one which caused her to top herself, if you insist on your idea,' he continued relentlessly. 'What's this all about?'

I shuddered. 'We talked a lot about Hans. A lot, as you know. Gretel had admitted to me she had made it all up about Hans. That is why she came to see you and withdrew her testimony.'

The police officer shook off his hat into his hand with a deliberate and practised movement and placed it on his knee, which he had pushed tight together as if they cold. He was cold, cold and baffled and he was getting nowhere with me. 'You do not understand, Miss Epstein. Gretel never withdrew her testimony. Yes, she did come and visit us, but that was after Hans had been released by us. We had decided we could not make the case stick and had held him too long anyway. We simply did not have the corroborating evidence. He had gone before she arrived at the Station. Just timing, all down the line. When Gretel learned he had been released, she left the Station immediately, without saying anything else to us. Why did you say this?'

It was my turn to be silent. I recalled, distinctly, being told that Hans had said Gretel's visit had ended in his release. Pieter had said it had been my meeting with her, which had made her return to the Station.

In a few words, the whole mood of the meeting had changed. Up until now, I could accept or reject his ideas. They had been mere supposition, his suggestions against my own. Neither could be proven right unless the other piece of paper, if it did exist, was found. The officer's words had changed everything. All at once I sensed the familiar fear in my mouth, my words issuing in jerky statements, and I felt sure the man believed I was the guilty person.

'Are you sure, officer? Could there not be some mistake?'

'Yes, there is always a possibility of an error occurring of course,' he replied honestly. 'Someone in my office was told and acted without my authority. The chances are, however, about five thousand to one. Everyone who reports in to the Station, is logged, their statements recorded and filed in duplicate. I would have known if Gretel had issued such a repudiation of her original charge, as the case is undoubtedly, the most important one in my patch, at present. We might have re-arrested him if she had come up with newer, stronger evidence.'

The policeman pursed his blued lips in his sallow face. It reminded me of one of the rats in the camp, rats fed well on human corpses.

'It was pure chance that we released Hans Maas at the same time, If, what you say is true, he must have talked to Gretel after he was released, that night, in fact, for she was dead by lunch the next day. It does not look good for him, does it?'

It was time for me to give up. I was, by now, confused and I had no idea if Hans was completely guilty, or totally innocent, as I desperately wanted him to be. I didn't want to think of the war being dragged back into the headlines just as we were all settling into peace again. Too many memories would be stirred up, like the mud in the canal. But, if he was innocent, why had he lied to his family by saying Gretel had released him? It would have been only too natural to tell the truth of what happened at the time. I shivered in the evening air, wishing the warmth of the stove on my face and the wheelhouse door locked against the world.

'I cannot help you anymore, officer. You will have to work it out for yourself. As far as I am concerned, I think Hans, on being released, imagined Gretel had done what I myself asked her to do. It would make it easier to explain to his family as well, wouldn't it? The decision to write the note is confirmation to me she could not go on with her lie. That's all,' I ended firmly. It was getting late and I hoped there would be sandwiches to make.

'Very well, Miss. But, we may need to speak to you again.'

'You know where I live, and where I work…and where I go for lunch.' Perhaps I had been wrong. This man frightened me almost as much as the Gestapo.

To cross the gangplank and to feel the deck moving beneath my feet was as near to heaven as I could imagine. I began to shake and stutter as soon as I saw Theo, and recounted the meeting, accompanied by much heaving of my chest and a shuddering of my bottom jaw.

'And, all I could think of was having sold fifty sandwiches.'

'Fifty! You darling boy.' I could not help myself. He had gone out, so quietly and nonchalantly, talking to his friends no doubt, suggesting, proposing, and beguiling the boatmen to buy a sandwich here and there. 'You could cheese to Edam.'

But, he shook his head.

'The word seems to have got out. You know how it is here. I decided fifty was enough. I did not know if we had enough bread, or fillings.'

The hug was becoming a ritual. How easy it was to slip away from the Gretel nightmare, into the warm security of our new plans for the future. I stopped. I was going too fast. Stick to sandwiches.

'We had better start right away.'

'There's a run on cheese and onion.' This was followed by: 'Do you want to tell me about it?'

Theo was getting better. The fact he was emerging from his own terrifying ordeal was real. I wanted Doctor Hertz to see for himself, but not until I felt Theo was really ready to stand up to his questioning. Theo was asking about me, and was concerned for me instead of worrying and talking about his own fears. The paranoia of his hypochondria was fading. The good Doctor had told me the first signs of recovery, if they were to come, would be when he stopped discussing his own concerns, giving him the time and space to review the rest of the world he lived in, without slipping back into the deep hole of his mind.

'I met that policeman again, after work. It is why I am late. I don't believe he has a single clue as to whether Gretel killed herself, or not, but he is certainly trying every thing he can to muddy the picture. I don't know if it is simply the way he works, to see if something comes to the surface by itself, or just that he is genuinely baffled with the whole thing. He said he would want to see me again which makes me think he is still in the dark.

'Their car has been circling the harbour almost all day, backwards and forwards endlessly as if petrol isn't expensive enough, as it is.'

I cut the cheese into slices carefully, determined not to let the problem throw my sandwich production off-key. Nonetheless, had the policeman been right about part of the letter being missing? And, why had Hans lied, *if* he had lied? Neither problem could be passed on to Theo. I just could not risk him slipping

The Potato Eaters

back just as he was starting to show real progress in his rehabilitation.

'I put the pram in the water today,' he said casually, laying the cheese onto the bread, his tongue hanging out in his concentration.

'The pram? What pram?'

'The little dinghy. The one I keep in the stern covered by canvas.'

I went on with my work, having nodded my head, as if I knew all about the boat, which, in fact, I had never seen. 'That's good, Theo. Why have you done that?'

'Well, it's the time of the year, before the sun dries the timber too far and opens out the clinker planking. The water will soon swell the wood back tight together. Besides,' he added even more nonchalantly, if that were possible,' besides, I can't get out to the centre moorings can I, without it?'

'I wondered how you would do it. Can we handle the extra business?' The last few words were spoken with a strangled cry. I pretended I had a piece of cheese stuck in my throat. Theo responded by banging my back as if he were knocking rust off the side of *Kuijpers*. This time, I managed to utter a genuine choke.

'We can, if I go into production before you get back from work. I can cut the cheese, prepare all the fillings, as I shall know the quantities by then, which just leaves the bread to arrive when you get back. Then, I can cover it all up, so it won't get dry. I need to be able to cut bread as thin as you, as well.'

For an answer, I handed over the knife and watched him slice off four rounds. He improved remarkably quickly between the first diamond wedges to the fourth, though I had to show him how to keep from pressing the soft bread into a flat sausage.

'Only thinner, Theo. We need to keep the profit margins up.'

'Can I come in?'

The interruption came from Jos, who stood in the lobby leading to the companionway, hand raised to knock. I don't know how long he had been standing there, and I hadn't heard him come down the steps. Usually, I would always know when any member of the Family arrived, by the heavy tread of their boots.

'Come in,' said Theo. 'Where is the Family?'

'Still eating. I wondered if you and Mae would like a drink later. I can see you are busy now.'

'Yes we are,' I said shortly, slightly annoyed by the intrusion to our privacy. But that was silly. It wasn't as if we were lovers…or anything. Theo however, had already plumped an arm around the other.

'You will soon be buying our sandwiches.'

'Possibly,' Jos replied warily, eyeing me carefully. 'Course, Mama keeps us very well.'

'Only joking,' I said. 'Sorry Jos, we cannot come out. We have so many to make before bedtime. Why don't you and Theo go across the road and bring in a jug of beer?'

Both the men bounded towards the steps. 'Good idea,' responded Theo, looking back as he reached the steps. 'Let's go.'

'Have you any money? And what about the jug? Or does it get given to you in the landlord's own carrier?'

Both men looked sheepish, and I was annoyed with myself for the condescending manner in which I had spoken. They returned ten minutes later, and we sprang our three glasses together with a bang, making the white froth, or was it called foam, slide down the sides like a river in spate when it is caught in a backwater for a moment.

'So, what do you want to discuss?' I spoke, while laying pickle on a slice of bread with growing expertise.

'Why? Do you think there is something special to talk about?'

'Yes. You have not come over before…just for a drink, that is, and on your own, so, there must be a reason.'

Jos frowned, and shrugged his shoulders. Then he smiled at me, which made me uneasy, wondering what he wanted to say. I was still nervous that someone in the Family might say or do something to Theo, to set him back. It was a rotten thing to think, but I had had experience of their help before. There was no doubt he wanted to talk without the rest of the Family being present.

'It is about Gretel… the police, and all. Why are they asking us all these questions, probing into our lives? Their car, is always there, up on the quayside, looking down on us, snooping and prying? Just for a suicide, after all, nothing else. It doesn't make sense, does it?'

'She had a rich and powerful father, Jos. When money and influence at that level comes into play, it can stir up a real hornet's nest, let alone the mire, which also comes to the surface. I can imagine Gretel's father has been to the Chief of Police for Amsterdam, top man anyway, and told him to sort it out…pretty damn quickly.'

'Have they spoken to you much?'

'Twice,' I replied too swiftly, as I wiped the onion tears from my eyes. 'Theo, hand me a cloth please.'

'What about?' Jos insisted on carrying the conversation forward. 'I'm sorry to go on so, but Hans has been through hell, and we all want to make sure the police leave him alone, once and for all.'

'Well. The police are not sure whether she committed suicide, or whether it was a cover-up, a murder made to look like suicide.'

'That is terrible, if it is true. But the note was addressed to you, so why were the police asking you questions?'

'Perhaps I was the only person she could trust, or talk to, and I was the last person she spoke to, officially that is. There may have been someone later …Money can isolate you, Jos. No friends, only people trying to get to know you, to marry into the family for the money.

Theo, I think you had better pop out and get a refill. Take Jos with you, I'm paying.' The two men were out of the cabin as soon as I pulled some coins from my purse. As soon as their feet cleared the deck overhead, I wiped my hands on my apron and walked into the boiler room where we kept old newspapers drying for the stove. The paper was our one luxury.

It was there, staring me in the face, set in an imitation torn edge as if it were a piece, torn from a larger letter. Little did the editor know he might have been showing it as it really was, so I re-read it again.

> *I shall not be able to meet with you today. You are the first person I feel I could trust and I really wanted to talk with you in the park. I am very frightened, as there is someone else involved in the problem.*
>
> *Having thought it over, I have changed my mind on everything I said, and I do not want to discuss it anymore. There's no point any further…*

Jos had been right all along. It *had* been in the paper. I had been too busy with sandwich-making to notice it. He had been telling the truth and I was ashamed I had doubted his word. Happily, I returned the paper to the pile and went back to chopping onions, while I sipped my beer.

A frothing jug of fresh beer preceded Theo, who shambled down the steps sloppily, spilling some of the precious fluid. I sighed. However much he improved, he would never be a naturally tidy man. The loss of beer stock was much to Jos's annoyance, however, though I noticed he did not offer to mop it up. It was, after all, woman's work.

Almost as soon as the beer was divided up, the conversation picked up where it had been left before. 'Do you think the police have finished with their questions?'

'I really don't know, Jos. You are asking a lot yourself for someone who has no connection at all with this affair.'

'What did you speak about, I mean, you and Gretel?'

'This and that.'

'Did she talk about Hans and the war?'

I paused. His persistence was strange, and it annoyed me. All I wanted to do was to drop the whole matter, and although I understood why he was saying it, it did not make the problem any better. The recurring image of her dead face was beginning to haunt me each time the subject was raised. I was frightened my own nightmares would return, for this could interfere with my work at the bakery, where I felt I was really beginning to make a place for myself. The last thing Theo needed was for someone to imitate his own shouts and cries at two o'clock in the morning.

'Possibly... this and that,' I repeated.

Food, scraps of bread and cheese were falling off the table and onto the brick floor, which encircled the stove. As I bent to pick them up, Jos retorted quickly. 'It is nothing to do with me, Mae, as I said, Hans is my brother and I want, somehow to get back at the police who put him away for so long. I think it was wicked, really wicked, keeping him locked up when he had done nothing, but because we have no position in life and no real money, they can just push us aside as if we had no rights at all. If we could afford a lawyer, it might make them much more careful in the way they conduct the rest of this investigation. This is why I need every little crumb of information anyone can give me, so I can use it against them. Hans has protected me all of my life and now I have a chance here, to show the way I feel. For the first time I am in a position to be of use, when in the past, I have always been the youngest, the one who isn't old enough to understand.' He sounded bitter, I could see. His words, together with the newspaper article confirmed in my mind, there had been a number of stupid mistakes. As my father had often said in the long past: 'You add two and two together and always come up with five.'

'I'm sorry I have bothered you with this. There's no reason to discuss it again. It is finished, ended,' he said with considerable finality in his voice.

I bent over, smelling strongly of onions and kissed him on the cheek, using the pressure of my lips to make him understand I was sorry. 'I must finish off here. Why don't the two of you go off, for a last beer? One only mind, as Theo has to get up early if he is to deliver this lot on time.'

Mollified, Jos led the way, followed closely by Theo. As they disappeared, up the steps, I leant back against the mast step, where it came down through the cabin roof, and eyed the lurid picture of Jesus. It carried a cross with gold-coloured spears of light radiating out in exact equal distances from each other, on every point of the compass. No doubt, Theo's grandmother would have enjoyed the pious scene, though, in these days it had become fashionable to throw such pictures away, replacing them with more modern images of the Christian faith. The dismal scene made the room oppressive, so on the spur of the moment, I took it down and hung up one of the large copper pans on the same nail. I hoped Theo's God would not mind, for the surfaces seemed to spring into life as it caught the firelight. It warmed my mind and banished the terrors now beginning to creep in with the evening shadows across the street. Tomorrow, I would tell the police they had got their story wrong. Jos needed almost as much help as Hans.

* * * * *

Mae left early the next morning, only stopping to reassure herself that Theo was awake. His bed looked inviting, and she struggled to pull herself away from the idea of climbing in beside him. But, the Manageress wanted to discuss her plans, and she needed to be there to give her a good impression.

The air was full of dampness and dense fog. Wet smells lying in the streets, since the first autumn rain of the year before, had washed down the gutters and into the canals. There was the smell of earthworms and sodden cardboard, mixed in with the acrid tang of tugboat smoke hanging low, along the street. The bands of gossamer clung to the huge piles of rusting cogwheels and American ration cards lying discarded by the street side, forgotten articles of war along with the forgotten men who had thrown them there. The thick murk blurred the water's edge where it met the granite quayside. Bollards, each looped with rope, stood out spookily, only coming into sharp focus when a bystander could touch them. Where the mist cloaked a cold object, it condensed immediately, turning iron and steel to a molten sheen, ropes into frail cobwebs and canvas into clammy sheets of cardboard.

Mae's mind was concentrated upon the idea of buying a new skirt. She had just enough money saved, and it would be the first real purchase she would make since her return. When she had lived in Rotterdam, Mary, her mother's old cleaner had pulled out things for her from a drawer in the attic. The skirt she wore that morning was one of them. The trams rumbled above her, bringing in the workers who lived outside the city.

She wondered if Gretel's father would be driving in, perhaps to talk to the police; it made her pause to consider arranging a meeting with him. But, she pondered, would there be any point in seeing such a powerful man, a man who could ensure the Chief of Police was personally involved in the investigation of his daughter's death.

The mist alighted on the fine hairs, curling out from her headscarf, before settling as tiny beads on her forehead and nose. It felt fresh and cool on her face. Footsteps echoed eerily behind her, though she could not see who the people were. It might even be the Family trying to catch her up. Her mind turned to Theo and wondered how far he had gone in his deliveries as he had calculated he would need two trips, dividing each into equal length, to reduce the time. Mae had told him, in no uncertain terms, if he were to miss a delivery, causing his customer to go to sea without his lunch, it would be very unlikely he would be given a second chance of an order. Besides, the sandwich would be wasted.

Mae turned off the road to take the shortcut to the Station. Here, the harbour mouth narrowed to a few metres width, and dove off to the right, to lead under the railway tracks as a long tunnel. Grass grew through the cobbles and fell, lank against the stone walls, which rose up as supports to the high arch of the bridge. The mist here was heavier as it formed a cocktail with the smoke of the arriving trains: it made the air more difficult to breathe, and Mae found it an unpleasant experience. More footsteps behind her had increased their striking rate, heavy, iron-studded boots, harsh and hollow in their sound, reminding her of jackboots from five years earlier.

For the first time she had made the daily walk, Mae began to feel uneasy. She looked back. Silhouetted at the end of the tunnel, a darker grey in a washing day cloud of lighter tones, she could see the huddled up bulk of a man with his head down to ward off the soaking mist. He was striding out as if he were late for an appointment. Something in the set of his body rang vaguely in her mind; the sort of nudge at her consciousness, which said, I know this person, but could not pin the image down. It stirred muddled memories from the long past even before Rotterdam. The person looked up for an instant, seeing her hesitate, and increased his speed until he came almost abreast of her just as she cleared the tunnel. He began to move towards her with great speed and she could now see why his head had appeared so deformed in the half-light. He was wrapped up in a dark scarf covering his face completely. Only a pair of eyes gleamed dully as they focussed upon her.

Mae began to run, but he reached out and took hold of her with a sudden, shocking movement, a totally unexpected action despite her initial sense of edginess.

'What do you want of me?' She demanded, realising, as she said it, what a ridiculous question to ask. The man said nothing. Instead, he pinioned her arms behind her with one hand as the other sought to clamp itself over her mouth. Slowly, he began to force her body down to the canal edge.

Mae had one chance and she took it without thinking of the consequences. She bit down hard into the arm holding her face, feeling the bone, exulting almost in her puny action, aware she was able to do something in her own defence. Certainly her fight back produced a growl of pain, allowing a temporary relaxation in his grip. Frantic of his reaction to her own attack, she kicked out, twisting her head from side to side in an attempt to free herself.

In the distance, up the incline from the tunnel, and heading, God bless them, in her direction, was the bread van and the brothers, on their way to the quay.

She screamed out: 'Help me! Please help!'

Without a moment's hesitation, the two men jumped off the moving wagon and began to run towards her. As they did so, she felt the man release her, finding space to leap away, his metal shod soles ringing like a blacksmith in the tunnel. Then he was swallowed up in the mist as if he had never existed.

Trembling, and breathing in great draughts of oxygen, she tried to calm herself by smoothing down her hair. Her breasts felt raw, and bruised from his clumsy clawing.

'Hey, lass. Are you alright? He's got away for sure.'

'Yes, I'm fine. Really I am. After my bag, no doubt.'

'It seemed more than that to me,' said the first, while the second man shook his head. 'He was trying to push you in the water.'

'Push me? How do you mean?' For an answer, he turned her round. Her feet were still placed almost on the water's edge, on the granite coping rather than the cobbles. Mae trawled up her pictures of Gretel, her drowned face in the ooze of the Amsterdam canal. The man who had held her would have been strong enough to have held Gretel down until her struggles had ceased. She realised the man had made no attempt to snatch her purse. A train sounded mournfully above her, echoing her mood. Out in the mist, was a person who had probably killed Gretel… almost certainly killed her, she corrected herself. He was still about, hiding out, somewhere behind the thick veil of the fog, still stalking the harbour. For whatever reason, he wanted Mae out of the way, seemingly, permanently.

'I'm fine,' she repeated, giving a semblance of a smile, as she attempted to control her breathing.

'We'll call the police.'

'No! No, it is not necessary.' She held up her chin in reassurance. 'I'm quite all right and can continue perfectly, so I will call in at the Police Station on my way to work. Thank you so very much,' she added resolutely. She held out her hand to both, by way of ending the conversation, and stepped around the horses, which had come to a halt alongside their masters without bidding, and awaited instructions.

One of the two men shook his head, perplexed. 'Well, I dunno.' But Mae was already striding up the incline in a determined manner, putting space between them with every pace she took. At the crest, just before Central Station she turned and waved to them both. Baffled, they climbed up into their wagon and *'hey-ooped'* the horses into action, continuing to shake their heads at post-war modern womanhood as they did.

By this time, Mae was walking past the entrance to the Station, hoping her heart would begin to slow down before she reached work. She knew she had just been involved in an attempt to murder her. She was positive it wasn't a wasted effort of rape, or a plan to steal her handbag. Any fool could see she had no money. What she did recall, with startling clarity, since her two rescuers had drawn attention to it, was the pressure on her body by the man, forcing her in one direction: towards the canal and under the water. She now understood why the man had waited until she was clear of the tunnel, instead of attacking her in the relative security of its darkness. The canal did not run through the short cut.

As she turned in the street, where the bakery was sited, she reconsidered her thoughts on going to the police. The whole mess of Gretel's death would have to be resurrected. There would be increased suspicion on everyone, including Hans again, and, anyway, would she ever be believed? Would not the police think she was making the whole story up, by altering the scent trail away from where they were following? And they knew she had made up the tale that she was Anna Maas. She dismissed the idea as one dashes water into one's eyes to clear a heavy head. Theo had told her it was a good remedy after drinking too much beer the night before. A stubborn image remained, however, an image of the man as he had disentangled himself from her as he jerked his arm from her mouth. He had had a powerful build, a working man in fact, with heavy steel shod boots and rough clothes. He had come from the harbour and run off again, also in the same direction as the boats.

It was Mae's turn to shake her head. The man was a sailor, a seaman, someone close to where she lived, someone perhaps, she knew or had met. Rotterdam had a port, as well, a large one. Someone she had met there, perhaps? One thing in all this fright cheered her up, as she tied the white apron behind her. She was now not at all sure it was Hans, the main suspect. Despite similar boots, Hans was much taller than her attacker unless the person had remained bent over all the time. She smiled for the first time in the day, and banished any thought of reporting to the police.

'You look pale, Mae,' said the Manageress as Mae brought the first tray of bread into the shop. 'Are you sure you are not doing too much at nights with this sandwich making?'

'No, Madame. It is the time of the month,' she lied. 'I am ready for anything. I want to start a first trial run of sandwiches today. Just thirty rounds, popular fillings so there will be very little risk. It will give us a chance to feel out the market with no wastage. I have prepared a pricing policy...here,' she indicated, pulling out a hand written list.

'Excellent. We will have them typed up into properly made labels. They must appear as professional as the cakes themselves.'

Mae was in the shop half an hour before her own lunch break when a young man in a smart suit and a white shirt arrived and glanced at the glass shelf.

'Good idea,' he said. 'Just like the English ones. I'll take a cheese and a pickled herring.' He was overheard by two more office workers behind him.

'Have you any salami ones?'

'No,' Mae replied, but if you buy cheese today I will have salami tomorrow. You can also order the day before so they will be waiting for you. There will be no need to queue. If you become a regular, you can open a weekly account so you will not have to bother to pay each day. Get you out quicker for your lunch break.'

'Terrific,' said the spotty-faced youth. Mae saw the Manageress frown, but the woman did not comment until after the rush, as she was going out to lunch herself. 'We cannot open accounts for anyone, Mae.'

'These 'any-ones', Madame, are the basis for our future business. These are the training managers, management material, in the offices across the road, who will tell their staff where to go.

We will know just where they work. We will charge them two percent extra if they do not pay up on the Friday. All we have to do is to say we will tell their employers.' She buttoned up her coat as if to close the conversation. The other woman threw up her hands in the air in helpless resignation.

'If you go on like this, you will be sitting on the Board.'

'No, Madame,' she responded, seeing at that moment in time, exactly where her life was to lead. 'All I want is a chain of shops...like my father had. Then I will rest and I will have shown my father that I was able to do this.'

Mae stepped outside the shop and slipped down to Dam Square. It was becoming a habit, though she needed space around her for a while after the bustle and pressure of the shop. The extra business of the morning had taken all of her thoughts away from the misty canal walk for a while. She had to seize, head-on, the idea of someone wanting to kill her. It was foremost in her mind, as she had to walk back through the same tunnel later in the evening, if she did not want to take the long route back through the old Jewish quarter. And, which was worse, she wasn't sure.

She could see her father dealing with difficult problems in business by always going out to meet them'... at least half-way, if not further,' he had always stressed to her. If Hans was innocent, as now seemed likely, despite Gretel's fears, it left a number of questions. What, or who was Gretel so frightened of? Who was this person she had written about? Was it a man or a woman? And, was there a connection with the early morning attack on herself, or had it been coincidence? Questions, questions, whirled through her head. The key to it all, she recognized, was the absolute certainty she had given away a piece of valuable information, say to the police, which was vitally important to someone else at the same time, but what? When she had eaten her lunch and turned back towards the bakery, she knew there was nothing of worth she could give to anyone. It could only, therefore, be that this someone believed she had given out vital information. It brought her back to Gretel. Gretel had to be the key to the problem, and she was dead.

Mae left work as soon as she was able to cash up, receiving further encouragement from the Manageress. 'Go on like this, and we shall have a visit from one of the Bessels' Family. They will be anxious and want to know more about you. I hope you have some long- term plan to tell them: they like permanence.' The woman was still hedging her bets until the new venture was properly established. Mae disregarded the comment and tossed her black hair onto her shoulders, freeing her head from the restrictive headband. She had been risking more than a fledgling business venture for eight years.

Instead of going aboard the *Kuijpers*, she stepped over the gangplank to the *Anna Rosner*.

'Well, hullo, Mae. We had a lovely evening with you,' said Pieter, giving her a hug. If he harboured any grudge against her, he was keeping it very private. She shook hands with Hans unable, as she did, to prevent herself from glancing down at the Family's boots. Pulled wide open at the tops, the laces hung down while the tongues lolled limply as if they were dogs after a long run. The soles rested well off the deck, kept there by the heavy nails and studs, which were designed to grip the muddy fields. Pieter's were by far the largest, which Mae recognised by the brass tags to his laces, a small affectation to match his taste in waistcoats. Hans caught her stare, intercepting her almost guilty stare, with his own intelligent eyes.

'Not for your dainty feet, Mae. They are for strong big men.' Was he mocking her? She could not tell and tried to distract him.

'Come and have a drink with me, Hans.'

'What? Just me,' he replied, looking across at his father and sisters. Mama and Jos had to be out shopping, for they had not yet come home. The cabin seemed larger without them.

'Go on, the two of you,' Pieter gestured towards the deck above, pleased at the sudden return of good relations between the two boats. 'Supper in an hour, Mama says.' He had addressed himself to Hans.

As they crossed the gangway, a wind was rising with the fading light, enough to warble its way through a dozen mastheads and their rigging, They vibrated and thrummed in concert, causing them to act like harp strings in the deteriorating weather. The musical overtures made the gulls protest in reaction, screaming and cackling like demented women as they paddled from foot to foot towards them, believing food was imminent. One ejected a stream of white slime at their feet in majestic offering, and as payment for the morsels to come. They cocked expectant heads at the two before dismissing them from their eternal search for food, while the boldest simply squawked cheekily.

'You haven't got me out of prison just to have a drink with me, Mae, have you?'

'Maybe not, but I like this sherry I have been introduced to.' She hesitated. 'Can we try another bar?'

'Sure. Let's go to the Brown Fox,' he said easily. It was close to the corner by the tunnel under the railway lines, and adjacent to the cold, dark water at the other end of the tunnel. It was not the best location Mae had had in mind.

It was a brown café, all wood and brass, where the paint had been rubbed from the painted wall panels to leave well-worn patches gleaming through underneath. In the corner stood a large, stone sink, chipped and worn with age, piled with dirty glasses. Steam was curling up from hot water, and soap suds created by old pieces of soap stuffed into a small, wire basket gave a lie to the, otherwise, dirty look of the place. A poor copy of Rembrandt's father by the artist, hung lopsidedly over a stove. Unconsciously, Mae straightened the frame, which raised a smile from Hans's face. The lighting was low, pools of it illuminating the tables, but nowhere else. It suited Mae.

He sat, sipping his beer, froth from the head beginning to run through his fingers. Mae studied him from the rim of her glass, waiting. At last, slightly unnerved, he raised a question to break the silence. 'You must have had a reason for this meeting. You and me, without Mama and Papa...Theo even. What does he think of you and me, alone, drinking, I wonder?'

'I'll get his dinner in due course. Now...tell me where you were, early this morning?'

Her sheer nerve worried her own belief in herself. What if, she wondered to herself, what if he *was* the man wrapped up in the headscarf and she had mistaken his height? It would be easy to do it, upset as she had been, with her only thought on survival, that of getting away from the rough hands. Could the good-looking man straddling the high-backed chair in front of her be a potential, or a real murderer? She added the stress to her thesis, remembering Gretel. If she was proved correct, she had to begin to ease herself from the bar and to the boat without Hans coming for her in the darkness.

'This morning? I left early, very early, without the rest of the Family. We weren't picking today. The fog was too thick to see anything, you see? Jos went into town, followed by the girls, shopping, I believe. Papa cleaned the engine room to try and match Theo's, and Mama did some baking. Why?'

'What time did you leave?'

'Six. Six-ten, something like that. I was in no rush. Why?'

'Where did you go…first,' she continued relentlessly. It caused Hans to pull out a paper packet of cigarettes. He jerked one out expertly, and directed it in the general direction of his mouth. She accepted the next one. 'Where?'

'I went to *Oosterpark*. There is a good flea market there every day now. I went to buy a leather jacket.'

'*Oosterpark*,' said Mae pensively, rubbing the side of her nose as she had seen the policeman do several times. The pause unsettled Hans.

'That's east of here, isn't it?'

'Yes.'

'Away from Central Station.'

'Yes, look, what on earth is this all about, Mae?'

'Nothing,' she replied fatuously. 'Can you prove it?'

His eyes flickered fear for the first time. 'Something's happened, hasn't it?'

'Many things, Hans. The world, for a start, is twelve hours older. We are all a bit older, closer to our graves.'

'I can, as a matter of fact.'

'What?'

'Prove it, I mean. Anna and Suzannah met me. They were looking for summer blouses.'

'You said earlier, you only believed your sisters went shopping.' She ignored his open mouth waiting to make a comment. 'What time was this?'

'I get it. This is just a practice for another of those police interrogations. You know, Mae, this is just like the Dam Square police…about seven,' he ended, seeing impatience light in her face.

'An hour after you left?'

'Yes. I was there before the girls. As they weren't working, they stayed in bed until Mama made them get up, I expect.' He smiled encouragingly. 'Any more?' He was back in control.

'Just one. What were you wearing?'

'Well...what you see now. I haven't changed. Sorry, I did not know you wanted to go out this evening or I would have put a clean shirt on for the interrogation.'

She glanced down at his feet. He had on a pair of worn, black shoes, laced up tightly. The caps were dusty, but were well polished under the layer. The doubts flooded back into Mae's mind. This was the third time she had drawn a blank. And sitting here with her, he now appeared about the right height. 'Oh, this is so silly.'

'I'm sorry, Mae. I don't know what you want of me.'

'Nor do I. Walk me back, please.'

'But I haven't finish-'

Reluctantly, he drained his, still half full, glass and rose, pushing the chair back against the wall to make space for her. It was a small, but polite act. 'I thought we were going to make an evening of it...end up with something special.'

'Another time, Hans. I need to see Theo. And he will be ready for his meal.'

'That reminds me. No one has seen Theo today. After his early morning round of the harbour, that is. He was up very early, wasn't he?'

'He has to. To take the orders.' She felt a spark of adrenalin begin to pump her heart faster. 'He's probably aboard.'

'No. Mama called with a cup of tea at about eleven this morning, she said. He had not come back by then.'

'I expect he went shopping.'

'No,' Hans repeated, annoyingly and worryingly. 'His basket was on deck when I got back from town. It was tied to a stay...as always.'

Mae began to increase her speed. 'You don't think he has been taken ill again, do you? He has been so much better, almost as if he had never had the illness.'

'The doctor said, didn't he, we would never be able to plan when it might return? He said it could be triggered off by almost anything. A single silly act, a small, seemingly trivial stress laid onto his day, a scare, a sudden fright, anything.'

'But, he did stay away the other time.' It was a wishful comment.

They reached the quay and she began to jump the ropes one by one, in a rhythm of a hurdler. One-two-three jump, one-two-three jump.

He wasn't on the boat. It had the sort of emptiness about it, like the last time, which told her at once he had not been back for some hours. Eventually, she gazed across the harbour towards the *Ij*.

'Hans! Hans! What is that? Out there…on the far side, in front of the trees?'

'It's a boat, I think. A dinghy, maybe. But, it's so dark it could be anything.'

'Yes,' she answered fearful for the real answer in her mind. She ran to the stern. The canvas cover was stacked against the gunwale, the pram gone. The *Kuijpers* dinghy had disappeared from its normal stowage. 'It's his, Theo's,' she said.

'What? The boat out there?'

'We must get it, please.'

'It may not be his, you know.'

'Please, Hans.'

'It doesn't matter, does it? It's floating, empty.'

'We need it back anyway. Please.'

The two scrambled onto the Family's small punt, where the water covered the bottom a clinker board in depth. There was a single oar, which Hans used expertly to scull his way across the basin. It was quite a distance, and Mae strained her eyes impatiently as the gap narrowed between the two craft. As they approached, Hans called out.

'It's alright. There is no one aboard.' And, after a short silence he confirmed, 'It is *his* dinghy though.'

Mae's heart sank to the bottom boards. She connected the facts together. Theo was not at home when he should be. It was his dinghy; it was adrift with its painter trailing in the water, and it was dark. He should be preparing the sandwiches for the next day's sales.

The tiny boat lay in the water, surrounded by spilt diesel, which sucked greedily at the timber planking. It swayed and rocked on the slight swell, abandoned and forlorn.

There were no oars.

OUT INTO THE BASIN

The water is as green and black as broken bottles in a drum. This deep moves without ceasing, but always towards the main canal with its grey, bitter cold setting. The sea swirls and sucks at the granite walls, which threaten to move inwards at any moment, to crush the boats. The watcher is unable to make any decision to move out onto the water, for the threat of being dashed to death, or drowned in the green foam, are not the problems he faces: but, the curving sky beyond the proscenium arch of the bridge and the dread of the return of his illness brings indecision.. Like taking an object out of a box, he is also able to put it back in its place. It means he is better; better than he has been since the creeping sickness began. Small synapses in his brain are beginning to spark again, creating the proper connections, as if a telephonist is plugging in her callers sequentially, one by one. His fear is that she will pull one of the cords out of this progression, when the time is up on a long distance call.

This, then, is his balancing trick, a juggler playing with time and imagination, all the while knowing he has most of the known world waiting to see if his juggling balls will tumble into the sawdust ring. It is better, they think, than his real trick of keeping them all in the air at the same moment.

All at once he finds himself grasping the oars. His back faces the direction he wants to go, ideal for him for if he has to look towards his destination, he will probably fail at the first obstacle. The water here by the other boats is oily and slack; it heaves itself like a whale, back up the side of the jetty before making for the bottom again. The repetition is helpful, for he can plan a rhythm to his work anything to take his mind off his real assignment, so he tries to think of the good things in his life, those that have come in the past few weeks. Mae for instance.

His rowing has a pulse of its own and he allows this to control his fear of being on the water, knowing it will help combat the terrors of the main stream, which is now very close.

Rounding a large tug moored in mid-water he is, all at once, heading for the tunnel and the Ij. It is the most frightening time of his life even though he realises he does not have to put himself in this situation any more. There is no one who can make him go further; no one who has any rights to tell him so and no one who can cure himself but himself.

Chapter Six

The darkness sank down on me as if it were a physical cloak of heavy wool. I reached out across the water between the dinghy and the *Kuijpers* pram straining to catch the edge of the gunwale. The smell of oil and diesel choked my throat coming perhaps, from a spillage somewhere in the outer harbour, for it was enough to calm the crests into treacly movement. I was aware of the mournful sounds of late returning barges as they ploughed their way up the *Ij*, towards their allotted berths. In the light of a masthead lamp close by, I saw my face, white and sick looking in the reflection of the water, a few centimetres from my nose.

'I've got it,' I said, feeling rather than seeing the boat at that level. Just then, a light winked on allowing me to look directly into the pram. It was empty, as Hans had said, except for a piece of paper. By the light of Hans's match I could see it was an order, a large order for sandwiches. Theo had covered most of the harbour. Strangely though, some of the orders were for boats registered in berths numbered in the two-hundreds.

'Oh, shit!' I said to myself. I could understand exactly what had happened. 'It's Theo's list, Hans. He went rowing to the centre moorings.'

'So. Where is he then?'

'You don't realise. He left the quayside. He left the shore. When your father tried to make him do that, when you were in prison, he went berserk.'

I stared, afraid to look down to the black, oily surface. If he had fallen in, there was no sign of him now, though he was able to swim, I reminded myself, which heartened me to some extent. But the tide backed up again in my mind. If his thoughts had snapped while he had been out here in his boat, without me to help him calm down, he could easily have drowned, or frozen to death, in his frantic panic.

And…it had been me who had suggested, so blithely, he had to work out a solution on how to reach the new, larger market where it sat, tempting him, towards the middle of the harbour. The 'two-hundreds' were the most lucrative boats, bigger craft, more crews, more money… and the furthest out in the stream.

All at once I knew why the Jews, as a nation, were so reviled by the rest of the world. It was our obsession with money. My obsession may have taken Theo to his death and, if so, it would be my own fault to have lost most of the reason for my existence.I felt blackness envelop me. This might well be the third death I was to be involved in?

'Oh shit, shit, shit!' What had I done? Hans tied the painter to the stern of his boat and took the scull. Neither of us said a word as he propelled us with consummate skill towards the direction of the *Kuijpers*. I watched the masthead light swinging from left to right in equal sections as his strong arms shortened the distance in a few minutes. I could see how far Theo must have come, even allowing for the drift of the boat

I found it difficult to climb back on board, only doing so when I received a rather unseemly push from behind. Hans's powerful thrust against my backside caused me to arrive on deck rather quicker than I had anticipated.

'I'm going to tie up. We will have to initiate a search. He may have gone ashore, or is still visiting one of the boats. The boat may have come free by itself you know.'

'No, Hans. The list is today's list. I cannot believe he would have left it, or dropped it without trying to get it back. He believes in this catering venture as much as I-'

'Ahoy-ee.'

'What's that,' I asked.

'Ahoy-ee.' It came again, very faint from across the water.

'It's Theo,' I screamed at Hans. 'Theo!' I shouted. 'Can you hear me?'

But, the silence came back down like an invisible cloak settling about us, leaving me to interpret the slaps and gurgles of the wavelets off the sides of the boats as the call from Theo, or, equally, the cry of a gull taking it out on another.

Hans came aboard, followed quickly by Pieter.

'I thought I heard Theo.'

We all listened again, all feeling a trifle foolish as we stood in line, craning our necks towards the opposite side of the harbour, and the wall formed by the night. The cold made me hunch my shoulders as I held onto a stay. Pieter rode the swell, allowing his knees to buckle and stiffen to the rhythms. I imagined, once, I heard a distant call, a halloo, but it was almost certainly my imagination.

'It's too late for anyone to do anything tonight,' said Pieter. 'Come and stay with us.'

'No, thank you. I want to be here when Theo gets back. Besides, there are all these sandwiches to make.'

'I'll come over later and help,' said Hans quickly. He seemed quite insistent. Something nudged in my wits, telling me not to accept.

'Thank you. It will help pass the time. I suppose he may have gone to the cinema.' I said instead.

For supper, I nibbled a bit of cheese as if I were a mouse with a fussy taste. Hans came clomping aboard, smelling of fried food. His walk was so different from Theo's. I knew who it was immediately.

'Hullo,' he said, without knocking, which annoyed me. It seemed to be a habit of the younger members of the Family. 'Any news?'

'No. Here, you cut the cheese.'

He picked up the long knife, which was used for anything and everything. It was razor sharp as the edge caught the lantern light and Hans's eyes for a moment. His thumb felt out the point of the blade carefully before he took hold of the string bound handle in his left hand.

'I didn't know you were left-handed,' I spread the bread with pickles as I asked the question. Vinegar filled the room.

'A sign of genius, you know.'

'So, why aren't you up there, talking with Aldous Huxley?'

'Who,' he asked suspiciously. The knife bit down through the hard cheese as if it had been heated. He went on: 'Earlier, in the bar? What was all that about? You know…what was I wearing today…and all.'

'Nothing, really. I was attacked this morning...in the fog. In the tunnel, the one which leads to the Station-'

'Attacked? Did he get away? Were you hurt?'

'I don't know who he was...or she for that matter,' I added this in to confuse him further. Otherwise, I would have told you. I do know his height. He likes garlic and his hands were rough, like a picker's.'

'Or a seaman, I suppose.' He said it without properly understanding my train of thought, or was it just to throw me off the scent?

I no longer cared less what I said to him. Theo was missing, possibly drowned and I was doing nothing about it. If he was dead, I wanted to join him, let the cold water numb me like the last time, and close over my head forever, thankfully. The reality then hit me, as if cold water had really been thrown into my face. What if? What if Theo really was dead? Who would his boat belong to? Neither to hear his soft breathing in the middle of the night, nor to feel his gentle kiss goodbye on my cheek in the morning when I went to work. Just when he was getting better...

Hans was watching me very carefully, studying each word, each phrase as though waiting for some further revelation, knife in his left hand, a lump of cheese in the other. 'There is something, isn't there? Ever since I came out of prison you have been different with me.'

'I spoke to Gretel about you. She loved you very much you know. She died, I believe, because she couldn't face the future, even with her comfortable life. In the end, she was just a rich, pretty girl to you, wasn't she? Exciting, I'm sure, but completely out of your class. Was this the reason for chucking her out?'

So, that is what it is all about. Yes, I enjoyed Gretel's company, especially in bed,' he added maliciously, 'but it was all to do with her father. He refused to allow me to go on meeting her. He threatened to cut off her allowance, which, as I am sure you are aware, was large. Gretel didn't seem to mind whether he did so or not. She did love her father very much, of that I am certain, but she was frightened of him at the same time. Can you understand that, Mae? When I told Gretel it would be better if we did not see each other again, if only to preserve the relationship with her father, she went a little crazy, throwing valuable things about her apartment onto the floor.' He stopped, breathing heavily as if he had been running or had climbed a steep flight of stairs too quickly

So, I had been right. They had been lovers, sleeping together. I imagined his rough body with his coarsened hands against her own white smoothness, lying in silk sheets, warmed by radiators with carpets and fine curtains and pictures surrounding the bed.

Hans was continuing. 'She threatened to go to her father. Tell him things…about the past, the war. Not just about me, about the others as well. I knew it was no good going on seeing her. The connection dies between you, doesn't it?'

'I suppose so,' I replied. I had never been in love, and never had the chance. 'So she went to her father and, I presume, it was him who told her to go to the police. No doubt he helped her with her statement. A few exaggerations, here and there.'

'Were they Hans? I just don't know what to believe any more. The police think you are a traitor. They have told me so and nothing I say or do seem to change their mind. Gretel then goes and dies in, to say the least mysterious, circumstances just after you leave prison, and the police have never stopped making enquiries ever since, including, I might add, to me on several occasions, as though I have been connected in some way myself.'

'Now hang on, Mae. I had nothing to do with her suicide. I was right to walk away, especially when she threatened me with blackmail. There are things you know nothing about in all of this mess.'

'I didn't say I thought it was suicide. I think they believe you murdered her.'

The silence, one of those long, deathly hushes where dust appears to stop moving in a light beam, froze me to the spot. A few seconds went by as his hand tightened perceptibly on the knife handle. I unbolted myself from the floor and moved as casually as I could to the opposite side of the table. 'What did you say? Are you inferring…?' And then he lost control of himself.

'How dare you, you…you little Jewish brat!' Hans's voice rose in pitch until it ended almost in a shout. I wondered if the Family could hear him and offered up a prayer they might come and investigate. God in heaven, what had my stupid mouth got me into this time?

'Listen Hans. I wasn't inferring it was you, only that-'

'Like hell you weren't.'

There was a bump on the side of the hull making Hans start and turn his head towards the noise. My prayer had been answered. I took the chance and ran for the companionway steps. I leaped up, three at a time, with all the hounds of hell after me and ran straight into the outstretched arms of Theo.

'What on earth is going on?'

'Oh Theo,' I managed to gasp. 'Where have you been? I've hardly started the sandwiches and we've been searching for you across the harbour. I thought you had drowned.'

He held me tight, just as I had planned it at night in my imagination. My heart was banging against his chest in a wild mix of demented fear and supreme delight. I could not make up my mind, which was the stronger.

'Hullo Hans,' he said over my shoulder, receiving no comment on his arrival. 'What are you doing here?'

'Apart from making your sandwiches…looking for you, as a matter of fact. We found your pram drifting in the basin on the far -east side.'

Ignoring this, Theo went on:' I heard shouting when I arrived, right through the hull. What's going on?' He continued to hold me, his arms wrapped around my head to shut out my fears and keep my chest from disintegrating into a large number of pieces.

'Mae was upset as she thinks I have been involved in Gretel's death, or rather murder. It's a lie, a damned lie,' he shouted out defiantly yet defensively. 'Here, take your bloody knife and make your own sandwiches.'

'Thank you for your help.'

Hans pulled the wheelhouse door shut with a bang causing the compass binnacle to vibrate.

'Where have you been? You cannot just go away without leaving a note for me.'

'I know. Let's have some tea and I'll tell you all about it. I've lost my list though.' He shook his head in frustration at his failure.

'No you haven't. I found it in the boat, quite by accident as it could have blown out at any moment. That's when we thought you had been drowned.'

Theo smiled thankfully. 'Here's the rest.' He pulled out another piece of paper.

The Potato Eaters

We sat opposite each other at the table, our mugs cracked and chipped in front of us. I placed new mugs fairly high on my shopping list for the next week. 'So, where were you?'

'I've been out there, Mae. Alone, on the water. Taking my business to the middle harbour owners. The 'two hundreds'. 'Do you remember, telling me I had to work it all out for myself...how to get to the boats...for the sandwich orders. So, I got into the dinghy and held tight to the hawser. To start with I felt quite sick, like I was really going to be sick, but after a while I began to feel better, like when you drink hot rum. It started in my hands and spread to my head. So, in the end, I got out an oar and paddled around the *Kuijpers* to get used to the idea, holding onto the side of the boat, ropes, anything to make me feel safer, so to speak. At one time, when some people stopped to look at me, I pretended to be examining the side of the hull for damage. It needs painting, you know.'

We both laughed, though tears were streaming down my face, splashing onto the tablecloth. 'Then, I reached across to the *Anna Rosner's* hawser, and so on, until I had put about a hundred metres between myself and the boat. I began to think everything was just...dandy, I was cured, and so I began to row further out. Then, when I was as far away from the *Kuijpers* as possible, I was suddenly violently sick, which made me lose the oar, so I was stuck out there anyway.'

I could hardly believe what I was hearing. He was so rational. His voice was still halting, though I began to suspect this might be a characteristic of his even before he had been taken ill, and he stopped frequently to draw deeply on his cigarette. I took it from his fingers now and drew in the smoke into my lungs. I forced it down, wanting the harsh rasp on my throat as if to punish myself for making Theo take his life in his hands. It had, in my mind, been quite literally that.

'I drifted for ages, waving my hands, shouting...well, screaming at times but all the people had gone to work. I was so frightened because I saw I was drifting towards the *Ij* and wasn't sure if I could have stopped myself when I went through the tunnel. There seemed nothing to stop me, not even the harbour master was about. I was saved by the family on the big steel barge, on the far, east side. I got an order from them too.' He held up the piece of paper on which was written: Two rounds of herring and onion. Berth 264. 0630 hours. He paused for a long time. Each time I tried to fill in the silence he held up his hand. Eventually, he said: 'I have to go back, don't I?'

For a moment, I did not understand him. 'No, of course you don't.'

'I do, Mae. I must.'

I saw his point. He had several orders for the middle berths. He would have to deliver these orders, and each time he delivered an order, he might well pick up another. It was self-perpetuating and I had always thought this is how it could be. Either he continued to take orders and deliver them, or he must not go out in that sector again.

'I'll get up early. Well, earlier. It won't take ten minutes. You can do all the hard ones, on the far side. How did you get back?' I asked, having forgotten, in the heat of Hans's departure to find out.

'The family brought me back. Dropped me off. I shouted for quite a time, you know, but there was no answer. It was dark when they came back from work and found me on their deck. I just froze for hours, not moving, not knowing what to do. Johann, I think his name is, rowed me over. I heard shouting as I came aboard, nasty words by Hans, and it seemed to me that he was extremely angry. Is everything all right between the two of you?'

'I have no idea,' I answered, wanting to forget his name calling, and the implied threat of the knife. It was a confusing picture and I could not tell whether my relationship with Hans would survive at all. I had not said goodbye to him.

'I'll have a word with him now, if you wish.'

'No!' I was adamant this time. I had to give his mind a rest to toughen it up further, and allow his brain to come to terms with what he had achieved today. It must have taken a mental battering in the boat, and by the sound of it, on the steel barge, for he had been away for hours, all day in fact. I studied his eyes for tell tale yellow flecks but all I saw were soft grey reflections. 'Come on, Theo. Lets get down to production, after which I will cook supper. Work first, eh?'

He nodded, picking up the big knife.

'Tomorrow is my first half-day off. I'm going in, in the evening, to pick up the bread and other things but I will not be at the bakery after half-past eleven.'

Theo smiled, pleased for me. 'Can we go out on a date together some time?'

'I've some personal matters to attend to first,' I said, afraid it might upset him. 'We could go for a drink later. What about we walk up town…Rembrandt Square. There's a lot of music and dancing there.'

This seemed to satisfy him, so I began to slice rings of onion, looking up occasionally to see he was doing his work as professionally as he was able. On the shelf, in a jar, was a large pile of cents and half guilders. We were in business.

* * * * *

It was raining. Warm spots began to settle on my face as I looked up into the ragged sky. I had an appointment at twelve, very close by in a shipping office where I now stood, looking up at the enormous stone façade with its plate glass windows. I walked into a reception as large as a ballroom.

'Meinheer Neumann, please. I have an appointment.'

The young, bespectacled face of the clerk threw a curious glance at me, as if to demand what on earth I could be doing, wasting his illustrious boss's time. I noticed he wore a black armband, and the office was over-filled with flowers, I guessed from the funeral. Nonetheless, he picked up a telephone and mumbled into the mouthpiece. 'Please wait a moment.'

Within two minutes there came a voice beside me. 'Please come into my office and take a seat, Miss Epstein. May I bring you some coffee?'

The voice emanated from a man in his mid-sixties. He was tall, overly so but strong, with a powerful neck and a face tanned by years of sea winds. His frame was attired in a superb light grey, herringbone suit, the type of material, which he could only have bought in England. His tie was blue silk, shot with black. On his feet, a pair of shoes gleamed dully with soft leather, cross-stitched at the sides in a very modern way. For a moment I thought he might have been wearing perfume, like the Americans in the war, after shave they called it, but I'm sure, in the end it must have been the flowers.

I shook my head at the offer. 'No thank you, Sir. I'm sorry to take up your time, but I need to resolve a few questions in my mind…about Gretel…and all,' I ended awkwardly, sounding rather like Theo, and cursed my recently acquired inability to stand up to the rich businessman, 'I'm so sorry about Gretel. I hardly knew her, you know?'

He frowned, though not at me. 'It's a puzzle, which remains with me as well. I was on the point of contacting you anyway of course, but I have had all the funeral arrangements to meet and relations have only just left. You see, dear Gretel always spoke of her friends to me… always you understand. I had never heard your name mentioned at any time, until after her death. Afterwards, the police themselves were the first to raise your name. Then, there was the letter.'

His city office looked down and over the harbour and the railway station. Wide and panoramic, it had windows, which covered almost the entire waterfront. On one of the deep sills, was a telescope mounted on a brass tripod. I could just make out the *Anna Rosner* shielding the hull of the *Kuijpers,* though I could see her funnel rising above all of the other clutter in the basin. I couldn't see Theo and wondered if he was covering the far side berths again. I turned back to the man with the sad eyes, carrying dark circles below them. It appeared as if he had taken the death of his daughter very badly.

'I wasn't a friend in any sense of the word. Not, that I was an enemy. I mean…I only got to know her slightly through someone else, who did know her.'

'Who was that, if I may ask?'

I hesitated. 'Hans. Hans Maas.'

'That scumbag. I'm surprised, Miss Epstein you associate with such trash.'

'I live near him, Sir. He has always been extremely kind to me since I arrived back in Amsterdam. You can hardly ask me to transfer my allegiance when he has always acted with the very best of intentions towards me.' I meant every word of it and I used considerable emphasis on the words to make him understand I was not going to agree to every thing he said, just because he was a very rich man. Hans had not been in the *Anna Rosner* when Pieter had tried to take it to sea.

Gretel's father frowned again then pursed his lips as if in agreement with my comment. 'So, where do you fit into this particular crossword? I've lost a darling daughter and I am told she committed suicide.' He almost spat out the last three words, an action which turned his face into a mottled pink and blue. 'Never in a hundred years did she kill herself.'

'What then, *Meinheer* Neumann, do you think did happen?'

He lit a cigarette, American Virginia without offering me one. 'Why, she fell in, of course. The cold would have got to her first. Steep sides, no one about. She literally froze to death-'

'But, what about the letter, the one she sent to me?'

This did upset him. He banged a fist onto his desk, more in frustration with himself for being unable to express himself clearly, rather than being angry with me for interrupting him. 'It is not a suicide letter. It is simply a letter telling someone she cannot make a rendezvous that day…that's you isn't it? '

'Did you know Gretel had taken back her accusations concerning Hans?'

'Rubbish! I know all about it. She just did not want to see him shot.'

'She told me she couldn't face you, you know. She loved you too much to see you involved and hurt.'

His face softened. 'She could always talk to me. My door was always open here for her, any time to the day.'

'But not about Hans evidently. She loved him too. She-'

'No! She didn't love him. Not at all! How could she? He was just a common potato picker.'

'*Meinheer* Neumann. Men and women throughout history and from all differing walks of life have found themselves in love, often with disastrous results. History is littered with them.'

He began to drum the fingers of his left hand on the box of cigarettes. 'Why have you come here, Miss Epstein? To lecture me, or what?'

'Some one tried to kill me, Sir. I believe there is a connection between Gretel's death and the attempt on my own life.'

I let him ponder on my words for a moment or two. He looked quite startled for the first time and, momentarily he lost his urbane composure. 'That hardly seems possible. Are you sure this wasn't some form of bungled rape? And connected with Gretel? Absurd.'

'I can assure you, this was no fumbled rape. I almost ended up in a canal myself. I was saved only by the quick action of two men who were close by. You see, I am the only link between Gretel and Hans. That is a fact, what ever you want to say.' Whether you like it or not, there is much, much more to this whole business than you realise. Agreed, I don't believe Gretel did kill herself, but I differ from you in your claim that she slipped and fell in. Even if she had, there would have been boats near by: ropes, and things. People would hear her calls for she would not have died instantly. It would take three or four minutes to die in the cold. So, why did no one hear her?'

'You know a lot about death, Miss Epstein and you are implying a form of death I find very difficult to believe in.'

'I have recently come back from Auschwitz, Sir. Yes, I do know a lot about death, especially dying in the cold.'

'Ah sh-. I beg your pardon, Miss Epstein. I did not know.' He put his head in his hands and left it there for a considerable period of time. I wished I had taken up his offer of coffee. The fingers returned to the drumming on the desk. 'You do realise the seriousness of the charge you are implying?'

I looked across the harbour again, seeing the wakes of a dozen small boats criss-crossing each other. A magnificent glass-domed clock on the mantelpiece began to chime the hour. Each note became absorbed into the thick curtains and carpets ending up as muted tones.

It was at that moment, some one out there gave a sign of approval to something, though what it was I have no idea. It might not have been for me, as the slim sunbeam shone down onto the dome of St. Nicholas's church. As it wasn't a synagogue, I became certain it wasn't for my notice. Pity in a way, as I needed some sort of moral support. For far too long, I had had to fight on my own for everything. I wanted some one else to help me from time to time, just to agree with me occasionally, would be nice. But the sun shone down in a shiver of white steel and remained fixed on the roof. Was it all about Theo?

'Miss Epstein.'

I brought myself back to his world. 'Yes. Yes I do.'

'It only leaves murder, doesn't it?'

'Yes.'

'Have you been to the police with these fears of yours?'

'No. They are continuing their investigations though.'

'But surely, on a suicide…or an accident?'

'I'm not sure Sir; in fact I have no idea, as they do not tell me anything. They do seem to be taking a very long time to end the investigations; meanwhile they continue to ask me questions. I hardly know what the Amsterdam police department think about all this, but I do know I would want a great deal more evidence than a torn letter and there is none, is there?'

'The people who rescued you. They are witnesses aren't they?'

My mood stirred. 'Yes. I know them, owners from a local bakery. They ride by most days of the week delivering to the boats on the waterfront.

'It is a very small start. Look, I cannot do anything more myself. I do not want the newspapers to get hold of this story, as they will turn this whole mess inside out and plaster their results on the front pages. My name, you know, will ensure that. Perhaps you may be totally wrong on the other hand, but, if you do find out any thing new, you must come to me. Let me know straight away. I can help you in ways that you on your own could not achieve. Do not talk to any one about this except your boyfriend, and he should not talk to any one himself. I can unplug the bottlenecks as they arise, just as well as I can build ships you know.' He smiled thinly. One of the main reasons for existing, in his life, had disappeared forever leaving a void not even his money would be able to fill.

The cold air outside the office was in sharp contrast to the Virginia tobacco warmth I had just left. His words came as a tonic lifting me up again, and I was certain I could call on his powerful support at any time, provided, of course, I had the evidence to back up my rather mawkish statement.

I felt an arm around my waist making me jerk around in alarm. 'Theo!'

'I've finished work. Mevrouw Kroller had a baby last night so her husband wasn't there when I delivered my sandwiches. Herring and onion.' He held up a greaseproof bag. 'Lunch?'

We sat on the slope to the innermost basin just in front of a double row of trees setting off the front of Central Station. It faced south, so we could turn our faces to the sun while we munched the fish. Somehow, with one slice of bread piled on the other the food tasted better as it remained fresh and soft. It was a good meal for a tugboat man in the middle of the day. No wonder they were selling well.

'What were you doing in the Neumann Shipping Line offices?' Theo's voice was not nearly so lucid today, I noticed. He was unsure of himself, and scratched his head self-consciously, knowing, as he asked, that he was prying into my own private world.

'I was meeting with Neumann himself. He is Gretel's father.'

A look of extraordinary relief passed across his thin face. 'Of course, I hadn't realised the two were connected.'

'I felt I ought to meet him, as I was almost certainly one of the last people to have talked to Gretel.'

'Of course.' He repeated, squeezing my hand. 'I understand, really I do.'

I loved his naivety in being unable to cover his emotions. His fondness for me was written across his face as clear as if it had been tattooed. 'How many orders?' I said to change the subject. I did not want to have to lie to Theo, easily enough achieved, but I was not going to continue with the discussion at this time for all sorts of motives. In many ways, he was not yet able to receive the truth, where it could slow down the convalescence of his mind.

'Fifty-six. Some are asking for different or new fillings. I didn't know what to say, until I had spoken with you.'

This was where I found it frustrating. It would always have to be me who made the business decisions, at least for the foreseeable future.. 'I saw some cheap salami. What about ham from the bone?'

'Ham is very expensive.'

'What if we ask the butcher to slice it very thin and we mix it with cheese. More cheese than ham but the tuggies are on limited incomes and they will think it very grand, don't you think?'

'But ham,' repeated Theo.' No one eats ham, least not in these parts.'

'Not yet,' I said firmly, to make Theo understand I was quite prepared to try new and risky ideas as part of the venture. Theo was a traditionalist through and through, so even if he had alternatives himself he could find them difficult to sell unless I was urging him on. I smiled at myself. Here I was…a Jew, arguing for, and blatantly promoting the merits of ham with a Christian.

'I want to buy a bicycle Theo, with a big basket for the sandwiches.'

'Why?'

'We have to speed up deliveries in the morning for as the orders increase so will the morning round slow down. You might be twenty minutes behind at the end of a run. We have to get them out earlier.'

'You are becoming a bit of a bully.' He smiled.

I rubbed his shoulder closest to me. He had forgotten the reason for me being in this part of town, or he no longer cared. I realised then, for the first time, how much he trusted me. Break that one more time and he might never come back from hospital.

After supper that evening, we sat back, both smoking the same cigarette. This way, we could afford one packet a week. I could not help comparing the coarse tobacco taste, and smell, with the pale, grey smoke of the Neumann office. 'Are you ready?' Theo asked eventually. I had been basking in mindless revelations, switched off from the rest of the world.

'Ready for what?'

'Rembrandt Square. We said we would go, didn't we?'

I was about to tut-tut my teeth together until I saw his expectant face. 'All our profits are going to disappear if we do this too often.' But I did not refuse. I hadn't been into town, not properly, since the beginning of the war.

As we walked out on deck, having finished preparing the sandwich production, I saw Hans leaning against the wheelhouse door of the *Anna Rosner,* whittling away at a piece of wood. At the same time, he was staring back at the quay, as if searching for something, or someone. I wondered if it was a girl coming to meet him for the evening.

'Evening Mae. Evening Theo. Going out?'

'Yes,' replied Theo shortly. We both wanted to be alone that evening, and neither of us wanted his or any one else's company. 'Family well?'

'Yes thanks.' He kept his eyes locked onto what ever he was studying while he spoke. It was a rather rude gesture I thought, not like Hans's usual mood and I realised the row in the cabin had done some lasting damage.

Walking through the long, dark tunnel this time, I was thankful I was snuggled tight to Theo's arm. His shambling walk was slower than my own bird-like steps, but he out-paced me all the same. It meant our thighs came into contact every three steps or so, but I didn't mind. One day, he might take one of his hands from a pocket, and take hold of one of mine.

To get to Rembrandt Square, Theo took me through the New Market and across the *Amstel*. Unconsciously maybe, he kept well west of the *Middlelaan*, where I had first seen him, and where Pieter had picked me up from a puddle in the freezing ice. I did not want to see the dark, empty houses, those few which remained, with the dead eyes of the windows like skulls sockets, and the door frames, like the doors themselves, long since stolen for firewood. I wanted lights, bright and shining, and music, loud and sweet, to take away the shadows from both our lives.

We had been right to choose here. Around the Square, there were a number of bars. From some came the sound of music played on a variety of instruments. One song was French, a mournful love song I had heard played on the wireless in the bakery. In another, three Dutchmen strummed guitars with more enthusiasm than ability, but it did not seem to matter. It matched the mood of the Square and the people, like us, out for the evening and ready to enjoy anything out of the commonplace. Girls with cheaply bought, poorly applied lipstick, and youths with their hair slicked down with grease, stared out at us from the comfort of their hard won chairs in one bar, engaging themselves in people-watching while coveting the space in front of them. They made way for us readily enough, however, when we pushed open the door. Theo chose a space more for the fact there were two chairs together recently vacated, rather than they were near the music.

While he went to the bar, a garish construction of chrome and brightly painted wood, I sat drawing in the thick clouds of tobacco smoke which filled the room and made my eyes water. The friendly chatter of the Amsterdam young folk surrounded me. Strange, I realised, I could divorce these unlined faces with their puffy hairstyles and leather jackets, from my own thoughts whenever I wanted. Most of the drinkers around me were of my own age: none of them though, had brushed against life's edges yet; not, that is as I had done.

The Potato Eaters

The smoke formed ribbons of grey and blue as it curled towards the ceiling, coiling violently each time someone came or left the main door. Only over the bar counter itself did it disappear, as an electric fan split it into a thousand blue tufts, as it was inhaled by the spinning blades. I imagined the bar-girl, drawing beer from the row of pumps, would be sticky with nicotine, by the end of the evening.

A guitarist edged through the tight throng and took her place on one of the bar's high stools. In sitting down, her skirt edged up her thigh, much to the delight of the male population, who jeered and whistled, but it did not seem to affect the girl's composure. When it continued, preventing her from playing she tried, unsuccessfully to pull it down and opted, instead, to press her knees together. Theo returned, his left arm extended as high as it would go, as he clasped two glasses of beer, navigating a route through the crowd. I had decided sherry, nice as it was, was too expensive for us. It was a lady's drink, something Gretel might have drunk, I suppose, when she was with her father before dinner. It was not for me, a girl who had only managed to regain her registration papers, and thus country of origin, with the help of a single friend from the past. Without that confirmation to the police, of who I was and where I had come from, I might well have been sitting in a refugee camp somewhere, stateless, with only a tattoo for identification.

As Theo negotiated a space to sit down, having successfully steered his way through a jumble of legs, a face in the street outside the café materialised for an instant, before being lost again in the tide of evening drinkers. He had walked on, quite unconcerned, apparently unaware of my presence, but I was sure I recognised him: it was the same bloody policeman. The coincidence of meeting here at this time was too high.

'You were a thousand kilometres away, Mae. I called out to you several times to see which kind of beer you wanted to drink, but you were in some kind of trance.'

'I'm sorry.' I was contrite, and meant it. 'It's so noisy in here I could not hear you.'

'Nor see me,' he chided. 'I got you Heineken.'

'Good, good,' I repeated, anxious not to upset him. What the devil was the policeman doing in this neighbourhood, well up-town from his own patch?

'This bicycle idea. I think I can get one, but it doesn't have a cross-bar, so you could use it if you ever needed it.'

'Never mind that, I can ride a bike with a cross-bar anyway. How much?'

He smiled. 'Nothing.'

'Nothing? Nothing. Like, it cannot be legal. No one gives bikes away.'

'One of the tuggies. He never uses it. It is one of those delivery bikes that butchers use. It has a metal panel under the crossbar, which you can write on…like a company name for instance. And a big, low basket in the front.'

'Ooh!' I kissed him on the edge of his mouth and smelt and tasted salt and beer. 'We can paint your name on the side. I'm quite good at lettering.'

Theo paused, eyeing me up, wanting to raise a special subject, something private in his mind. I waited as well. He had to make up his own mind to get it out on the surface.

Finally he said. 'This *Meinheer* Neumann. What does he think about Gretel's death…and all? Does he think it is suicide?'

I told him all about the meeting, describing first the beautiful office with its marvellous view over the harbour. Then, Gretel's father, in detail, down to the black hairs, which curled out of his nostrils. Father had been forever plucking such hairs out of his own nose, with a pair of fine tweezers, making his eyes water. I explained to Theo, we had both believed murder could be a possibility, as it was the only form of death matching all of the circumstances, despite the note. This piece of paper was only confusing the real story, I was sure, in fact, it was the note which had become the mystery itself.

'What if,' said Theo pulling out the sentence as he mulled over an idea, 'what if I was to do some investigating? You said the man who attacked you ran off in the direction of the harbour…came from there as well, didn't he? Maybe I can walk round as I deliver the sandwiches, ask questions, discreet like, of course. I'm there each day and I feel he must come from this area.'

'Sort of as a detective?'

'I suppose so. You could help me at the weekends. We could call on all of the small boats, one by one, and you could see if you recognised anyone. During my walks, I can tick off the boats, those which could not be involved for one reason or another. The younger boat owners, wives, ladies, those types of people.'

'Why not older people?' I knew why, but I wanted him to tell me.'

'You said the man ran off quickly. I imagine he must be fairly young to do that, don't you?'

I did like the way he was responding. This was a rational man, a thinker and not the confused youth of several weeks ago. 'I hadn't thought of that. It is a terrific idea. Wonderful. And keep a sharp look out for the police, the one who does all the question-asking, particularly.'

While he was lighting a cigarette for both of us, I sorted out the right words to broach another subject. 'The boats...in the centre of the basin. How do you feel about them now?'

He drained his glass in a deliberate way before answering me. 'I have absolutely no idea at all. I was very frightened, Mae, that first time. The next time, I could lose contr–'

'Then, there mustn't be a second time, Theo. No amount of profit is worth the loss of your health, and my state of mind, in having caused it in the first place.'

'But...I have to take the orders back.'

'You don't have to, if you do not feel up to it.'

'I might get someone to deliver them for me, just for a few days. There's the postman I know well.'

I was about to say the profit would be watered down, but checked myself just in time.

We both paused to reflect. Light from behind the bar, low down, was shining directly through six large glasses of beer. The barman was slicing each top with a large wooden blade to remove the froth, and top up each glass a little higher. It seemed a shame. I liked the foam on my lips. One by one, the glasses tilted back, as it found its owner's mouth, where the clear, amber liquid began to slide out of view. It was followed, of course by the ritual smacking of lips, and other sounds of appreciation, as the stress and strain of the day buckled into small smiles at first, grins spreading wider as the evening extended itself.

Theo returned to his subject. 'I must try it again...in my own time. The harbour is...safe...I think but, it is when I get nearer to the *Ij* entrance, with the open water beyond...that is when I get the shakes, just as if I haven't eaten for two days. Like the war and the cold winter.'

I couldn't to tell him Auschwitz had been like this every day I had been an attendee, only far, far worse. 'Take your time.' I emptied my glass. I still had to make most of the conversation, as he wasn't the slightest bit interested any further in my work. 'Now, take me home, Theo. We need an early start in the morning.'

That bastard policeman. What was he following me around for?

* * * * *

It was swinging in the wind from the short foremast. It was the cat which had first stolen onto my bed in the *Anna Rosner* the night she had arrived in the harbour. Mae had seen it a few times, a stray but one that had once had a good home, as she herself had had. Now it hung, stiff in the cold, its fur spiky and at odds with the once sleek body, its eyes bulging. The suddenness of finding it here on the boat made her feel sick inside.

'Oh God! Now this.'

'It is only a cat,' said Theo trying to soften the scene.

'No, no it isn't Theo. Someone knew that I had been kind to it, fed it a few times, given it a stroke. This is a warning it could happen to me.'

'Surely, not-'

'What other possible reason cold there be. This is more that a cruel joke by the local children.'

'We will get the police in…find out who did it.'

'It is a waste of time. Nothing will be achieved.'

'Well,' he persisted. 'They could try and find out who did it. If there is a connection then we may find out more about who tried to kill you."

There's no point, Theo, besides I thought we, or rather you were going to do just that. You will have far more time than any old detective.'

'I don't think you like the police, do you?'

Mae did not reply. No, she did not like the police, was all she could have replied. Theo cut the ct down and threw it into a dustbin on the quayside before joining Mae in the wheelhouse, feeling the boat had been invaded. It was tainted, like dirty boot marks over a freshly scrubbed deck, and there was only one person she could think of who could have done such a thing.

Mae let Theo climb down the companionway steps first, and followed until the two of them were outside the main cabin. Theo slid into the darkened room, outwardly fearless and composed, inwardly, however, wondering just what he could or would do if a blow were to come from behind the door. Mae followed, jabbing at the door to the engine room with a finger, as if trying to remove a spider from the edge of a curtain. There was nothing there and no one appeared armed with a cudgel.

When a reaction came, it arrived unexpectedly, several minutes later as Mae was stripping the table of the sandwich remains following the production run they had completed before going out on the town. It came as a knock at the wheelhouse door.

'I'll take it,' said Theo, already making for the steps. 'You wait here, just in case.'

When he returned, he brought in tow a tall man in a superb tailored suit. His silver hair contrasted with his tie and his tanned complexion. Behind him, came a burly man in a grey suit, and cap, who turned out to be a chauffeur.

'*Meinheer* Neumann!' Mae was, understandably startled, having been cleaning the table, head bent down when the three men entered. The big man seemed to block out all the available light from the cabin creating shadows in each corner. 'What can I do for you?'

'It is quite alright,' he said to his driver,' please wait in the car.'

'If you say so, Sir.' The man retraced his steps without another comment, though his face showed his unhappiness at leaving his boss in such surroundings.

'Can you possibly spare me a few moments? I realise it is quite late.' He addressed his words to Mae. 'I can see you are busy.'

Signs of power and money always made Theo anxious. 'Of course, *Meinheer*. Won't you please take a seat?'

'Only if you will.'

All three found space around the table. Mae kicked a bread crust further beneath her chair. Theo turned his face expectantly towards Gretel's father. 'So?' said Mae, to start off the meeting.

'I have been thinking a great deal of what you said, Miss Epstein. I remember falling in love with my wife, such a long time ago now. Her parents really hated me as they thought I was a gold digger, if you know what I mean. Got where I did, my way you see. Always honest though,' he added, holding up a hand as if to reinforce his statement, only partially believed by his listeners. 'I've never broken the law. My parents were strong Dutch church. In the end, her parents allowed me to marry. It was a great day, I recall.'

He paused to take in the cabin for the first time, seeing the brightness of the copper pans and the clean crochet work on the table under his large hands. Eventually, he grunted with some long lost memory. 'Perhaps, just perhaps, Gretel really loved this man. Let's just imagine, for one moment she did. This leaves us with two options to consider. The first is this...this bum, Maas, loved her back. He would, therefore, have no reason to kill her at all, would he? Second. He did not love her, or fell out of love with her after a time, it happens. This could give him a reason-'

Mae cut him off before he could continue. 'Why? They were not married, not even engaged. He could just break off the relationship at any time to suit himself...as she could as well. That isn't motive enough for murder, is it?'

Neumann pulled out his silver cigarette case and flipped open the lid. Twelve Virginia cigarettes nestled there, held in place by a bright blue elasticised band. Mae tried to read the inscription engraved upside down, but failed. The cabin began to fill with smoke from the combined effect of the three smokers.

'You make the treatise worse, not better, madam. You see, which ever way you turn and look at it, Hans Maas is not the central character in this unholy mess.'

Mae grimaced, trying to exhale at the same time as interrupting. She began to cough. Finally, she managed to say:' I agree with you there.'

'So, who on God's earth could it be, and for what reason? I never really knew Gretel's friends, even though I knew their names. You are the only contact I have. I don't know where to start.'

Theo stared at the floor. 'It must all go back to this business with the Germans in the war.'

'You're right there, lad,' Neumann said, seizing on the idea as a drowning man will clutch at a straw on the water. 'I could start my investigation on that. There must be a connection with the past somewhere. I have a number of contacts in City Hall and one of them must have a lead into the archives section.'

'But…if the police have not been able to lay charges, what can you find out that they do not already know?'

'It's my first lead, Miss Epstein. I do have certain contacts who will work in a rather different way to that of the police, if you know what I mean.' Mae didn't. 'I was given my first lead in buying a ship when I had nothing to go on. Just information. From little beginnings we may be able to build a picture to find out who really killed my daughter.'

He rose, shaking hands gravely with the two of them, adding a tiny, but significant old-fashioned bow as he withdrew from the cabin.

'Go up with him,' Mae whispered to Theo. 'See him off. He is a good man.'

She reached for the greaseproof paper, sighing. 'Will I ever get the chance for a clear run at this catering business?'

* * * * *

Theo stepped off the deck of the *Kuijpers*, loaded with his first delivery of the day. Dawn had broken into a backdrop of half greys and whites, its stillness leaving a flat calm to the water. It created a tension in the atmosphere, causing the oil and diesel to slop uneasily on the surface, almost as if it were waiting for something momentous to happen. Sheet lines slapped mastheads in a series of lazy tattoos, to match the ebb and flow of water lying in the bottom of the *Anna Rosner's* dinghy. The normally raucous gulls had also sensed a change in mood to the day, wishing for the wind to rise and lift them above the overnight, homebound trawlers cleaning out their holds. Both would bring a temporary increase to the bird population of the basin.

'Whoa-ho Theo! Off so early?' It was Jos, up well before the rest of the family. His eyes looked tired with blotchy hollows beneath them, resting like soot on his skin.

'You look tired,' said Theo to underpin his thought and rather stating the obvious.

'I couldn't sleep. This business with Hans is not finished yet, you know. That policeman is still about I hear, on the opposite side of the water, continuing to make his enquiries. Sometimes, I see him watching this quayside through his binoculars and always trained on Hans when he leaves for work. I think he believes Hans is guilty but does not have the evidence, so is attempting to trap him into doing or saying which will incriminate him.'

'I have to go, Jos. My clients are waiting.'

'I'll come with you, keep you company. I expect the fresh air will do me good, as well. Besides…' he paused, keeping his eyes directed towards the horizon, 'there is something I have to ask you.'

'Ask away,' said Theo beginning to feel uncomfortable, 'but keep up with me. These tugboat men get up very early.' He walked on, shouldering the heavy bag, which contained the carefully wrapped packages. Mae had become quite expert in folding the ends so they would not pull out. Despite his height, and his long legs, Jos had to increase his speed to keep up.

'Why do you think the police are still around?' He asked over Theo's shoulder.

'I have no idea.'

'I simply have to find out. I must try and help, as this is wearing down the whole family. Even Papa is becoming quiet. Do you know…in the war, Hans would go into the streets and play his whistle. Sometimes, he would make a few cents and always, he would give them to me.'

'What? And not for your sisters, as well?'

'Well, of course, for them too. The point is, he did not keep them himself.'

But he was talking to an iron bollard, blocking his way. Theo had jumped onto a steel-decked barge, which lay very low in the water. A young, married couple, the woman with a young baby in her arms, came out to greet him.

'Morning Theo.'

'Morning to you both…sorry, to you three. One cheese and onion, and one cheese on its own. Same tomorrow?' He took the money offered.

The couple looked at each other. 'I hear you are doing ham. Is it very expensive?'

'News travels fast. Ham and cheese mixed. Eight cents more.' The couple nodded. Theo could see Jos was beginning to become impatient. He began to write out the order methodically and laboriously, his printed handwriting neat, if executed agonisingly. He eventually touched his forelock. 'Until tomorrow.'

He jumped onto the quayside, suddenly feeling strong and in control of himself, a servant of no one, a mood he hadn't experienced for years. He knew if he was to go out on the *Ij* one day, he would find it very difficult to control his emotions such an enormous step would create. He did know, however, it was sufficient at this time, for him to consider rowing out into the middle of the harbour again.

Jos continued as if he hadn't broken his conversation for the past five minutes. 'That Gretel woman had a nerve, didn't she? Making all of those accusations. She only did it because she was stood up. All women are like that I think I expect you find them the same.'

'I dunno. I don't know any that well.'

'But, what about Ruth, Mae?'

'Well...she is different, isn't she? She's not like other girls I knew at school. She's...' he stumbled over words again, attempting to find the right one and becoming muddled, 'so efficient.' He waved a hand across the air in front of him, as if to brush off the wrong words to make way for the correct one.

'Bet she is no different between the legs,' replied Jos crudely, giggling. 'I expect you know all about it.' He jabbed Theo in the ribs, an action he found merely increased the other's speed further.

'We sleep in different parts of the boat, Jos. There is none of that...sex stuff.'

'I bet,' Jos repeated, but Theo was gone again, this time to stroke the soft noses of the two big baker's horses that had been hitched to a hawser,

'Strange business of that girl of yours,' said one of the brothers. 'Did she report the attack?'

'I believe so.' Theo did not want to lie and felt uncomfortable, but for some reason, he felt it was important they believed his viewpoint.

'Good job. Get the police on to it as soon as possible. They must have a good description of the man, from Mae. They'll soon find the bugger.'

His brother, identical in looks and dress except for having an enormous nose to distinguish him from the other, put in his own proposal. 'Men like him want their balls cut off. Castrate 'em, that's what I say.' Jos turned to go, bored. 'Come on, Theo. You'll never get these delivered.' 'You are right,' Theo replied briskly and began to run, leaping ropes and bales of goods dumped haphazardly on the quayside. The light was growing stronger by the minute, as tints of yellow began to suffuse the greys and whites of the horizon. He hadn't enjoyed the crude conversation of the other man. His grandparents had always moderated their language in front of him, and he suspected it had not altered much when they had been alone and out of his hearing. It would have been a rare occasion when a swear word in the most dilute form slipped out in conversation. His grandmother's wrath could, and would have been something to observe from afar. Crude humour was not a subject to have been found on the *Kuijpers* before the war.

He thought back to Jos's words. He had seen Mae naked, once or twice, when the curtain had not been pulled across properly, and neither would have wanted to draw attention to the fact by pulling it further into position. He would, though, study her when she lay asleep. She had the habit of often lying with her feet tucked up tight into her chest, so her body was chastely covered even without the quilt. A spasm would, sometimes flutter across her face, a grimace of intense pain, or fear, reflected in the furrows around her mouth. It would cause her legs to react, stretching out sometimes in front of her, so he could gaze upon her bare torso. He felt like a voyeur, though this did not prevent him from continuing to stare at her. So, he would remain, hardly breathing, attendant upon her until a cloud would obscure the moon again, to merge the bedclothes and her body into a series of inky blurs.

Jos had gone, he was surprised to note. He would be late to catch the picking lorry, and, no doubt, Pieter would clip him one over an ear none too lightly but Theo liked the way he had defended his brother. He felt sorry for Jos. It could not be easy living in the small boat with his parents still under their direct control on a daily basis. He felt he was a good man, pressurised into living the life he did, as did Hans, as there were no other options open to them. Neither had any money to give them the independence they sought. Jos would now find himself in trouble because he wanted to spend twenty minutes away from the suffocating closeness of the family. Theo wished he had a brother to care for him at times, or, he corrected himself, that was until Mae came along. When he returned to the *Kuijpers,* from his second delivery, Mae had gone to work. He inhaled the air of the cabin, sensed her warmness still hanging in the room, painting its own picture of her. He glanced about restlessly and knew he had to try again. Paying the postman wasn't going to work, for he couldn't cheat himself even if he was able to fool Mae, and he wondered if he had been clever enough to deceive her. Her eyes were often in the back of her head. Besides, paying the postman in beers was not a commercial operation, and there seemed no point in doing business in the middle of the basin if he was not to do it himself.

Out on deck, the weather had changed since the early morning. The wind had arrived, causing pieces of paper to toss about like autumn leaves; the small eddies, suspending wood shavings and dust, swirled across the scrubbed decks of the boats to stain the new washing. The local gulls padded after him flat-footedly, believing there might be food. They squawked at each other, in the same way as one fisherwoman would do to another, as they manoeuvred for the best site in the marketplace.

He sighed deeply as he climbed over the side and lowered himself into the tiny dinghy. It was so small, just two metres in length, while the bow was blunted as if it had been hit head-on in a crash with a large steamer,. It gave the appearance of a wooden coffin, bobbing uneasily over the water. He tried to ignore his description of his boat: it was difficult enough as it was.

As he had primed himself yesterday, Theo pulled on the stern rope until he was clear of the tug. With a strong, final heave, he allowed the boat to drift around the stern of the *Anna Rosner,* where he caught hold of the next rope. His hands, he knew, were shaking as if he had contracted Parkinson's disease; his palms were wet with sweat, despite the keen wind which was cutting into his thick jersey. 'Christ! What am I doing?' He realised he had blasphemed. 'Bugger,' he completed the phrase, and felt better, if not safer.

The next craft in line was a massive barge, broad in the beam, like an old washer-lady. The high gunwale cut out a lot of the daylight as he pulled himself along her length. His absolute mission was not to look ahead. Once or twice, passers-by looked down idly in a disinterested fashion. When they did, he busied himself fitting the scull in position, and permitted the pram to rock free of the ropes. Little by little, he progressed along the harbour wall until he was at right angles to a series of large boats moored tight together, so much so their sides squealed and groaned in friendly companionship as they compressed the rubber tyres placed there as fenders. The wind was now causing the craft in the basin to rise and fall into the greasy troughs. One bow would raise itself, followed by the next, and the next, as if they were horses jumping a fence in a race. Oil and water slopped against the steel-painted sides and coloured the surface in petrol glints, a hundred dragon flies all meeting at one point. Above him, the clouds were now shredded, the same shade of pale grey as the seagulls, beginning to stack above the masts moved to obliterate the towers of Saint Nicholas and Central Station. He sighed yet again. It was definitely going to rain and he had forgotten to bring a jacket. Eventually, he made it to the six boats and delivered the packages on time. These tugs were on the perimeter of the middle basin berths, Ahead lay, moored the biggest and the best boats.

Using all of his strength, he jerked on the last rope in the line, turning to stand to face the stern, so he could not see the entrance to the *Ij*. He had memorised the location of the boats out in the stream as he began to scull, closing his eyes as tight as was possible to the vast sheets of heaving water and the opening on the left where the exit tunnel mouth lay. A quick glance at it to position the whole basin in his mind made it appear to be a giant whale's maw, and as terrifying.

'God... give me strength. God... give me strength. God...give me...strength.' He continued the mantra with each roll of the scull. He could see the blackness on his eyelids and the dark, evil just out of reach on the horizon of his thoughts. When the sickness began to move towards him, beginning to press him into a corner, forming up behind him like a column of soldiers marching up his back, he snapped his eyes open, dreading, but needing to discover, what was ahead. Surprised, he found himself well out into the crossing, with his course accurate and on line for his destination. It was a fine piece of navigation, for he had not

The Potato Eaters

opened his eyes once. The boat ahead dipped into a trough, then rose as if to acknowledge his imminent arrival. It brought him cheer as he closed his eyes again.

Quickly he found temporary moorings with his clients and delivered his sandwiches before eyeing the larger craft further out.

'God…give me strength,' the repetition sounding like a priest with a rosary in an endless loop. In mid-phrase, he felt a sharp thump of wood on steel, throwing his direction askew and unbalancing him.

'That's not very seamanlike,' came a voice from above him. Theo threw up a rope and an older man made fast with a series of rapid half hitches. There was a small iron ladder close-by so he could negotiate the deck with more grace than his immediate contact with the craft.

'Sorry.'

'Have we lost much paint?' Another voice materialised above, though edged with humour. The big boat, all steel and probably a hundred years old was so rusted there appeared to be not a single spot of paint on the entire surface. Only the brass work remained bright and the deck boards scrubbed white, being areas, Theo supposed, which could be reached with relative simplicity. The first man, with a white mop of hair, standing erect as if it were a brush, straightened up from his task.

'Visitors?'

'Visitor,' said his companion. 'Steered straight at us. He was sculling as if all the demons in the world, and more, were after him.'

'Almost certainly true,' said Theo under his breath, though taking the time to shake hands with both. Quickly, he explained his mission while they listened in silence until he had finished.

'Seems a good idea, young un, but, we never go to sea. Boat would break its back now if we moved across the basin, so we are moored here for-ever, retired, all three of us, so to speak. As we have no need to get up early in the morning and Benjamin brings back fresh bread every morning as his exercise, so there's no sale, I'm afraid.'

Theo turned to go. This was one sale he wasn't going to win what ever he said. And they, being out in the basin as well! 'Thanks anyway and I am really sorry I banged your boat.'

'Come and have a Geneva. You did your best and we don't welcome many visitors here, save the harbour master from time to time who always wants to know what we intend to do with the boat once we are gone. He has a point, as it will have to be salvaged on the spot.

'You've come your distance, besides, it is going to blow and rain any moment. Wait until the storm passes or you will get very wet out there without a coat.'

Theo gazed across the gulf he had travelled, appalled at the area of water which separated him from the *Kuijpers*. Boats were disappearing into a grey veil as he watched. A sudden splatter on the deck announced it had arrived, and the three men moved to the wheelhouse, which could have accommodated ten in comfort.

Benjamin led the way to the main cabin on the same level, the room being far lighter than his own with many more areas of glass. In fact, they were windows rather than portholes or scuttles. There was a large rag rug on the floor and rows of different china mugs, suspended on brass hooks screwed to the ceiling. It gave him the impression of a bar. As always, a large table, edged also in brass and highly polished, dominated the space. It was spread with books, the sort without any cartoons or pictures inside and, almost certainly they had prefaces and bibliographies. More books lined the end wall much as wallpaper will do in another house, overflowing onto the floor in piles but showing, nonetheless, there was some sort of order in their stacking.

'Benjamin studies,' explained the other, still unnamed. 'I'm Michiel,' he said as if answering Theo's query. 'Benjamin never stops asking questions about all sorts of silly things.'

Benjamin merely smiled, quite used, obviously, to the comment repeated *ad nauseam*. He poured out three Genevas with a practised hand, into three tiny glasses. His arms were much tanned despite the earliness of the year spreading to his face in the form of freckles.

'Here's to your little venture. I'm sure it will go well, despite us.' And, after a pause, while the two of them studied their guest he said: 'you must be Jon's grandson…from the *Kuijpers*?'

'Well…yes,' said a startled Theo, choking on the strong gin. 'How did you know?'

'I knew you were ill,' Benjamin went on, quite unabashed at drawing attention to Theo's troublesome condition, which often embarrassed people trying to talk about it. 'You live on your own, next to the Maas family, don't you?' It was a statement.

'Yes. They are my friends.'

Michiel gave a non-committal grunt. 'That's hard work...what they do. But, they keep the *Anna Rosner* shipshape, I'll give them that.'

He could have been a trifle more encouraging, thought Theo. He was clearly holding something back 'Do you know them well?'

'No. Not really. Well...before the war, we used to see them much more regularly. Used to have a drink together occasionally. That's when we would run ashore ourselves of an evening. Those boys of his liked a drink or two.'

It was the signal for opening up the tall clay bottle again. The clear, oily liquid flowed up the sides of the glasses as rain began to beat against the glass with a sudden fury. It caused all three men turn to gaze at the storm, typical seamen, gauging the weather before putting to sea.

'Here it comes. Said it was a-coming.'

'It didn't need a fortune-teller to see it was going to storm,' replied Michiel. 'I could smell it an hour ago.'

'I smelt it when I got up this morning,' countered Benjamin, determined to win the argument.

Theo's eyes roved around the cabin, taking in the Swiss cuckoo clock and two large pictures, both of big ships.

'We both used to be engineers. Big ships,' said Benjamin, seeing where Theo's eyes were fastened. 'Do you read at all?'

'No. Never seem to have the time. Besides, this job keeps me busy right up to bedtime.'

'I guess so.'

'You say you know the Maas family...and the two sons.'

'Yes. And a pretty daughter, that Suzannah.' Benjamin's face filled with smiles and his faded blue eyes winked in acknowledgement.

'Did you drink with them much?'

'With Hans, before the war, that is. The other one, what's his name, Jos, was a bit young for that family. Hans was something of a handful, wasn't he?'

'How do you mean?' Theo was immediately alert and curious.

'Well…stories and things.'

'Stories?'

Michiel took up the conversation. 'There's stories, about the war, and the Maas family. Those boys could often be seen watching those bastard Germans parading in Dam Square. Most people, of course, stayed away on those events but, the two boys always liked to see those pigs goose-stepping through our streets, waving their banners, and the like. They could be seen on their boat from time to time, practising the Nazi salute, in fun, maybe, but it upset many of the local watermen hereabouts. They did it too often for it to be treated as boyish pranks.'

Theo stayed silent, using the excuse to drink so he could mull over the man's words. Were these just words, bandied about like the boxes of fish landed each day or was there something more, the sort of news he had suggested to Mae he could find? Hans was, once again, back in the circle of light, the spot-light distinguishing him above the other members of the family. Whichever way a discussion fell, the eldest son of the Maas family re-emerged to throw doubt and mistrust on his plea that he was not and had never been a collaborator.

Theo's mind did not move at the same speed as Mae's, and his reasoning was slower. Though Doctor Hertz was satisfied with his progress, to the extent he had eased down the drugs, he was still sufficiently dosed up to have his reaction times to such issues slowed down considerably. Hertz had promised to remove the treatment altogether if he continued on with Mae's help. Meanwhile, he had to stumble along trying to keep pace with two intelligent engineers.

'What did Pieter and Elizabeta do about it?'

'Very little, Theo. Pieter is a proud man. He refused to listen to the voices, some of whom, of course, were malicious, no doubt about it. He is a successful man in his own way, makes him feel he is superior to the rest of us in the basin. Folks don't like it, do they? So, the one or two stories grew, they got bigger, and more fanciful. The truth is then bent and, in the end, no one knows what is real and what is just a lie. 'He poured himself a third drink and took half of the glass at one drink.

'Hans was arrested as a suspected collaborator-'

The Potato Eaters

'And freed. No evidence,' said Theo quickly. 'All to do with a jilted girlfriend.'

'Funny though,' Michiel said, 'he gets off and she is found in a canal the next day.'

Theo was beginning to feel dizzy with the gin. He was not used to drinking in the day, and not at this pace even in the evening, and not gin anyway. The two old men gave the impression of being impervious to the quantity they had consumed. They allowed the clear liquid to run down their throats like wartime orange juice to a child.

'Where did you first hear these stories…about Hans?'

'The first time was when it all went round the harbour, both sides it reached, almost to the Station. You know how it travels here…faster than the water post.'

Theo did know. The news of his illness, that he was again in the special hospital, had been known on the far side of the basin, almost as soon as he had been signed in, by Doctor Hertz.

Benjamin was continuing. 'Pieter Maas heard his boys were up at Dam Square, watching a parade. He went up there and pulled them back to the *Anna Rosner* by their ears. He didn't seem afraid of the Germans. They just sat back and laughed at his antics. But…the trouble was, the boys went back. They were fascinated by the bands and the flags, the parades, the sort of things the Nazis did well. We all love a band of marching men, but of our own forces, not the…occupying forces.' He almost spat out the last words, unable to bring himself to say the word conquerors.

'I must go. The rain has stopped. Are you sure you do not need any sandwiches?'

'No thank you son. But we will tell the visiting boats. There are several moorings here. And…good to see you are so much better. At one time, we believed you were lost to the hospital forever. Word was you were never going to recover.'

'More harbour talk for you, eh?' They all laughed.

As Theo climbed back into the dinghy and wiped the thwart dry, he realised what he had said. It was harbour talk, an idle nation with nothing to do but speculate, while the Germans ran their country. What if two teenagers played at pretending to be soldiers? Boys had run away to war since time immemorial.

He had moved fifty metres before he realised he was in midstream. The shock of it froze him to the scull. Back across the water, he was being watched by his two, new companions, who gave him a friendly wave. Though he could not let go, he waggled the oar in a semblance of a goodbye, concentrating on keeping the course as straight as possible.

'I can make it. I can make it,' he breathed out loud and hoarsely. His bowels felt loose, looser than he might be able to control. The only thing, keeping him from fouling his underpants, was the realisation of what Mae might say when she washed them. She wouldn't know, he speculated, for he could just throw them overboard before she came home. Nonetheless, he concentrated on holding on to his bowel contents, despite the fears arising from the water.

He made it back, sweaty and shaking as if with the ague, where he to clung to the *Kuijpers* hawser for several minutes, below the quay edge and out of sight of passers-by. The Family had all gone to work long ago, so they could not see him clutching to the rope with his head bowed in total exhaustion. Just now, the last thing he wanted was for Hans's voice to echo above him, asking him what he was meant to be doing, or Pieter's bright enquiry, well-meaning and kind, but making him feel small, insignificant and useless.

Now he was safe, his language switched from the godly to the earthly. 'Shit! Shit! Shit! What on earth am I doing, boating about, selling sandwiches to retired boatmen?' The outburst went as quickly as it came, for he felt a mood of triumphant success flood over him. He wanted Mae to come back so he could tell her what he had learned.

Mae, on the other hand, was far from happy.

* * * * *

I couldn't see what I had done wrong. A few minutes after I arrived at work, the Manageress bustled in rather urgently, giving rapid instructions to my work mates to take over the running of my duties.

'But, the sandwiches, Madame Who will organise them?'

'They are taken care of Ruth. You are to see two of the Directors at eight o'clock this morning. In fact, as soon as they arrive.'

'Why? I mean, what do they wish to talk about? Is it something I have done?'

'I really don't know, Ruth. I was told to ensure you are ready to see them when they arrived and, on that, I could assure them, as you always seem to be here before anybody else. If I were you, I would take off your cap and brush your hair. Leave your apron on, though.'

I could not grasp any of it, and it alarmed me. The woman was calm, I must admit, polite, nice even, with a slight smile on her face, but she was giving nothing away if she did know the real reason. I wondered if she might have become jealous in some way and had got me into trouble with a Director on some silly charge or other. The bloody sandwiches and the quiches had just taken off like one of those jet planes, with a queue forming daily as if it were the war all over again. Two queues, one for bread and the other for lunch time snacks. That cannot all have been bad, though it could be construed, I suppose, the shop was running rapidly in the opposite direction to its original intentions.

'You should go up now, Ruth. You can wait in the secretary's office at the top of the stairs.'

I had never been to the first floor before. Only management normally trod this staircase: them and the spotty-faced accountant, a nephew of one of the owners. He had given me an owlish look once, burdened as he was at the time with a pile of ledgers. He could not be the reason for my summons, for I hadn't spoken one word with the brat. Perhaps I should have? Maybe I should have bobbed in front of him, while opening the door, and said: 'Good morning, Sir'. Oh God, give me strength, I repeated to myself, needing considerable strength of mind in a fast fading future. I could not afford to lose this job. No, it was the bloody sandwiches, it had to be. Buggar.

I walked up the staircase, whose treads were covered in highly polished linoleum. The handrail, in brass, gleamed fresh from its daily rubbing and without the day's fingers and hands yet upon its surface. At the top were two doors. One said BOARD ROOM the other was marked PRIVATE SECRETARY. Across the small hall was a third door, slightly ajar. It was a toilet but, it was only natural I suppose, the owners would wee privately rather than use our all sex toilet at the back of the bakery.

The secretary I had seen as a background figure, moving rather purposefully in one direction or another. She did not mix with the rest of us and rarely acknowledged me. At this moment she did not catch my eye. I was, without a doubt, in serious trouble.

'Epstein? '

'Yes.'

'Sit over there. *Meinheer* Mathieu has not yet arrived. When he does, he will be joined by *Meinheer* Willi.' She sniffed into a handkerchief before starting to type on a modern looking machine. I could not help noticing on the opposite side of her desk to the typewriter, a brown folder. On it, in clear lettering, was my name – EPSTEIN R. Mejuffrouw.

Just like all Germans, the super-efficient Dutch had a file on everyone. Last time I had a file it was even slimmer than this one. It had AUSCHWITZ-BIRKENAU – WOMEN and a black stylised eagle stamp at the top. This one could hardly be better.

'*Mejuffrouw* Epstein, isn't it?'

A man had come out of the Board Room. He was almost as thin as I was, but very tall, so tall he had a permanent stoop which aged him prematurely, with the same subtle hint of money I had noticed with Neumann. I could see, as he held out his hand to shake mine…surprising me…that his watch was of gold. He limped.

'My name is Mathieu Bessels. I am the Director of Production for the comp-'

'Yes Sir. I know who you are. You are my direct boss.'

He laughed the easy laugh of the super rich, with little to worry him, certainly not at my level of discussion. 'You appear to be taking over my job. In here, please.'

So this is what it was all about. The secretary looked briefly into my eyes, before dismissing me completely. She knew, she knew, the bitch.

Inside the room, a large polished table, gleaming like the brass handrail, filled the room so it glowed, and showed off different grains of the inlaid woods. Father had had something similar. Conscious of my surroundings and desperate to hold onto my job, I had lapsed into the Dutch accent of my old school. I was about to open my mouth again when we were joined by a second man. He was older, greyer, but having the same quirky and characteristic bottom lip which retained a fleshy swell as though he was forming a pout.

'Willi Bessels. I am the Managing Director. Would you please sit over there, on the opposite side of the table.' So saying, the two men sat facing me, easing themselves into the leather chairs with familiarity borne of long use. I didn't dare place my hands on the table for fear of leaving a blotch of greasy fingers on its pristine surface.

'Now…Miss Epstein,' began Willi Bessels. 'Thank you for coming. You have not been long with us, have you?' He used my title, Miss, rather as a German likes to be addressed as von. Here we definitely go, I knew. 'No Sir. But I enjoy the work very much.'

'Yes, yes. Our shop manager has given me her report.' He tapped the same brown file I had seen in the secretary's office. 'It is your new ideas I want to talk about.'

'It was nothing really, Sir, just a silly idea. I thought perhaps-'

Mathieu Bessels interrupted me with a wave of his hand. 'But, they are not nothing, if you understand me. They have had a considerable effect upon our traditional business.'

I had never been able to work out double negatives. I always had to subtract one of the noes, then work forward from there. I never could understand why people spoke like that. 'I could stop the production Sir. Go back to cakes and breads.' It was my silly idea, nothing to with Madame.' I felt I had to be loyal to her, for she had helped me a lot.

'You still misunderstand me. We not only want you to continue, but we want to expand production. We are going to open five more retail outlets, each with a special lunch counter and are negotiating with some of the big stores for them to provide such a service to their customers.' Father and son both paused, both waiting for me to react.

I was dumbfounded. So anxious had I been to hold on to my job I had blanked out any thought of receiving good news. And now they would think I was an idiot for not working out a double negative, for goodness sake. 'But Sir. Where do I come in all of this? You said you want me to continue in what I am doing.'

Bessels Senior leaned over the table to emphasize the importance of his words. 'We want you to develop your ideas and to supervise all six of our main outlets; that is, here in the City, the new five, also the shopping stores production. Later, if this proves a success, we will open more and you can take these on as well.'

I could not think of a single word to say. All the years in the camp and the grim period in Rotterdam were forgotten. Bessels Senior saw my unsteadiness and misread the hesitancy. 'Your pay will of course, be increased significantly. And you will receive an advance…so you can go and buy yourself a suit. A production manageress must always look smart in front of her customers. We will agree all the details in the next few days, if this is satisfactory to you?'

I blinked, rather like a chameleon does when it is trying to make up its mind whether it can be seen on its carefully camouflaged branch, or not. As I stood up, Willi Bessels said: 'You are of the Jewish faith, are you not?'

My heart plummeted again. 'Yes Sir.'

He paused for a long time, finding it difficult, I think, to find the correct words, or any words, which might allow him to speak appropriately to me. Eventually he said: 'What the Germans, and aye, some of our own people, at times, did to you as a race…we shall never be able to make amends for…it is right and proper I now have the opportunity to apologise to you.' It was a curiously old-fashioned speech, followed by a half bow. Stupidly, I bobbed back at him like a pantry maid and threw a quick smile. Yes, it was late, very late, but nice all the same.

I shook hands with both men and headed for the door. The secretary continued to bang away at her typewriter. That was all she ever would be, a machine, unthinking, unable to contribute a single original thought or idea.

For the rest of the day, I worked in a kind of trance, spending money I did not know if I would receive or not. Father would have been very angry, at least, annoyed that I had not asked what my increase would be. He would have asked for it in writing, before agreeing to any proposal. I hadn't done that either.

With evening, and the closing of the shop, I thought of Theo, and bread and sandwiches. I had nine loaves as well as a variety of fillings. They pulled heavily on my shoulders. Outside, it was much darker than usual as a storm began to pile up across the polders, cutting off the Spring evening sky with a black and purple band of cloud. The wind had risen enough to make the dust in the street form thin lines along the pavements, rather as if it had leaked out of a bag with a small hole. The canvas sides of the delivery lorries bulged like barge sails causing those moving on the roads to sway dangerously. In my minds eye I saw the basin, and wanted to be home.

'Stormy, eh?' A voice in my ear, followed by my bag being pulled from my shoulder made me jump. It was just before the tunnel, which had become shrouded in deep gloom. The wind moaned down its full length accentuating the scene. I clutched for the strap, missed and turned.

'Hans! It's you.'

'Yes, me. I'll carry your bag. It looks heavy.'

'Thank you,' I answered, concerned and now in some fear.

'Actually,' he went on, 'I wanted to see you, to apologise. I said some terrible things the other day to you.'

'You certainly did. You called me a Jew. That was the worst.'

'But…you are a Jew,' he parried, trying to hide behind his statement.

'I know it. But it was the manner in which you said it. It never goes away, does it, this hate for the Jews? It is like the common cold, remaining in the gut of ordinary gentiles, waiting to come up out of their throats. You Hans are no different from the rest.'

'I said I was sorry.'

'If I was to turn round one day when you are in mid-conversation and called you a dirty little gypsy, who grubbed about in the earth all day long, how would you take that?'

He sucked air in hard before rallying. 'I wouldn't like it one bit.'

'I don't want apologies, Hans. Far better men than you have tried, and failed, to apologise for what has been done to my people. Today, all we want is to live our own lives in peace, without fear. It is quite a small thing I ask.'

'You needn't be frightened of me,' he whispered, as we entered the tunnel. I laughed, the sound echoing hollowly. 'Even with a bloody big knife you were waving at the time?'

'Sorry,' he repeated, thumping me on the shoulder as if I were one of his gang of boys at school. 'Your language is awful.'

'No fucking worse than your own,' I retorted spitefully. I wanted to use more adjectives, to make him sit up and understand what I was trying to make him see. If he was going to attack me, he would probably wait until I was almost clear of the tunnel. He could see if anyone else was approaching. The rail embankment above shielded the entrance from the boat owners, but, he would be hampered by the heavy bag: it might just give me time to get clear. I was sure I could easily out-run him so to be certain of the best chance, I distanced myself from him and moved forward a pace. As we neared the end of the tunnel, he speeded up until we were shoulder to shoulder again. I had very little room left for manoeuvre.

The wind came back strongly as we moved onto the quayside. Hans was relaxed, cheerful almost and showed no signs of agitation. The harbour, though, had turned into a heaving maelstrom of choppy water. Each boat was acting independently of its neighbours. They corkscrewed, causing their sides to collide alarmingly, prevented from real damage by the fenders placed there for that very reason. One boat was protected from itself by two pieces of old mattress. Another, further out, had elegantly plaited rope fenders. Sheets and shrouds screamed out as if in torture, becoming entangled with the shredded clouds. I was bewildered by the change.

'It's coming from nowhere.'

'No, it's been building all day. You stay in so much at work in that office of yours, you never see the weather.' He shook his head, convinced this was a bad thing.

I stopped in my tracks, safe. I could be seen by others. This route was not the one Hans would have taken from the lorry. 'Why did you come out of your way to meet me?'

'I told you. I wanted to say I was sorry.'

'There's something else.'

He turned to study my face. 'You're a bright girl, Ruth. It is Gretel's father. He is at the *Kuijpers*. He's in his car, parked nearby.'

It was my turn to stare. 'Have you spoken to him?'

'I suppose it was one way of describing what happened. He found it difficult to bring himself to talk to me. Theo is out, but it is you, anyway, he wants to see. Lucky girl,' he added a trifle sarcastically. 'He's got a lot of money.'

'And some very sophisticated women in tow,' I replied tartly. The idea of *Meinheer* Neumann…and me together in a hot, sticky situation appeared ludicrous to me. 'Is this why you came to see me?'

'I would like to know what he has to say to you. Perhaps you could tell me after. She was my girlfriend once, you know.'

'It all depends if it is private or not, doesn't it? Thank you for carrying my bag, I said, relieving him of the load.' I began to hurry. 'I'll speak to you later.' It was important I sever my discussions with him, for I needed to be alone when I met Neumann.

Hans disappeared into the wheelhouse of another tug. Alongside the *Kuijpers* was a black Renault, like the French police use. It brought back memories again.

'Hullo *Meinheer* Neumann. I heard you were looking for me.' I spoke through the window where he was alone.

'Would you be so kind as to spare a few moments for me? I have some news for you.' So saying, he had opened the passenger door, assuming, as so many rich men do, I would acquiesce easily. I did.

We shook hands awkwardly across the steering wheel. 'I have had a report back from my secretary. He has spent the day researching for me. He asked quite a few questions.'

I might have known this man would have a male secretary. I had never heard of such a thing before, but then I had not seen much of life anyway. 'What sort of news?'

'The building, the one Gretel said she saw Hans Maas come out of. It is on the *Herengracht*. Typical of the Germans, they took the smartest addresses. It was a kind of meeting place. The lower ground floor rooms, street level that is, were knocked into one, so fifty people or so could meet together. Nothing was advertised, no signs, no door-plates, no guards or anything, you understand? Inside, upstairs, were high-class prostitutes.'

Ah, a German brothel. They were all over the place.'

'No,' said Neumann firmly. 'This one was different. Young Dutchmen were encouraged to go in, have a drink, and meet with others like themselves. Girls were arranged for them upstairs. Even boys…' he slowed and stopped. 'Yes, I'm afraid so. What ever your taste, so to speak. I had heard there were some fairly nasty stories coming out of the place at one time. It became a meeting place for the young, the disaffected, the poor, seeking to jump on the ladder, but very low-key to the outside world, very discreet.'

I wasn't sure what low-key meant, but he painted a fairly dismal picture. I understood exactly what he was implying.

'And Hans used to go in there?'

Neumann frowned as if unable to understand himself. 'No. That is the strange part. He wasn't a member there. Oh yes. It was a members' club, typical of the German character to keep strict records.'

'So if Hans didn't go there, it puts him in the clear.'

Again he frowned. 'Strange, he wasn't on the members list. Of course, he could have been a guest while they sized him up as a potential recruit. Gretel was very clear she had seen him there that day.'

I felt relieved. 'Are you sure you looked over all of the lists? Perhaps there were other lists which have gone missing-'

'It wasn't me who checked, young lady, but my man is very efficient and thorough.' He looked amused and began to light one of his cigarettes.

'I'm sorry, I didn't mean-'I was embarrassed, but it was also important I made sure. 'He might have faked his name...altered it in some way.'

'I don't think so, Ruth. May I call you Ruth? All callers at the house would have been obliged to identify themselves through their identity card. The Germans would have wanted to begin the process early, as soon as they had a potential conscript. Maas is a common name too, isn't it? There are quite a few.'

As I listened to his words, I surreptitiously drew in the delicious Virginia smoke. Maas. It wasn't that a common name, in fact. 'I have to know who all the other Maas's are. I must have a list; a written copy would be best so I can tick them off, one by one.'

'Anything else at the same time, Madame?' Neumann enquired, continuing to smile. I could see I was still dictating my requirements rather than ask for them.

'I'm so sorry. It is important.'

'I cannot see why. You met my daughter twice. You came from out of the blue, spoke a little with each other and planned a third rendezvous which Gretel never kept...poor darling.' Neumann's eyes glazed over. He pulled hard at his cigarette before pulling down on a loose eyelash. 'Gretel's dead, but still you go on asking questions which make no sense.'

I butted in. 'You forget, Sir. Someone tried to kill me. Of that I am positive, quite sure and I am not wrong.' I banged the dashboard with my fist.

'I do remember, Ruth. But what has Hans Maas's possible, but probably unlikely, membership of a questionable club eight years ago have to do with Gretel? Even if Maas had been involved at the *Herengracht* address, it is a matter of record and the police knew this. They obviously have seen no connection between then and now and have recognised the fact by setting him free.'

'I know...I know. But, the real problem is the connection with the collaboration with the Germans, which led to the death of the resistance fighters. One thing leads to another, Sir, and who ever killed Gretel, knew this too.'

'*If* she was killed. It could be we are both wrong in all of this. She made a terrible mistake by accusing that gypsy boy and couldn't face me. It does happen,' he ended, his face softening. I could see his mind was beginning to find ways to reject the harsh realities of the possibility of murder. Anything would be easier to accept than this. 'Or,' he said helplessly, 'or she just slipped and fell in.'

I dismissed this idea as nonsense. We had been through every option available to us several times. 'I tried the two baker brothers, the men who came to rescue me in the tunnel. They say they were still quite far away when the man, who ever it was, ran off. It was very foggy that morning. We are just left with the list. It is all we have to go on. I need this list with all the members, not only the Maas names. Maybe some name or other could activate some memory or other from the past, a link perhaps with someone we both know?'

Neumann came back from where ever he had been, stalking across Gretel's cold grave, desperate for her to sleep undisturbed.

'I'll get the lists for you, Ruth, if in return you will be good enough to let me know if you find anything which bears on this.

And, if asked, you simply cannot recall where you got the list. There are already a number of names on the list, names you read about every day in the newspapers. Big men, powerful men, all prepared possibly, to go to extraordinary lengths to ensure their name is not brought to the light of day. I had to dig very deep to get the first. The Police would have had a bigger job, being controlled by many of these men.'

'So how–'

For answer, Neumann patted his pocket and reached across me to open the car door. 'We will be in touch, no doubt.'

As I climbed out, Theo came up clutching an entire salami. He had been to town. He touched his forehead with two fingers before turning them towards the big man behind the windscreen. He was answered by a confident wave.

'You smell of expensive tobacco,' was his only comment. I kissed him on the cheek, noticing a curtain had been drawn back on the *Anna Rosner*.

'I've got so much to tell you,' he went on, as he set the salami down on the table. I bought this as a bargain, and to meet the demand for smoked meats. There are so many orders for salami sandwiches I thought we would save money.' He faltered for a moment, wondering if he had done any wrong with the large purchase.

'You did absolutely right,' I said smiling as much as possible to make him believe me. 'What things? Do tell me.'

'I'll tell you when we eat. Did you have a nice day?'

I had almost forgotten my conversation with Bessels since meeting Neumann again. 'Not bad, I suppose.'

We ate stew off-cuts from the butcher up the road. Bits of lamb, trimmed to make the shoulder nice and round for a prized customer, allowed us to eat well for a small sum. It was my habit to smile at the butcher whenever he served me, while his wife who took the money, wasn't looking. Theo dropped a slice of bread into his gravy, then, wiped the plate until it was gleaming. 'I heard some news today. I couldn't sell them any sandwiches because they are retired and don't go to sea, but they know the Maas family…have done, in fact, for a long while.'

'Which boat?'

For an answer, he pointed through the porthole across the harbour, out to the central mooring area. His finger bobbed in the air until it located a big, rusting barge. All of the accommodation was built onto the main deck.

'Right out there. Oh, Theo. Did you get right out there?' It was another huge step for him; almost three hundred metres directly out from the quay *and* towards the entrance to the *Ij*. It had meant he would have been as far from land as anywhere in his small world. He could see me thinking over his words. Perhaps alarm showed on my face.

'It was…special. A special journey. A long way to go, with more sales than ever today. I met two nice men and we had a Geneva …or two.' I leaned forward so I could brush some breadcrumbs off his chest, too happy for words. 'Well, three in fact,' he supplemented his remark. 'They told me a few things, stories and things,' he repeated himself, attempting to recall the meeting exactly. 'The boys used to go and watch the German troop's parade. They would goose step around while practising the salutes.

'I expect they were making out to be silly when the Germans weren't about. Making out they were fool-'

'No.' Theo was adamant. 'That wasn't what Benjamin said. It appears they spent a lot of time watching them parade, even speaking to the officers on a number of times.'

This was news. 'We need to have more words with this Benjamin-'

'And Michiel. They live on the boat together. But watch out for the gin measures. They are quite free with it.'

'We'll go and meet them this weekend and take something as a present.'

'Some of this stew?'

It wasn't such a bad idea. Two old men living together on board must give rise to a great deal of boredom in their menu.

I shivered as I cleaned the plates. It was all like a giant jigsaw. I felt all the pieces were available but not necessarily turned up on the board. One day they would fit into a picture but, at the moment, all the pieces were tinted sky blue. I needed another colour to start tying them together. And…someone out there was, equally as keen to see we failed.

'We need to know more, Theo.'

'It was harbour talk…they emph…emph-'

'Emphasized?' I suggested.

'Yes, you know how it is. All tittle-tattle on the waterfront. Benjamin and Michiel know of my illness, so I expect they know all about you as well.' He ended with a smile, which I found enchanting.

I was sure he was right but it was another small piece of news which needed to be followed up. 'That is why we need to see them. Besides, it will be an excuse for you to take your girl out on the water.'

'So long as it is not on the *Ij*.'

'Absolutely. Not on the *Ij*,' I stressed. It might have been the Atlantic Ocean.

We had been making sandwiches for half an hour, chatting to each other from time to time, as some small incident or other of the day cropped up, when I believed it was the right time to give Theo my news.

'I'm in management now.'

He hardly heard me, least of all understood.' 'Management?'

'At my job. I've been promoted. I'm going to be in charge of six shops. More money too.'

He stopped slicing and stared at me. 'I've been home two hours and you have only just told me this.'

'It is nothing sensational, Theo.'

He shook his head in annoyance. 'But, it is, silly. It is fantastic news.' He put his knife down. 'What does this mean for us? You will be going away, I suppose.'

'Away? Where to?'

'You know. More money. You can get an apartment of your own.'

'Now you are the silly one. I like it here. Besides, the rent is cheap.'

'You don't pay rent.'

'Specifically, but, I cook and clean for you. Those must be worth something.'

'Something, I suppose.'

Men could be such pigs at times. Just when I was considering what to throw at him, he burst out laughing. 'A lot of money, I should think.'

I couldn't smack his bottom, as he was too big. I was interrupted from continuing by a bang on the steel deck above.

'We never seem to be alone,' said Theo, picking up the knife again.

'It's Elizabeta.' It was Mama, alone, climbing down the steps carefully.

'Hullo children. I want you to come to dinner on Saturday night. We don't have your company these days at the table. Theo, you look well,' and aside to me she added: 'you've put on weight. It suits you. You really are very pretty, Mae.'

'*Very* pretty,' Theo burst in having overheard the stage whisper, but in retreat as soon as he had uttered the words.

Gravely, Mama nodded her head. 'Quite right. *Very*. So, you will come?'

'We will come, Theo, won't we?'

'Absolutely,' he replied. 'I've been out-'

'Theo's been out in the harbour, by himself,' I said, unable to stop myself this time. It was important Mama was not given all of the details of his meeting. 'Here and there.'

'That is wonderful. You must tell us all about it. Saturday at, say, six."

Theo blinked his eyes, as a frog will do. Despite his medicines dumbing down his reaction times, he had quickly caught my drift. When she had disappeared up the steps, labouring at each tread, he turned back to me. There was a half-smile on his face.

'I wasn't going to tell her...honestly, but this whole thing is becoming like a detective story.'

I let him prattle on. He seemed to have forgotten someone had tried to kill me and warn us off. I could not make out if he really did not care enough, either for himself or for me, or if it was something else which had yet to surface in his complicated brain waves. There was so much torn, scrambled tissue up there needing to heal itself before I could be sure of his intentions, I just had to wait.

'It's cheese and pickle isn't it?' I put this in to bring us back to the real world.

As he cut cheese, using his maddeningly slow but now accurate technique, he spoke again of my job. 'You being a manageress...and all that. It doesn't mean you will leave, does it? Your cooking and cleaning...it's worth twice what you would be paying in rent, so I should be paying you.'

We both laughed, gawking into each others eyes across the chopping board.

I couldn't tell him of my plan. Not then.

SHE'S DERANGED, YOU KNOW

The water lies as if in a trance, becalmed as a clipper is sometimes on its race from Australia. The trees bend over benignly, fronds hanging close to the wavelets breaking on the beach. The sky has never seemed so blue, inviting everyone who wishes to participate, to sit and dream of the good things in life.

It had seemed at times, as if these days would never come. So dark they had been, black, almost, framing the corners and bending the light so it turned in on the watcher.

As if by magic, the sea crumples into a roar. All of a sudden, the wind is blowing, tearing at his clothes and hair, making him blink back the tears. He understands only too well the awful realisation, that the pretty picture he had been believing was real and actual, was in fact a cardboard sham, a Hollywood film set, all timber props and false doors, the reality as thin as the thickness of the paste walls. He begins to scream. He cries for the lost future; the hope which extended as far as the horizon; the love in his chest which had begun to flutter like a young, delicate bird and, most of all for the lost saneness of his mind. He was falling again..............

CHAPTER SEVEN

'Message for you, Mae. There is an envelope in the bakery.' One of the bakers had slipped his head around the door frame. He rather liked her though he knew she could be tough. Only the master bakers' were allowed to address her as Mae, all the rest had to call her Miss. She was, he knew, going places, carving a niche out of life for herself, and favoured, it was rumoured, by the Bessels family themselves. At times, when the shop was quiet, she would come out to where they would knead the dough, and demand to know the exact ingredients; how hot was the oven was another; how long does it stay in for? Where did the seeds come from which stuck to the rolls? And the bloody weight of just about everything. As if he knew: it just happened, as his father had taught him, and his father before that.

Then would come the second batch of questions, quickly following after the first so there was little time to think. He found there was no time to make up the answers so he just told the truth. 'What-ifs' he called them. What if this oven were to be turned sideways? There would be room for another…here. What if the marble pastry slabs were moved half a metre nearer the oven doors? Would it mean the shelves could be loaded more quickly? Or would the heat be too much for the dough? To cap it all, the two Bessels, the family Directors, the men who held your job in the palm of their hands, were often around the bakery these days, especially the office where she sat. They were always close to where she was working. They too asked questions or made quick, surreptitious notes in the back of polished leather notepads. The pens were gold, the ink black, jet-black for some reason, with powerful strokes, making statements every time the caps were screwed off.

Mae had an office. Only a small one, with a glass wall which faced directly onto the production line. There was a door with her name in black on a white card and a spare chair, though no one had sat on it yet: there was never enough time to rest one's feet. If there was a problem, Mae would be out of her chair and dealing with the issue as soon as she was informed, demanding politely, but firmly, what was being done to alleviate the crisis, so the production line could recommence with minimal delay.

'Thank you. I will be right there.' A message. There was no one she could think of who might want to send her something.

The thick envelope had a neatly typed label on good quality paper with Private and Confidential at the top. Otherwise it remained anonymous and shed no clues.

'At last!' She exclaimed, looking around her as she pulled out a sheaf of papers, all written in a neat hand. Who ever had made the copy had very neat handwriting. The sheets comprised rows and rows of names, registration numbers each with the last known address of a member. Neumann had not left his calling card, not even a compliment slip, nothing, in fact to identify him with the lists, though they were quite clearly from his staff.

Mae retreated to her office and closed the door. After all, it was her lunch break.

She flipped through the sheets, feeling guilty. The copyist had spent a great deal of time ensuring the work was accurate. Typical of Neumann's attention to detail, she guessed.

There they were! The 'M's'. There were, surprisingly, sixteen names under Maas. None had the name Hans attached.

'Holy Moses!' Mae exclaimed aloud. There was no sign of Hans, but the given names Pieter and Jos were both there. She pulled her head down until it almost touched the paper in disbelief. In precise, pale mauve ink with the 's' of Maas ending in a slight flourish, as if the writer needed to make the reader aware, he or she had a character about them which required recognition. Maas....Jos and above, Maas...Pieter, both of the tugboat *Anna Rosner* of *Oosterdok*, Amsterdam. The address tallied with the names.

Mae looked up, suddenly fearful someone might be peering in on her, who might have learned her secret. Pieter? All along she had been thinking of Hans.

She looked down again at the innocuous lists. Pieter had registered in 1942, paying his subscription for two years. She noticed it had not been renewed. Jos had joined in late 1944. Maybe it was the joining up age, which had prevented him from signing before? Everything else revolved around the age of 21: perhaps sex as well, with German prostitutes?

She scanned the sheets, looking for other clues. Her eyes popped occasionally as she recognised a big name among the many others. Neumann's name was not among them though, no doubt an efficient secretary would have left his out if it had been needed. She abruptly felt sickened, for a number of the names were of those prominent in declaiming the Nazi atrocities. These men had demanded the maximum penalty to be brought against those caught and tried; a convenient way of removing the problem forever.

It was Saturday. She had promised to eat supper with Pieter and Elizabeta. Instead of just one man to consider, she now had three problems. Theo simply would not believe her, she was sure, even with the lists he would find it difficult to believe Pieter had something to do with this, and Jos had just been a youngster. Perhaps, she wondered, perhaps the whole family was involved? And there appeared no point in raising the subject to him when he returned to the *Kuijpers*. It was also the first time she had been entrusted to close down the bakery for the night and hand over to the night watchman. With her former manageress transferred to the new bakery in *Baarn*, and the Bessels family never calling in on a Saturday, she had been lectured on her responsibilities for securing all of the buildings on the site. It was not just the shop she had to check. The bakery, the stores and a number of outbuildings which housed the delivery vans, were also subject to her scrutiny. She counted each lock in turn to ensure she had covered them all, finally backing out of the rear staff door. As she bent down to secure the final bolt, there was a tap on her shoulder, causing her to jump up as if guilty of some misdemeanour. It annoyed her, especially as she recognised who it was.

'Oh damn! I mean, excuse me, officer. You gave me a start.' It was the police officer who had been investigating Gretel's death.

'Forgive me *Miss Epstein* but I did not know you were responsible also for the security of one of Amsterdam's best bakeries.'

'Yes,' she said tartly, unwilling to go through the whole explanation again. 'I'm in management these days. I'm handing over to the security guard.'

'Congratulations,' he replied, though his eyes showed their disinterest in the news. 'Do you have any information for me?'

'No. I assumed you had completed your investigations satisfactorily. I read nothing more in the newspapers, so I gathered everything was as it should be.'

'A curious phrase, if you don't mind me saying so,' Lifting the big bag of bread up to her shoulder, Mae wondered if he thought she was stealing the end of the weeks production. 'As it should be,' he repeated. 'Why should it not, be?'

'I have paid for this bread, officer. I have an arrangement. I don't know if it shouldn't be...I mean, look officer, double negatives always muddle me up. I'm in a hurry as I am going out to dinner.'

'I won't keep you long. I just need to know if you have been making any enquiries at the official War Crimes offices.'

Mae coloured, glad of the dark, and turned away quickly, as if to leave. 'I can honestly say, I don't even know where this office is. Is it in Amsterdam?'

The policeman deliberated, studying her suspiciously, wondering if she was making fun of him, but he could see she was in control of her emotions. 'They are in the Hague.'

'Oh,' she replied, relieved. 'How on earth could I find the time to go to The Hague to find an office? I work all day from an early start and get back to start cooking as soon as I leave here. Surely these offices of yours only open when I am in the shop? War crimes, you say? Are you suggesting the Gretel Neumann affair is not only continuing but is, in some way, connected with war crimes?'

'I'm not suggesting anything, Miss, though someone has been making waves, and large amounts of money have changed hands I'm sure. Someone has been buying information to see files, not due for release for another twenty-five years. He – or she is not entitled to the information-'

'There you go again, officer. Where would I get a large amount of money from?'

The man grunted, somewhat mollified, and shrugged his shoulders as if to say he was in agreement but wanted help. 'Well, let me know if you hear anything...'

'Of course. Goodnight. Happy weekend.'

So, she said to herself as she pushed through the Saturday crowds. There were those going home after work and as many others coming into town for a night out. Thoughts of having a drink were far from her mind. The case had not been closed: it could not be suicide. The police would not be spending all of this effort for a single girl throwing herself into a canal. It happened often enough anyway. But it made no difference to Mae's thinking, for she had abandoned the idea as soon as it had been raised on the first day.

Theo met her near the entrance to the tunnel. 'I thought I would meet you,' he said as soon as he had relieved her of the heavy bag. 'We are going to the *Anna Rosner*, tonight, to eat,' he ended rather unnecessarily.

'Yes, I know. I want to wash first, all over. I wish we had a bath.'

'Grandmamma used to take me to the City baths from time to time. When I used to smell rather strong.'

Mae liked the idea, especially after a long day in the hot office with the constant smell of yeast. She enjoyed the fresh air with its own scent along the canal walk, allowing her to release the pressures of the day in a slow uninterrupted way. 'I might just do it myself one of these days, though you would not be able to scrub my back there.'

'No, I won't.' He had not picked up on the humour of her words. When she had a bath, or rather a strip wash, Theo had to sit out on deck or go to the shops. It was the only time she could dry herself properly. 'The baths are divided into men and women sections. Each cubicle has a bath and they give you a towel and a tiny piece of soap. It's so narrow in there that my elbows touch each side at the same time as I got out of the bath.'

'I shall go next week. After work, I think. Then I will come back and make you supper.'

'I don't smell, do I?' Theo enquired, caught up in the same idea to be clean.

'No, not at all, though I am surprised we don't both smell a bit.'

'That's alright then. You would tell me, wouldn't you,' he said looking at her directly.

'If you smell strongly, as you call it, though it sounds rather like a rat or a dog, I shall boil up a lot of water on the stove and I will wash you right then and there. I can't have a Dutchman smelling like a manure heap. I leave that to the English.' Remembering, with a start her plans, her face changed to a grimace.

As they crossed on to the *Knijpers*, Pieter gave a cheery wave from the wheelhouse, where he was engaged upon the task of polishing all of the brass work. 'Getting ready for our visitors.'

Theo waved back. 'See you in half an hour.'

Mae ducked under the forepeak to change her blouse. She had two spare these days, and all three were different shades. She liked to think they were subtle colours, unlike the Maas family choices, as often as not, vivid and outrageous, cocking a snoop to most of Amsterdam fashion. She pulled out her clothes such as they were, and put them neatly together in a bag. She re-entered the main cabin, buttoning up her front, the action of an established housewife, quite used to having her husband regard her half-naked breasts and bare stomach with reasonable equanimity.

'It is strange, Mae, very strange. It is at times like this, I feel in control of my life. I can look at you as if…as if I was long married to you. Then, at other times, like at night, I want to look…and touch, and feel-'

'It is only natural, Theo. I also want to touch and be felt. We have got ourselves into a somewhat ridiculous situation, not a normal married relationship, nor just of friends together for the evening. I'm old-fashioned enough to want to be a virgin when I get married. Like my old school friends, it was our dream. At other times, I think, what the hell: life will never be the same for me in the future.'

Ridiculous, she said to herself. Quite ridiculous.

Theo nodded and was about to speak in reply, slightly disappointed with her words, but she had placed a hand in front of his mouth. ' I do not mean you, it is just I am so muddled at the moment with a massive problem ahead of me so you must excuse me if I say something silly.' Theo shrugged himself into his jacket and turned to adjust his lapel in the mirror on the end wall. It permitted him a full view of her face, worried and concerned, biting her lip in frustration. It was strange, for she seemed much more wound up than just being unsure of a sexual relationship which might or might not occur as a prospect in the future. She was tense, markedly so and refused to make eye contact with him as she would normally do.

When she left for the bakery in the morning, or after she had arrived back, from her new, responsible job, he could see she was totally in command of herself and her emotions. Perhaps she was becoming involved with him to a degree she found difficult to control. He could understand she must have had precious little sex education in Auschwitz, while, before the camp she had been too young anyway to merit such attention or to learn the facts of life.

As Mae tucked her blouse into her skirt, she wondered what she would do if Theo had decided, then and there to take up her offer to sleep with her. She could hardly cry for help. Her main fear was her lack of knowledge of just how the act was performed. Her mother had told her nothing other than to say when the time comes, you will know exactly what your man will want of you, a mysterious and perplexing statement, which confused her further. She had seen a man's penis before, in fact hundreds, more than most women would see in a lifetime of lovers. She had, of course, seen Theo's. She had stared blindly across a quadrangle on arrival at the camp as the men, all naked, had run and paraded for their captors. She had no idea what an uncircumcised man would look like, only that men came in all sizes of long, thin, powerful and swollen, pink and purple, flaccid, yellow and white. Yet, she could not imagine, even remotely how this dangling piece of flesh came together with her own secret source of delight for a man, at least in order for her mother to stifle a cry of ecstasy in the night.

Mae had learned one new thing in the past few weeks. She had discovered the sheer joy of touching and being touched in return. She understood how it must be to be touched all over her body, at will, both sides consenting to the others movements of fingers and palms. Adagio movement she had come to realise, never allegro.

Theo was sitting, waiting patiently for her. He did not rise as she combed her hair in order that he might do it for her, nor even make the suggestion, which could lead to sex later that night. His action or non-action was disturbing her thoughts. 'Ah, well, Theo,' she said dejectedly, brushing a hand down his jacket to remove any hairs or fluff, 'you look good enough for either Suzannah or Anna.'

Suzannah, or Anna maybe, for an evening out at dinner. She would be able to look across the table at them, and Mama, dismiss them from her troubled mind. Across the same table, however, would sit three men, all of whom could have tried to kill her. Pieter? Surely not with his waistcoat and his ready smile. But…could it be his smile masked his real nature? Jos, yes he could have done it, but he would have been too young to have become properly involved with the Germans. And Hans? She had no idea, and she was no further forward in her reasoning. It left her with the only action she could take. Resolving the state of affairs needed a desperate, near impossible response she knew: she patted Theo's arm realising there would be four men at the table, one of whom had been recently described as officially insane. Tears flickered on her eyelids so she placed her back firmly in his view.

As they climbed the stairs, Mae stopped and turned. 'Go on ahead. I've forgotten something. I'll be right there.'

The *Anna Rosner* looked, as she always looked, immaculate and shipshape from forepeak to sternpost. The small burgee fluttering at the masthead was new, home-made by Anna or Suzannah, he guessed. The edges of the narrow gangplank had recently been re-whitened, along with the lifebelt secured to the wheelhouse cabin wall. Theo gave a short tap on the deck.

'They must know we are here,' said Mae, arriving behind him. 'I saw Suzannah looking out of a port.' As if to answer her she heard a disembodied voice: 'Come on down,' which sounded like Elizabeta, though it was followed up straight away by Pieter emerging on deck clad in a spotless waistcoat of canary yellow sporting a red check line. Its buttons were gold, or rather, gilt, so they caught the evening light, one by one.

'What do you think?' He exclaimed, holding out both arms to hug Mae who, instead, turned her head to allow three pecks on the cheek to be given, seeing his hair was rather long for these days of fashionable shortness, and a shaven neck.

'Its…fantastic,' she answered, disentangling herself to allow Theo to shake hands. Mae noticed, with warm pleasure, how he looked Pieter right in the eye as he did so. It was normal for Theo to look down or away automatically when meeting people or making conversation, so the shadows filled his eye sockets, fearing someone might laugh at him or at least, make comment on his regular disappearances into hospital.

'You look good, boy,' said Pieter approvingly. 'This girl has done a good deal for you.'

'Yes,' mumbled Theo, and then, louder, 'she has.'

'Come on down. Elizabeta never stops talking about this business venture of yours. You see, she always imagined she was the early riser. You seem, however, to beat her by at least half an hour.'

'I hope I don't–'

'Of course not, dear boy. She is so pleased for you.'

'Pleased for whom?' Elizabeta asked, coming to the bottom of the stairs. She also, had gone to considerable lengths to look smart and to make the evening special. Jos, standing behind her, had slicked his hair down with water and the girls had taken off their aprons. Mae's heart plummeted and she felt a tremor in her fingers, difficult to control, so she kept them in her pockets until the last minute for the staircase.

 She felt sick in seeing these kindly people taking so much trouble…and yet, one was a killer, of that she was sure.

'Where's Hans?' Theo said, casting his eyes about the cabin.

Pieter winked an eye as if to impart some wicked proposal. 'Gone for cider, lots of it. At least, three large bottles, we thought. Makes an evening a bit better than normal, doesn't it? Maybe, afterwards, us men could go to a bar.'

'We will see how good you are first,' said Mama archly and in full breath, making the comment without breaking her stride. She fluttered down over her stove, lifting saucepans one by one, applying nods to each as if they were her friends. A wooden spoon was thrust into the largest pot, steam emitting from its lid, and the throat-catching aroma of hot garlic. Theo's nose twitched at the mixture of smells.

'Here's Hans,' said Anna. She had glanced up at the porthole as she heard footsteps on the gangplank. Pieter went to the stair to help him down with his bags, having to bend low as he passed under the threshold beam. A small item, it nagged at Mae's mind. Pieter was the same height as Jos and both were shorter than Hans.

'I've got some cider, beer as well,' he added, eyeing his mother's face. 'Seemed like a good idea at the time, instead of going back later.' There was no riposte. She had all of her family together again. She patted a chair for Mae.

'Sit down my love. I must say, you do look well, both of you, for that matter. Do I hear right, you are in management these days?'

'Yes,' Mae answered shortly. This was a sensitive subject. 'But, all I am doing is what I did before really.'

Pieter shook his head. 'Really? The Bessels family is one of the shrewdest traders in Dam. I hear they have given an office all to yourself, and most of the staff call you Miss and jump up when you go into a room. If that is true, they have done it for one reason only. They see a chance to make more money-'

'And expand,' said Jos.

'You all appear very well informed,' Mae was mystified. 'The job is so new I hardly have time to sit down in my chair. I'm usually in the shop where I started.'

Pieter stopped himself from continuing, realising she was intending to continue to play down her role. 'We did not mean to pry, Mae. Jos has been round to the bakery for some of those spices you use, and heard you had been promoted.'

'I just do not want it to become a big thing, that's all. I don't feel more grand, or important, so let's leave it at that.'

Mama patted her hand fondly. 'Sit down everyone. So long as you feel you want to come here, Ruth, we will love to have you.'

Suzannah was rather in awe of her. 'I would love to do something else…other than picking flowers, I mean. But what could I do?'

'Anything. You just need to want it more than anything else in the world, and stick to it. Learn the job properly.'

'I would like to help other people, I think.'

'What about being a nurse, or a teacher?'

Pieter tut-tutted. 'What about my family organisation? I need a team. What would we do while Suzannah was off, prancing around a lot of kids, or soothing some poor fellow's brow?'

'We all need education, Pieter. More, now we are at peace. You can see out there, every day things are getting better. Machinery is taking over at the bakery and there are machines to cut the flower heads off the bulbs, others to pick the potatoes. Besides...in a few years...or so,' she went on hurriedly, realising he was being retired well before his time without having left the cabin or made another comment,' you will want to ease up a bit, so will Elizabeta. Then, the team is broken up anyway. So, Suzannah and Anna will have nothing to fall back on.'

Pieter sought out intangible nuances in Mae's face he might have missed in the past. It was as if all of the Family were seeking her advice. 'I had never seen it quite like that before. But, my sons-'

'Don't be absolutely certain about it, Papa. It is a hard life and, as Mae says, machinery has begun to take over from all of the old ways of doing things.'

Mama's top lip trembled. This was not the talk she wanted to hear. It implied her family were on the brink of dispersing to all different parts of Holland 'Potatoes!' She declared firmly. 'Potatoes with cheese and chives. There's mutton stew to follow with leeks and carrots.'

The standard period of appreciative silence followed. Eight noses sought out the idle coils of steam as they rose from the huge dish; the brown skins resembled an old Indonesian woman's face; Mae recalled vaguely a picture from an old school book, which had illustrated pictures describing the Netherlands colonies in some detail. The double slash on each potato, scored to form a cross, oozed, ejected and spewed forth the white, creamy flesh, over which expensive butter floated, running down every crevice to await discovery from a probing fork.

To Mae, as she surveyed the expectant faces of the Family, this had become almost a ritual, a religious ceremony whereby these delights were released each week to be weighed up in the mind. These had to be smelt, compared with previous evocations, being absorbed into the brain before there was the inevitable assault upon the waiting dish with unabated passion. She marvelled they never tired of the dish... and she hated the atmosphere of happiness. It would all end in tears.

Her short reverie was interrupted. 'To two very good friends.' Pieter held up his large glass of cider and raised it, a trifle self-consciously, and rather too high, towards Theo and Mae.

'Nice to be here,' mumbled Theo, lapsing back, embarrassed at being toasted in such a fashion. The Family turned to Mae for she had not acknowledged the toast.

'Bugger,' she said in her mind. 'I really thought I had had all the worry I needed in this world', knowing the commitment she was just about to make. She put down her knife and fork with great deliberation. 'I very much regret I cannot accept the toast. Though I find this very hard to say, I feel I cannot go on any more in being dishonest to you. You see, I am almost sure one of you tried to kill me the other day.'

* * * * *

Somehow, the move from being told what to do, to ordering other people about, was bringing me the greatest peace of mind I had ever known, certainly since before the war.

I found I could think about the camp from time to time, without the automatic mechanisms immediately beginning to close out the images, like a camera shutter set at its fastest speed. The pictures were set now, and I could focus on a peaked cap or a death's head badge without the vitriol stirring my stomach and making my heart beat increase its rate.

My life had developed along two strands. On the one side, I was rapidly falling into contentment, one I had never known, not even when my parents had been alive. My work, Theo, the *Kuijpers*, and my life on the waterfront, with its kind, hard-working people. It was the sort of life I wanted to continue to be a part of. The other strand was as if I lived on the dark side of the moon, a world full of unknown terrors, black craters with bottomless pits, unassailable mountains, crevasses and the thought that something might crawl out of one of them to face me at any moment. This atmosphere threatened as soon as I began to think of Gretel, or the big man with bigger boots, who had wanted to kill me. What surprised and shocked me was my unwillingness to tell the police, or to let them become involved in any way. Surprised perhaps, but I knew why. My father had taught me to respect the police at all times, but that was a hundred years ago in another life and another age. I did not want my happy life to become embroiled with the fear of the past, nor did I want to look back over my shoulder as I had done for three years. I had abandoned all of this in nineteen forty-five and I had no wish to return to sleepless nights and the daily dread of waiting for a bullet in side of my head.

Then, one day had merged with the next. It would matter not which of those awful days I plucked out to give an example. A day in November in nineteen forty-four, seeing the grey dawn break over the dark spikes of the conifers, a time when I had had to struggle into my still damp, almost wet and bitterly cold clothes. I can recall, exactly, the feeling as my shirt settled onto my bare shoulders so they flinched of their own accord and tensed like a pair of starved greyhounds at the start of a race. Of course, I wasn't running anywhere, least of all to a gate called freedom. The other women would be shuffling behind me, groaning at the agony of their sodden clothes, and the crackle of the frost beneath our feet. Two women, both in their sixties, had died in the night. You could tell by glancing at them quickly as you went past their beds without slowing. They hadn't moved, their limbs had taken on a pale, sickly colour, greasily shining in the glow of the single light. One of the women had her mouth open as if to try and swallow one last gasp of air before death itself caught up with her. The gold teeth would be gone in an hour, along with her long hair. I imagined there was a half-smile on the other's face, reminding us all she had cheated the fear of the gas chamber, or worse, drowning in the latrines. Neither woman would ever have to stand in line again, waiting to be called, as the cold clamped feet into blue lumps of clay.

'Epstein! Officer duties. You are to serve breakfast.' I was lucky again for the kitchen was warm. It would allow my clothes to dry out properly. As I ran towards the inner gate, I heard a bang behind me. Another shot, identical to so many in the past, it hardly made me react at all. It was at the gate, I had the chance to stop and turn my head casually, as I waited for the guard to let me through. What I saw made me want to scream aloud. I wanted to call down God's fire and thunder upon my tormenters. I wanted only to die as well.

Mother was lying in the mud with her right arm sprawled across the frost line where the shadow of a hut had slowed the rate of melting. Otherwise, she lay flat on the ground, feet turned in, her head immersed deep in the slime, so there was hardly a contour formed by her body. The German who had shot her, looked across at me as he holstered his still smoking pistol, jeering. He knew who I was and the relationship with the dead woman. But, I didn't have to scream, or call upon God's fire. Mother had gone and would never be tormented again. Father was dead, I was sure for the same reason and, if this was true, there was a good chance they would now be already reunited.

'They've gone home,' I repeated over and over again, as I struggled to keep my balance in the slippery mud. A young soldier, he could hardly have been eighteen, already committed to a thousand awful acts, looked at the tears coursing down my cheeks and frowned. He had no idea the dead woman behind me in the mud was my mother. Surely now, he seemed to say, I had got used to the sudden way in which so many people departed from this camp? Just a Jew, another dirty Jew.

How could he possibly have known how my mother had spent so many hours each week at the hospital as a visitor? But, her help had not ended with a few trite words and platitudes to selected patients. She had often called at their houses with milk and bread, or a pot of jam when she learned a family of a patient was in trouble. It wasn't a Jewish hospital either, just a normal place for everyone to go to when they were sick. If the Nazi party had never existed, Mother would have gone on with her work and no-one would have known nor cared much, if they had been told she was a Jew.

I don't know how I managed to get through serving that breakfast. The ultimate wrench came with the arrival of the officer who had killed my mother. The smell of cordite still hung on his clothes. It was a day which has remained fresh in my memory ever since. I seriously considered diving for his pistol and shooting him, not in the head, but between his legs, to destroy his manhood and bring him down to my level, a whimpering wretch who also wanted to die.

I did not shoot him. For one thing, the flap over his pistol holster would have prevented me pulling it out quickly enough to take aim before the other officers shot me, or, more likely, before the man grabbed my hands. For another, I did not want to die. We had heard, through contacts, the Allies were advancing along a number of Fronts: it could only be a matter of time, we were told. Hang on. I wanted to live more than anything else in the world. I wanted to go home and see and hear normal things, walk where I determined to walk, speak when I wished and wake in the morning without the dreaded fear of a new day.

So I passed him by and studied his neck with its short hairs sticking out at all angles from the purpled flesh, and tried to smile.

And so, I lived. The smell of cordite softened. The image of Mother lying flat in death, faded. It brought me the resolve never to be pushed around again. I wanted to work until I was in a position where I would give the instructions and make the world move in the direction I wanted it to spin. It was why I was determined I was not going to visit the dark side of the moon, or scale any vertical mountains. I was not going to be caught unawares again in a long tunnel in Amsterdam Docks.

* * * * *

The potatoes arrived on the table direct from the oven, which belched heat and steam, until Mama kicked the door shut with a blue-slippered foot.

The Family's eyes were locked onto the pile, each examining size, or the amount of butter which leaked out of the split skins. Some reckoned on how they could scoop up the butter from the bottom of the serving dish without appearing too rude in front of their guests.

It was as if the cabin were a church, and the table the high altar to which the Maas Family paid regular homage. The steam caused the surrounding faces, close hauled to the bowl, to waver in and out of focus, excepting, of course, Pieter, who sat immobile, intent upon the third potato down from the pyramidal top. This one had been carefully positioned earlier to allow me, and Theo, I am sure, to take first and second choice, leaving him direct access to this third one, brimming full of its coating of yellow, and surpassing all others in the dish. Finally, Pieter captured his potato enabling him to concentrate on standing to serve the first flagon of cider without fear of losing his treasured helping, pouring a full half litre for everyone. Anna smiled at Suzannah and winked at the boys. Everything was just perfect.

To this day, I do not know how I found the strength to say what I did, planned though it was since we had been asked to supper. It was as if in violent reaction to the soft family scene with everyone loving and happy, that I stood up. The talk had been light in preparation for the serious business of eating. Serious talk could come later, if indeed it ever reached the stage when anyone found it necessary to discuss matters within the newspapers or the price of vegetables in the market. I stood up.

'I very much regret I cannot accept the toast. Though I find this very hard to say, I feel I cannot go on any more in being dishonest to you. You see, I am almost sure one of you tried to kill me the other day.'

Mama had been concentrating on serving out leeks and carrots and had not heard me at all, for she merely smiled and nodded her head as one does, in agreement. The girls nudged each other nervously, unsure if they had taken in my words correctly. Theo rubbed the stubble on his face in a slow, sanding motion. Jos blushed, as if in embarrassment and looked decidedly alarmed, fully understanding the import of my words. Hans just chuckled. Pieter, as only Pieter could, put down his fork and spoon in mid-bite, a critical action at anytime, to fold his arms across his chest.

'I don't think we follow you, Ruth. Is this a story from your past, perhaps?'

He knew from the way in which I continued to stand, when all others sat, and by my face, cold and calm, it was not the case, but he also knew he could not cope with my statement. Above all, he did not want to make a fool of himself by repeating the awful day when he had tried to take the *Anna Rosner*, to sea.

As if in slow motion, I could see Theo rising from his chair. I held out a finger, not too rudely, I hope, though it was meant for him to stay in his seat. This was my own, personal business and had nothing to do with Theo. He also was tall, boot shod and lived on the waterfront: I remembered he had often been in a mentally wild state many times before in the past, and still could not account for many of his actions.

'Please Theo. I do not want to cause trouble in front of these dear, kind people, but,' I turned to Pieter, 'you must understand, I was attacked in the tunnel the other morning, very early. The man tried to push me into the canal, in a manner, similar to the way Gretel was found by the police.'

'I thought she committed suicide,' Mama answered quickly, frowning in concentration and not comprehending.

'It was made to look like suicide, Elizabeta. She was pushed in and held down. It's quite easy in this water temperature. A strong grip is all you require, the sort of grip which comes from pulling up potatoes.'

The silence hung in the sir like a guillotine itself. 'But…her note?'

'She never wrote she was going to kill herself, did she? She said she was taking the only way out by leaving. You see, she loved someone so much she could not bear to see him shot, or placed in prison, possibly for all time. It was merely chance, I think, a terrible, terrible chance for her to write her note to say she would not be meeting me. She was a well brought up girl. She needed to let me know she could not make our meeting. She knew we had had the same kind of schooling where such matters are a part of life. It even fooled the police for a time.'

'I think we have got off the track, haven't we?' Pieter said icily, folding his arms before refolding them in the opposite direction.

I had never seen that done before, believing everyone folded their arms either to the left, or to the right. My mind was wandering again. 'The two are very much related, Pieter. I was attacked by someone who knew my movements. I was up very early. Someone who wore large boots, caked in mud and, someone who came from, and ran off in the direction of the quay.'

'It could apply to Theo as-'

'I know and I agree,' I said peevishly. I had hoped they would not raise his name. 'I didn't say it wasn't Theo. It is just harder for me to include him as…' I was saying it all, as there seemed little point in leaving out the other, important points in this drama'…I think I am in love with him.'

To say there was a pause for digestion was something of an understatement. I recall a girls' book at school where the pause was described as pregnant. This could be such a time. The only thing to move in the cabin was the steam as it curled over the fast congealing butter. Theo's mouth opening to object to my words fell wider until he resembled a fish. He finally closed it with an intake of air. Pieter looked directly into the eyes of the three other men in the room, seeing only answering defiance.

'Not me, Papa,' said Jos.

'Nor me, Papa. I know I am linked strongly to this girl and I did see a lot of her at one time but…to kill her, for what reason, for Gods sake? Papa, I give you my word, on the bible if you wish.'

'I wish it. Mama, bring me the bible.' He thundered out the words with such force his blood suffused in his face. It made him ugly. The cockiness had gone.

Elizabeta stumbled forward, thoroughly frightened, so much so she couldn't speak. She refused to make eye contact with me.

'You swear,' he said to Hans as he grasped his son's right hand to force it down on the book.

'I swear, Papa.'

'And you,' He turned on Jos.

I had had enough. I just could not tell who was speaking the truth. 'One of you in this room has to live with their conscience for the rest of his life. You also, Pieter. It could have been you. You have the muddiest boots, are the same height as your son, and you are always up before the rest of the Family.' I turned to Elizabeta.

'I'm so sorry I spoiled your meal again. It appears to be a habit of mine. But, you have to realise, being followed by someone who is trying to kill you and almost succeeding, to wonder when you are going to be jumped on in the tunnel for a second time, waiting for a push in the dark. It is like I was back in Auschwitz, living hour by hour. I am not prepared to go through with it all again. Goodbye everyone. Theo, you can reach me through the bakery.'

I walked out of the cabin and climbed the companionway stairs. Not a sound followed me out.

* * * * *

It wasn't until Mae's footsteps could be heard on the steel deck above, that uproar ensued. Pieter pushed aside his plate with a savage blow. It spread butter and leeks across the crochet tablecloth. Hans rose slowly, watching Theo for his reaction, almost afraid for his guest who remained in his seat, oblivious to the tears and the swear words. Finally, Pieter crashed a fist down onto the table before taking up his usual position in such circumstances, with his back to the stove, legs astride, arms folded.

His first words were calm, icy and very polite. 'Theo. I realise you are not part of this continuing charade, but I would ask you to leave straight away. My advice to you, should you wish to take it, is to have nothing to do with that...lady, anymore. She can be very charming, but she is obviously completely deranged...her experiences in the camps no doubt, but it is not the first time she has insulted me and Mama in our own home...and she, a guest.'

Mama had turned too. 'She may have left for good and good riddance if it is the case. Anna, Suzannah, I don't want you to raise her name or speak to her ever again. I advise you, Theo, to make sure she has really left. It will only upset you if she comes back to the boat after a few days, or anywhere near the harbour for that matter, and it could put you right back in the sanatorium...couldn't it?'

Theo was already walking away, very close to tears, seeing his whole world beginning to disintegrate in front of him. Why did she go and say such a thing today? If only they had stayed on the *Kuijpers*. Pieter was right though: Mae had shown some very strange ways and treated the Family's kindnesses in a dreadful manner. It had to be the war, he realised. Her mind had finally broken, probably as a result of her mother's murder, an act, she said she had witnessed. Twisted, distorted, tortured in her mind, her ability to hang on to her sanity and control her emotions, was obviously far less successful than his own. She should, in normal circumstances, have been seeing Doctor Hertz herself. It was a strange idea, but he began to feel he should be making an effort to bring her to the sanatorium, to visit her and, when better, help build up her resistance, until she could cope with the day to day problems. It brought some comfort to him as he climbed up the stairs in silence.

He went out on deck as shouting broke out below. A stiff wind was whipping wavelets on the surface, the taste of salt on his lips. It stung his eyes and rattled a loose chain on a nearby masthead.

She had returned to the *Kuijpers* only to retrieve her clothes, which she must have packed before the lunch. It was as if the boat's soul had gone, whether temporarily or forever, he had no way of knowing. On a sudden impulse, remembering her last words before they had left for lunch, he leaped down the companionway steps, arms locked rigidly into his shoulders hands on the rails, so his feet cleared the flight in one jump.

There *was* a letter. It was propped up on the vase of paper flowers on the table. Theo felt sick, frightened to open it, yet terrified not to learn the truth. Around him, the cabin shone in the warm beeswax; it gleamed through the white crochet cloth as if they were droplets of molten gold burning through ice. His bed was made so neatly he could have bounced a cent coin on the tight sheet. More mindful still, however, was the string, which held the dividing curtain in place at night. It was coiled, too neatly even for her fastidious loving care, almost saying to him, this isn't wanted any more; store me in the kitchen drawer. Was there never to be any more glances through the gap in the curtain when the moon shone, and her breathing settled to an easy rhythm? He opened the envelope, his fingers a slight blur to his eyes.

> *My dearest Theo*
>
> *You will not understand my actions today, nor do I expect you to. I was unfair in saying I believe I am in love you, when you could not respond. Unfair also, because I want desperately to know if you feel the same way about me.*
>
> *I have to know also, however, who it is who wants to kill me, and why. This, to me, is the real reason for being as frightened as I am. It is the not knowing why? For any future of any worth together, I must first resolve this.*
>
> *I have arranged for the bread to be delivered to you each day. You must not stop the business now, just because I do not happen to be around you at the present time. You have the ability to go on, and to expand upon your contacts and have the time to make the sandwiches properly so they will want to come back time and time again. Cut the bread thinly, wrap the greaseproof tightly.*
>
> *One day, soon I hope, we will both know the truth – I promise you that if nothing else.*
>
> *Your loving Ruth*

And, she had inserted all the correct punctuation, and made the same declaration of love, as she had done on the *Anna Rosner*. It had all been planned some time before.

For an eternity or so, it seemed, he sat on the bed reading and rereading her letter. She loved him…but she didn't trust him. Was this what she was trying to say? Or, was it solely, she loved him but had to find out who was threatening her on her own. If the second case was the true one, why had she left him and what could she achieve on her own by leaving the *Kuijpers* and the harbour, where all the problems were focussed?

When he eventually got up from the quilt, he found he was quite calm, as if he had passed through the eye of a storm at sea, and the waves glinted again with the hint of a sun. Without thinking, he reached out automatically for the knife and began to slice bread, determined they would be as slim as anything Mae could achieve. While he spread pickles, he leaned over to where he had laid her letter, ignoring the faint shouting coming from the direction of the *Anna Rosner*. He wrapped sandwiches tightly in greaseproof paper as she had taught him. Across the cabin, not half a metre away, was where she always stood of an evening, pursing her lips from time to time as she reviewed the orders before glancing back, satisfied. She would read the reactions on his face until she would bend to her tasks again.

When he went to bed that night after a long afternoon, he lay with his head on his hands as he stared across to the empty couch and the unfamiliar light, which shone through the starboard scuttle: it had been screened each night by her curtain arrangement.

Theo wanted to relieve the mounting pressure. He knew how, but his grandfather had caught him in the act once, to his intense embarrassment. He had said only: 'It's wrong, Theo. It is a sin.' The calm words had stopped him playing with himself, preferring better to wake to a distant memory of a soft dream. He wasn't at all clear why it was a sin, for his grandfather had not stopped long enough to explain what he had meant. Theo had felt at the time, they were both as uncomfortable as the other, both wanting to get away from the scene as soon as possible. So, he allowed himself to make ready for bed and certified himself for dreamless sleep, seeing her letter, which still brought him hope and drove away the demons.

The wind had dropped the next morning and the cloud cover minimal. It enabled the sun to pour down onto the basin. The unexpected heat made the wooden decks creak and expand in sympathetic response having dried the overnight dew on the cobbles so it left dark, damp lines around each stone block and made them easy to count if one had been so minded. It did not surprisingly, interest Theo for he left the six o'clock weather forecast halfway through the announcer's words, to deliver the first batch of greaseproof paper parcels.

As he passed by the *Anna Rosner*, he could see no lights burning. It would be at least half an hour before the Family arose. Piled on top of the dustbin on the quayside, were a number of jacket potatoes, all split open and disgorging grey, stained flesh, surrounded with a greasy film of dust-covered butter. It told a story...of a precious meal abandoned midway through its course.

The water slopped and slapped uneasily below him as he made his first deliveries, having to do so without the lingering touch of her lips upon his left cheek from her daily kiss she bestowed upon him. It was treated almost as a good luck talisman, rather than for any special association. Or was there, he wondered on reflection? Now, with the knowledge in her letter, he could see it was her way of telling him she cared, her own hunger only half-formed but there, waiting to emerge. Instead, he dipped his face into the enamel bowl and brushed his teeth with more vigour than usual. He had breakfasted on her letter, reading and rereading the words, as if each alone were a precious stone to be examined under a strong light to make sure there was not a single flaw inside. He then placed it inside a wooden box on the pot shelf, which ran around the room.

Out in the harbour, the steel blue sky of the early morning reflected the boats in mirror image of their hulls; the greasiness of the water made the fine lines of the rigging form sidewinder snake patterns on the surface.

Theo still had six craft in the centre of the basin to deliver to, despite the lack of interest from the retired couple on the big barge. It would never become easier he realised, as he climbed down into the pram, for the sweat was already forming on his brow and his palms were wet against the scull. If he lived to eternity, this detachment from the shore would always be agony, a torture touched with guilt. He was, after all, a seaman, trained to go to sea at a moment's notice, whether the weather was benign or rough. It was a salutary lesson. If he was to make the delivery of sandwiches his life's work, he would always have a period of each day when he would be terrified out of his mind.

He had his eyes closed particularly tight, when he collided again with an object.

'Damnit boy! That is the second time you have hit my boat.'

Theo opened his eyes to see Benjamin looking down from his neat, highly varnished inboard runabout, the rubbing strakes were unmarked, gleaming brass screws ran in parallel lines and the painter had been boiled white, coiled as it was into a tight spiral on the foredeck. It was in sharp contrast with the beaten up mother craft. He realised he was upside down in the bottom of the pram with one foot over the gunwale where he had fallen.

'I'm sorry, Benjamin,' he said attempting to pull himself to his feet with as much dignity as he could muster in such a tiny boat. 'I wasn't looking where I was going.'

'Too bloody right. Of course you couldn't see where you were going. Your bloody eyes were closed tight, that's bloody why.' He leaned over the side of his boat to examine the immaculate sheen to discover there was no damage. 'Hmm. It seems you damaged your pride more than my boat. What brings you here: we don't want any sandwiches you know?'

'No, but your neighbours do.' Theo pointed to the line of boats dead ahead.

'Go and get rid of your deliveries and come back for a glass of something. We wanted to talk to you anyway. It's important.'

'I have about half to three quarters of an hour for the rest of my rounds. Can I come in, say one hour from now?'

'We'll be here. We are not going anywhere.' Without further ado, Benjamin engaged the motor for a brief moment and placed the tiller hard over. The boat responded instantly, like a horse with new oats, and turned upon itself. He cut the motor as soon as he had started, allowing the nose to touch the big steel barge lightly. It was a simple, yet fine act of seamanship, repeated hundreds of times a day in the harbours, yet it never failed to impress Theo of the skills of the local people.

'One hour,' Theo called back, mystified but interested while realising he had to do the trip all over again. Twice in one day. He was so involved in what the two men had to say, however, he sculled off quickly, momentarily forgetting where he was and succeeded in colliding with his first customer's boat.

'Damn! Damn!' He exclaimed, but the bargee chuckled as he took the package.

'Same again tomorrow, Theo, but I'll do without the bump if you don't mind. If you do this every time you deliver my lunch, there will be no paint on one side of my boat.' This was a slight exaggeration for the tug had hardly less paint on it than that belonging to the two engineers.

Slightly chagrined, Theo continued on his deliveries and went back for the second load. This he could do much more quickly as all the clients were accessed from the quayside. He renewed the orders and returned to the pram moored alongside the *Kuijpers*. Yet again, he aligned himself up with Benjamin's barge and made mental calculations on distance, drift and the wind. He had calculated well, for by the time he opened his eyes the boat was nudging the rusted side with a faint squeak of a rope.

'Better,' came a voice from above. Framed in the clear blue of the sky, he could see a hand held out over the water. It held a glass filled to the brim with what could only be Geneva Gin. All at once Michiel's face connected with the arm. Theo felt much better as he grasped the safe world of the ladder and the massive deck above, despite its distance from the shore.

'Good morning Benjamin. Good morning Michiel.' He had the glass thrust at him before taking a proffered chair on the deck, a rattan cane frame which had seen service in the Far-East many years before it came to rest in Amsterdam.

'Too hot inside. Well…young man, young Theo I should say. What's up with you?'

'Good and not good.' He wondered how much news had already filtered out into the basin. 'My girl's gone…but she says she loves me all the same.'

Benjamin looked at Michiel before frowning and lifting his eyebrows into a large question mark. 'I see.' He assumed there was much more to tell and explain.

'Well…I don't,' began Michiel. 'What do you mean, she has left you?'

'Left me, moved out. Gone away.'

'Ahh! Yes, I see.'

'Mmm,' said Benjamin.

Theo moved quickly, to add to the discussion, seeing the doubt still writ large on their faces. 'But she says, in fact she writes, that she loves me.'

'Mmm,' said Michiel this time.

'All clear to me,' said Benjamin, following up, not to be outdone. 'Clear as canal water in summer.'

The two pensioners burst out laughing, before trying to sober up. It wasn't that Theo was upset. It was their own news they needed to pass on.

'We are sorry, Theo. We did not mean to joke at your expense. We are both delighted that...she loves you.'

Now, to business. Michiel and I listened to what you had to say, about the Maas family. It stayed with us and we got to thinking, Michiel and me. There is one in particular in the family, either one of the boys or even it could be Pieter. Whoever it is, sails up the *Ij* every week. Not strange in itself with such a family, but there are stories about collaborators...funny things.' Benjamin threw back his Geneva with a practised movement as he handled the bottle.

'Collaborators. What, war time ones you mean?'

'Yes. There's a whole mass of them still wanted by the police. Many went underground at the end of the war you know.'

'But Hans was cleared by the police. At least-'he frowned, 'at least, he was released, insufficient evidence.'

'There you go then.' Michiel was in no doubt about Hans's guilt.

'Funny things?' queried Theo, sipping his gin as if it were a sherry, his thoughts lost on Mae for a long moment. Benjamin darted a glance at Michiel who nodded his head.

If you ask me, Theo, Hans is helping to move some of these traitors out of the country. The boat we believe he has been seen on is large and powerful. It is certainly not his, yet he has been piloting the vessel as if it is his own. It needs a very good seaman to handle such a craft and Hans is just that, isn't he?'

'Where does the boat go from?'

'West of here, in *Westerdok* a little bit further up the *Ij*, and he sails west as well.'

'The North Sea Canal?' There came a scene of cold, grey water, kilometres from anywhere...threatening and malevolent.

'Exactly,' said Michiel. 'Hans could deliver a man onto a waiting cargo boat and they are away...anywhere in the world once they pass the locks at *Ijmuiden.*'

Theo began to get very excited. If only he could catch Hans in the act, so to speak, it might ensure he was thrown into prison for a very long time, and remove any fear Mae might have of a stalking murderer. It would mean she could come home to the *Kuijpers*. He became more agitated by the minute.

'I have to catch this man...doing it,' he said. 'It is very important to me, probably the most important thing in my life.'

'Follow him, then, any Tuesday,' said Benjamin. 'You cannot miss the boat; it is moored by the entrance to the *Westerdok*. Big bastard, thirty metres, steel and timber job with a big hold. Carries the name *Affaric.*'

'Why such a big barge to take a man out to sea?'

'I don't know, Theo and I may be wrong in all of this, don't forget. But, a large barge, loaded up, will cause no eyebrows to rise on the canal.'

'Big bastard,' Michiel reiterated, reminding the other that size was strength. He added a touch more Geneva to their glasses. 'You be careful, young man. You could be dealing with extremely dangerous men and an even more dangerous cargo. They have absolutely nothing to lose.'

'All of a sudden,' said Theo accusingly, 'you seem to know quite a bit about all of this...Hans and this boat.'

Benjamin remained unabashed by the accusation. 'Sure I do...now. I took the inboard over there in the morning to check. Her bow is turned out, ready to go. I had just returned when you bumped into me...for the second time.'

'Oh, I see. And tomorrow is Tuesday, conveniently,' Theo murmured, half to himself. 'The *Affaric* you say?'

'Big bastard.'

Theo sat in his dinghy under the lee of the barge. He felt the sun bouncing off the water, so it struck his forehead, and began to burn his lips. Having shaken hands with some enthusiasm, he began to realise just what he had decided to do. There was no way in which he could venture upon the *Ij*, let alone steam up the broad reaches of the North Sea Canal. So...how on God's earth could he find out what was going on?

There was a way, he knew. Mae. 'Mae must help me. She will want to help me,' he gabbled to himself as he made for the quayside in the shortest distance, and time, possible. The pram rocked wildly with a mixture of misjudged scull strokes and correcting turns to keep him on course, but he made rapid progress.

He hadn't been inside the bakery before. It smelt good; reminding him he had missed his breakfast. It was busy with shoppers selecting the crispest rolls with considerable care.

'Yes Sir?' Said a girl with rimless glasses and a pigtail tucked up inside her cap.

'Can you get a message to Mae, er Ruth for me, please?'

'Miss Epstein, do you mean?'

'Er, yes.' Theo stumbled, beginning to falter, out of his depth. 'Say, it is Theo, and to meet me outside at her lunchtime.'

The girl looked at him curiously, attracted by his blond curls over his eyes. 'Theo you said. Alright. If she comes it will be at twelve, but I cannot guarantee anything. Does she know you?'

'I have no trouble that she will not recognise my name.' Theo grinned for the first time as he began to regain his composure. Other shoppers were looking anxiously over his shoulder, wondering what was the hold up. 'Thank you very much.'

Now there is a nice man, she thought to herself, as she moved on to her regular customers. As soon as she was able, she excused herself to the other girls and went to find Mae. She knew that messages had to be passed on as soon as possible and accurately to Miss Epstein. The girl knocked on the office door.

'There was a man, Miss Epstein. He has gone now, says his name is Theo. He said he needs to see you, outside at twelve o'clock. He seemed as if he had something urgent to tell you.'

'Very well,' said Mae, surprised and warmed. She had not thought Theo would come to the bakery, however hard pressed he felt. Not, at least so soon after she had left. She felt a stab of concern, in case she had set him back again in his recovery process.

He was waiting for her on the opposite side of the street. He was studying each person as they left the bakery like an expectant puppy, which pricked up its ears at the slightest sign of attention. She was surprised again when he walked up quickly with a fleeting smile, but with a serious, underlining mood.

'I need to talk. Something's come up.' No kiss. No welcoming touch of the hands was offered.

As Mae led the way to the Square, where something different seemed to crop up almost every other day, she made mental notes. His shirt was clean and his black lace-ups were still polished just as she had insisted he present himself to his clients. His eyes were calm, though she could see he was under pressure: there was a tension about him she had not seen for some time. These were new signs; bad signs.

He sat where Gretel had smoothed her immaculate dress across the green painted timber slats of the bench. Looking into his eyes, and unconsciously pushing aside a small wisp of hair for him, she found it difficult to believe he could be Gretel's killer, just because he wore boots and was taller than Pieter.

'So…what is so important?'

But, despite his eagerness, there were many other things to say first. 'You look good, Mae. Where did you sleep last night?'

'On the settee in my office. Are you managing?'

'Yes, but I miss you already. Yesterday, you said you loved me. Did you mean it, really mean it?'

She sat back against the bench, the better to examine his face. 'I have never been more sure of anything in my life Theo. And…I want to come back to the *Kuijpers,* very soon. But, I am so frightened. The tunnel, each day; not knowing if I am going to be attacked again. I need this time to work it all out in my mind.'

'I could walk you through the tunnel every day, you know that. And meet you every evening.'

'I know Theo. But it is the time you make your deliveries.'

'Fuck the deliveries,' he answered.

For her reply she placed a hand over his mouth. I have taught you words that do not come easily to you. You need the business, Theo, not for the money but the assurance it is bringing you, especially on the water. You have self-esteem here in the harbour again. Folks are saying, 'Theo's better. He is working again."

'Benjamin,' he blurted out. 'Benjamin says one or more of the boys, maybe Pieter, are possibly smuggling collaborators out of the country. On Tuesdays,' he added, as if it had a special significance, or that stating a particular day would bring credence to what he was trying to say.

'Slow down,' said Mae, holding up her hand again. 'Who told you what?'

Theo recounted the whole story, word for word, trying to recall exactly the narrative the two men had relayed to him. He did not want to exaggerate. 'I think Hans has never stopped his nasty work. I think he kept his contacts after the war had ended, so he became a natural to give these men, probably buddies of his in the war, safe passage out of the country.'

'Every Tuesday?' Mae repeated. 'That is an awful lot of collaborators-'

'I thought about that. I think he is pretending to run a proper business on a regular basis, so he can be accepted by the local boatmen, and the Harbour Master. Occasionally, he slips a man or two through the net.'

It made sense. 'Yes, you could be right. But, if this is the case, he might not have anyone aboard on Tuesday.

Theo screwed his eyes tight. 'On the other hand…he might.' Benjamin was very certain he would take the boat out anyway to maintain a routine.'

'So what are you suggesting we do?'

'I felt you might have an idea.'

'We could follow his boat, or whoever it belongs to, and watch him to see if he makes some sort of rendezvous.'

There was a silence, allowing the traffic noises to intrude into the small world they were occupying. Theo tried to digest the last word. 'Hmm. It would mean going into the North Sea Canal, wouldn't it, Mae? I could not do it.'

'I know, I know. I wasn't thinking of you. It is too big a step to take. The harbour, to start with, then it will be the *Ij* one day and, later, the big one.'

'But…but, who are you thinking of to take my place?'

'Me, of course, who else?' She glanced up, took in his curious expression with its hurt in the eyes. She reversed her thoughts at the bat of an eye. She had a plan and she could not afford to hurt him now. 'Not yet, not on my own. We know he goes each Tuesday, you say. We must plan something properly. If there is someone else on board the boat, the police will need to be notified.'

'If there is no one, the police will never believe us again.' It was Theos turn to be negative, though he was comforted by her words. They had to plan, and Mae was good at planning.

'I know, it is why we have to check him out first. Then, if we are right, we will call the police and have him arrested.'

'Does this mean you are coming home…to the *Kuijpers*?'

She took his arm. 'Not yet. I can't for the same reasons I spelled out on the boat. Hans smuggling collaborators out of the country, if it is true, may not be anything to do with the person trying to kill me.'

He hadn't thought of that at all. He had made the natural assumption the two were directly connected. On impulse he said: 'I miss you so much, Mae.'

And she wanted to say the same thing. It hurt thinking about it that a vessel throbbed visibly on her temple. She wanted to go to the boat, now, but she knew it was impossible. She had found a room close to the bakery, which was cheap yet clean. She would get by, but it would be a cold, dismal room without the smell of cigarette smoke and the soft squeal of the hawsers creaking above the cabin roof in concert with the movements of the boat.

'I must go. Kiss me,' she said, rising to her feet. He kissed her tentatively, never having been told to kiss anyone in the past, and never having had the miraculous touch of soft lips yielding to his pressure. 'I'll speak to you soon about this matter. The bread will be with you at five this afternoon. Marie goes home past the boat.'

She blew him a kiss and walked off quickly without turning her head back. He did notice how she glanced about nervously, almost anxiously, if anyone came too close to her or crossed the road towards her. It was the first time he had realised how jumpy and frightened she had become. Slowly, he exhaled, realising he had been holding his breath since she had left.

'I love you,' he mouthed to the world. 'I really love you.'

* * * * *

By the following day, I had a plan at last. Fully actioned, it had sprung to my head just as I was discussing ideas with Theo. I was so eager to put it into effect I had to bite my tongue, and tasted blood for my efforts.

I could not tell Theo. He would insist on coming and my plan might include the North Sea Canal, and I couldn't take the risk of him having a panic attack while we watched. The North Sea Canal ran all the way to *Ijmuiden* on the coast, to the furthest point west of the *Ij*, leading out from Amsterdam. It was all one giant, tide-less stretch with the level of the water along its sixteen kilometres controlled by men and not the moon. It was, virtually, one enormous port, where boats could stop off at any point legitimately, to collect and deliver cargo. I saw what Benjamin had seen. Hans's boat, a cargo barge, and, in fact, a home to a bargee, could ply up and down the canal and through the locks at *Ijmuiden*, where a delivery could be made on the blind side of the port in a matter of minutes.

I had to see the boat for myself…that was enough to start with.

The afternoon passed quicker than I expected as I received a visit from Willi Bessels, my Managing Director, to brief me on a new shop. The Family was planning on expanding into the outskirts of the city, the suburbs as they were called. He filled in the details.

'What do you think, Ruth?'

I hesitated. He was, after all the boss of the company and had much more knowledge than me. 'Well…'

'Go on; say what you want to say.'

'Well Sir. Bread, cakes, yes. But not high quality cakes and certainly not the sandwich and quiche business we are building here.'

'But…why ever not? The sandwiches I mean.'

'There are plenty of houses in the area, in fact, there are hardly any other buildings but houses, reasonable stock but blue collar workers-'

'Yes, yes. Thousands of potential clients.'

'But, no business, Sir. The people who buy our sandwiches are all office workers who have travelled in from this area. Out there, the suburbs are empty in the day, either the men are in the city, in offices or at *Schipohl* airport, now that that is expanding with a big building programme planned. There is no money for expensive luxuries with these people, so cakes, but not our specialities. These people are still recovering from the war, and haven't a great deal of loose change. They are fussy about their bread so, good quality but they will be looking for value for money.'

Willi Bessels sat down in my visitor chair, frowning and pouting as I shot down most of his plan. Then he rose quickly and slapped his thighs simultaneously with his hands, an old-fashioned gesture I had not seen for years. 'You are absolutely right. Do you know, I spent a hundred guilders on a consultant to advise me...wrongly as it turns out. Next time, I would like to come to you, if I may? Commission you separately from your normal working hours.'

I was flattered he had asked me whether I would like to receive him in my office, or rather his, for he owned the whole building. 'What ever you wish, Sir. You are my boss, after all.

'Hmm. Sometimes I wonder, young lady. Maybe I am getting too old. We need young blood in the Board Room. Goodnight...and thank you for your advice.' He walked out, closing the door, making me see him in a new light. He wasn't quite the ogre he was made out to be by all of the shop girls.

As soon as he had gone, I folded my files away in a drawer and locked it carefully, for it contained the strategic plans for the bakery for the next three years. I slipped out the back door hurriedly. Not far away was a store the kind that sold rather dubious goods, but some useful ex-Army and Navy clothes. I had left my bag at work leaving me with nothing to carry. As a precaution, I had removed the pair of cheap earrings I always wore, something my mother had traded for in the camp, for my birthday.

'Now...for the *Affaric.*'

West of Central Station, where the enormous barrel vault comes to a sudden end, the slim docking piers stand out into the *Ij* like the tines on a giants rake. I crossed the *Singel*, where the mainland swells out into the water as if it were heavy with child. The area still showed conspicuous signs of the war. Rusted barbed wire was attached to massive X-shaped steels forming barricades. They were piled haphazardly, one upon the other, exactly where they had been dumped in joyous delight, the day the Germans left the city. Green shoots from weeds, forced their way through the brick roads everywhere. The sidings, running parallel with the Western Dock, carried brown stains of rust on the rails. Occasionally, an unaccompanied rail wagon trundled in spiteful protest down one of the myriads of lines, to come to rest forlorn and alone. They were being abandoned by the shunters as night came on, for there were no lights in the area to help them do their work. The lack of street lighting helped me as I did not wish to advertise my presence to anyone: I only wanted to watch and observe. The moon was due in an hour according to the newspaper in the bakery and I probably had plenty of time. As I neared the docks, the sparse traffic finally gave up as it diverted itself down other side roads, on the way home for the night. The cranes squealed to a halt grinding themselves to a sudden, restful silence, save for the wind through their cables. Over everything came an arctic stillness, the kind of hush that makes one want to hold ones breath for unexplained reasons. I did hold my breath as I neared the dock, stupidly believing someone might hear me. A single toot on a steam whistle, well upstream of me, was the only break in the tranquillity over the whole of this derelict scene, temporarily disowned by the people who worked there.

'Oh shit!' I couldn't help it. Emerging from a huge pile of railway sleepers, so big they had blanked out my view completely, I almost ran into the side of a big barge. She was a big bastard, almost thirty metres from sternpost to stem. She was steel-sided with a timber superstructure. Most of the length was made up of a hold, which was only half covered with shallow sloping deck boards. To its rear, the large wheelhouse spanned the full width of the craft. Her name was chipped, but readable, and proclaimed to all she was the 'Affaric'.

There was no sign of human activity, either on the boat or on the quay. The granite kerbs to the finger dock were almost exactly the same height as the narrow deck which ran both sides, alongside the hold until they collided with the bridge shack. With no tides to design to, the quay height had been made to match that of the boats. I stepped across as though on stepping stones in a river. By now, of course, my heart was hammering in my ribcage enough to dry my tongue, so it began to stick to the roof of my mouth. I was on the boat, which the two retired engineers had said could be connected with Hans, but I had not planned to take it any further forward and no ideas of what to do now I was here. There had been considerable doubt in my mind I would ever have found the barge. I looked around in a vague manner wondering what I should be looking for when the decision, was taken out of my hands seeing that a car had begun to turn into the quayside road about two hundred metres away. It slowed and finally came to a stop close-by. Two men climbed out of the back seat, their voices low, almost muffled, and as soon as the door was closed the car moved off again and was soon lost to sight behind the sleepers.

Seeing the car approaching I had been left with no options, so I leapt over the coaming to the open section of the hold to land, luckily, two metres lower on a pile of sacks. They smelt of daffodil bulbs. I hefted a few aside, so I could make a chamber of sorts before letting them fall back, to half-cover my burrow, and blessed the idea of buying a balaclava as I needed my face turned up to the sky. Almost as soon as I had found my new home, I heard two sets of voices.

'Stay in the wheelhouse all the time. Try not to show your face at the portholes. I'll cast off myself but you can hold the engine on quarter power for me.' So saying, I heard a rumble, which died before reviving itself. I could smell half-burnt diesel fuel, and heard footsteps running along the decking close-by, up to the bow.

What the hell was I meant to do now? I could give myself up, say I had lost my way and decided to take a nap. Or continue to hide and see what would happen: a much more dangerous idea, though I had more chance of finding out the real reason for the night trip.

I decided to take the second option, despite my reasoning, for it had suddenly become infinitely safer.

I had recognised the voice above.

* * * * *

Theo's mood had changed dramatically. He had been almost euphoric when he had left Mae. His lips on hers all be it but briefly, the surrender to the slight, but insistent pressure had caused an extraordinary transformation in his whole attitude to life. As she had walked away, seeing her trim back fully erect, shoulders back as she had been taught in school, his only need was to tell Doctor Hertz he did not have need of his services again.

But it was back on the boat, hosing down the deck with seawater when his humour began to change. His mood had not altered because of a return, however small, of his illness. The horizons stayed level and distant, the sky had not turned to purple and black and his mind remained clear. It changed because he had lived with Mae long enough to understand her character. She had been quick, too quick to suggest there was plenty of time to plan how to deal with the Affaric. Normally, such a proposal would have flung her into a flurry of planning and scheming, sheets and lists, each a suggestion for him to select the best. It was, she always said, a partnership. And…she had never cared for the police, or been concerned if they were involved or not. He knew she had not returned to the police station after her attack. All of a sudden, she was making just such a suggestion. It was strange and it did not add up in his mind.

He frowned to himself. She had kissed him softly for the first time, not just a peck as an aunt would proffer. Instead of, as usual, offering her forehead or cheek, she had brought her lips to his, touching, pressing, lingering, if for a fraction of a second longer than necessary. She had blown a kiss in public, a declaration, perhaps, of her feelings for him. A kiss such as this, however, also had another meaning…one where she was unsure of the future, enough to need the comfort of his touch. She was a courageous girl, he knew, but there were limits and she seemed as if she might have reached them now. Mortified, he paced around the deck while he shook his head in the old, familiar way. He knew exactly what she was going to do. She could be sitting in her office at this moment, making up one of her plans without him. Her quick brain would be throwing up risk options against counter-risk. Timing would be important; she might even consult a newspaper to see if there was a moon and, if so, the time it was rising.

He began to stride across the deck boards more rapidly, towing the hose behind him, his mission quite forgotten, though water continued to issue from the nozzle. Eventually, he threw it aside. His frustration was the greater for he had dawdled on the way back to the *Kuijpers*. Time had been wasted. He turned into the wheelhouse and climbed down to the cabin where he scrabbled about for an old bakery bag. On it was a telephone number for the branch shop. He patted his pocket to check his change before running across the gangway towards a phone box close to the tunnel. Feverishly almost, he dialled the number with unpractised fingers causing him to redial twice.

'Come on, come on,' he shouted into the mouthpiece as if it were an animate body.

'Can I help you Sir?'

'Miss Epstein please.'

'I'm sorry Sir. Miss Epstein has left for the night. Everyone has gone. This is the night watchman speaking.'

Theo banged down the phone, failing to thank the man. He half-ran, half-walked back to the boat, alternating his mood from urgency to a mood of despondency. He changed his speed as often as his mind focused on an idea, before rejecting it in favour of another.

Something dark and deep down inside him began to stir, as if shifting its weight to make a statement at the same time. Theo knew it well, very well indeed: so did Doctor Hertz.

'Oh Christ!' He arrived back on deck again, quickly pivoting his head so he could stare across the water towards the *Ij* and the North Sea Canal. If she was going-..

His eye caught upon the big barge where Benjamin and Michiel lived.

'They can help me: their boat, their boat,' he half giggled at the simplicity of the idea. With rapid strokes of the scull, he ploughed a furrow through the evening misty water. Returning boatmen had to alter course to allow the pram to continue, once it became clear that the boat, and the man who cackled incoherently to himself, had no intention of giving way, least of all to larger craft.

Once again he approached the familiar hull and tied up to the mooring line. The two men were waiting for him, expectant faces, wise though, knowing Theo was in deep trouble and needing help urgently.

'Something we can do for you, Theo?' Benjamin said quietly. He nodded at Michiel who went to the wheelhouse for a bottle. Seated, a drink in front of him, and secure now he had made the passage safely, Theo pondered on how he could broach the subject. It all sounded rather foolish now he was among friends.

'Spit it out then, Theo,' said Michiel hurriedly.

'It's Mae. I think…she is in danger. I mean real danger. Well…she's gone.'

'Gone where?'

'I don't know, but I think it's to see if Hans is meeting someone on his boat tonight. Like you said, perhaps a collaborator? I rang Mae's office but she had left for the night. She never leaves her work at this time of the evening.'

'So she hasn't come back to the *Kuijpers*?'

'No. She is not living with me at the moment; I told you…but not living like…'

Benjamin nodded his head sagely. I understand what you mean. So, maybe she has gone shopping.'

'Yes. No. Don't you see? I know her so well. I told her about the boat, and Hans. She said,' Let's plan it all out, bring in the police, all that sort of thing.'

'Very commendable.' The two men sat, arms folded, waiting, then:

'Well?' asked Michiel as the conversation appeared to have slowed almost to a stop.

'She is not going to do any of that. Shopping I mean, at this time of night. And, she hates the police; they remind her too much of the camps. I am sure she has decided to go down to the Docks to find out for herself. I'm sure,' he added with unusual vehemence, something the men had not seen before.

'This is crazy,' Benjamin answered, wishing he hadn't used the word. He got up and stared out at the harbour as if, in some way, he could see all the way round to the North Sea Canal. 'If she has it could be a very dangerous thing to try.'

'I've been trying to tell you since I arrived. It is why I am here. I want to borrow your inboard for a short while. I'll pay for the fuel and I wont damage it…so I can go and find her.'

It was Michiel's turn to join his companion on his feet. 'If you don't mind me saying, Theo, you appear somewhat shaky in a pram one hundred metres from the shoreline let alone-'

'I can manage.'

'On the *Ij*? On the Canal?'

Theo hesitated for a brief moment. 'I will manage it, don't you worry about me. Just let me borrow your boat.'

The two men looked across to each other. Both had, anyway, made up their minds individually. 'We are coming with you, Theo. There is safety in numbers and three men in a boat will have less chance of being recognised by Hans, if it is Hans, and he is there. We can be a fishing party. Michiel knows the Canal like the back of his hand.'

Theo could see the argument and began to realise they were right. It made sense. Besides, the mere thought of being on that stretch of water by himself made him tremble and sweat, even as his eyes scanned the water in the harbour.

'Give us two minutes.' Benjamin turned back to the inner cabin as he began to throw a few things into a sailor's bag. They wore duffel coats besides adding more sweaters to the growing pile. Their caps were automatically included and Theo wondered what they would do if, one day they had to put to sea without them. A torch, a rope and a case wrench followed. As they climbed down into the launch, Michiel passed down two fishing rods.

'Makes it look authentic.'

Theo had no idea what the word meant but he strapped them down so the ends overhung the prow, where they could be seen by any onlooker.

'I think we must go with caution, what ever we do,' said Benjamin. He bent down with the starting handle. Through Michiel's legs he could see Theo sitting, one hand spread either side so he spanned the full beam of the craft. His back was ramrod-straight, his knuckles clenched to the timbers, eyes closed as if in prayer.

'All right, Theo? Take it very easy. Hold on to one of us if you wish. There is nothing to be frightened about or to be ashamed of-'

'It's so silly,' Theo whispered, as if he were just arriving in a church for a solemn Mass. He did not trust himself to let go of the thwarts which might allow him to move closer to the men. Still, with his eyes squeezed shut like two clams at low tide, he found it easier to conjure up a mental image of Mae as he remembered her earlier in the day. As the boat's engine broke into life with the burble of a watery exhaust, he clamped his fingers even tighter to the boat's sides. As the noise increased, the boat began to rise and fall. He forced his mind to concentrate on counting every single event he had ever experienced in his life with her.

Michiel threw the helm over hard to negotiate the passageway under the railway lines ignoring the SLOW restriction pasted up by the Harbour Master. Theo sensed, rather than saw the steel beams pass over him in the dark, aware also he was in the *Ij*. This was a different motion, one he knew well, for the water was deeper, much wider here and exposed to the wind. He began to gabble to himself, small white flecks of foam appearing on his lips.

Benjamin looked on with concern on his face at the far younger man who was beginning to show the first signs of catatonia, face grey and yellow like window putty when it is first applied. 'Should we go on?' He asked Michiel.

'Yes!' screamed Theo, over-hearing the words. 'It is just my way of holding on. Speed up, it's getting very dark.'

The engine note increased again. It isolated the slap-slap of the bow wave as the water was now unable to move out of the way fast enough, so instead it sliced through the surface leaving a Vee-trail of foam and froth.

Benjamin jammed his hat down until it met the thin, silver line of hair, surrounding his bald head. He pulled out a pipe from one of the deep pockets in his duffel, at one with the water and his boat. A few minutes later, as they passed the bulk of the Station, the moon came up and the remaining daylight slipped away.

* * * * *

I was stunned. All the while I had thought that, somewhere, however slight, Hans had to be connected to this nightmare. When I had tried to see the best in him, his image had always slipped surreptitiously back to the idea he was somehow involved. There was so much discussion on what he had done rather than had he done it in the first place, that he had become the main suspect in the whole story.

But Jos! The younger brother, the one who wanted to help Hans, too young for the war, hardly old enough to be worthy of consideration!

He remained at the helm, supremely confident in his control of the enormous boat. Out on the water, away from the Family, he was quite different to the man I had known in the harbour. Slowly, by adjusting the sacks carefully, I could look back to the wheelhouse where he and a much older man, stared out over the bow, as if to see through the black night and over the horizon. Both smoked cigarettes and continued to talk in a quiet murmur, snatches of which drifted down to me as the wind, or the boat changed direction from time to time.

The man beside Jos was not Hans, I was fairly sure. He was huddled up inside himself, hidden from the world by a dark coloured balaclava pulled down over his head, making quick, jerky movements with his body. I was reminded of a jackdaw kept in the local café, constantly on the search as it reacted to every movement around it. That was not Hans's mannerisms. The man above me was, quite clearly under considerable stress, frightened almost of his own shadow, as though he had been living with it for some time. A man, perhaps, who might have lived out of other men's view for the past five years, intent on keeping away from the police and the various Nazi hunting groups which had proliferated since hostilities had ended.

Without warning, a heavy dose of dust, blown from a sack by an eddy of wind, forced its way up my nose. There was no way in which I could stop myself sneezing loudly, causing my shoulders to jump up and down in sympathetic response. It made my head vibrate...and my heart to stop.

'Who's there?' I heard his familiar voice as I went to ground, seeking the steel lining of the boat's hold. 'Who is it?' I heard again, but more muffled this time.

Someone jumped down into the hold and began to walk across the sacks with difficult strides. He walked almost directly on top of me.

'I don't know Jos. May have been nothing.'

Jos grunted, only half-satisfied. 'We don't have time to search the whole hold. You need to get ready. There's your ship, dead ahead, about a kilometre. She's making for the sea locks at *Ijmuiden*. You'll be in the North Sea in a couple of hours. I'm going to come up astern of her on her starboard side. There will be a sea ladder boomed out for you to catch. Don't miss it or you'll go down under the ship. The screws will pull you in and then you'll be fish food and coloured sea water.'

'Thanks,' said the other, still muffled and shivering in expectation while eyeing the boat in the distance. He was staring almost straight at me as I came closer to the surface again, but I was sure he could not see me. He had the moon dead ahead, rising from a low angle, making the shadows around us intensely black.

After a few moments, the man climbed back up an iron ladder from the hold and went back into the wheelhouse. By shifting slightly, I could turn to face the bow, but I was too far down to see anything but the night sky.

'Damn!' I wanted to see the ship's name. I was obliged to lie within the sacks, unable to move, unable to hear anything of use. There was very little point in me being here if I could not progress things further. Almost as if realising my thoughts, I heard the engine turn to idle and back into reverse, then forward again. With the slightest jar, more of a rubbing together of two friendly objects, we came into contact with something fairly solid, certainly heavy enough not to get out of our way. I had to admire Jos's seamanship.

'Good luck. Don't send me a postcard.'

'Thank you Jos. Not much longer and you can forget having to pick another potato.' Then the man was gone. The *Affaric* went into reverse, swinging as it did so, to port. It was heading back the way it had come.

All at once I realised I was on a boat alone with a man who had tried to kill me not long ago. I had no idea what I should do, though by lying still I had a good chance of remaining undetected until we docked again. But…I had to see the name of the ship before it disappeared from sight.

So, I began to move forward as quickly as I could, until I got to a point where I could raise myself up. As I did so, I felt a stinging blow on the shoulder, which propelled me forward. Trying to rise, I stared up into Jos's face. He grabbed me by the waist. It was as if iron fingers were clamped around me which he transferred up to grasp my breasts in a painful embrace. For an answer, I kicked backward and upward. I felt my heel sink into something soft, followed instantly by a relaxation of his hold on me.

'Jesus Christ!' He yelled at the top of his voice. I took the opportunity and reached out for the ladder, sought and found the rungs and pulled for the sky and the sea like a demented being.

On deck, I found the boat to be idling in midstream as it began to slew towards the south bank, uncontrolled in a sixty metre arc. Upstream, beginning to pick up speed was the enormous bulk of an ocean-going cargo vessel, its derricks rigged for sea. I couldn't see the name on the stern plate as I found the moon had thrown shadows down towards the water. All I could see was silver light on a funnel, which had two red and black bands. The bridge was cantilevered out both sides and painted such as it was, in white. There was no sign of the other man.

It was all I could take in. Jos hit me again, this time making me sink to my knees with the pain. I felt sick and dizzy.

'Kick me, you Jewish bitch.' He must only now have realised who it was on his boat, for I had covered my face with the balaclava. He hit me again and again, mostly in the chest and the face. I fainted.

When I surfaced into consciousness a few seconds later, I found myself being pulled back across the deck towards the wheel house. So I bit his hand.

He swore again, loudly, before repeating the blows. I was, finally, unable to distinguish whether it was his blood in my mouth, or my own trickling down from my forehead. Why hadn't he pushed me into the canal? He could run me down at his convenience, chop me up in his screw for…fish food and coloured water.

I became aware of another noise, separate from that of the *Affaric's* engine, which had been placed at maximum revolutions. I was half lying, half sitting, propped against the wheel-house wall, feeling as if I was a marionette after work, something hard as iron digging into my backbone. Jos was at the wheel with one hand in his mouth sucking what looked like a nasty cut he had sustained recently. His feet were straddled wide to take the slight bow wave action. Suddenly, for no apparent reason he screamed out. 'I've got Mae here,' into the darkness, rather than directed towards me. 'Turn about, or I'll put her into my screw.'

I had no idea who he was speaking to. His wild eyes and spittle at the corners of his mouth told their own story. I had seen them all before, in the camps. It was often the scene after a shooting party had had their fun, pre-empting the need for several dozen inmates to take the walk to the showers, where they would have stoked the fire in the tall chimney and lit up the underside of the clouds at night.

I pulled myself up painfully until I could look over the coaming, and out over the canal. To my absolute, wonderful delight, a small inboard passenger boat was standing off some fifty metres, as it bucked and swayed in the wake of the *Affaric*.

But, to my further amazement, however, was the sight of Theo standing up with his shoulders hunched up in fury. I forgot about the danger, my predicament with a madman. I saw only my beloved Theo, astride a boat… in the North Sea Canal for Gods sake! With him were two much older men. They had to be Benjamin and Michiel. I was so delighted I whooped and cheered as if I were at a football game in the cheap end of the stand. I made an attempt to wave my arms, but Jos hit me as if I had been an annoying little wasp in his line of sight, and I went down again to the steel deck.

Across the water I could hear Theo's voice. 'Leave her alone you bastard! You've nothing to gain. There's nowhere for you to hide or run to. Give yourself up.'

'Back off Theo. Turn around and don't stop until you get to the basin. If not…I'll kill her, I can promise you that.'

One of the older men spoke. 'You are trapped here, Maas. You know as well as I do, the canal is surrounded with locks. There's no escape. We can simply call in the police to man every one.'

'I mean it,' yelled Jos, shaking spittle from his mouth as if he were a dog with rabies. 'Turn around…now!' So saying, he let go the wheel and reaching down, pulled me to my feet, before kicking open the bridge house door. I was held by one arm over the water. I felt the skin under my arm tearing with the force he exerted on me. If I hadn't eaten so much in the last few weeks it might have been easier for me, being lighter than I was now. As it was, the pain was intense.

'Now! Now! Now!' He screamed to the three men watching me, as he began to relax the hold on my body.

THE GREY OF THE SEA,
THE BLACK OF THE NIGHT

The water level hereabouts never changes, regulated as it is by the Water Ministry. It does though, flow from the North Sea, fed into the canal in small amounts as each ship and boat enters the lock. The water is grey and dark and cruel, carrying the souls of millions of sailors as they spill through the gates, souls who have died from war or just storms and typhoons as they sailed their ships across the Atlantic.

The water is worse as night comes, for the darkness turns it to inky blackness, like the black of the plague on a man's body and the stink of diesel turns to the smell of corruption.

The scene changes from water to dockside, yellow light throwing perspective all askew. Shadows on the quays waver and hold unknown terrors to those who walk at this time of the evening, for there is nothing here save the groan of the boats as they rub against each other for comfort. The quay side stretches into the far distance. Cobbles turn into pebbles, as they recede into infinity, until they turn a corner behind a warehouse, bending in the sallow beams seeking the old days, when nothing was as it should be.

The fear now is supreme, without description, as it goes beyond the limit, defying every adjective and noun in the Netherlands Dictionary. He, anyway, is torn between killing himself to relieve the awful fear, and taking a supreme risk of achieving his goal while his sanity hangs on a gossamer thread. A successful end, he knows, will be like a burst of light...if only he dare go on.

CHAPTER EIGHT

The motorboat cut through the slight swell with the ease of its hard chine and the high sheen of its varnish. Moonlight highlighted each point where the foam appeared, alighting on the churned up water at the stern post and either side of the bow, as if it were an arrow seeking a target ahead in the dimness. Outside of this white radiance, the water reflected only the night sky, an intense black, like coal without its dust coating, or charcoal in the art class at school.

Benjamin was determined not to prevent his enjoyment of his pipe, despite a growing tension of what might be found further up the canal. Theo was lying down on a thwart moaning to himself quietly, yet every now and then, he would raise his head to reassure himself the boat was heading North-West up the wide canal. The silver skin on its surface buckled and separated, only to rejoin itself together again every few moments.

Michiel occupied himself by examining the outer quays, noting the registration numbers of the ships moored up. Flag staffs flew peacetime colours: lights gleamed out of portholes without any need for blackout against passing bombers. The Dutch, he noticed, were returning to their old habit of leaving their curtains pulled back, letting the world take a critical or appraising look at the insides of their homes. The enormous energy of the people was again being deployed anew into export and expansion.

He shaded his eyes from the moonlight. Ahead, a self-propelled thirty metre barge was heading towards *Ijmuiden* at the maximum speed permitted in the waterway. He could see one man walking along the narrow deck before he climbed down out of sight into the hold.

'Affaric! Got you, you bastard! Benjy, there it is, just off the port bow. Big bastard.' At his voice, Theo lifted an arm from the bottom of the boat where it had been lying, careless of the bilge water, to prop himself up higher.

'Yes,' he exclaimed with growing excitement. 'It's her.'

'She's slowing down. Look. She's negotiating to come alongside that big cargo job ahead of her-'

'I think she may be transferring someone.' Michiel throttled back his engine.

He could see only two figures, both in dark clothing, intent as they were, on bringing the barge alongside the other, which towered over them like a rusty cliff. He could not help but admire the seamanship of the Affaric's helmsman as he manoeuvred the barge towards a boomed out sea ladder, despite the fact neither of the ships had slowed, causing the water between them to boil and erupt upwards in a dangerous series of eddies.

'He's jumped,' said Theo. 'One of them has gone.' As he spoke, the barge went into reverse and to port. Neatly, it swung around the vast stern, rising and falling by its nose in the wake of the twin propellers.

'She's not there,' Theo said, bitterly disappointed. Somehow, he had imagined she would be there, on the deck…or somewhere where he could have seen her. It was a silly idea, he realised. She would not have been in Hans's sight. The story of Hans and this boat could well have been wrong anyway. This might just be the transfer of a pilot, or a late arriving crew member. It happened every day of the week. Mae could well be…anywhere but here. It was ridiculous, he knew.

Theo craned his neck forward as the barge swung past them, heading back, but the solitary man at the helm had a scarf around his face.

'It *is* the Affaric.'

'Come on, Theo. There's little more we can do here.' Benjamin knew he could not board the other boat even if they had been alongside. The boat was too big and could crush the cockleshell they were in, in a trice.

The barge was coming abreast of them when the man at the wheel jerked his head in surprise towards the hold, before leaping out of the wheel house and running towards the narrow deck. A few seconds later, Theo could see the reason why he had run. A second person had appeared, hauled up from the hold in a series of savage jerks.

'Oh God! It's Mae. I'm certain of it.'

The first man had begun to hit the new arrival, raining in blows by using his foot as a weapon. All at once, he screamed out loudly before buckling forward onto his knees. Benjamin chuckled grimly. 'She's kicked him in the goolies.'

'Do something,' Theo yelled frantically. Mae, if it was Mae, had collapsed onto the deck.

It was impossible to come alongside the fast-moving, lightly loaded barge, as it had no ladder, not even a rope to cling onto. Theo knew well the dangers of falling, this close. Any person would be sucked into the screw from which their body would emerge in dismembered form.

'Do something!' He repeated and began to beat the thwart with massive blows of his fists.

'There's nothing we can do, son. That man up there knows it too.' Benjamin also showed his frustration. 'Hang on…he's shouting something.'

From over the noise of the combined engines they could hear the hoarse, panicky voice of a young man.

'Oh, my God! It's Jos…it's not Hans! It's Jos!' Theo had never been more sure of himself. 'Leave her alone, Jos. You've nothing to gain, there's nowhere for you to go. Give yourself up.' Jos was screaming back, threatening to kill her. 'Oh God! He's holding her over the water. He's going to let go, let her fall into the water by the screw. Turn back, Michiel. He's mad enough to do it.'

As soon as he had spoken, the inboard lost way. Jos shouted out. 'Go home. I'll be watching. If you don't, I'll let her go, I swear I will-' At that, he spun the wheel into a blur of spokes. The barge began to come round, churning the moonlight to froth.

'He's coming for us,' shouted Benjamin.

'I don't think so,' Michiel replied as the *Affaric* made a turn in the wide canal heading back again towards the North Sea and the fast disappearing cargo vessel. As the barge passed the motorboat with five metres of sea space between them, Theo could see

The Potato Eaters

across to Mae whose face was streaming blood from a head wound. Her hands were held together, almost as if in prayer. Theo rode the wash with ease, a man fully back at home in his environment. He thrust a fist out at Jos.

'We'll be back, you bastard.'

For reply, Jos laughed into the slipstream. 'Stay away, mad boy, and your Jewish whore won't get hurt.'

'It is he who is mad, you know,' Michiel said. He adjusted the throttle to idle. 'We must get the police.'

'Yes, yes,' said Benjamin, realising the danger they were in for the first time. 'This has gone on far too long already.'

'Drop me there…on that quay over there. You fetch the police. I have to see where Jos is taking Mae.'

'He can't get past the locks, can he?'

'That's just the point,' Theo replied firmly. 'He knows that as well, so he must be making for some other point on the canal.'

Theo had no faith in calling the police; at least, not yet. Mae could be dead by the time Benjamin and Michiel had explained sufficiently to the authorities, that they move a force down to the waterside.

As soon as the boat touched lightly against an old, rotting pier, he leapt ashore, ignoring the treaties to take care from the two men. He felt the firmness of the earth and the solidity of the stone flags beneath his feet and realised the hold on him was as strong as ever. There had been no change despite the time at sea; it was only his fear of losing Mae that had spurred him on across the water. Turning his shoulder, he saw the bow come up as Michiel pulled out the throttle to its maximum ratchet. The transom, in response, dipped into the engines wake.

'Quickly! Quickly! Damnit! Wait till I telephone you before you go to the police. I won't be long' he shouted to himself, watching the others for a moment, who were already speeding away, back to the *Ij*. Running with his stumbling gait, he found himself within a huddle of small houses, fishermen's huts built a hundred years earlier. Three bicycles leant against a wall of a small bar. Without pausing to consider the consequences, he snatched up the crossbar of the nearest, a smart job with back pedal braking and a pair of pannier baskets draped across the rear wheels. Just the thing for delivering sandwiches he realised, as he swung a leg over the seat.

The street, more of a lane, was cobbled, forcing him to veer to the kerbside where a thin strip of sand and grass smoothed his ride and permitted him to accelerate. He forced his legs into the pedals and threw his entire weight over the top of the handlebars, bound in some form of tape to prevent hands from slipping in the wet. On the opposite side of the canal, he could see the lights of *Zaandam,* an extension of the port on the North-East side. Here, if he wasn't careful, the *Affaric* could swing into one of the hundreds of spur canals which formed the complex of docks. Worse, it could turn to port, into *West Haven* with its enormous wharves. Ships here were jammed into every metre of granite quayside, tight packed as Portuguese sardines. The booms and masts of their derricks stood out against the dock lights as a fine web filling the entire space over the ships.

The bike's front wheel slewed to a halt. 'Damn! Damn,' came the usual expletives. It was not the security fence directly ahead to cause him to stop suddenly, for it had collapsed in a dozen places nearby. It was from his vantage point on the south bank he could see the barge turning to port as he had feared, though the boat was, at least, on the same side of the canal as himself, he realised. As he studied her wake, the barge came amidships and began to sail down the centre of the main waterway, as if the helmsman knew exactly the route he was to take.

Theo searched for a crossing but there was none to be seen which could bridge the width of the waterway in front of him. He would have to cycle the full length of the main spur, before turning north again, and making any attempt to catch up. Two hundred metres later, the boat turned, this time to starboard as it manoeuvred for a berth on its port side. Far away, Theo screamed his frustration, being able to see the boat but unable to be near enough to affect the result.

Desperate now, he urged the bicycle along the perimeter wire where he could see a clear gap sufficient for his borrowed bicycle to make good speed. Several times, goods, long abandoned, were propped along the fence, rusting and damaged, seeking to tear at any exposed part of his skin, his knees and knuckles especially. His shins too, were lacerated from the wire strands, snapped open from long disuse, now standing out from the fence with razor sharp ends.

Up the West side, he could look down on the entire length of the *West Haven* waterway system. In the far distance was the North Sea Canal. Of the *Affaric*, however, there wasn't a sign. The docks had swallowed her up, absorbing her like protoplasm, into the darkness of the night.

* * * * *

Just when I thought he was going to let me go, I was snatched back to an upright position as if I were a marionette, with arms on fire from where the skin had torn under the weight of my body, and the grip of his hands. I knew my face had swelled up for I could no longer see out of my left eye anymore. I gave up trying to make a comparison with my mouth, as to which was more damaged. My lower lip too, felt like an orange: it must have appeared so, to any onlooker, as well.

'Stay inside, you bitch,' Jos growled at me from the wheel. He attempted to wipe half-dried spittle from his cheeks, at the same time turning the barge westwards several times, having first looked back out of the wheelhouse. He grunted in satisfaction as the boat picked up speed again.

'You never had a single idea it was me, did you? Not for a single moment. Everyone thought it was Hans, darling Hans, though they didn't like to say so, did they?' He glanced aft again. 'They've turned damnit! They are going back, back to the *Ij*.' He hooted in triumph.

'You were told Hans was always out at night...with the girls. So he was. Hans has always liked his women. I was the quiet one, doing my duty, working for a new Europe after the war. You Jews, you are all so dim-witted, aren't you? You think, because the war is over, everything will be fine again, back to the old ways of lending money, making more money than anyone else, selling diamonds, ignoring everyone but your own race. You charge higher interest rates than anyone else and keep it all in the family instead of spreading it around. Well...your meddling in our affairs is an extremely dangerous thing to do. No one is going to give a shit when they find your body: I bet you won't make it to the newspapers, not worth even a small column.'

His words saddened me as few had done before, for it was probably the truth. I tried to speak clearly, though I found it almost impossible to open my mouth. 'But, Gretel did. You killed her, didn't you?'

He stared at me wildly, and for a moment I believed he was going to do something really stupid. 'I got her going one night. Told her about how Hans had cheated on her while he was seeing her, dating her. She told me she had seen me coming out of the young Dutch Friends Club. I told her she was up against very powerful people; people at the centre of government who would stop at nothing to make sure their names were not disclosed. I said she would regret ever having mentioned that address. In fact, the most stupid mistake ever. Silly bitch went out and wrote a letter to you saying she was going to run away to *Baarn* the next day and stay with her father. I found the letter when I stopped her by the canal and tore off the bottom half so it would confuse everyone. It was so simple, holding her down. She didn't have any strength…not like you. She was dead in half a minute. No more Gretel Neumann to tell the story.

'And it was you who tried to kill me…in the tunnel? It was your height that gave you away.'

Despite everything, Jos laughed. 'That day, you were lucky. Today…your luck has finally run out.'

'There's nowhere to go-'

'That's where you are wrong, bitch-face. I can leave whenever I wish. And I will now. Today I will arrange for a pickup and sort out my affairs. Until then, you are going to be my insurance. It appears regretfully, as if women are still able to be useful as bargaining tools in this brave new world of ours.'

Jos spat close to where I was lying. The phlegm quivered as if in anger, like a stranded tadpole trying to get back to its pond. 'I'm not interested in women. I prefer…people, men I can trust. Women always let you down in the end, like when you take them out for an evening. All they ever want to do is to turn their eyes upon everybody and hope eyes are on them. Gretel used to do that a lot. Men never do that sort of thing.'

It just fell out of my mouth. 'Are you a queer?'

He spat again, closer, real hate in his eyes. But he didn't have a word to replace it. 'I don't like that word. It doesn't mean what it should. There are very many good things about a man to man relationship. Comradeship, reliable company, that sort of thing-'

'Maybe Jos,' I managed to say through swelling lips,' but if everyone did what you do with your bottoms, there would be no children in the world, would there? The human race would just die out and you would have no-one to rule, would you.' I stopped. This was quite ridiculous. We were discussing deep philosophic arguments while the man listening and steering the *Affaric*, was certainly planning to kill me in the next few hours, if not minutes.

Jos removed his attention from me as he concentrated upon the maze of wharves ahead. For a quick moment, I thought it might be because Theo had decided to remain by the boat but, raising myself to the coaming, I saw lights along the port side. I had never been to *West Haven* but it had to be the Docks, directly opposite *Zaandam*, as they were. The area was flooded with low energy sodium lighting, casting gloom between the hundreds of hulls. Jos spun the wheel to a blur to bring the bow central to the main waterway. I glanced back, but Theo and the motorboat, my only hopes of salvation, were almost a speck in the far distance of the main canal and heading for the shore. They had given up, put off by Jos's threat to drop me into the water.

'Bugger!' I said aloud.

'Tsk! Tsk! Ladies from nice schools shouldn't be allowed to swear like that. In fact, not at all come to think of it. You had an expensive education as well didn't y-'

I interrupted him. 'What about the Family Jos? After all this, when you have dropped me over the side or whatever you plan to do to me, where can you go? Theo knows all about you. By now, he will be contacting the police.'

'You really are a stupid bitch. As if I want to go on living in the dross of the *Anna Rosner*, all the rest of my life and being told what I must and what I must not do by Papa and Mama. I've had enough Mae. I would have cleared out anyway, even if you had not come along to complicate matters. You see, it was all planned. My disappearance and all, only you won't be coming along with me.'

'I suppose you will be taking your Nancy boy with you.'

I really don't know why I said such things, a stupid comment really, for he hit me again, very hard, full force into my face with the flat of his hand. It hardly stung anymore, though the blow brought tears to my eyes, and I fell to the floor.

He disappeared from sight. A moment later, a huge derrick passed overhead, followed by a bump. I heard the engine run idle before it died away completely. Around me, in the silence, the dockside was bathed in this strange yellow light, which caused all the shadows to intensify themselves and become much blacker. The cobbled street was awash with the colour of golden bricks. I pulled myself to my feet glancing about to see there was no one about; with no sign of Jos I jumped to the quay side feeling as if my head and arms were on fire, but at least I could move. I assumed Jos must have thought he had damaged me enough to leave me for a while. The *Affaric* was moored with a single rope to a bollard with no attempt having been made to put out the rope fenders or to secure the stern with a rope spring to prevent it from swinging out into the waterway.

I heard an engine start up which made me break into a run…and a sweat. It had to be Jos for the place was deserted. I ran, waiting for the chrome bumper to smash into my legs before riding up the back of my head. I ran in fear for what he planned to do to me, but more than this, I ran in fear for what I knew he was capable of doing to me. I had come so far after the war that I didn't want to die now.

The glow from the car shone ahead of me, so my shadow snickered back and forth as it aped my frantic haste, bouncing off the piles of lumber and steel drums. At the instant of impact, I sensed rather than felt the vehicle swing past me. Some twenty metres ahead, it came to an abrupt halt sliding on the greasy cobbles almost out of control. It was an old van, once German with the insignia crudely painted out. Jos's legs, so much longer than my own, rapidly overhauled me as I tried to dodge and twist inside and around the stacks of cargo. It was like at school, if there had not been the deadly intent of the catcher. At length, we came to a position where we were face to face, separated by a street lamp with a feeble glow which highlighted his panting yet exultant mouth. He seemed oblivious of the need to be aware of other passers-by who, by now, might have thought something was seriously wrong and contacted the police. He didn't, for I knew he was quite mad, his mind switched off from the reality of the world. And I had worried about Theo.

'You and I are going for a nice ride. We are going to the seaside.' He hit me then, very hard on the side of my head so it made the lights flicker on and off as if someone was attempting to send a message in Morse code. It turned into a light switch as the source of power snapped off abruptly.

* * * * *

The West side of the docks was quite straight. It did not have the deep fissures and fingers of the opposite quay, so Theo was able to increase his speed significantly, driving his, now flagging leg muscles. There was real pain but he managed to hold it at arm's length, oblivious of everything else but his determination to catch up. He wanted the *Affaric* in his sights. He could plan what to do when he saw her.

Ahead, was a tumble of ships bridges and derrick masts. Almost in the centre of them, he saw a single moving light, a car or a van perhaps, swing like a searchlight from south to fix on a westerly point. Each mast in the area was illuminated in turn, allowing him to pinpoint each berth. Forcing his feet down onto the pedals, he swung into a small cobbled yard backed by a squad of tin huts. A grey coloured van spun on the oily surface. Whoever was driving was in a frantic haste: It could only be Jos.

'*Affaric!*' Theo roared like a bull, realising he had been very close to Mae. On the ground where the van had been, lay a black balaclava. He could see the red lights diminish in size, knowing he had lost the most important race of his life. He had absolutely no idea what else he could do.

* * * * *

I woke to the most extraordinary noise. It rose above the groan of the wind as it battered against the cabin ceiling. The slap of water was somehow distant, muted, almost muffled. With the strength of the wind I was surprised the boat was not more in motion. In fact, there was no motion at all.

With a start, I sat up, fully awake…on straw! The boat was not in motion because I wasn't on one. The memories of the past few hours tumbled down from the sky as they attempted to rearrange themselves in some sort of sequence in my brain. The first item to clarify itself was, if I was not on the *Kuijpers*, where was I? I knew I had left it after my party walk-out during supper with the Family. But, why straw? I had gone to my office to sleep...

'Oh God!' I added to the groaning. Realisation then, was total. The abrupt shut-off of consciousness, the chase through the docks and Theo, bless him, standing up in the tiny boat, defiant and desperate, held back from doing anything further by the two older men visibly having to restrain him.

The side of my head was being used as the base for a steam hammer. I had a headache, which was threatening to put me back into unconsciousness, so bad I wanted to be sick, but there was nothing in my stomach. I wretched blood and acid bile which stung my throat...and made me grunt again. My cry was echoed by the ghostly calls outside.

I was in a hut about four metres square, half of which contained piles of reeds and bales of straw. There were wood tined rakes and rusty chains on nails hanging on the walls lit only by the gleam of light through small gaps in the wooden planking. It was dawn, dampened by an intense fog, the sort often drummed up on the coast, blanketing out the rest of the world in a soaking wet mantle. The type of fog I remembered where it had lain in a dark tunnel with the sound of hobnailed boots behind me. I could see about five metres, sufficient to learn I had little hope of immediate rescue. The Docks had disappeared, so had the dim illuminated canal and the yellowed light. These were now replaced by clumps of marram grass, each blade bowed with the weight of water upon it. Sand was being driven against the planking of the hut which then collapsed into spirals on the ground. I could smell salt, sea salt, very strongly beyond the wall of mist. There was the murmur of the sea, a soft and continuous sound outside the hut.

My body felt as though it had been kicked and punched all over, which of course was exactly what Jos had done to it. I knew my top lip was split and the vision out of my right eye was partly obscured. On touching it, I realised it was dried blood, partly flaking where I had lain on the straw, so there was a good chance it was the blood affecting my sight and not major damage causing something far more serious.

It came again, a ghostly booming sound, not created by the sea, made more eerie by the fog and the fact I was alone. I began to wonder when Jos would return, for I was sure he would be back to use me in some way or other. There was no reason for him to have kept me alive if it was not to use me as some form of hostage. Theo and his friends would have gone straight to the authorities once they realised they could not get aboard the *Affaric* without seeing me dropped into the wash of the screw.

Poor Theo, he would be frantic by now and I wondered if his fragile mind had been able to withstand the imposed stress of the situation, he found himself. And...how did he find me? He knew, of course, where the Affaric was berthed as Benjamin had told him, but I had not given him the slightest indication I was going to try and find out about the boat. In other words, he had seen through my little story of waiting until the police became involved.

My thoughts turned back to Jos. Pieter and Mama, and the girls for that matter, would have learned of their son's attempts to kill me. With Hans, there had been no proof he had been involved in the exporting of collaborators to South America or where ever a safe country could be found. Jos, however, had nothing to hide behind. He had abducted a Dutch citizen in front of three witnesses, and had held her suspended over the water, as he had hurled obscenities at the world at large.

Mama would have moaned and cried. She would have beaten her enormous bosom with a reddened hand. 'Not my Jos, not my darling Jos?'

Pieter, I suspect, would have been deathly pale, stiff-lipped, with his back to the stove in his usual position whenever there was a family crisis. 'Don't talk about him, Mama. His name is not to be mentioned in front of me again.'

The girls would have sobbed, appalled and totally bewildered by the turn of events in such a short time.

It was getting much lighter outside. At once, I understood what was causing the booming sounds. I was fairly close to a lighthouse. It was a foghorn I could hear, not the ghostly sounds of a vampire or a werewolf. The men on the *Anna Rosner* had often spoken of their work in and around *Noordwijk*. There was a lighthouse there at the end of the sea front to the north and close to some bungalows. It bordered a wild area of massive sand dunes, covered in marram grass, the dune plants grown to keep the sand in place, and, of course, the sea from breaking through the sea defences and out into Western Holland. It was just possible I was close to the town, as Jos would have been familiar with the location and the geography: It was the centre for picking in Holland also, and he would have gone there often in the season.

A chain began to rattle harshly as it was drawn quickly through an iron ring. My heart began to hammer against my chest until it too, hurt. I looked round for something, anything to use as a club.

'Wie Gehts', he was using German rather than Dutch. He was smiling confidently as if he had not a single worry in the world. He held out a single bread roll. 'I advise you to eat it. It will be all you eat today.' Did that mean I had at least one day to live? How my past life had returned, catching up with events as familiar now as my life had been five years ago.

'You had better let me go, Jos. The police will be scouring the countryside today.' At least, that was what I intended to say but my throat had become glued to itself, so the words came out in an unrecognisable mutter.

He ignored my attempts at speech. 'Tonight we are leaving, you and I. You are my passport to freedom and a new life. If you do as I say, to the letter, I will set you free at the end of all this. If not-' he left the end suspended, like a cheap novel, but I understood, only too well his meaning.

I shivered in the mist, which curled like an autumn bonfire through the open door, the door framing freedom: the evil emanating from Jos was extraordinary. Young as he was, he had somehow managed to absorb a lifetime of wickedness into his blood and to become, instantly believable. I knew beyond a shadow of a doubt, he would kill me with his hands if needs be, while all the time maintaining the sardonic smile on his face as he did so.

For the time being, however, he needed me. It was my strongest, and only, card. 'Papa and Mama? They must know by now. I wonder how they are?'

He hit me in the face again, without stopping his chewing on a hunk of bread.

'Suzannah? Anna eh? What about your brother Hans? Hans, who you engineered the blame fall on, and put him in prison for weeks without regretting a moment of his time there.'

'Shut up, Jew bitch, for once and for all. What do you know of my family?'

'Only that you are prepared to sacrifice them to allow your own selfish principles to rule.'

'I almost had Hans once. Do you know, Papa thought seriously about joining the Party at one time when things were going well? He used to come with me to the club on some nights. It was only when the Allies landed, that he and Hans both changed their minds. Fair weather sailors, both of them. They didn't have the guts to stay with it when things began to get tough. There were so many others...just the same.'

'You are finished, Jos. You must know it, deep down inside of you. You will be hunted everywhere.'

He laughed, a high giggle, almost as if he were a schoolgirl. 'I told you, not where I am going, I wont.' His face changed again like the weather and the shifting brain patterns inside, caused him to switch from subject to subject. He stared down at me then looked back, outside the hut. 'Before I do, you might like to give me an exhibition.'

'Of what, Jos,' I said tiredly. Then I understood.' No!'

'Take your clothes off, or I'll cut them off you.'

'No.'

'You should be very pleased. Very few people ever want to touch a Jew. I'm young and healthy,' he added, rubbing his crotch with increasing speed and pointing to it in a crude fashion. 'Take your clothes off!'

He grabbed at my blouse, now tattered and filthy. I thought of the bakery waiting for my arrival. I would have to buy another blouse if I did manage to get away. The buttons ripped but the material was strong. In response, he threw himself down on the straw alongside me. With the hand he had pulled potatoes too often from the hard ground, he tugged at my skirt which yielded at last, leaving only my knickers to block his view. His eyes opened wider.

I managed to gasp out:' I thought you only liked schoolboys. What will your Nancy boy think when he learns you raped a girl, and a Jew girl at that?'

He stopped as though bitten by a snake, but not because of my words. Someone was standing in the doorway.

* * * * *

'You have to tell me where he might be, Pieter. I've told you the truth. It is all true, every word of it.'

Pieter tried to widen his stance further. 'How do I know you are telling a single word of truth? The whole thing is monstrous. Unbelievable.' But at the same time, he had never seen a more determined man in front of him, a man who was not going to go away.

Theo had arrived back at the harbour, exhausted from cycling from *West Haven* without stopping. He had managed to catch Michiel who had been waiting anxiously for a call and, after much trepidation, the two men had agreed to forestall calling the police until Theo had contacted them. Theo explained that with Jos in the position he was in, the sight of a uniform might well be the trigger for him to kill Mae.

'I have to get Pieter to tell me where he might be. He will never admit to a policeman where his son could be, but I might get it out of him. If I can't, call the police.'

Theo's hair was plastered against his sweaty face, exaggerating the bloodied streaks down his trousers and hands as he came aboard the *Anna Rosner*. It alarmed Mama and the girls, who could see only a wild man with waving arms and a crazy expression on his face. On hearing the first garbled words, Pieter ordered Theo back to the *Kuijpers*. Those first words had alarmed him, and he did not want the women to hear anymore.

'We cannot talk with the womenfolk here.'

As soon as they were inside the *Kuijpers* cabin, Pieter rounded fiercely on Theo. 'First Mae upsetting the Family, the whole family, mark you, and…she does it twice for God's sake. A day later, I find you jumping down my companionway, without a request to come aboard, talking a load of rubbish and looking as if you have been caught up in a roll of German barbed wire. Just look at you.'

'As a matter of fact, Pieter, I *have* been caught up in a roll of barbed wire. You are not listening to what I am saying. It's not Hans at all…its Jos.'

'It's Jos… what?'

'It is Jos who is the guilty party all along: he is the one who has been causing all the problems. It never was Hans. It was Jos all the time, with Hans probably covering up for his brother.' Theo snatched a couple of useful breaths of air, realising he had stopped breathing while he spoke. It was always the same when he became excited.

'So you said, but what proof have you got? Even the police could not find any evidence after several weeks' investigation.'

'They were working on Hans, not Jos. They never ever considered him, thinking he was too young, I expect.' He banged a fist on the polished table top to underline his impatience. 'You simply have to listen to what I am saying. Jos has kidnapped Mae on board a barge called the *Affaric-*'

'The *Affaric*, you say? Big boat belongs to the Van Loon family. Very fine family, made a lot of money during the war, I believe. Big in shipping, like the Neumann's. Your grandpapa would have known the family when they expanded right here in Amsterdam'

'I bet he did,' said Theo, pausing to let the other understand what was being said. At last, it seemed to dawn upon Pieter exactly what Theo had been trying to say to him. 'But proof, Theo. Proof.'

'Very soon, Michiel and Benjamin from the big flat top out in the harbour will be here with the police. They were witnesses to all these events I have been trying to tell you about.'

'The Suzie? Right astern of us?'

'Yes.'

'But-'

'They both were witnesses, Pieter, and their testimony will put Jos away for ever.

'You need to see Doctor Hertz, and soon.'

Theo continued as if not hearing the other. 'Jos was holding her, Mae, over the side, threatening to drop her into the water if we tried to board. He said he would kill-'

'Now hold hard, Theo. This is nonsense talk.'

Theo knew, for the first time in years he was sane. He was in control, not only of his mind, but of the drama and, no matter what the pain or the outcome was to be, life would never be the same again. He could still see clearly, Mae's bloodied face, held up in defiance, and recalled the exhausting chase across the docks. He was not imagining it: he was not mad, but Pieter had just one chance to resolve the matter.

'Pieter. In a few minutes, the police will be here. Then, you will have to listen to them. I'm giving you a chance to find Jos before they do. You may be the only person in the world who may know where he is hiding.' Quickly, and surprisingly fluently, Theo related the events of the night, the lead up from the evening, and Jos's escape in a van into *West Haven* docks. He showed his cuts and lacerations, explaining how he had received them. Pieter could not deny the bloodied skin and the torn clothes.

'The stolen bike is outside, on the quay-side. You know I have never taken anything from anybody in my life. Last night, if there had been a car, a truck or a bus, I would have stolen it to follow Jos. I need to know, Pieter, where he may have taken her. He is obviously using her as a hostage in case the police catch up with him.'

Silence followed. He could hear only the slap of water on the hull and the answering echoes from the other side. He realised he hadn't made the sandwiches and the tug men would have written him off, no doubt with a condescending smile, and a shrug of his shoulders. A good idea, but, Theo? Well, you couldn't expect him to keep it up, well…could you?'

'Pieter. Your last chance. The police will be-'

'Alright. *Noordwijk*. He might have gone to *Noordwijk*. Jos used to talk about it from time to time. Sometimes when we were picking, he would go off at lunchtime. Talked about a hut he knew, forgotten by the Germans. It was kept for reeds after the war.'

'I knew there must have been somewhere. How do we get there quickly? Before the police.'

Pieter continued to consider his options open to him. There weren't many. 'We cannot tell Mama. It might kill her, what with her poor heart and all. As this is all some awful mistake, which will soon be cleared up, there is absolutely no point in upsetting her by telling her about this…error.' It was a messy word, he knew, one he was not accustomed to use, but time was running out and he was losing faith in his beliefs, with every minute that passed. 'Well take the pickers' bus. We just have time.'

Theo headed for the stairs. 'We must hurry. If the police arrive we will never get away.' The words galvanised Pieter into urgent activity. He had lost his proud stance, his cockiness. He leaned forward to reveal his fancy waistcoat he always wore on a Saturday morning, now looking faintly ridiculous in the early morning light. In his haste to get away he trod on Theo's heels on the companionway stairs. 'We can go the back way.'

As soon as they had cleared the gangplank, they realised the mist had hardened into an impenetrable fog. It made it easier to hide as they ducked behind a mountain of goods ready to be shipped abroad. They walked and half ran, their steps muffled, to a concrete shelter where a group of men and women in muddied clothes were climbing into a lorry with a green canvas awning, spanning crude metal hoops. Most of those seeking extra weekend money, acknowledged Pieter with a brief, if respectful nod, seeing he was not in his working clothes. He was not usually to be seen picking at the weekends. There was not a lot to smile about at this time of the morning, particularly where it was difficult to see even across the width of the road. Besides, for them all, there was only the prospect of a long day in the fields, backbreaking work with little respite. No one challenged Pieter as to why he was without his family or why they had been replaced by the local madman. He obviously had his own reasons to be there.

Theo climbed up the back and found a seat next to two old men who should have been enjoying old age rather than the exhausting work they were seemingly obliged to do. Pieter made a point by sitting some distance away, close to the tailgate where he could see the road. He put his head in his hands to shut out any interference and to send out a message to the entire group, he was not to be spoken to. Once, he shook his head in disbelief. Otherwise, he did not catch Theo's eye for the entire journey.

Theo also had time to think for the first time in what seemed like ages. He had made up his mind that, if he ever found Mae alive and well, she would never leave the *Kuijpers* again or, only when he was with her. Already, he knew he could be too late.

It was when the lorry stopped for the third time, Pieter indicated for Theo to follow. The thick mist blanketed everything and coiled eerily a metre or so above the ground where only the grass was in sharp focus. The two men hung back to allow other pickers, who had also got off, to walk down a lane towards a large brick farmhouse where a crowd was collecting. A man was handing out numbers printed on cards. Instead of following them, Theo and Pieter walked past the gates and began to climb a slight hill, unusual for this part of the country. It was part of the massive dune protection designed to keep the sea from inundating this part of the coastline. Small neat bungalows were dotted about, each giving off that inexpressible air of a village settling back at last into its original purpose, that of a seaside resort.

'*Noordwijk*,' was all Pieter could say, managing to bring out a slight grimace as he studied Theos face. 'The fog should prevent the shipping from moving on the canal for the time being, anyway.' He grunted in some sort of satisfaction to himself. Theo understood. If no shipping was moving, it was highly unlikely Jos could have left the area, if indeed he had come here in the first place. He comforted himself by remembering Jos could only travel westwards. Pieter pointed, as they crested a rise, indicating a lighthouse standing at the end of the promenade. More than half was lost in the mist along with most of the bungalows; sand lay everywhere having been blown up from the vast beach, stretching away in both directions below the dunes. As if timed for their arrival, a booming sound issued from the top of the lighthouse. It made both men jump momentarily as they were taken unawares at the noise. It was loud enough to make Theo's ribcage vibrate, and his heart to match it in sympathy.

'What on Gods ear-?'

'It's the foghorn.' Pieter's wan smile said it all.

Within twenty metres, the village stopped for they had come to the edge of the sea front. Ahead, was a wild mass of clumpy dunes, their surfaces hairy with marram grass. The sand stuck to their boots from the soaking in the fog. Globules hung on every strand, particularly along the lines of rusting barbed wire, sporting faded notices in German and Dutch, warning the locals not to enter the area on pain of being shot.

'The Germans used to practise here…with live ammunition. There are huts hereabouts, which they used to shelter in when it was raining. Soft, they were.' Pieter sneered before clearing his throat noisily. He spat, showing his increasing nervousness.

'Is he somewhere here?'

'How should I know, Theo? I'm guessing as much as you. I just know he came up here a lot.'

The boom of the foghorn forced its way through the mist,

muffled and ghostly, making contact with the world, if only for the period of the reverberation. Theo fancied he saw shadows move in the near distance but, each time he turned his head to study one darker than the rest, it too began to lighten and merge with its neighbours. His breathing rate began to rise as the shapes collapsed.

'Hold it, Theo. We can't be far off. This damn mist makes its location very difficult to pinpoint, but I have been counting paces since the lighthouse. I reckon two hundred to three hundred metres.'

'There's one, Pieter. Over to your right.'

A timber shiplap structure sat in a hollow created by the bottom of two colliding dunes. The roof, though worn and covered with sand and lichen appeared serviceable, as were the walls. A single door, battened and braced to deal with all but the most ferocious attacks upon it by some determined intruder, was, strangely, ajar. It creaked once or twice as if someone was testing it or holding it open to prevent it from banging against the frame for there was no wind at all in the fog to make it do so of its own accord. Theo moved forward.

'No!' Pieter's whisper cut through to him instantly as a command, and not a request. It arose from a new man so unlike the old Pieter, who had sat in front of a table piled high with potatoes. This voice was cold, drained of any emotion other than the need to convey conviction and obeisance.

'This is for me to sort out, Theo. If it is Jos, and I feel sure it isn't, then I want to speak to him alone. He has to answer his critics. If it is someone else, I will call you up and you can come running. I might need your help.'

'What if Mae is with him?'

'As I say, it is for him and his father. Don't interfere. I'll come and call.'

'Very well, but if I think Mae is inside, there is nothing will stop me from getting her out, not even you.'

Pieter shrugged his shoulders, with understanding if not approval, besides, he could be of considerable help in a fight. 'Please give me a little time, that is all I ask.'

It took him two minutes to cross to the doorway of the hut. By then, the colours had been bleached out of his clothes by the distance, for the mist showed no signs of lifting. Half hidden in the sand, Theo could see a German helmet, discarded; he wondered, for what reason? Surrendering, dying, running away, or just tossing it aside as its owner made his own personal decision that the war was over?

Pieter moved up to the door opening.

* * * * *

Jos pulled back from my body as he tried to scramble to his feet. Shock registered on his face. 'Papa! What are you doing here?' he asked foolishly. All the arrogance had evaporated. It left him ashen and cowed, as if with a palsy, while he attempted to cover me up with straw as if I was some stolen treasure piece.

'Leave her be, Jos. Ruth, do your shirt up. Here,' he jerked some string from a hook on the wall and threw it to me. I dragged my skirt across.

'Papa-'

'Vermin! Bastard son!' Jos's words were strangled by his father's whiplash scream. He began to slap Jos across the face with the flat of a leathery hand, stinging, powerful strokes which reversed themselves after every other blow, so he could present his knuckles. Blood began to spill, first from his nose, then a lip. It would not be long before he began to look just like me. 'Bastard! You let Hans go to prison, when all the time it was you. You'll go to jail for a long time.'

'You don't know the half, Papa.' Jos answered, beginning to recover his composure. He warded off half a dozen aimed blows until Pieter stopped his assault, exhausted emotionally, as well as physically. 'When the police find out what I've been doing for the past three years, they will never set me free. And, the Jews: if they find out I told the Germans where they used to hide...' He let the implication die out like the damp mist.

'For God's sake, Jos. Where did you go wrong?' He shook his head at the empty air. 'What are you going to do? And, what were you going to do to Ruth?'

Jos reacted quickly, as soon as he saw his father in retreat. 'Just a hostage, Papa, until I could get away. I was just about to let her go when you arrived. I have got a boat ride out of here and Mae was to go free. Give me some help and I'll get away and never bother you again.'

I had heard enough. 'You forget one thing, Jos. I am here, and I have witnessed everything that went on. Have you forgotten you almost killed me on the *Affaric* and there are other witnesses to prove it? I will be able to tell the police how you got away…and where to.'

Both men's eyes turned upon me. There was a total silence. Always, always, my bloody mouth which got me into trouble. My mother always said it would be the death of me.

'What ever he has done to you, you cannot let them take Jos away, Ruth. He is too young to be shut away for the rest of his life, or something worse. Please, I'll do anything you want, if you forget this ever happened.'

'And my face? What do I say at work that is if I have a job to go back to?'

Joss face brightened as he saw me wavering. 'You could say you were hit by a lorry.'

'But, I will know that it was not the truth.'

Pieter held up a hand as he remembered why he was there. 'Theo is outside–'

'Theo!' I shouted.

'Theo is close by, and he will go to the police. But, if you are gone, and I am on the boat, there will be no proof.'

'Sorry, Pieter. Benjamin and Michiel both saw the whole thing too.'

Desperately, Pieter turned away, silent and inwardly frightened, fighting with himself and the situation he was quite unable to handle. Finally, after a long pause where his hands wrung themselves in some sort of silent agony, he put his back to Jos and caught my eye. In the same instant, he winked, quite deliberately at me. He was frantically trying to make me understand some point or other, or some plan he was devising. His eyes were pleading.

'Yeah. Benjamin from the Suzie saw me,' said Jos. Michiel was there as-'

'Then, you have really gone and done it. Ruth, call Theo for me, please. He is out there in the mist, across on one of the dunes.'

I got up from the straw very shakily. My eye throbbed worse than the pain in my ribs, so I was able to concentrate on one ache only. I held onto the door handle as the ground heaved. Pieter took hold of my hand. 'But, wait here. We have to talk this through, together.'

'Theo. It is me. I'm safe.'

Out of the mist he came running, joyfully. He hugged me, making small crooning noises in my neck. 'Mae, Mae,' he kept repeating.

I attempted to kiss him through my split lips. 'Jos is inside with Pieter.'

'I'll kill him. Ah!' he pulled from me aghast. 'Look what he has done to you.' Tears started down his face, streaking the sand sticking to his cheeks.

'I think Papa wants to save him from going to prison.'

'Never!'

'We cannot stop it anyway. The police will be on to him by now, I'm sure.'

'Ruth! Can you come, quickly?' It was Pieter, in trouble. Theo dashed towards the hut followed closely by me. If Theo was going to fight for me, the least I could do was to be beside him. As soon as I cleared the threshold, I felt a violent push in my back and found myself lying on top of Theo on the straw. My ribs throbbed with an agonising pain as I found out for the first time, at least one was broken. Pieter was already pulling the door closed. I had fallen for his scheme, and I was a stupid cow for believing he had a plan to resolve the matter.

'I'm sorry, I'm sorry,' he repeated, shaking his head in disbelief in what he was doing. 'But, blood is thicker than water.'

The room plunged into darkness and I hear the chain rattle several times as the two men made it fast. 'I will tell someone you are here.'

By the time we had got to our feet there was not a sound from outside. We could just hear the foghorn, but the mist was clamping down on the wilderness outside. Theo bumped into me as he walked towards the nearest wall where chinks of light shone through feebly.

'Quick, Mae. There are a couple of iron posts. I need to get one.' I felt myself being lifted into the air. Above me, resting on some crossbeams, I could just discern two metal posts among an assortment of other gear. The posts were made from angle iron, the kind to hold up mesh and barbed wire and keep chickens in. I grabbed one, fearful of falling to the ground with my damaged chest. As it was, Theo's grip caused me to bite my lip with the pain. He didn't know the extent of my injuries.

'Walk backwards,' I said. 'I cannot get it out.'

Theo obeyed, which made my body sway against him forcing him to clamp his hands tighter around me. I struggled for breath with the pain. The rod came down, however, along with a pile of loose straw.

Theo lowered me to the ground where I almost fainted, but he was unable to see my problems in the dimness. I stayed on the ground until I was sure I could stand without his help. He had taken hold of the rod.

'Stay there, Mae, in the corner.' At that, he began to attack a timber panel, showing more signs of age than the other walls. The wood began to splinter under his furious assault. A hole, and light, appeared simultaneously. Theo swung the bar sideways, and forced it behind a board so it acted like a lever. He was like a man possessed. With a crack, it gave way. Another followed a minute later to leave an opening the width of my body and less than a third of a metre in height. The trouble then became clear, for the hole contained vertical metal studs, obviously part of a series to which the boards had been nailed and which stiffened the whole structure. It had been set in concrete.

'Stand back,' Theo repeated, more determined than ever. He commenced his assault, launching blow after blow. Eventually, the lower part gave way but the rest remained, like a mule, stubbornly refusing to move. Half an hour later, he had hardly made an impression save for a series of splinters and chips in the opening.

I pushed Theo out of the way. 'It's my turn.' I lay down and eased my head under the splintered wood until I felt my breasts jammed up against me. For the first time I was pleased I did not have a bosom the size of my mother's, for I would have got no further. I forced myself on.

'Careful, Ruth. You are cutting yourself.' For some reason he used my real name. It was nice, and I wanted him to use it again. It spurred me on. Through a mouthful of dust, cornstalks and cobwebs, I told him in Yiddish to…keep quiet. The pain wasn't any worse than that from my ribs. All at once, when I thought I was going to have to remain in the hole until rescue came, the pressure slackened. My buttocks came clear of the restraining wood frame, leaving my head in the wet sand and the sharp-bladed grass.

'Whoopee!' I yelled like a child. It was an American expression I had learned from somewhere.

'Quick. The chain,' Theo called out anxiously. I needed no bidding wondering if the two men were going to return at any moment. I wasn't going to go running around in the fog, searching for a potential killer and an over-protective father, without some substantial support. Pieter had wrapped the chain around an iron hoop used as a handle, and the clasp. Otherwise, it was unsecured. As I pulled the chain through the eye, I felt a trickle down my spine. It didn't seem to hurt, despite the new cuts from the raw timber and I was covered in blood anyway. I was free, safe and Theo was with me. Nothing else mattered.

'Stop! Stop!' I shouted as Theo was bounding off into the mist. 'Stop and think. What do we plan to do?'

'Well. Get the police.'

'And tell them what?'

He looked at me, puzzled and tried to pat my back with his shirt tail. I made a mental note to give it a good soaking before it was washed. 'I don't understand, but you obviously have one of your plans.'

'Pieter tried to tell me something without Jos seeing. He winked at me. I am sure he did not want Jos to know. Somehow, he wants us to hold back, while he does something for him. Get him away, perhaps.'

'Exactly. So we must get up to the village. There will be someone there who-'

'No. We must get back to the *Kuijpers* first. We must explain to the Family what has been going on, Theo. They were very good to me and I owe them some sort of explanation. If Pieter is trying to make Jos give himself up, and that is what I think he is trying to do at this very moment, he will go back to the *Anna Rosner* first. They have always done everything as a family. Pieter will want to ask Elizabeta for her advice.'

As an answer, Theo shook his head but seemed no longer in the mood for wild chases. 'It's a long way back, forty kilometres.'

We stumbled across the wet sand, more by instinct than knowledge with the foghorn helping to guide us back to the village. The lighthouse loomed up like a funnel of an enormous liner, made more sinister when the mist whipped off the glass dome like smoke.

'We'll have to thumb a lift. There's plenty of lorries going into the city,' I said, as we walked clear of the sand at last, onto some paving. 'Let's go near the picking farms. There's bound to be a van.'

A van, a van. Even as I spoke, a white van came towards me. Theo ran into the road, waving his arms wildly. There was a single driver in the front, his head staring over the dashboard. As he came closer and rushed past us with no attempt at slowing, I could see a man, weeping, as his left hand continually beat the dashboard.

'Oh Christ! It's Pieter.' Theo recognised him just as he jumped clear but there was no answering recognition, either of hate or acknowledgement. We simply did not exist for him. Whether, with hindsight he just did not see us or didn't want to, I will never know, but the stolen van continued to career off down the slight hill as if a thousand demons were after it. 'I don't think Jos was with him,' he said. 'The van had glass panels at the sides and I'm sure Pieter was alone. '

Just what had the two men been doing while we had been locked inside the hut for an hour? Time enough for them to have got clear, for sure. It took us two hours to thumb a lift. It was the wrong time of the day, after the early morning deliveries and before the afternoon shifts. It was another hour and a half to get back to the *Kuijpers*. The truck had stopped all along the route, collecting bunches of flowers for the market. We had received a number of stares, particularly Theo. I think they thought he had hit me one too many times, but no one took it any further, and I remained huddled up as much as possible to cover my face. By the time we climbed down from the tailgate, rather stiffly, outside Central Station, it was mid-afternoon. We walked down through that tunnel together, Theo attached to my left arm as if it were handcuffed in position. As we broke into warm sunshine the City came to life and the buildings came into perspective. At that moment Theo said a shocking thing to me, the more shocking as it came straight from his heart, unpremeditated. I had not thought of the possibility.

'He's dead...isn't he?'

'Who?'

'Jos.'

'How do you mean, dead?'

Theo stopped to face me. 'Dead. You know, not breathing any more.'

I let air exhaust itself loudly out of my mouth. I must have looked ridiculous, mouth agape, blood all over my face, a broken rib, and bruises covering my body. I had only convinced the lorry driver to give us a ride saying I had had an accident with a tractor.

'Why? I don't understand.'

'Pieter. Pieter was crying. He was alone, driving like a madman. He must have stolen that van. Can you imagine, a normal Pieter, doing something like that? Pieter killed Jos as he couldn't accept what he had done. He winked at you to make you think he could resolve the whole thing. Instead, he had made up his mind nothing could be done, so the only thing left was to do away with him. He has buried him, no doubt in the dunes where he never will be found. No one goes there except to put things in the huts.'

The terrible thing about his words was that they rang with the truth. Pieter had made up his mind because there were no other options open to him. He was a proud man and he could not live with the idea of meeting friends in the harbour, knowing they knew his son was a traitor.

'Jos will disappear from the scene just as he was planning to do. In time, Papa could say he has gone overseas to find a new life.' It all made sense. But then: 'Surely, he would never kill his own son?'

'Think about it, Ruth. There's nowhere for Jos to go in *Noordwijk*. He has to get a boat. That's *Ijmuiden*. Pieter would not have been able to take him there and get back in time it took us to get out from the hut. Pieter would have had to contact Jos's friends to arrange a safe passage. He was alone, wasn't he? Pieter could have killed him easily. Jos would have been quite unsuspecting, thinking he had won over his father yet again. A piece of heavy timber would have been all it would take perhaps-'

'Don't,' I shouted.

I thought of Mama and Suzannah, little Anna reading by the light of the stove, Hans too. Would Pieter ever be able to hold such a terrible secret in his head for the rest of his days on earth? And, if not, what would the Family do? Every time he walked down the quay side it would be there in his mind, ready to come out one day, in a sudden flood of emotion or one too many drinks. Besides, there was the *Kuijpers* next door, and us knowing, or at least suspecting the worst of him.

It was the truth, it had to be. And Pieter had wanted me to understand he would do such a thing if I were to keep silent. We would have had to make up a story for Michiel and Benjamin, but, no doubt, I could lie myself through the day, to convince the police.

We walked slowly over to the Kuijpers, stepping over the hawsers one by one. Ahead, the configuration of masts and funnels was wrong; one was missing along with its burgee. It gave me the answer of how Pieter had resolved his terrible secret.

Where the *Anna Rosner* had once been moored, was now only a dark, oily rectangle of water. It was littered with floating rubbish on the surface, mostly potato skins. A mutton bone bobbed up and down on the slight swell, like a sea otter preening itself, but of the Anna Rosner itself, there was no sight. She was clear of the harbour, probably clear of the *Ij*, making way as she sought a new life for the pickers aboard.

The End